Sacrificial Princess and the King of Beasts

5

n Tomofuji

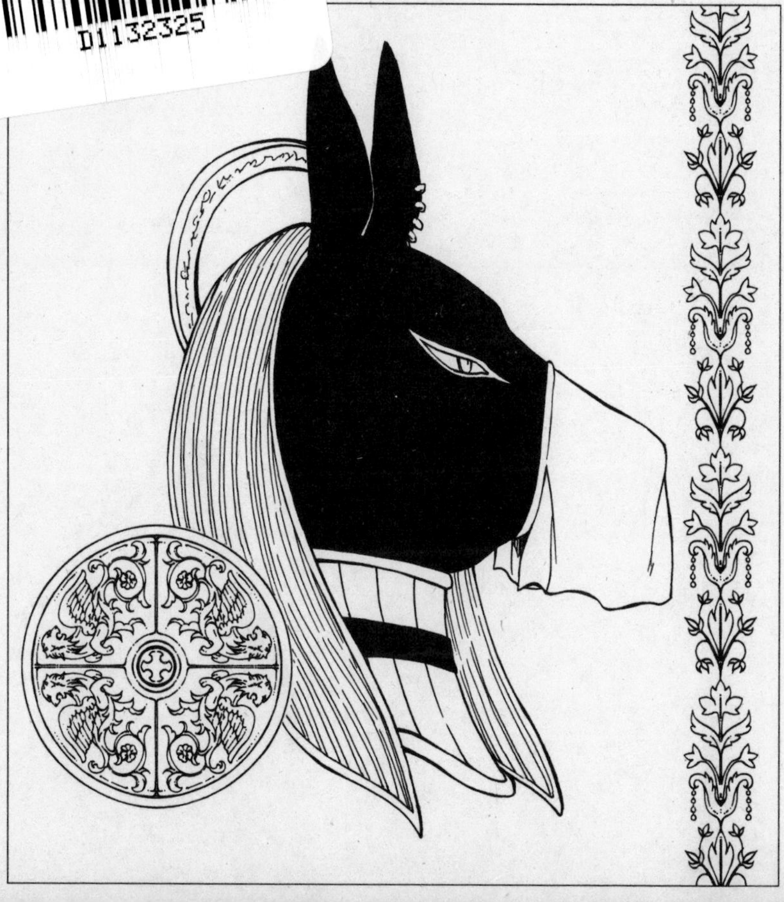

SACRIFICIAL PRINCESS AND THE King of Beasts

5

contents

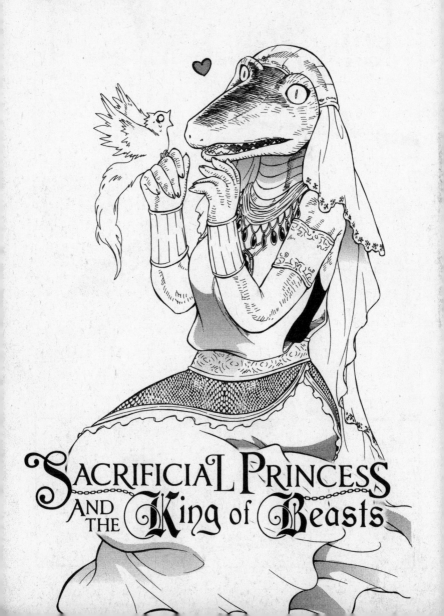

episode.24

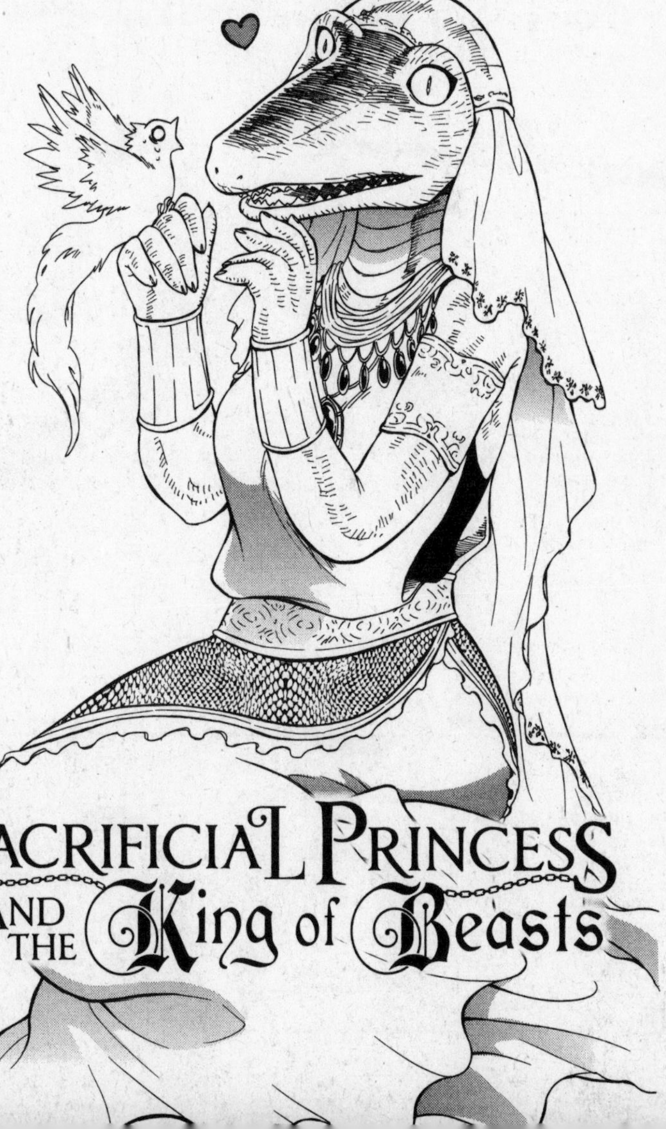

SACRIFICIAL PRINCESS AND THE King of Beasts

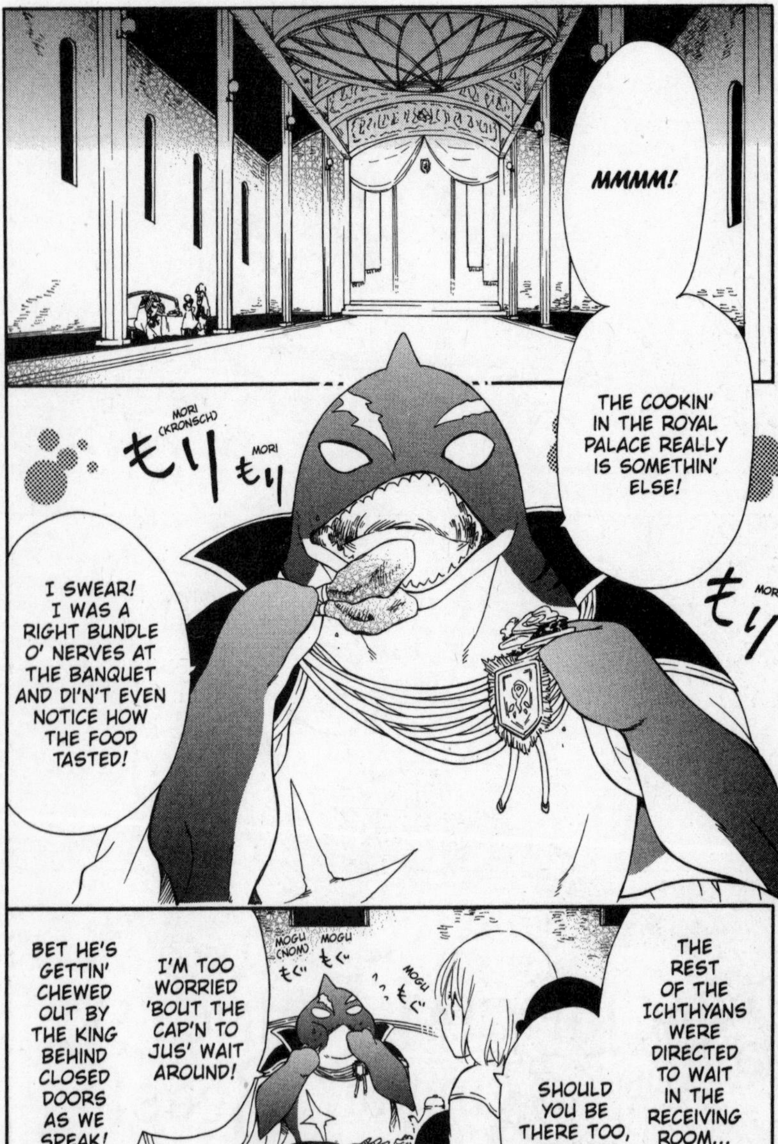
MMMM!
THE COOKIN' IN THE ROYAL PALACE REALLY IS SOMETHIN' ELSE!
もり MORI (KRONSCH)
もり MORI
もり MORI
I SWEAR! I WAS A RIGHT BUNDLE O' NERVES AT THE BANQUET AND DI'N'T EVEN NOTICE HOW THE FOOD TASTED!
THE REST OF THE ICHTHYANS WERE DIRECTED TO WAIT IN THE RECEIVING ROOM...
SHOULD YOU BE THERE TOO, SIR JOZ?
もぐ MOGU
もぐ MOGU
もぐ MOGU (NOM)
I'M TOO WORRIED 'BOUT THE CAP'N TO JUS' WAIT AROUND!
BET HE'S GETTIN' CHEWED OUT BY THE KING BEHIND CLOSED DOORS AS WE SPEAK!

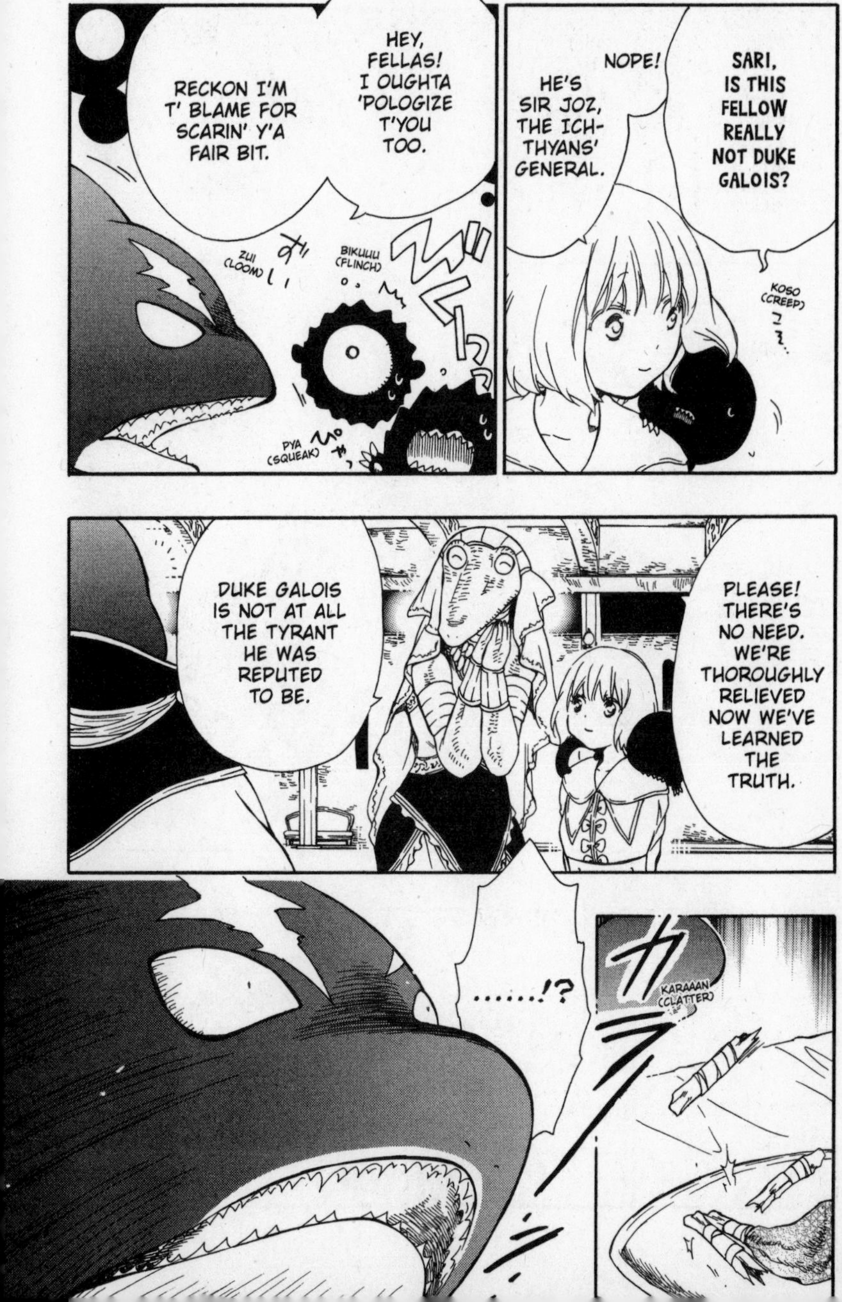
SARI, IS THIS FELLOW REALLY NOT DUKE GALOIS?
NOPE!
HE'S SIR JOZ, THE ICHTHYANS' GENERAL.
KOSO (CREEP)
HEY, FELLAS! I OUGHTA 'POLOGIZE T'YOU TOO.
RECKON I'M T' BLAME FOR SCARIN' Y'A FAIR BIT.
BIKUUU (FLINCH)
ZUI (LOOM)
PYA (SQUEAK)
PLEASE! THERE'S NO NEED. WE'RE THOROUGHLY RELIEVED NOW WE'VE LEARNED THE TRUTH.
DUKE GALOIS IS NOT AT ALL THE TYRANT HE WAS REPUTED TO BE.
KARAAAN (CLATTER)
......!?

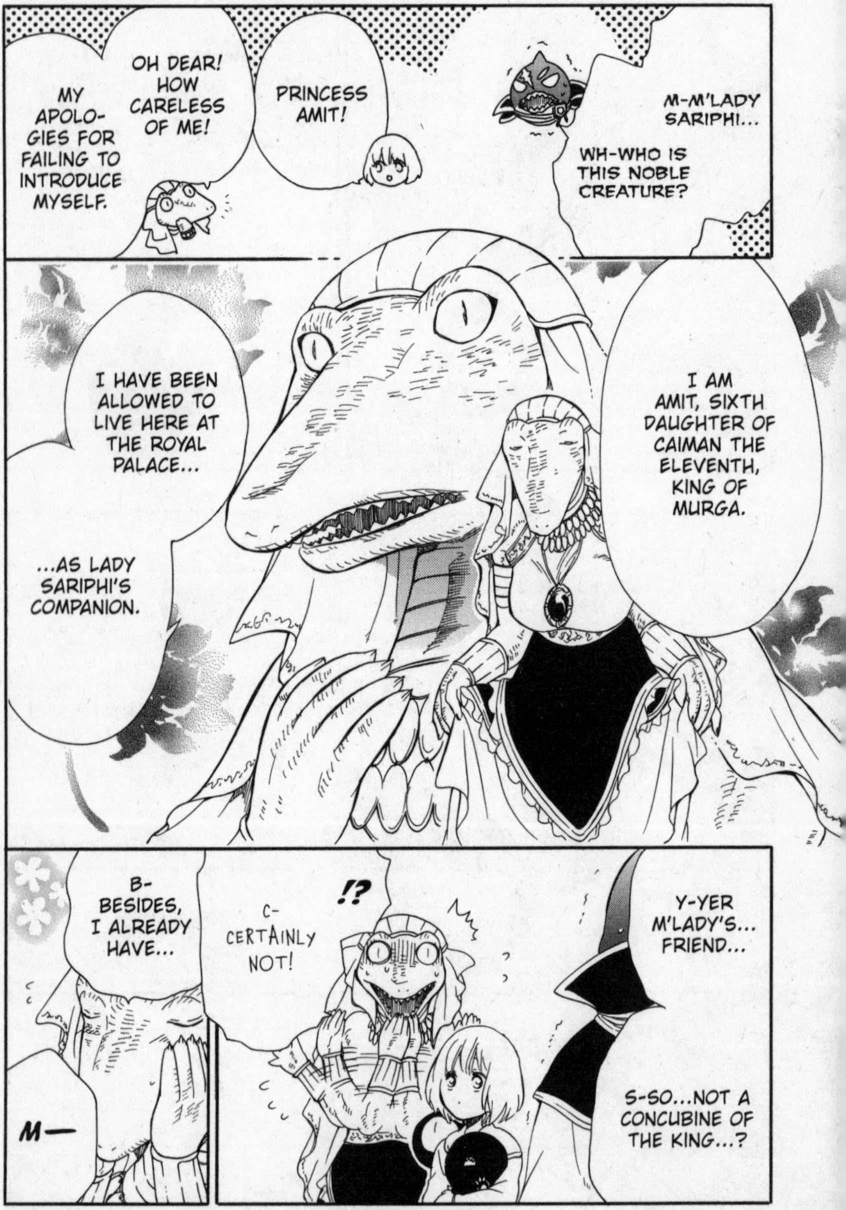
M-M'LADY SARIPHI...
WH-WHO IS THIS NOBLE CREATURE?
PRINCESS AMIT!
OH DEAR! HOW CARELESS OF ME!
MY APOLOGIES FOR FAILING TO INTRODUCE MYSELF.
I AM AMIT, SIXTH DAUGHTER OF CAIMAN THE ELEVENTH, KING OF MURGA.
I HAVE BEEN ALLOWED TO LIVE HERE AT THE ROYAL PALACE...
...AS LADY SARIPHI'S COMPANION.
Y-YER M'LADY'S... FRIEND...
S-SO...NOT A CONCUBINE OF THE KING...?
!?
C-CERTAINLY NOT!
B-BESIDES, I ALREADY HAVE...
M—

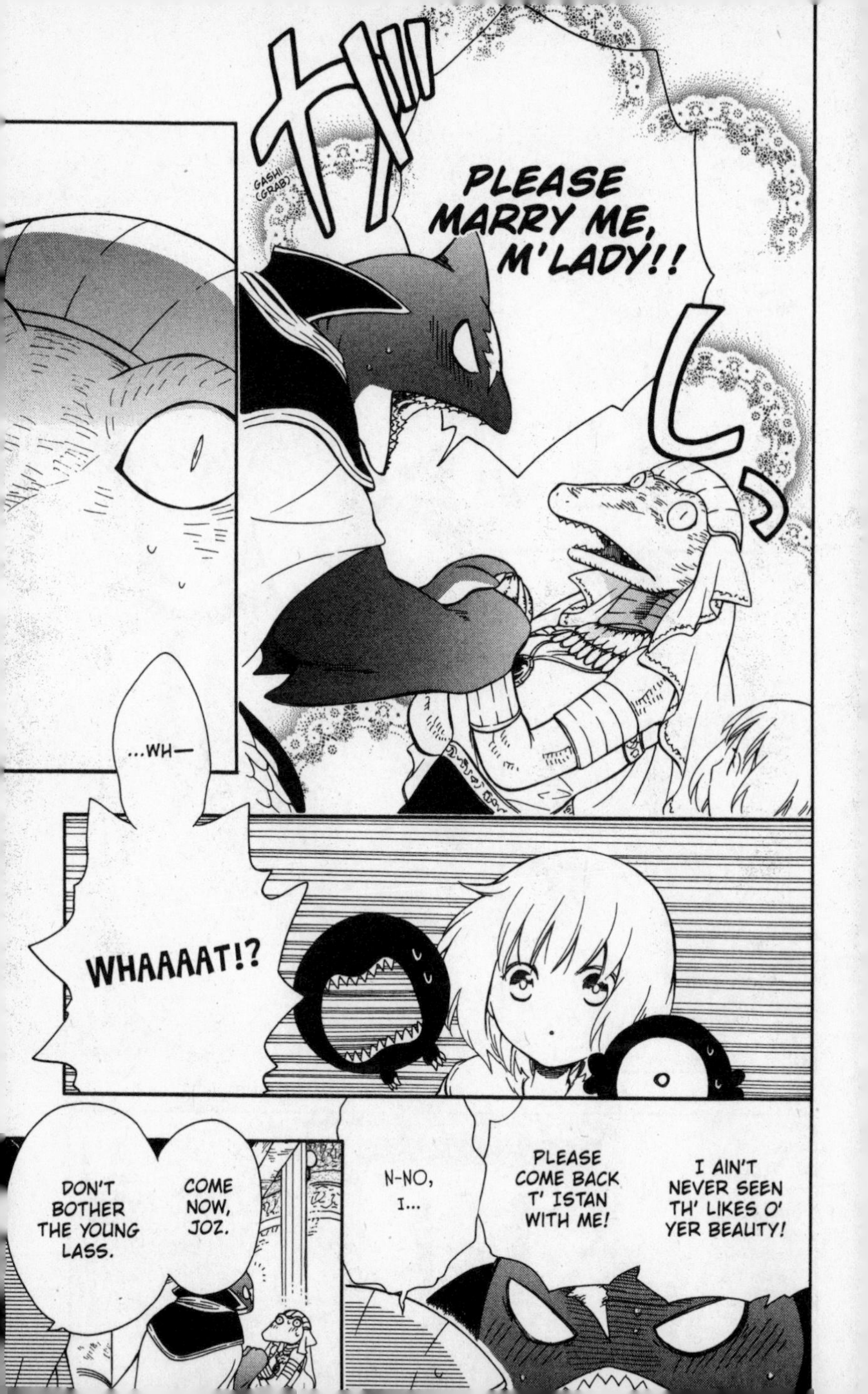
GASHI (GRAB)
PLEASE MARRY ME, M'LADY!!
...WH—
WHAAAAT!?
I AIN'T NEVER SEEN TH' LIKES O' YER BEAUTY!
PLEASE COME BACK T' ISTAN WITH ME!
N-NO, I...
COME NOW, JOZ.
DON'T BOTHER THE YOUNG LASS.

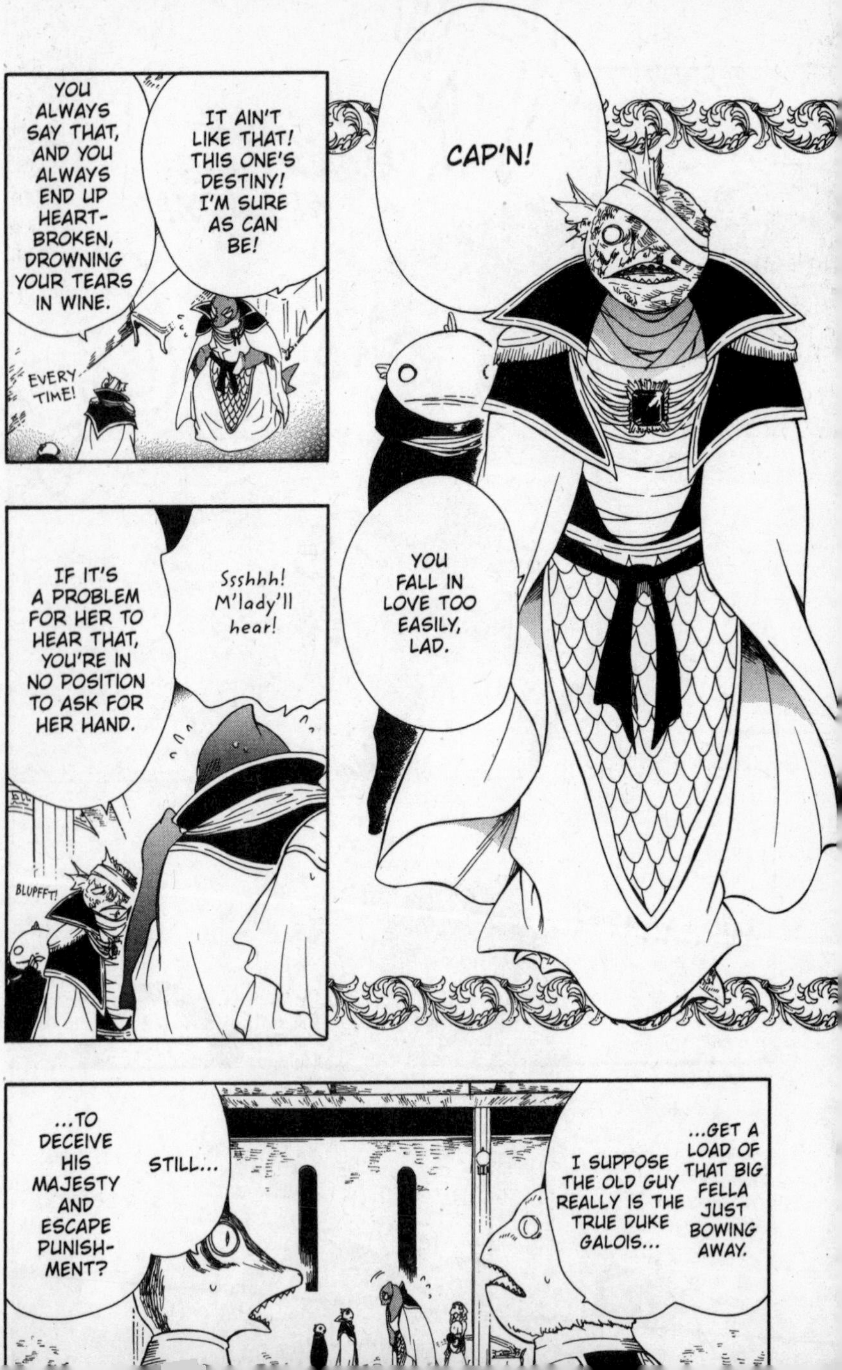
CAP'N!
YOU FALL IN LOVE TOO EASILY, LAD.
IT AIN'T LIKE THAT! THIS ONE'S DESTINY! I'M SURE AS CAN BE!
YOU ALWAYS SAY THAT, AND YOU ALWAYS END UP HEART-BROKEN, DROWNING YOUR TEARS IN WINE.
EVERY TIME!
Ssshhh! M'lady'll hear!
IF IT'S A PROBLEM FOR HER TO HEAR THAT, YOU'RE IN NO POSITION TO ASK FOR HER HAND.
BLUPFFT!
...GET A LOAD OF THAT BIG FELLA JUST BOWING AWAY.
I SUPPOSE THE OLD GUY REALLY IS THE TRUE DUKE GALOIS...
STILL...
...TO DECEIVE HIS MAJESTY AND ESCAPE PUNISHMENT?

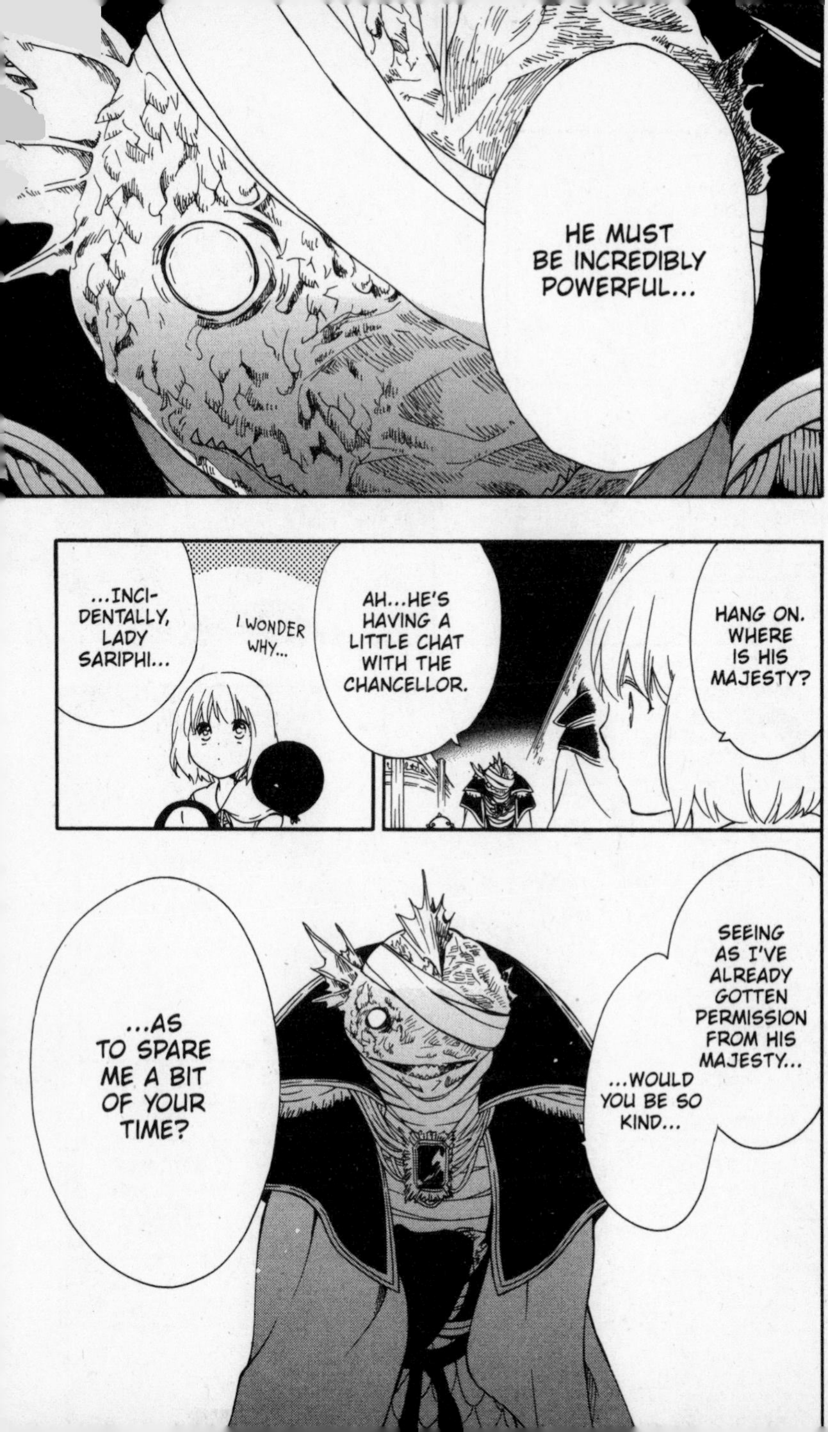
HE MUST BE INCREDIBLY POWERFUL...
HANG ON. WHERE IS HIS MAJESTY?
AH...HE'S HAVING A LITTLE CHAT WITH THE CHANCELLOR.
I WONDER WHY...
...INCIDENTALLY, LADY SARIPHI...
SEEING AS I'VE ALREADY GOTTEN PERMISSION FROM HIS MAJESTY...
...WOULD YOU BE SO KIND...
...AS TO SPARE ME A BIT OF YOUR TIME?

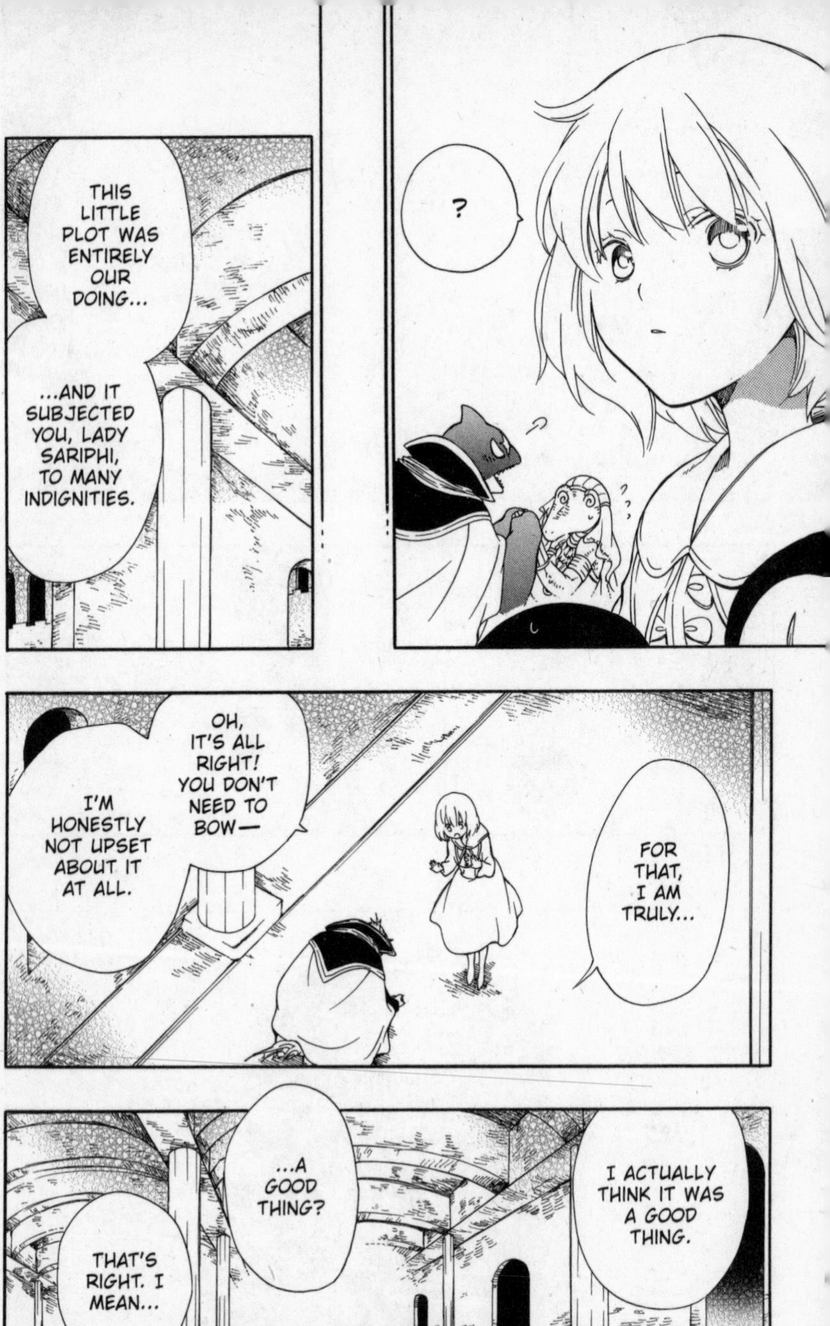
?
THIS LITTLE PLOT WAS ENTIRELY OUR DOING...
...AND IT SUBJECTED YOU, LADY SARIPHI, TO MANY INDIGNITIES.
FOR THAT, I AM TRULY...
OH, IT'S ALL RIGHT! YOU DON'T NEED TO BOW—
I'M HONESTLY NOT UPSET ABOUT IT AT ALL.
I ACTUALLY THINK IT WAS A GOOD THING.
...A GOOD THING?
THAT'S RIGHT. I MEAN...

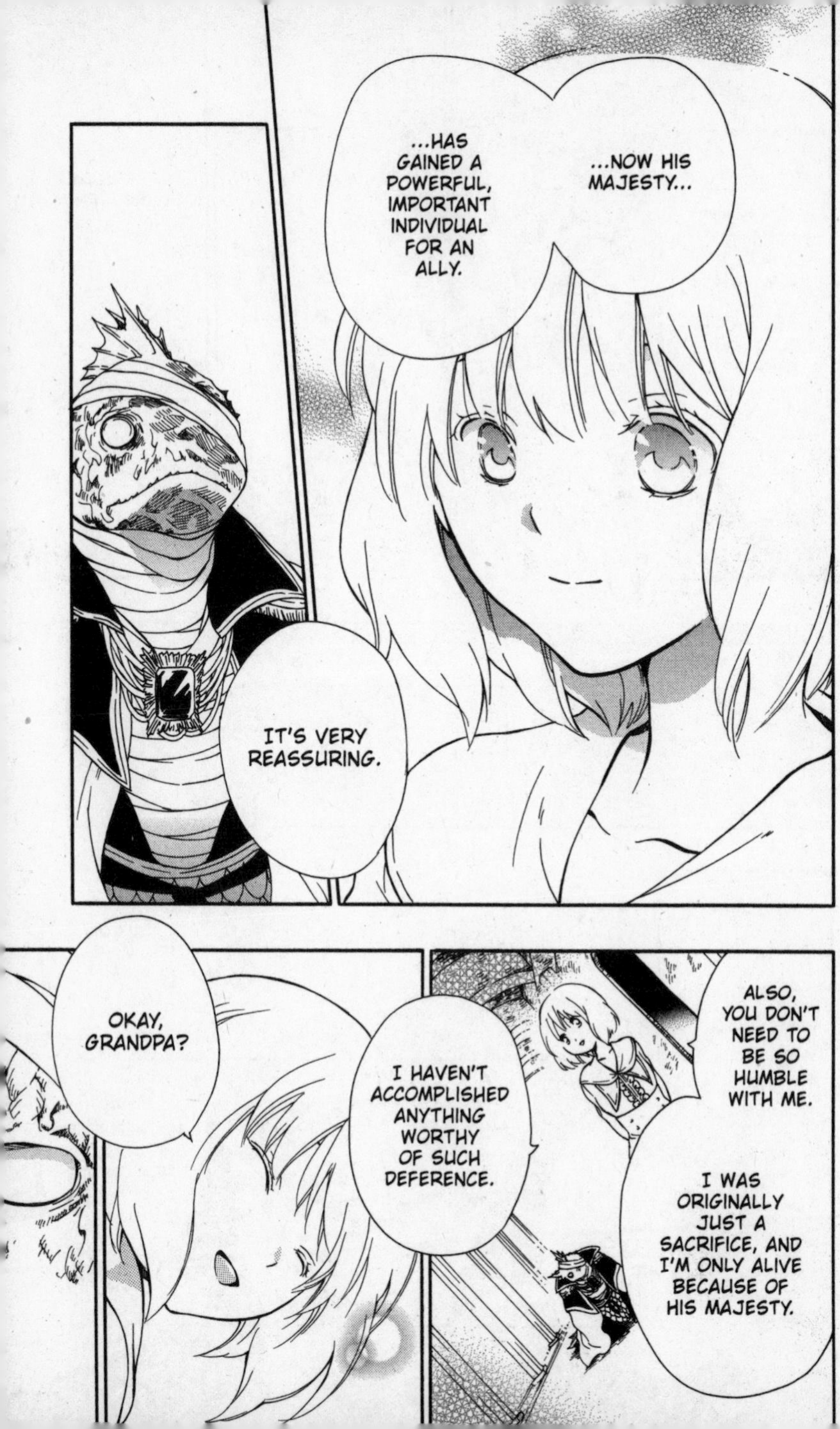
...NOW HIS MAJESTY...
...HAS GAINED A POWERFUL, IMPORTANT INDIVIDUAL FOR AN ALLY.
IT'S VERY REASSURING.
ALSO, YOU DON'T NEED TO BE SO HUMBLE WITH ME.
I WAS ORIGINALLY JUST A SACRIFICE, AND I'M ONLY ALIVE BECAUSE OF HIS MAJESTY.
I HAVEN'T ACCOMPLISHED ANYTHING WORTHY OF SUCH DEFERENCE.
OKAY, GRANDPA?

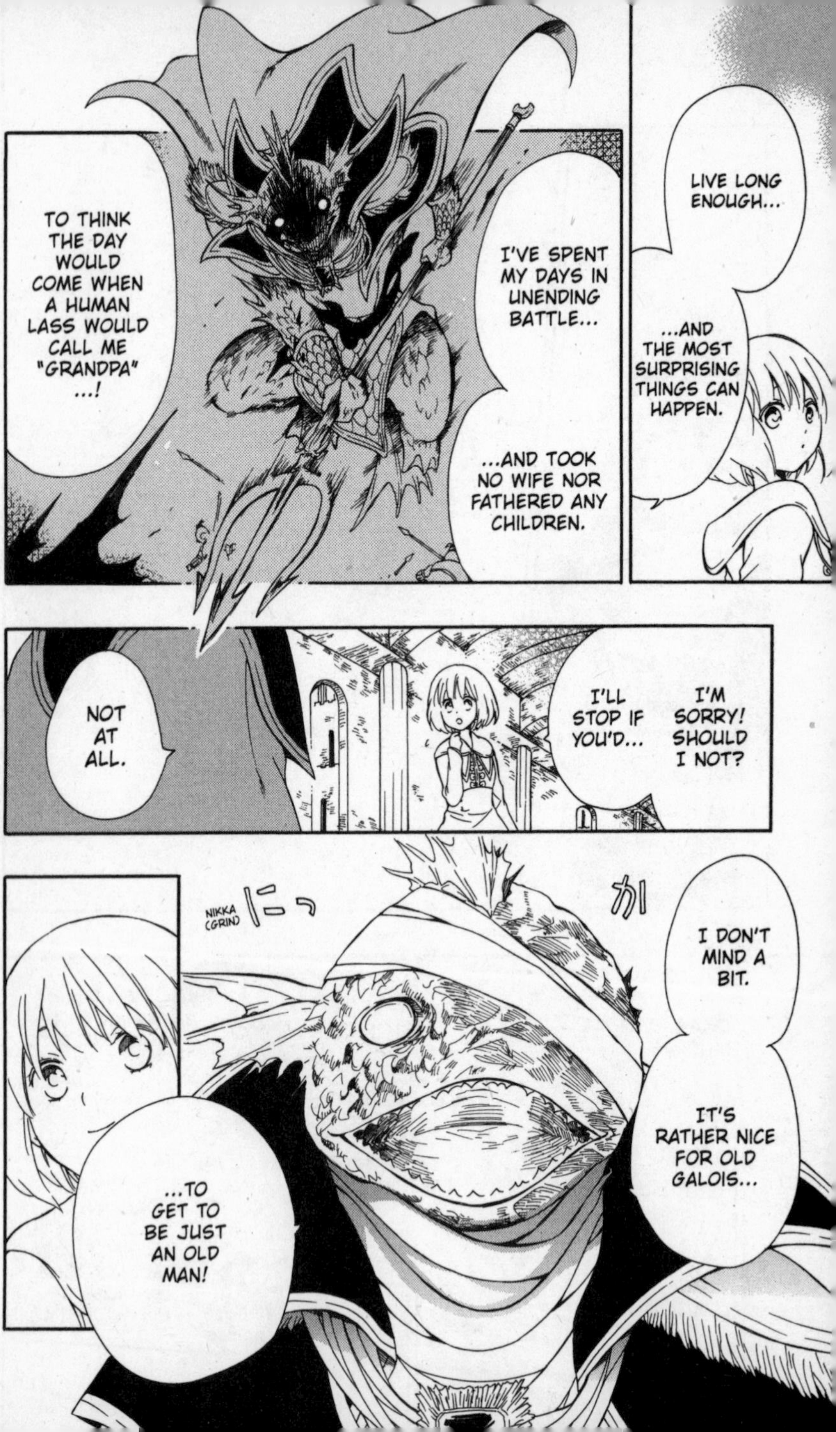
LIVE LONG ENOUGH...
...AND THE MOST SURPRISING THINGS CAN HAPPEN.
I'VE SPENT MY DAYS IN UNENDING BATTLE...
...AND TOOK NO WIFE NOR FATHERED ANY CHILDREN.
TO THINK THE DAY WOULD COME WHEN A HUMAN LASS WOULD CALL ME "GRANDPA" ...!
I'M SORRY! SHOULD I NOT?
I'LL STOP IF YOU'D...
NOT AT ALL.
カ
I DON'T MIND A BIT.
IT'S RATHER NICE FOR OLD GALOIS...
にっ
NIKKA (GRIN)
...TO GET TO BE JUST AN OLD MAN!

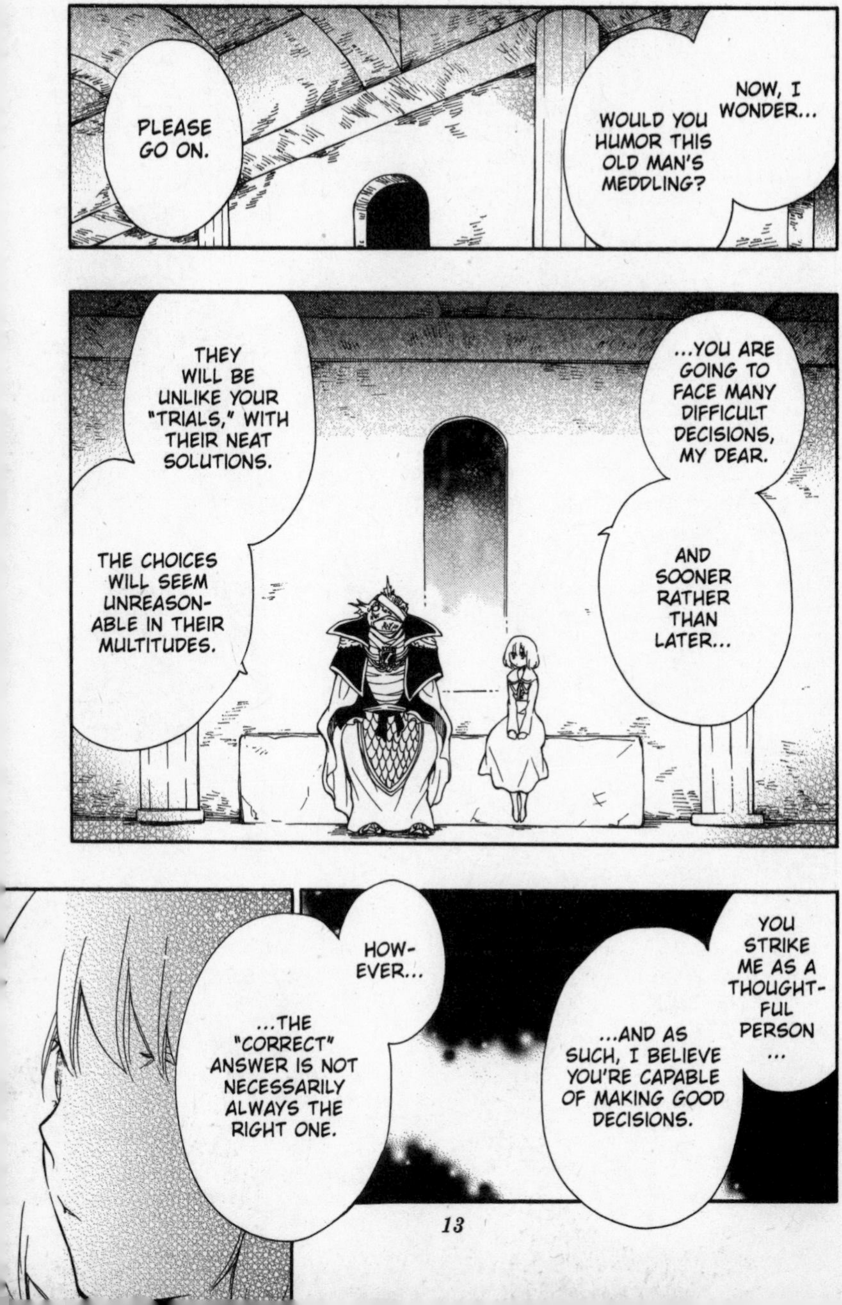
NOW, I WONDER...
WOULD YOU HUMOR THIS OLD MAN'S MEDDLING?
PLEASE GO ON.
...YOU ARE GOING TO FACE MANY DIFFICULT DECISIONS, MY DEAR.
AND SOONER RATHER THAN LATER...
THEY WILL BE UNLIKE YOUR "TRIALS," WITH THEIR NEAT SOLUTIONS.
THE CHOICES WILL SEEM UNREASON-ABLE IN THEIR MULTITUDES.
YOU STRIKE ME AS A THOUGHT-FUL PERSON...
...AND AS SUCH, I BELIEVE YOU'RE CAPABLE OF MAKING GOOD DECISIONS.
HOW-EVER...
...THE "CORRECT" ANSWER IS NOT NECESSARILY ALWAYS THE RIGHT ONE.

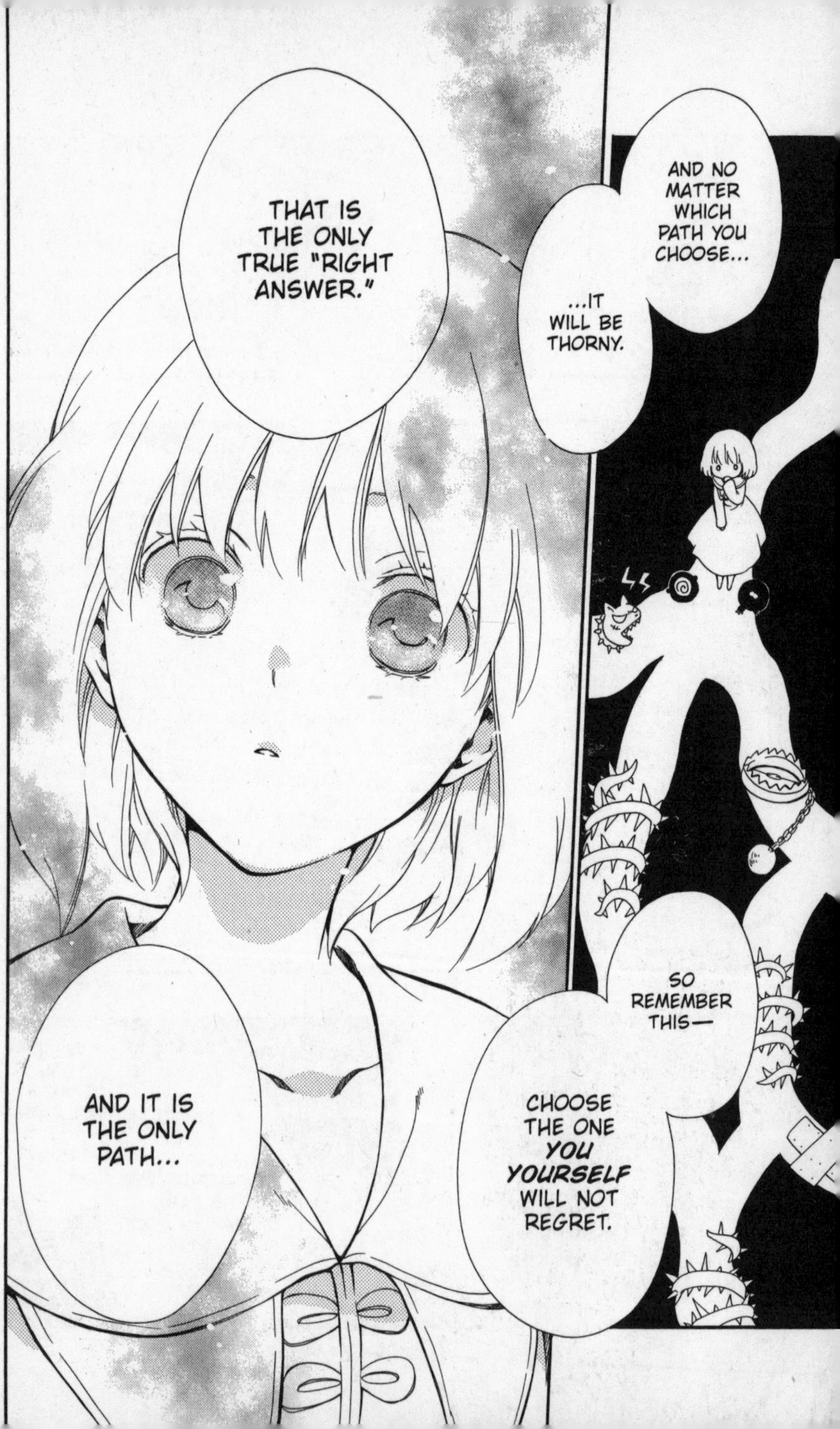
AND NO MATTER WHICH PATH YOU CHOOSE...
...IT WILL BE THORNY.
SO REMEMBER THIS—
CHOOSE THE ONE *YOU YOURSELF* WILL NOT REGRET.
THAT IS THE ONLY TRUE "RIGHT ANSWER."
AND IT IS THE ONLY PATH...

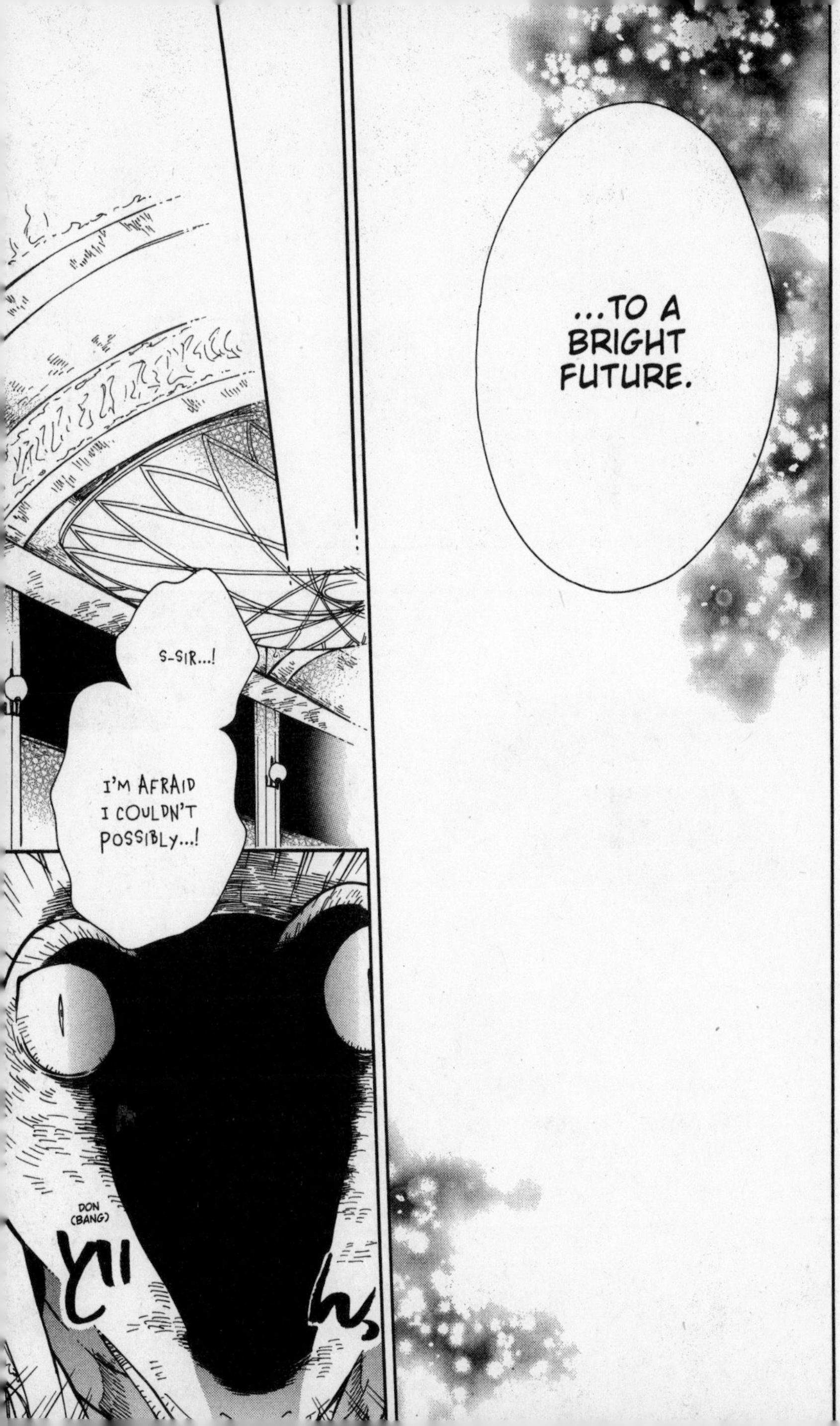
...TO A BRIGHT FUTURE.
S-SIR...!
I'M AFRAID I COULDN'T POSSIBLY...!
DON (BANG)

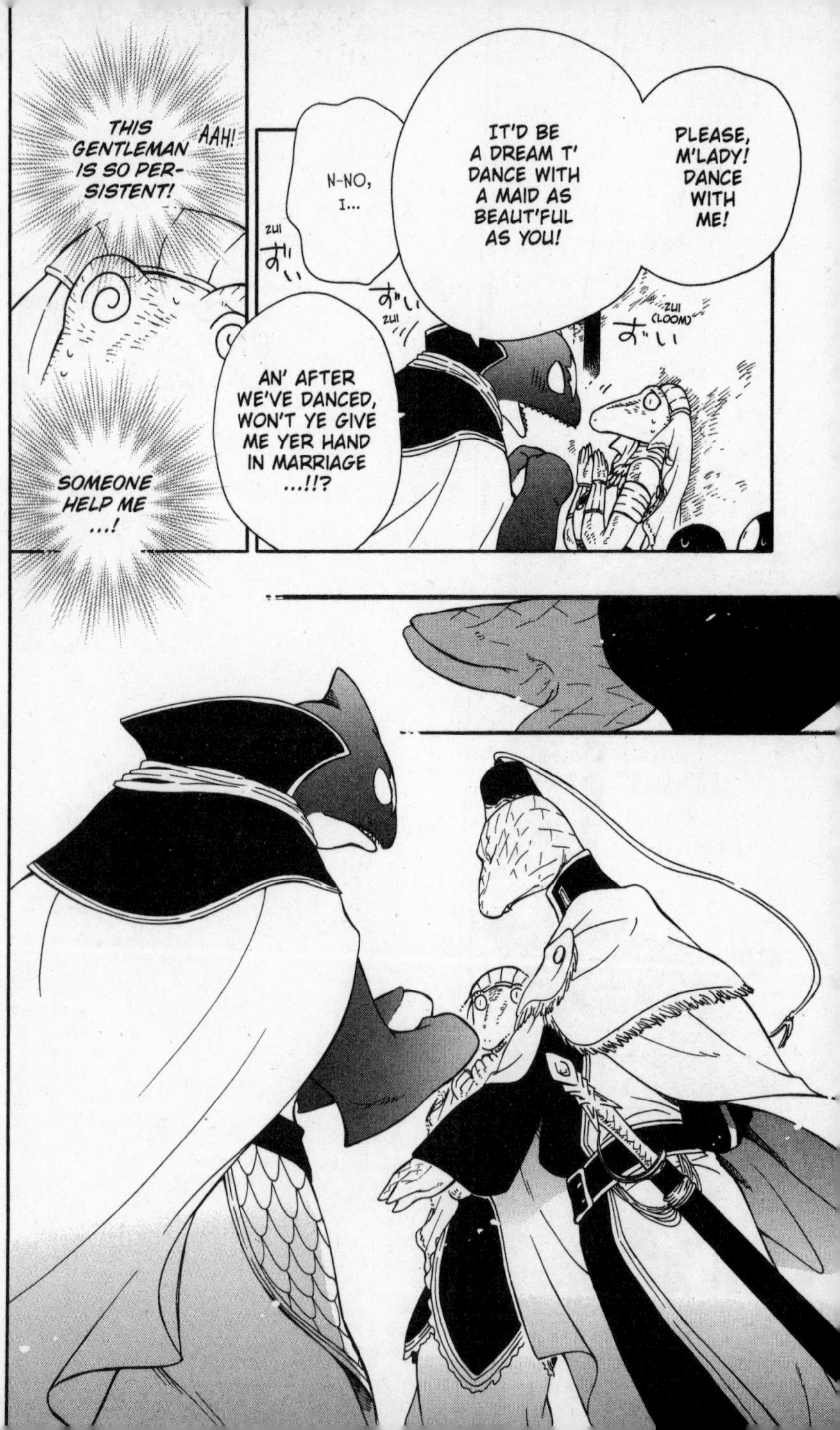
PLEASE, M'LADY! DANCE WITH ME!
IT'D BE A DREAM T' DANCE WITH A MAID AS BEAUT'FUL AS YOU!
ZUI (LOOM)
ずい
N-NO, I...
ZUI
ずい
ZUI
ずい
AN' AFTER WE'VE DANCED, WON'T YE GIVE ME YER HAND IN MARRIAGE ...!!?
AAH!
THIS GENTLEMAN IS SO PER-SISTENT!
SOMEONE HELP ME ...!

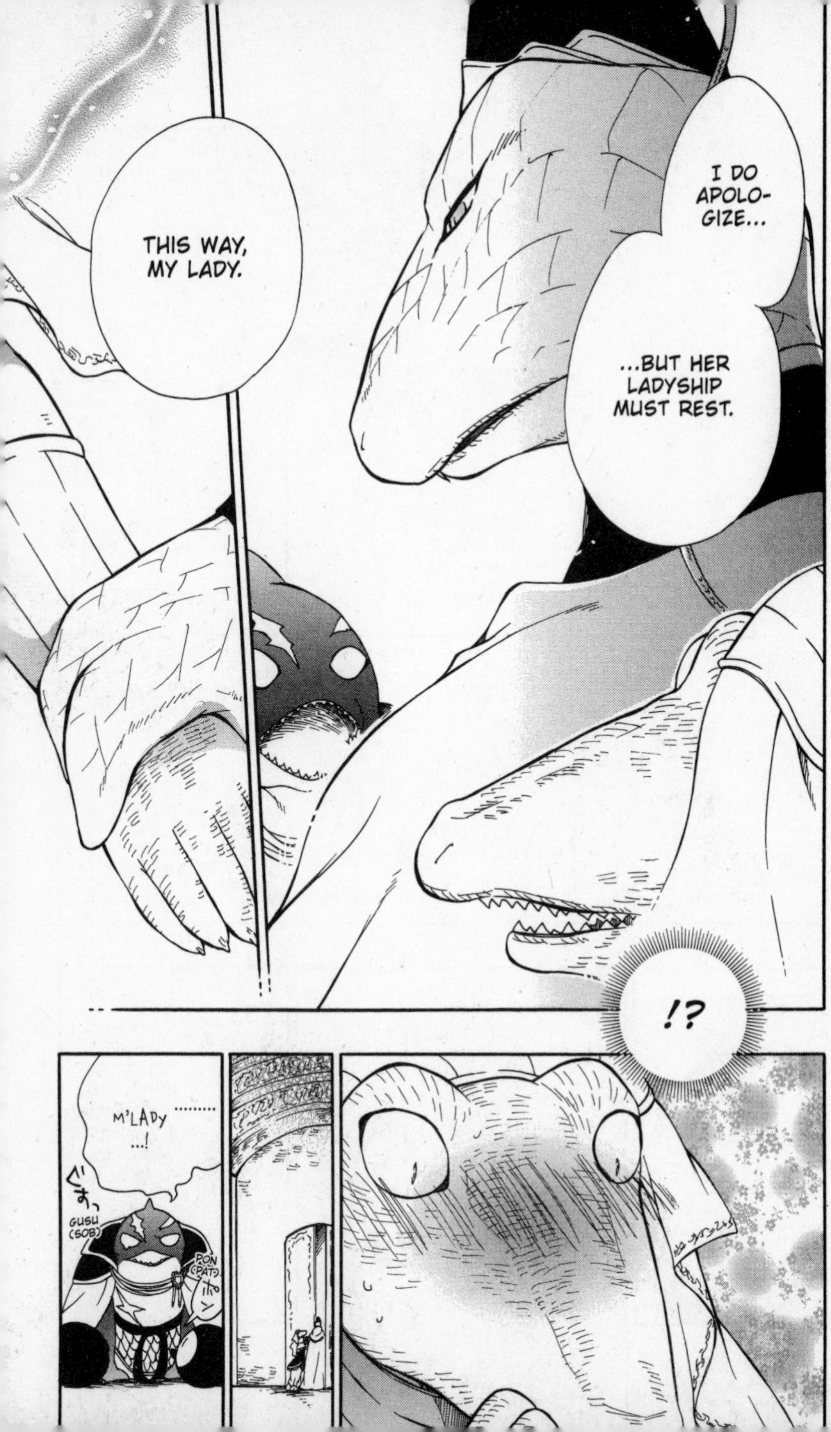
I DO APOLO-GIZE...
...BUT HER LADYSHIP MUST REST.
THIS WAY, MY LADY.
!?
....
M'LADY ...!
ぐすっ
GUSU (SOB)
ポン
PON (PAT)

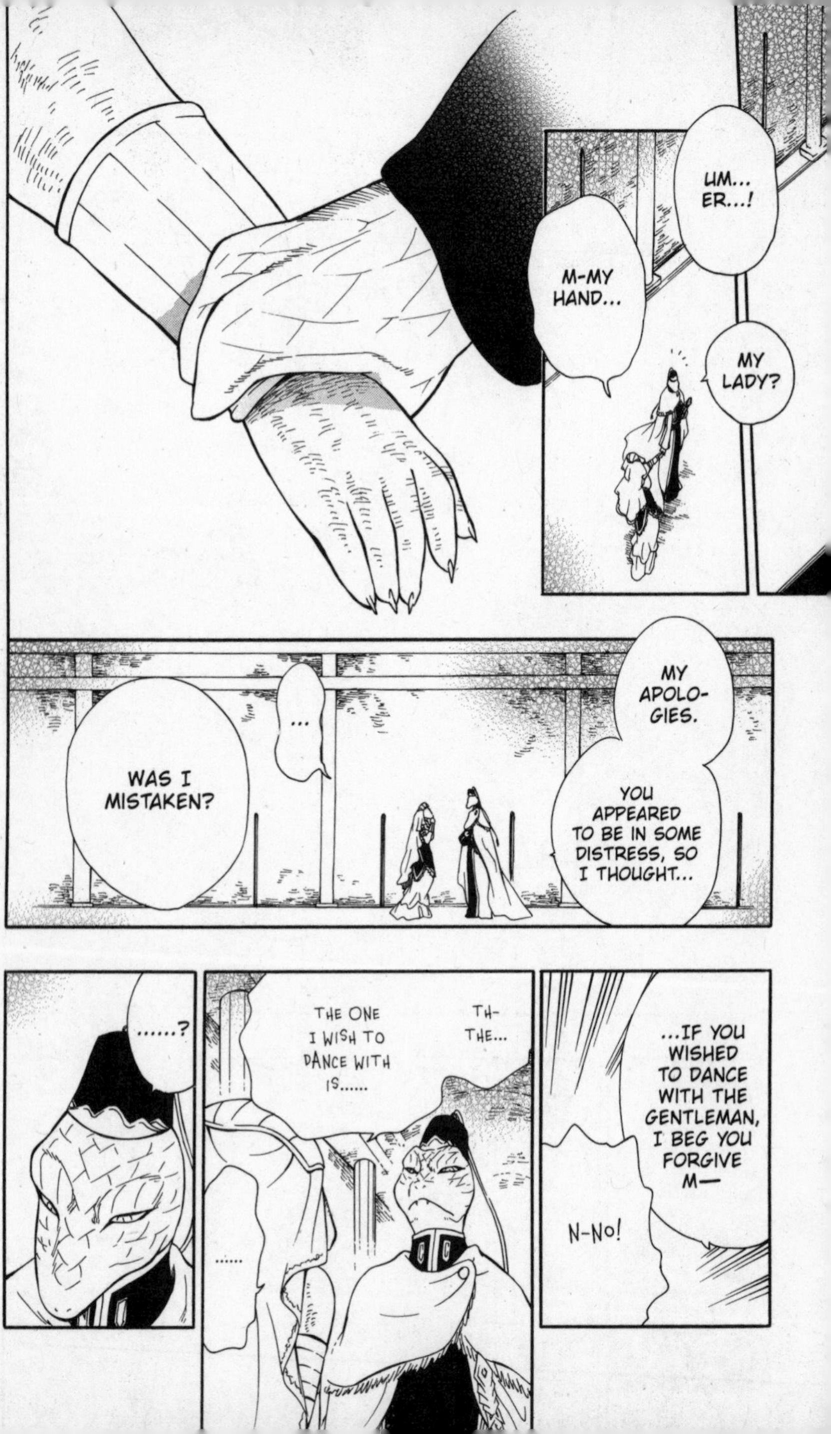
UM... ER...!
M-MY HAND...
MY LADY?
MY APOLOGIES.
YOU APPEARED TO BE IN SOME DISTRESS, SO I THOUGHT...
...
WAS I MISTAKEN?
...IF YOU WISHED TO DANCE WITH THE GENTLEMAN, I BEG YOU FORGIVE M—
N-NO!
TH- THE...
THE ONE I WISH TO DANCE WITH IS......
......
......?

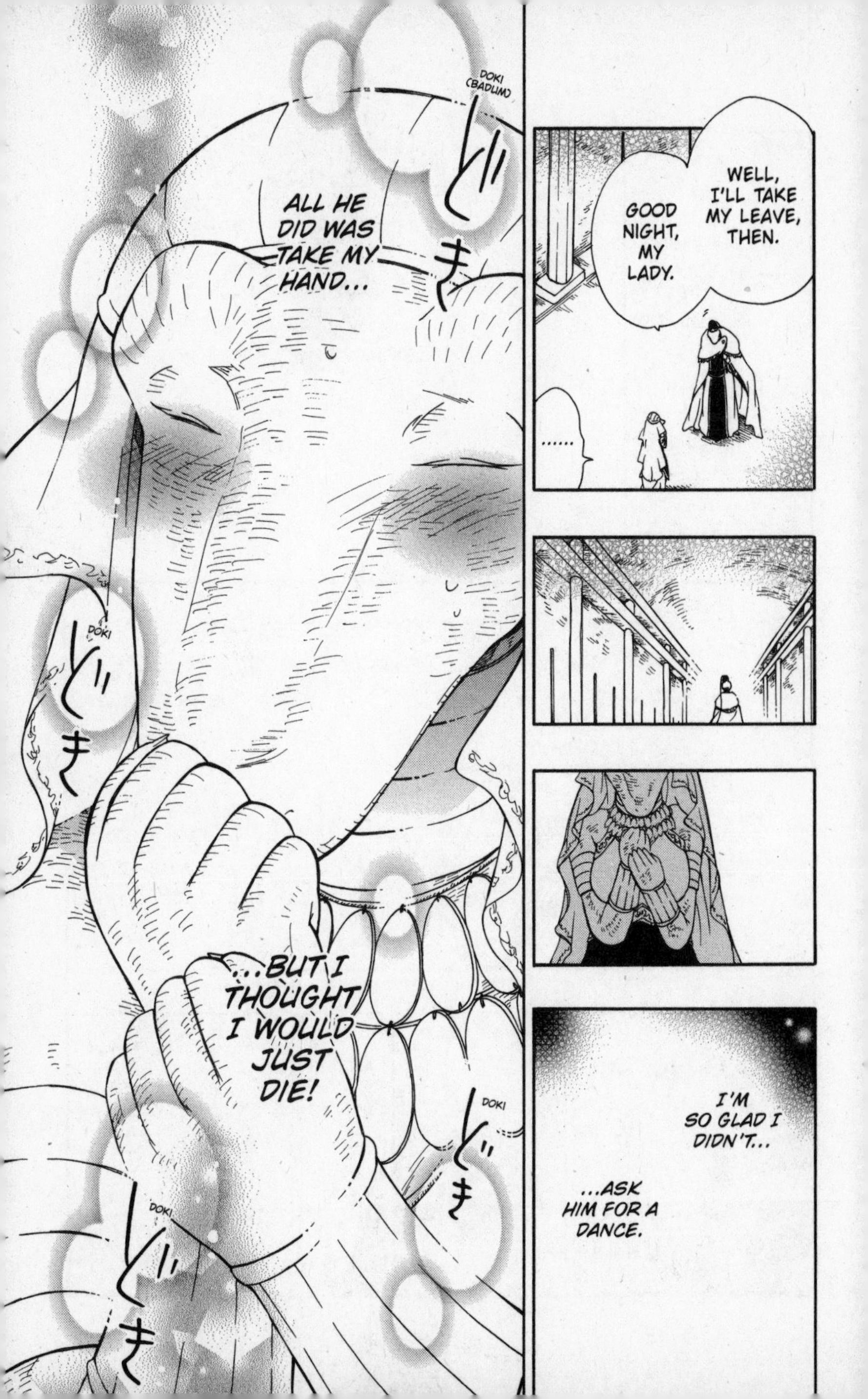
WELL, I'LL TAKE MY LEAVE, THEN.
GOOD NIGHT, MY LADY.
......
I'M SO GLAD I DIDN'T...
...ASK HIM FOR A DANCE.
DOKI (BADUM)
どき
ALL HE DID WAS TAKE MY HAND...
DOKI
どき
...BUT I THOUGHT I WOULD JUST DIE!
DOKI
どき
DOKI
どき

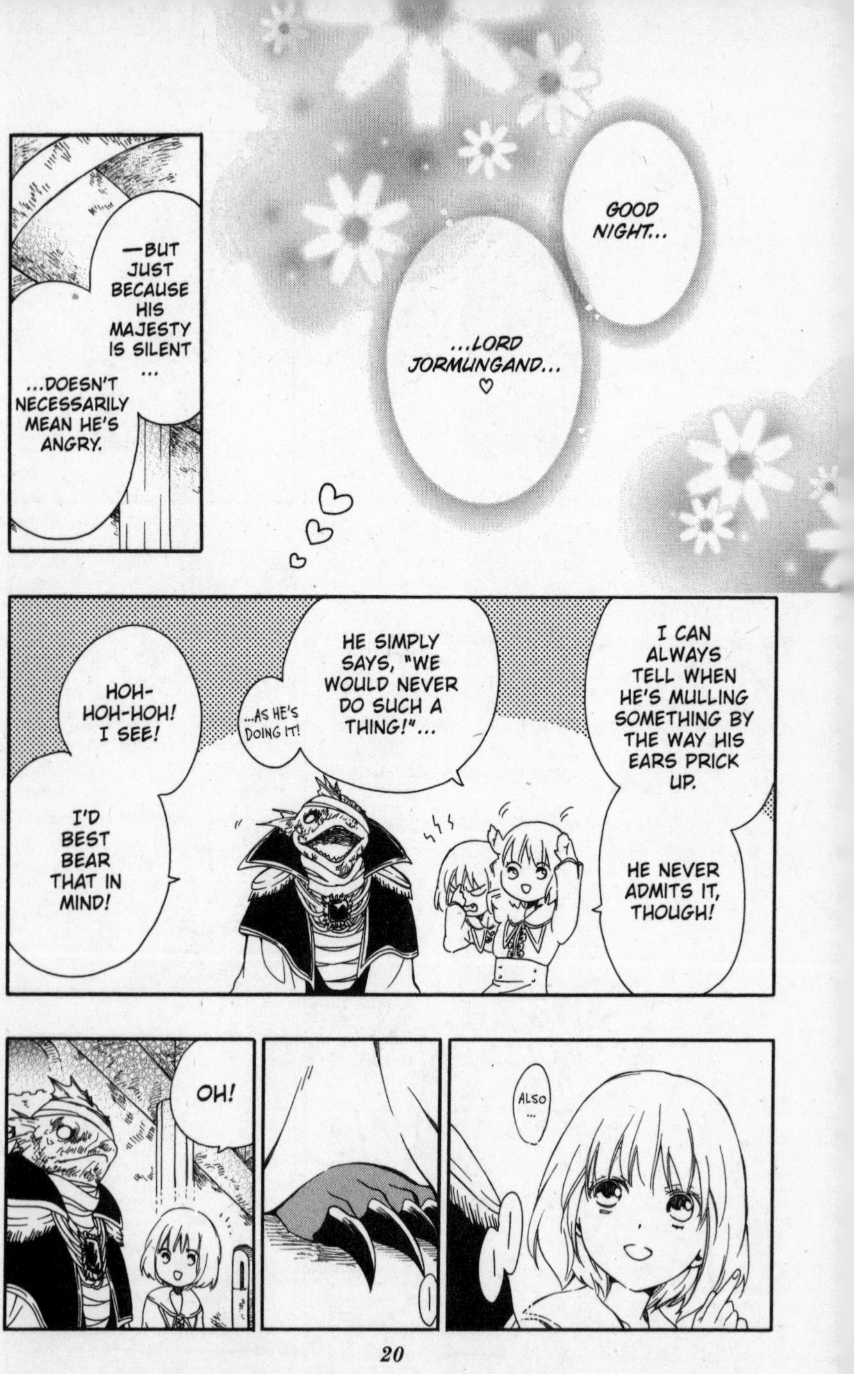
GOOD NIGHT...
...LORD JORMUNGAND... ♡
—BUT JUST BECAUSE HIS MAJESTY IS SILENT ...
...DOESN'T NECESSARILY MEAN HE'S ANGRY.
I CAN ALWAYS TELL WHEN HE'S MULLING SOMETHING BY THE WAY HIS EARS PRICK UP.
HE NEVER ADMITS IT, THOUGH!
HE SIMPLY SAYS, "WE WOULD NEVER DO SUCH A THING!"...
...AS HE'S DOING IT!
HOH-HOH-HOH! I SEE!
I'D BEST BEAR THAT IN MIND!
ALSO ...
OH!

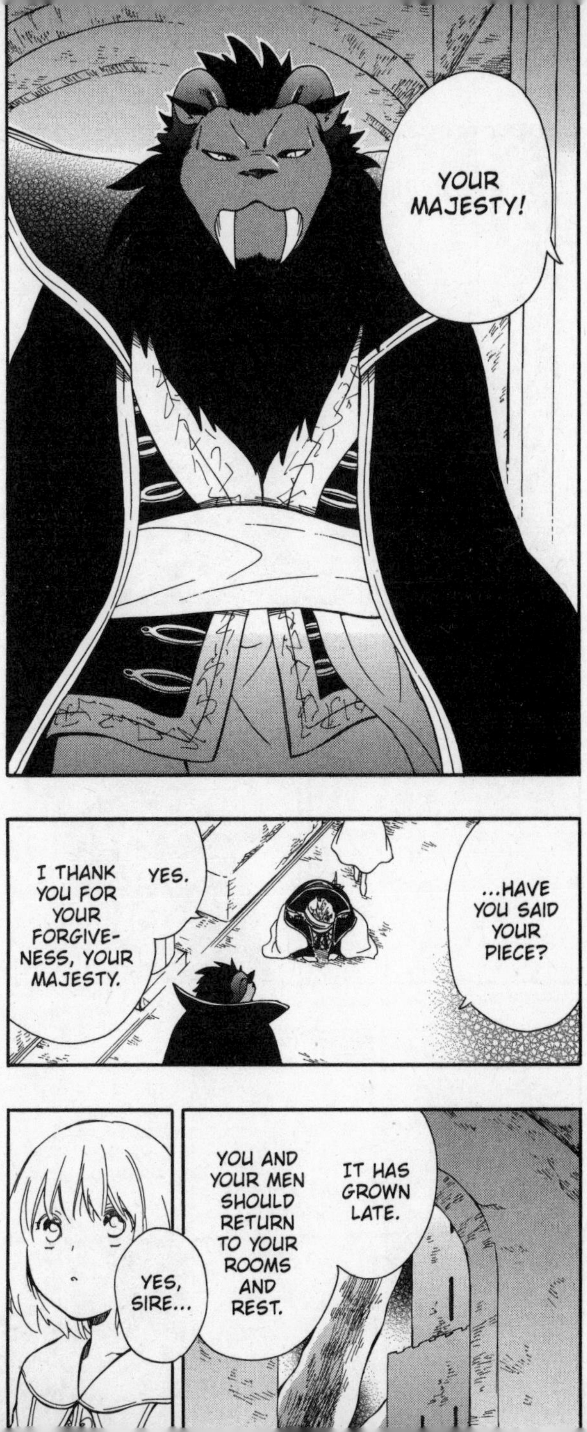
YOUR MAJESTY!
...HAVE YOU SAID YOUR PIECE?
YES.
I THANK YOU FOR YOUR FORGIVE-NESS, YOUR MAJESTY.
IT HAS GROWN LATE.
YOU AND YOUR MEN SHOULD RETURN TO YOUR ROOMS AND REST.
YES, SIRE...

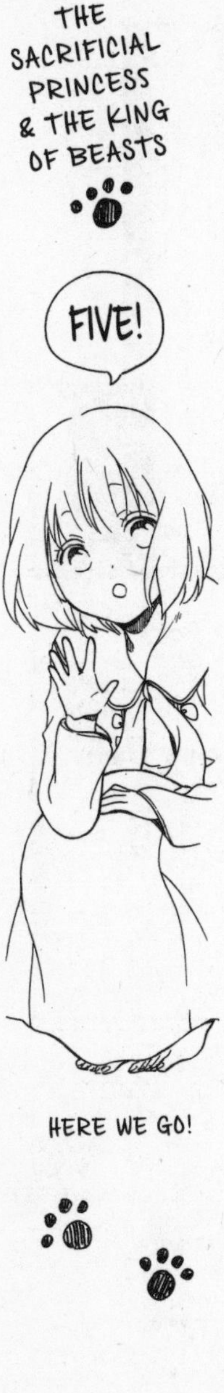
THE SACRIFICIAL PRINCESS & THE KING OF BEASTS
FIVE!
HERE WE GO!

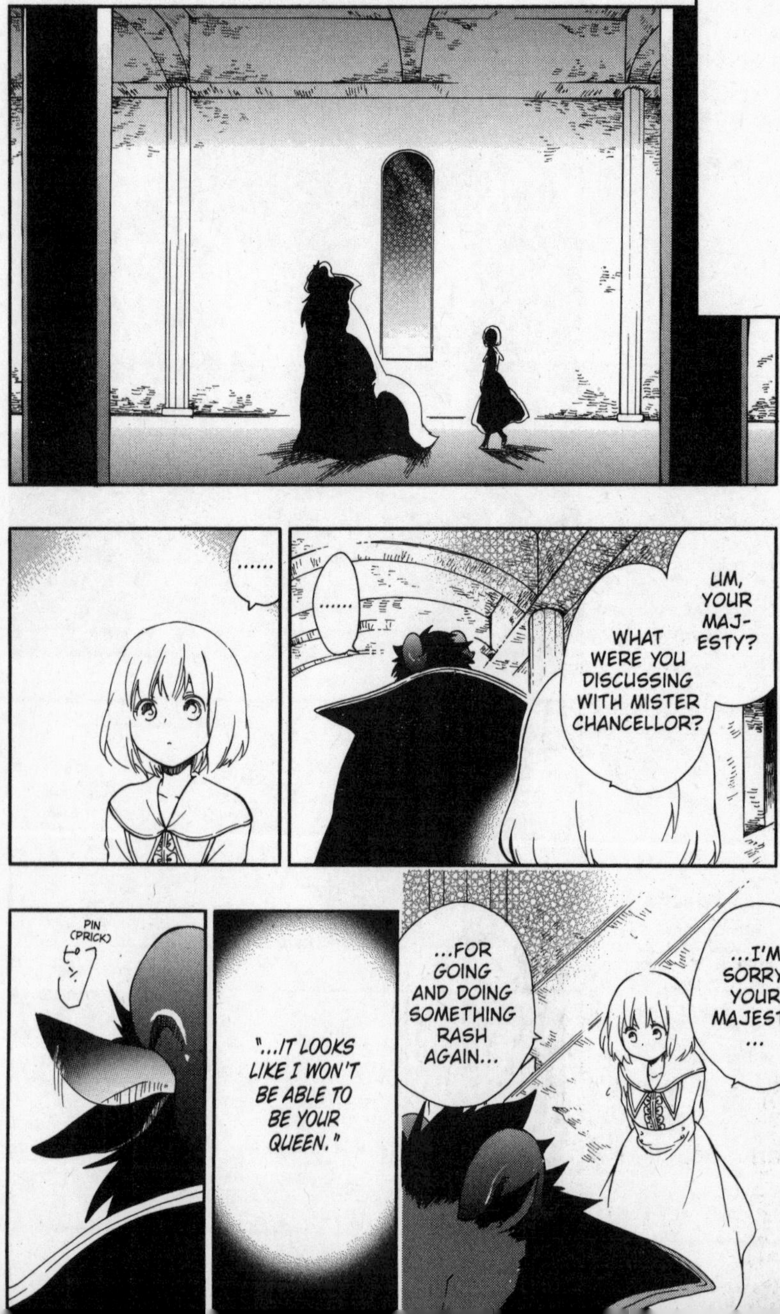
UM, YOUR MAJ-ESTY?
WHAT WERE YOU DISCUSSING WITH MISTER CHANCELLOR?
......
......
...I'M SORRY, YOUR MAJESTY...
...FOR GOING AND DOING SOMETHING RASH AGAIN...
"...IT LOOKS LIKE I WON'T BE ABLE TO BE YOUR QUEEN."
PIN (PRICK)

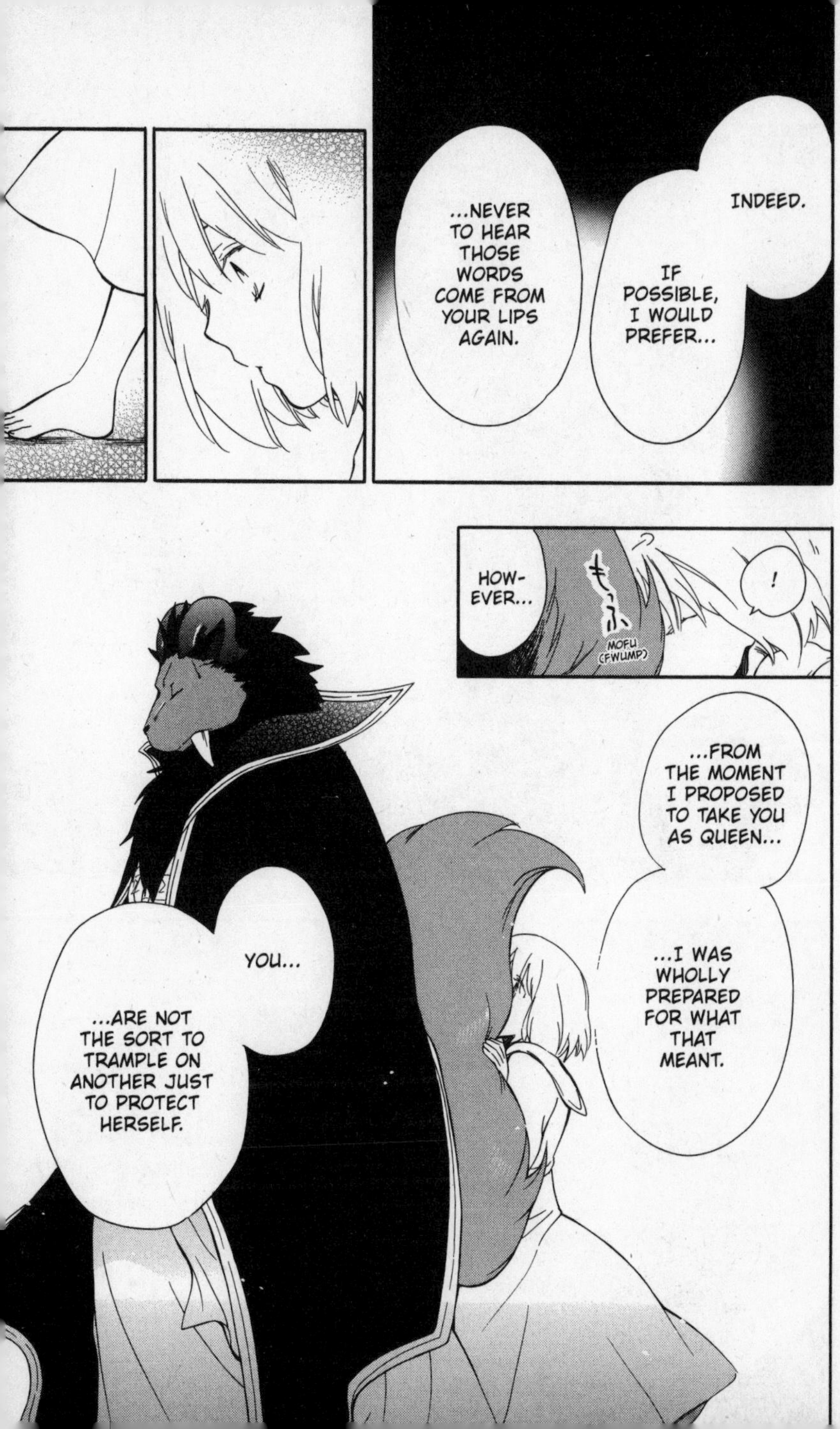
INDEED.
IF POSSIBLE, I WOULD PREFER...
...NEVER TO HEAR THOSE WORDS COME FROM YOUR LIPS AGAIN.
!
もふ
MOFU (FWUMP)
HOW-EVER...
...FROM THE MOMENT I PROPOSED TO TAKE YOU AS QUEEN...
...I WAS WHOLLY PREPARED FOR WHAT THAT MEANT.
YOU...
...ARE NOT THE SORT TO TRAMPLE ON ANOTHER JUST TO PROTECT HERSELF.

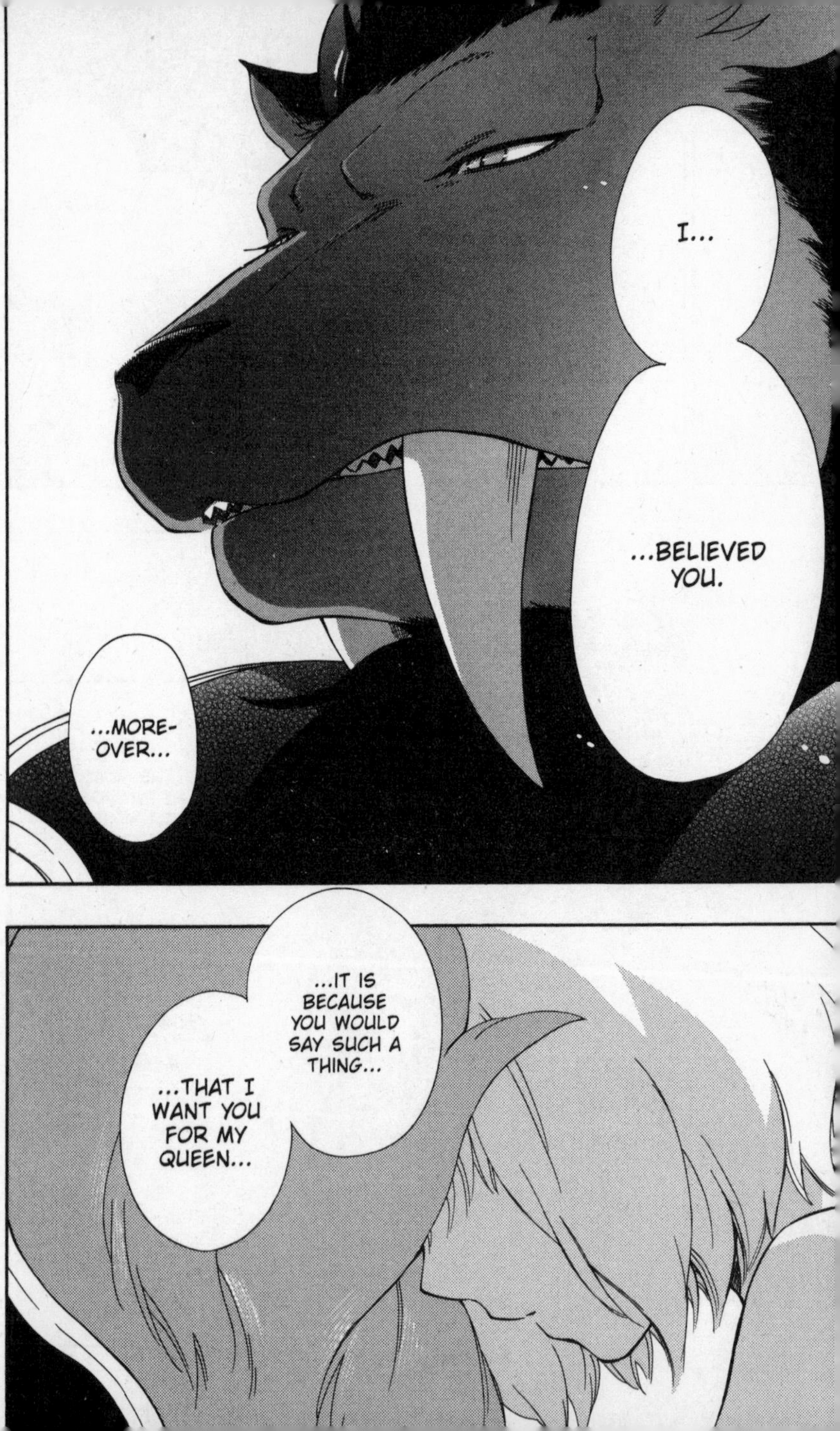
I...
...BELIEVED YOU.
...MORE-OVER...
...IT IS BECAUSE YOU WOULD SAY SUCH A THING...
...THAT I WANT YOU FOR MY QUEEN...

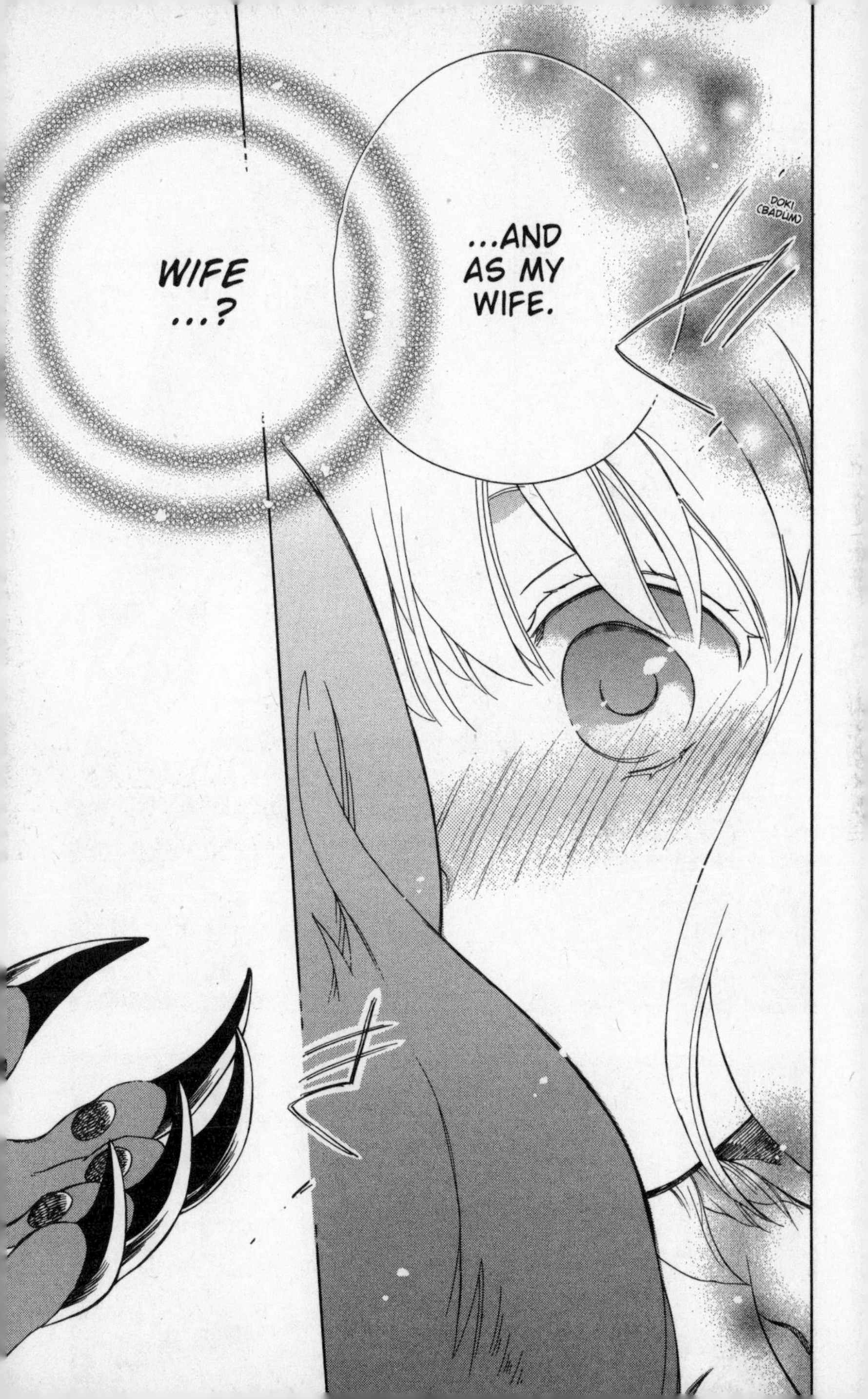
DOKI (BADUM)
...AND AS MY WIFE.
WIFE ...?

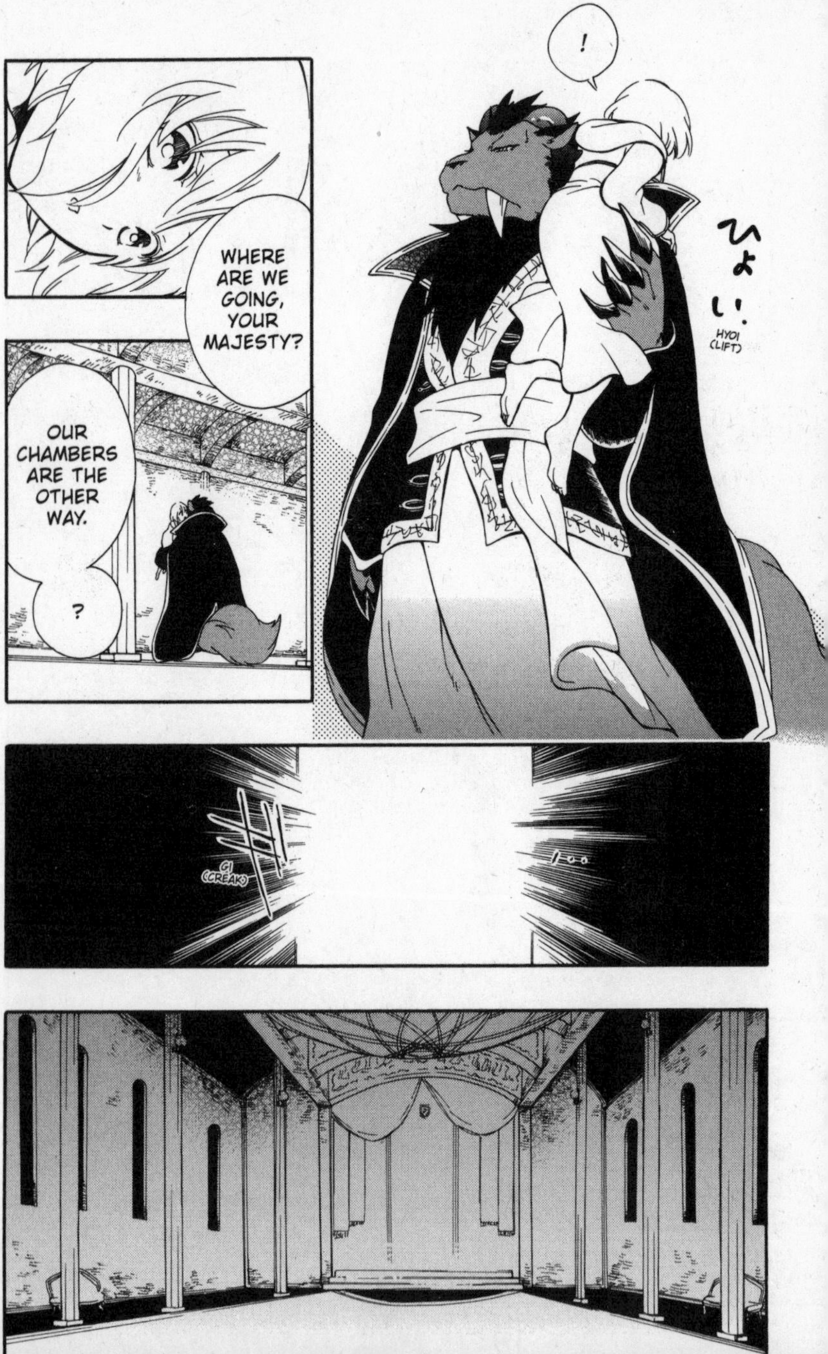
!
ひょい!
HYOI (LIFT)
WHERE ARE WE GOING, YOUR MAJESTY?
OUR CHAMBERS ARE THE OTHER WAY.
?
GI (CREAK)

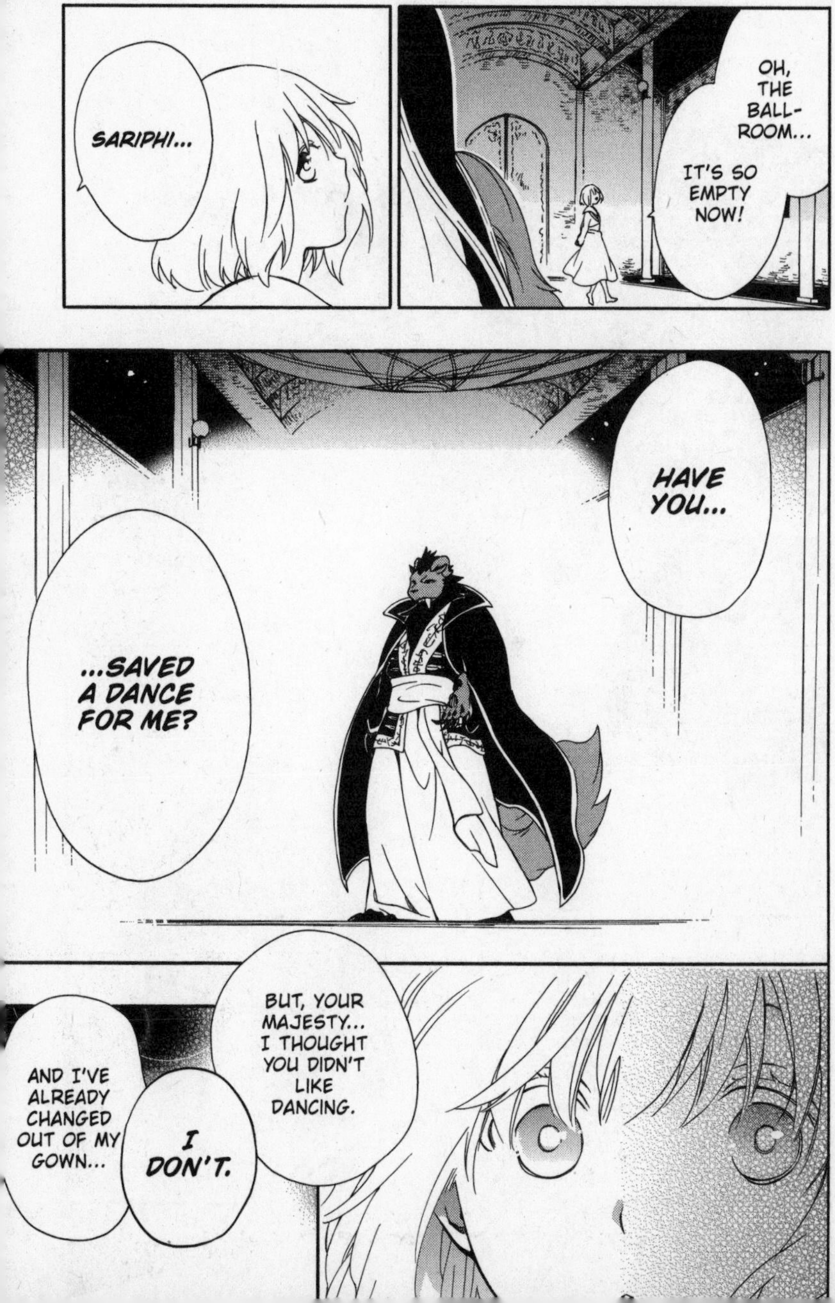
OH, THE BALL-ROOM...
IT'S SO EMPTY NOW!
SARIPHI...
HAVE YOU...
...SAVED A DANCE FOR ME?
BUT, YOUR MAJESTY... I THOUGHT YOU DIDN'T LIKE DANCING.
I DON'T.
AND I'VE ALREADY CHANGED OUT OF MY GOWN...

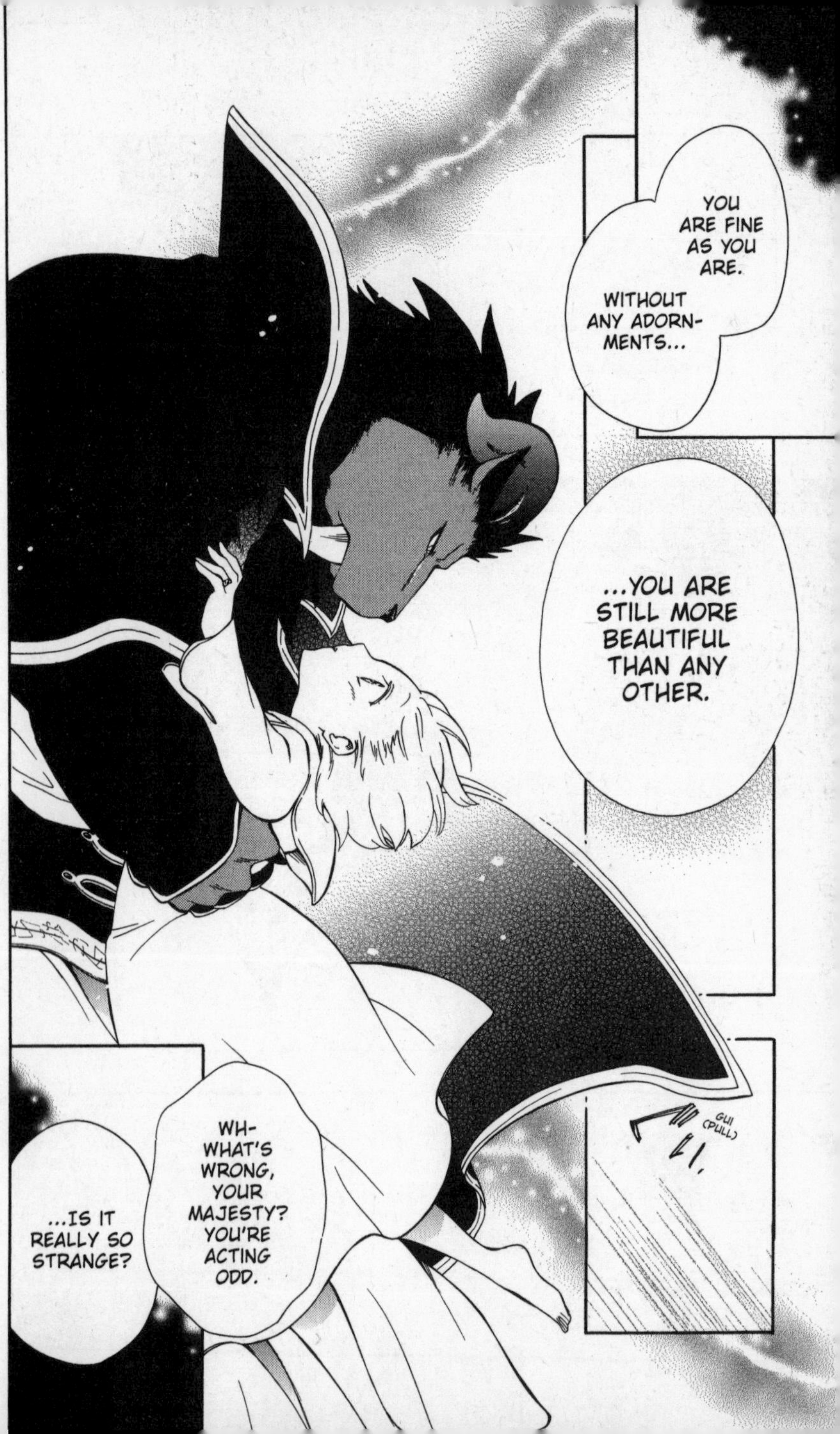
YOU ARE FINE AS YOU ARE.
WITHOUT ANY ADORNMENTS...
...YOU ARE STILL MORE BEAUTIFUL THAN ANY OTHER.
GUI (PULL)
WH- WHAT'S WRONG, YOUR MAJESTY? YOU'RE ACTING ODD.
...IS IT REALLY SO STRANGE?

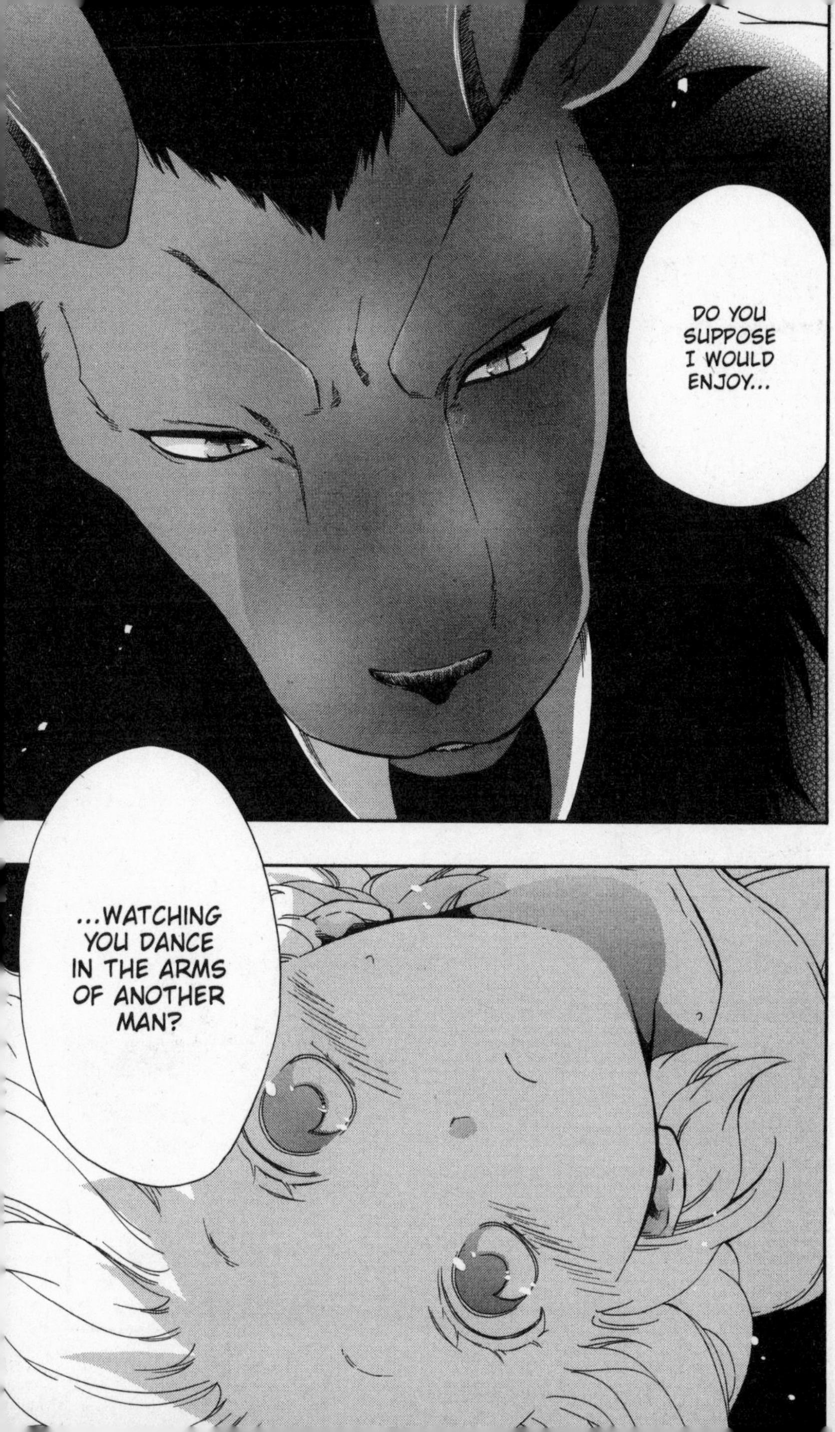
DO YOU SUPPOSE I WOULD ENJOY...
...WATCHING YOU DANCE IN THE ARMS OF ANOTHER MAN?

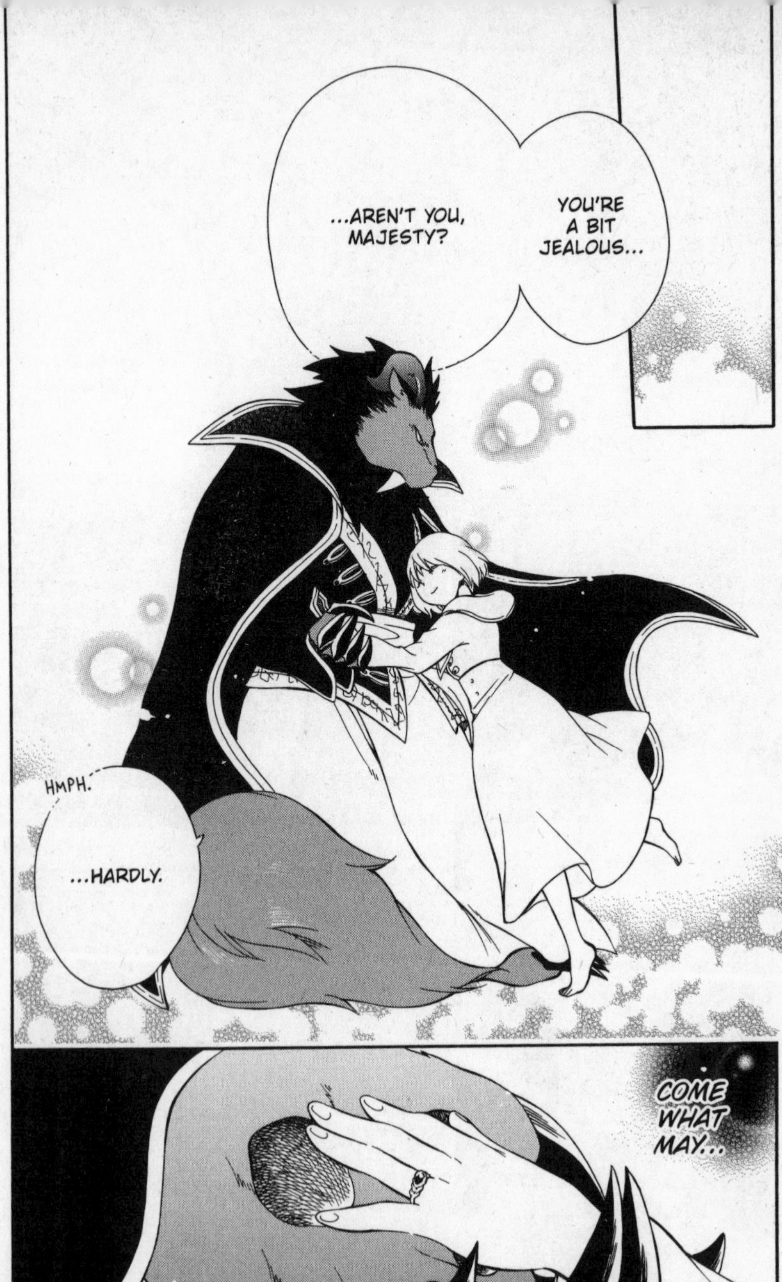
YOU'RE A BIT JEALOUS...
...AREN'T YOU, MAJESTY?
HMPH.
...HARDLY.
COME WHAT MAY...

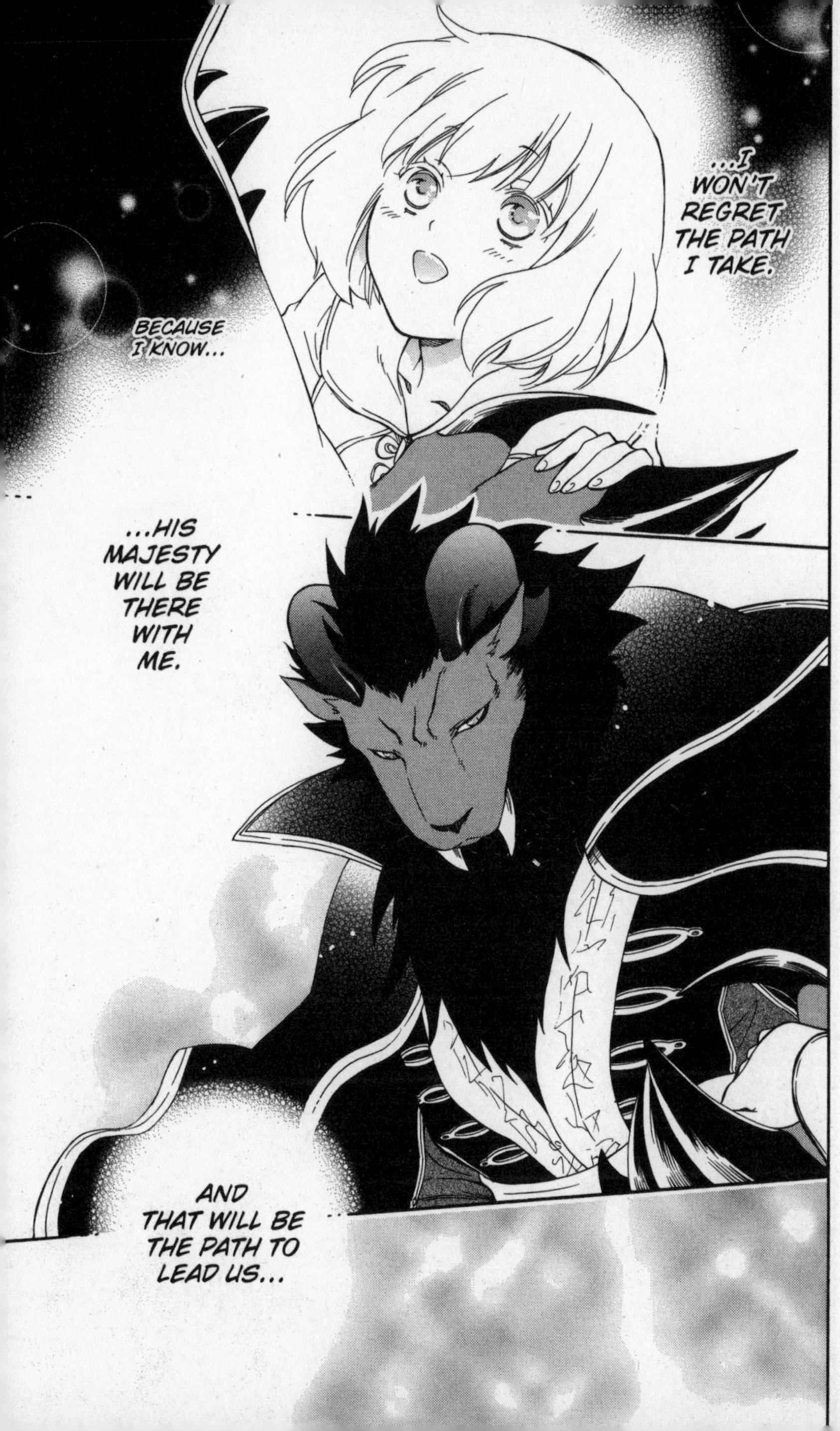
...I WON'T REGRET THE PATH I TAKE.
BECAUSE I KNOW...
...HIS MAJESTY WILL BE THERE WITH ME.
AND THAT WILL BE THE PATH TO LEAD US...

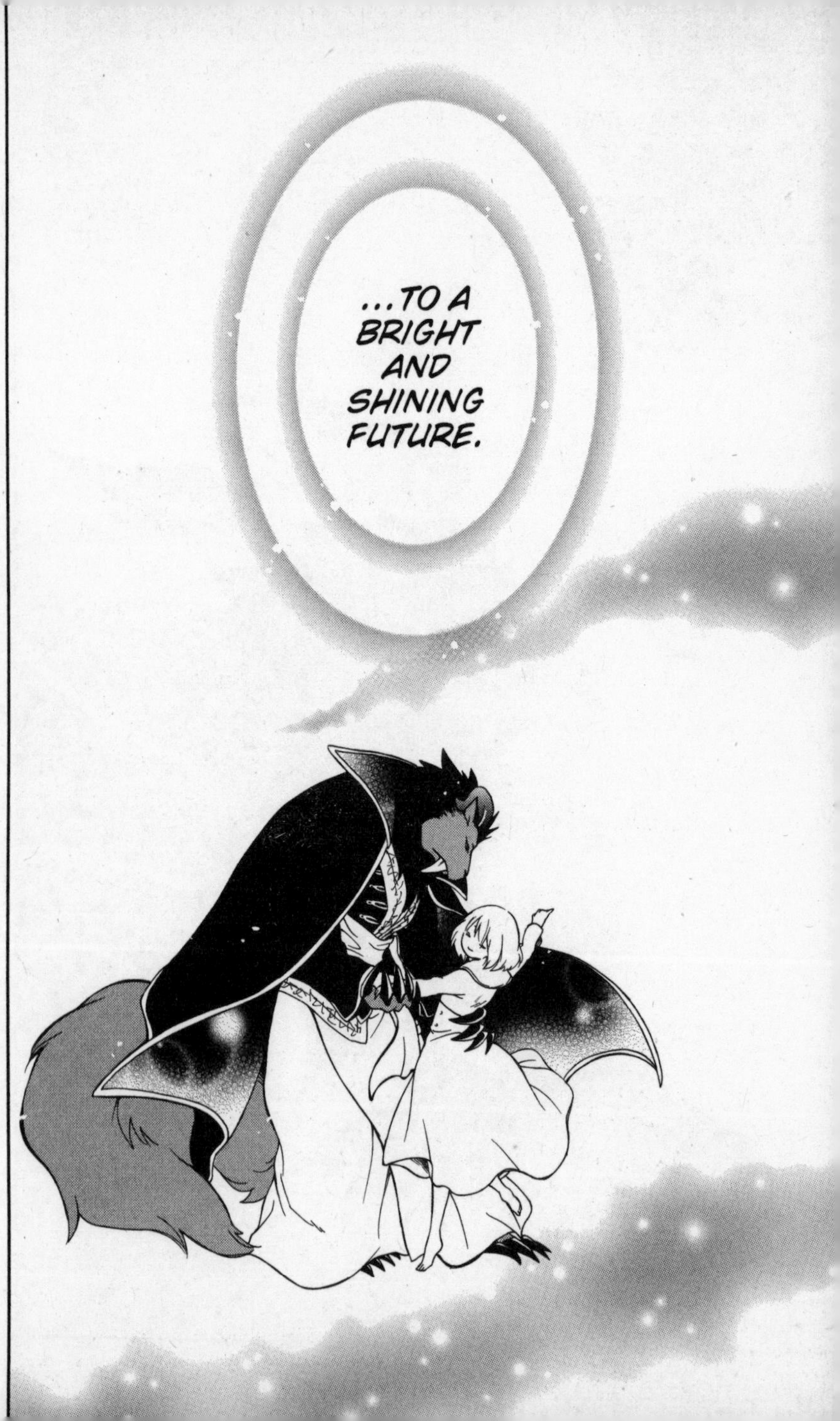
...TO A BRIGHT AND SHINING FUTURE.

episode. 25

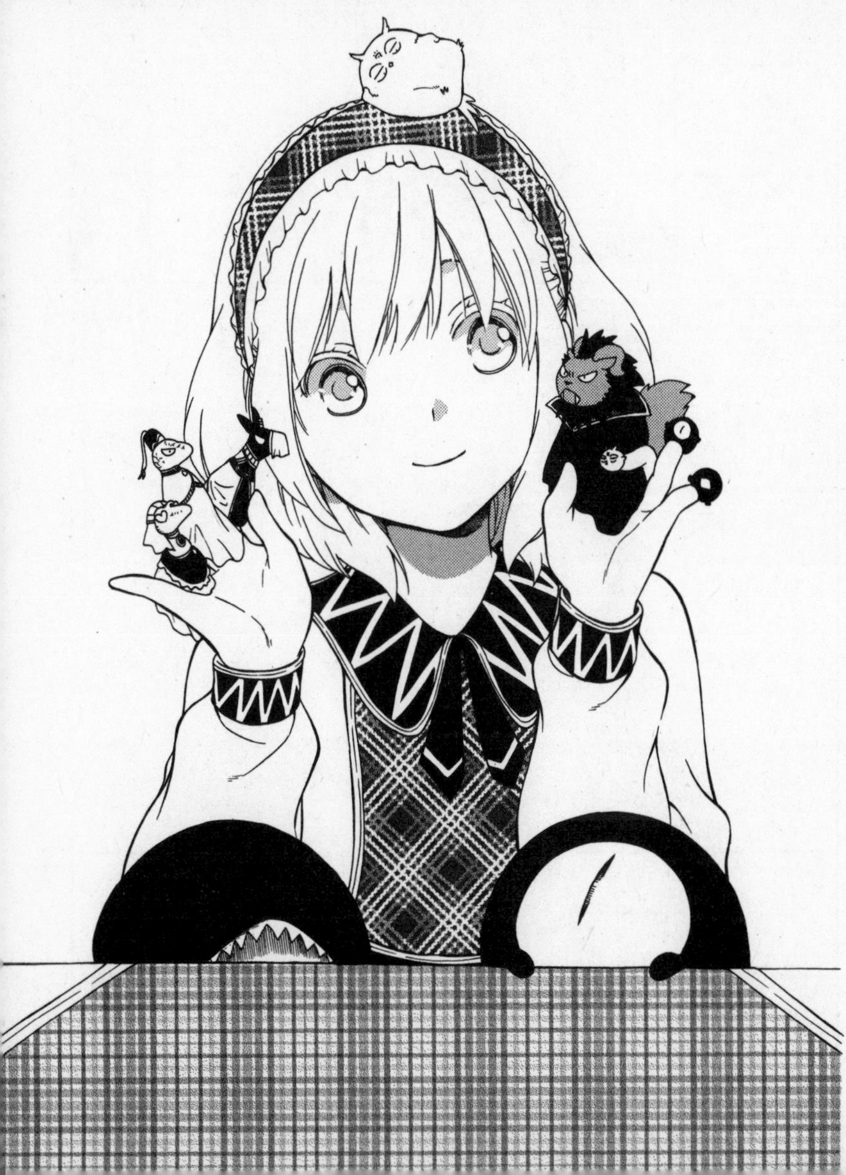

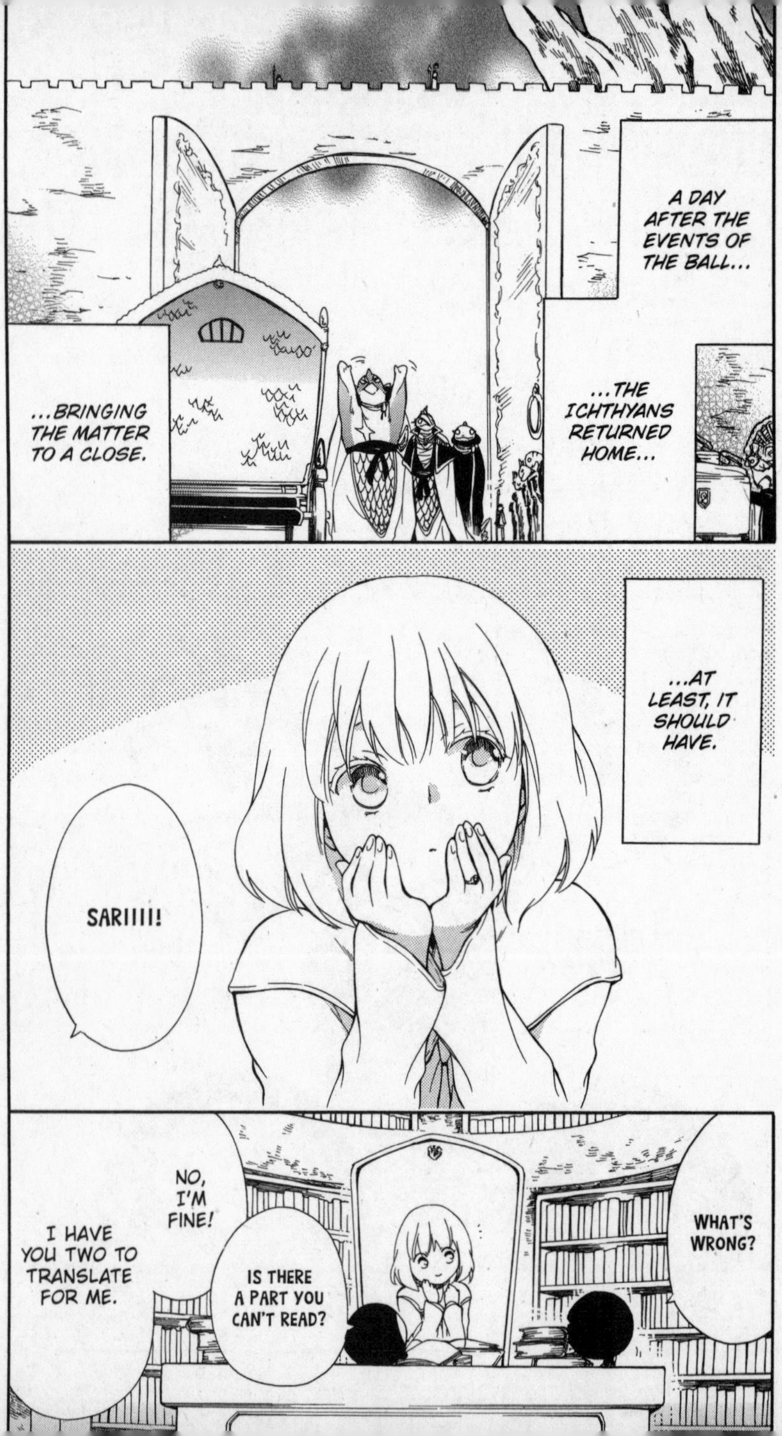
A DAY AFTER THE EVENTS OF THE BALL...
...THE ICHTHYANS RETURNED HOME...
...BRINGING THE MATTER TO A CLOSE.
...AT LEAST, IT SHOULD HAVE.
SARIIIII!
WHAT'S WRONG?
IS THERE A PART YOU CAN'T READ?
NO, I'M FINE!
I HAVE YOU TWO TO TRANSLATE FOR ME.

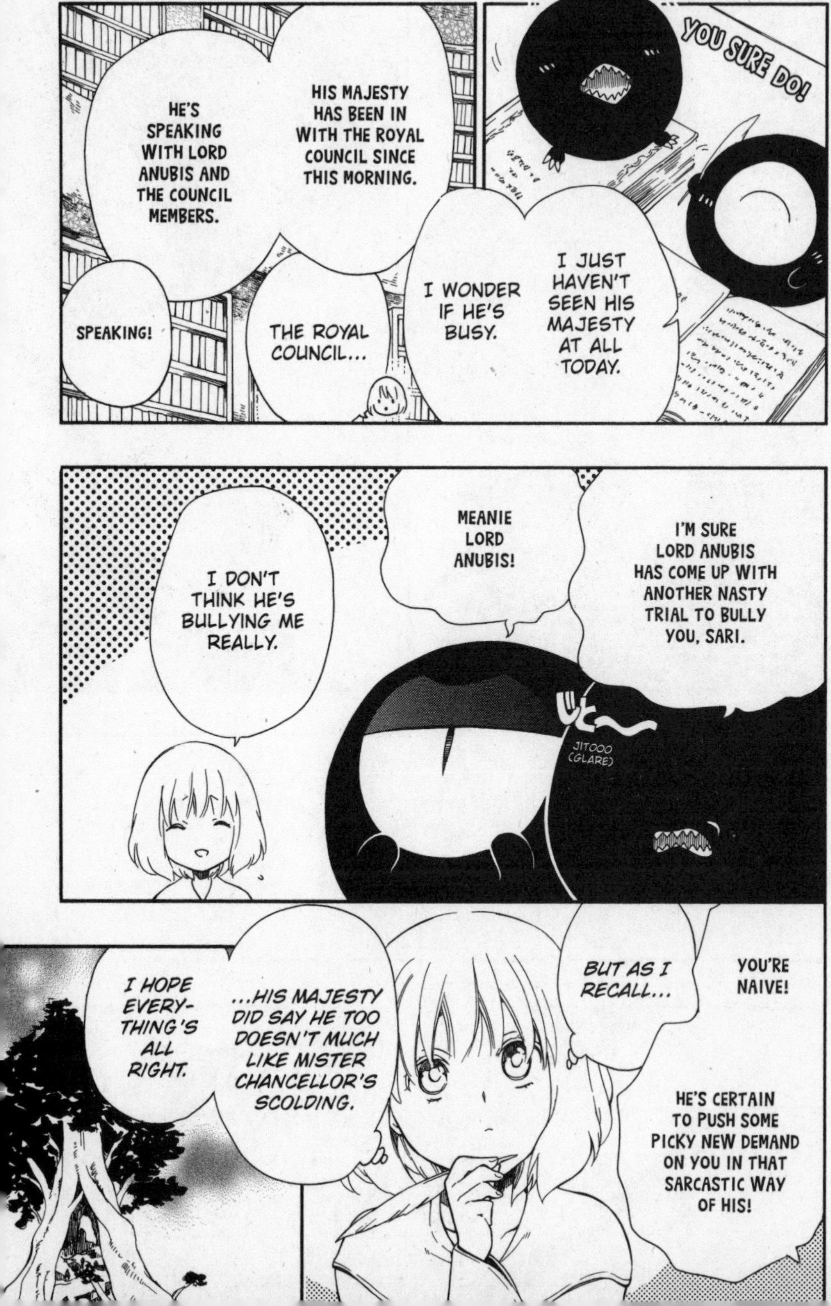
YOU SURE DO!
I JUST HAVEN'T SEEN HIS MAJESTY AT ALL TODAY.
I WONDER IF HE'S BUSY.
HIS MAJESTY HAS BEEN IN WITH THE ROYAL COUNCIL SINCE THIS MORNING.
HE'S SPEAKING WITH LORD ANUBIS AND THE COUNCIL MEMBERS.
THE ROYAL COUNCIL...
SPEAKING!
I'M SURE LORD ANUBIS HAS COME UP WITH ANOTHER NASTY TRIAL TO BULLY YOU, SARI.
MEANIE LORD ANUBIS!
JITOOO (GLARE)
I DON'T THINK HE'S BULLYING ME REALLY.
YOU'RE NAIVE!
HE'S CERTAIN TO PUSH SOME PICKY NEW DEMAND ON YOU IN THAT SARCASTIC WAY OF HIS!
BUT AS I RECALL...
...HIS MAJESTY DID SAY HE TOO DOESN'T MUCH LIKE MISTER CHANCELLOR'S SCOLDING.
I HOPE EVERY-THING'S ALL RIGHT.

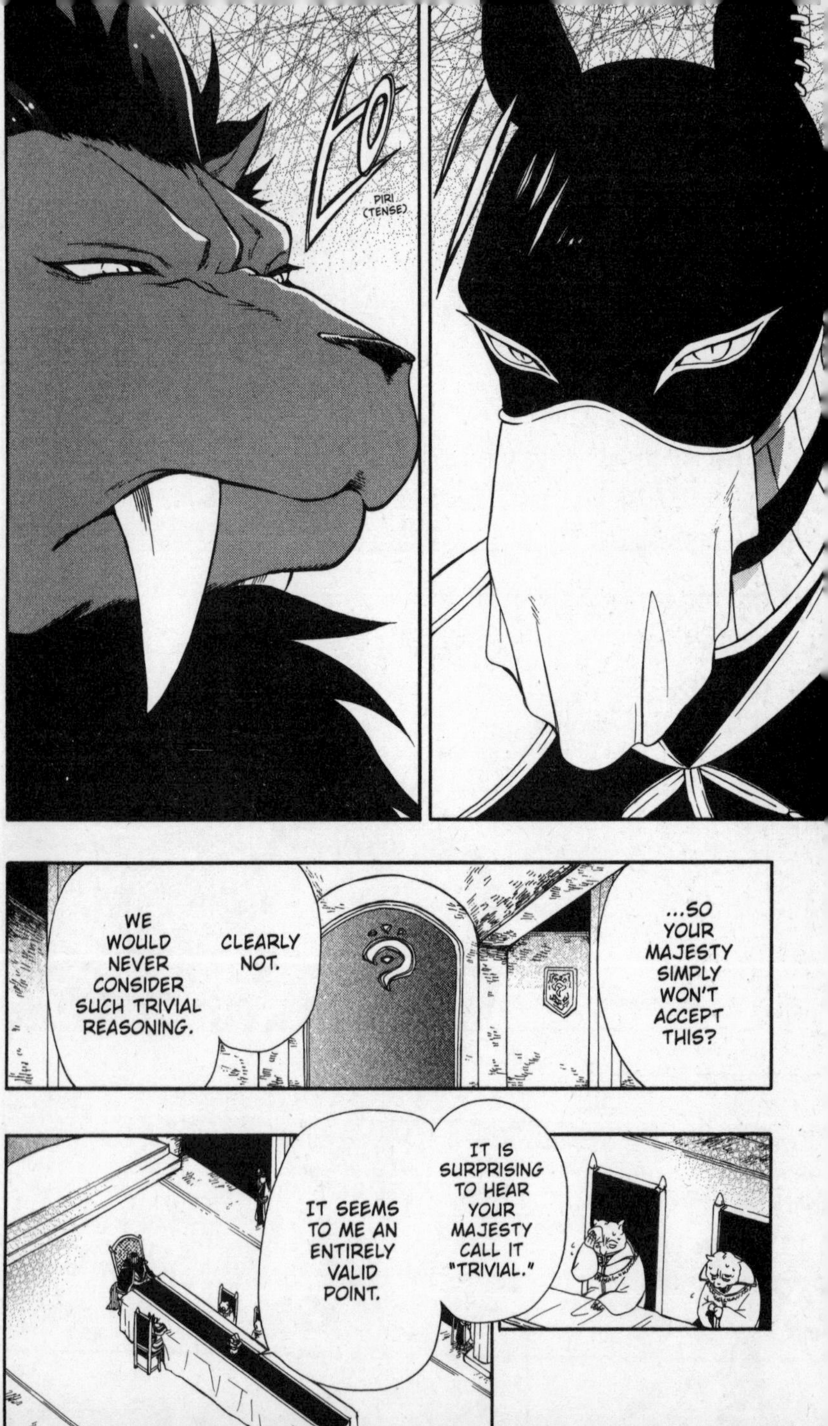
PIRI (TENSE)
...SO YOUR MAJESTY SIMPLY WON'T ACCEPT THIS?
CLEARLY NOT.
WE WOULD NEVER CONSIDER SUCH TRIVIAL REASONING.
IT IS SURPRISING TO HEAR YOUR MAJESTY CALL IT "TRIVIAL."
IT SEEMS TO ME AN ENTIRELY VALID POINT.

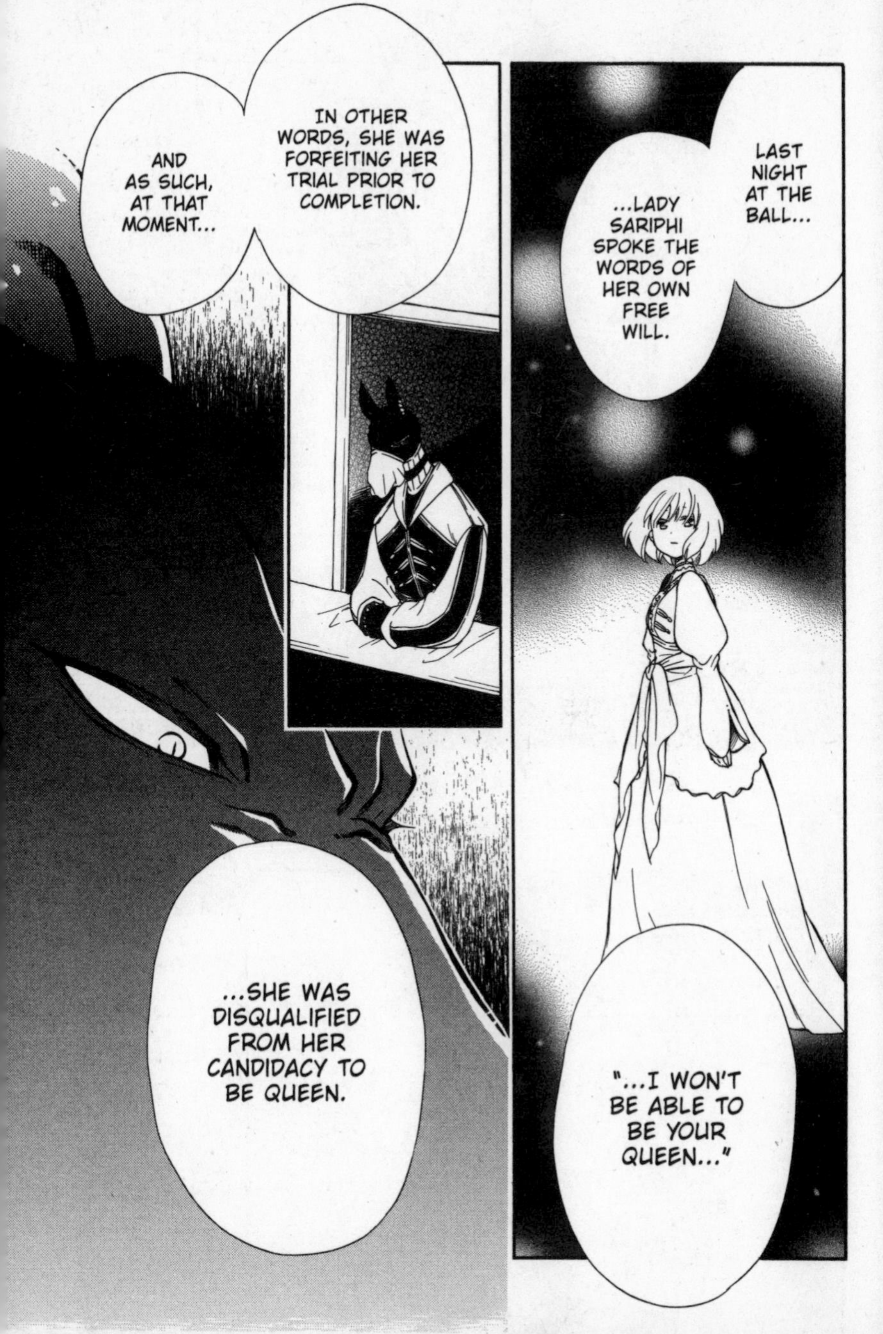
LAST NIGHT AT THE BALL...
...LADY SARIPHI SPOKE THE WORDS OF HER OWN FREE WILL.
"...I WON'T BE ABLE TO BE YOUR QUEEN..."
IN OTHER WORDS, SHE WAS FORFEITING HER TRIAL PRIOR TO COMPLETION.
AND AS SUCH, AT THAT MOMENT...
...SHE WAS DISQUALIFIED FROM HER CANDIDACY TO BE QUEEN.

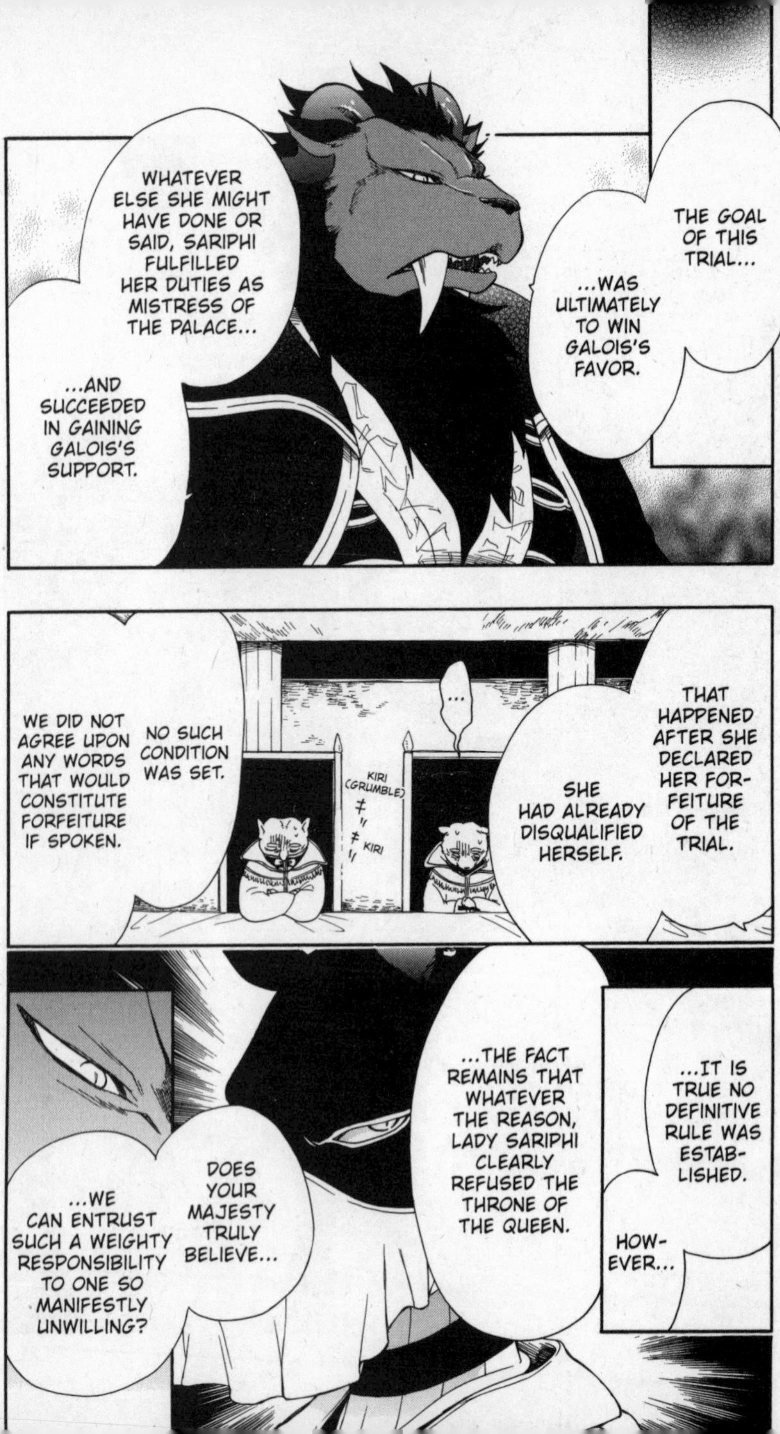
THE GOAL OF THIS TRIAL...
...WAS ULTIMATELY TO WIN GALOIS'S FAVOR.
WHATEVER ELSE SHE MIGHT HAVE DONE OR SAID, SARIPHI FULFILLED HER DUTIES AS MISTRESS OF THE PALACE...
...AND SUCCEEDED IN GAINING GALOIS'S SUPPORT.
THAT HAPPENED AFTER SHE DECLARED HER FOR-FEITURE OF THE TRIAL.
SHE HAD ALREADY DISQUALIFIED HERSELF.
...
KIRI (GRUMBLE)
KIRI
NO SUCH CONDITION WAS SET.
WE DID NOT AGREE UPON ANY WORDS THAT WOULD CONSTITUTE FORFEITURE IF SPOKEN.
...IT IS TRUE NO DEFINITIVE RULE WAS ESTAB-LISHED.
HOW-EVER...
...THE FACT REMAINS THAT WHATEVER THE REASON, LADY SARIPHI CLEARLY REFUSED THE THRONE OF THE QUEEN.
DOES YOUR MAJESTY TRULY BELIEVE...
...WE CAN ENTRUST SUCH A WEIGHTY RESPONSIBILITY TO ONE SO MANIFESTLY UNWILLING?

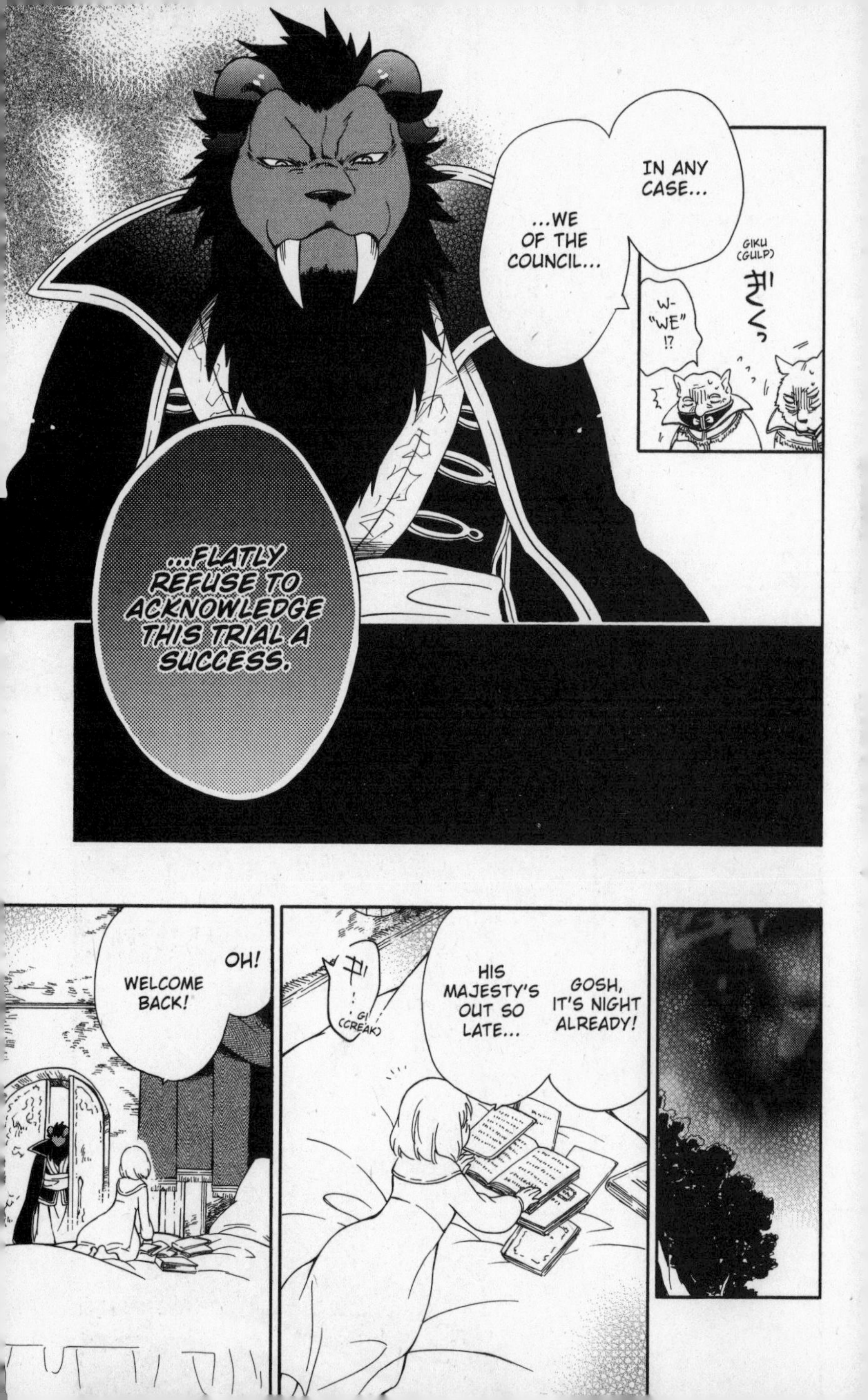
IN ANY CASE...
...WE OF THE COUNCIL...
GIKU (GULP)
W- "WE" !?
...FLATLY REFUSE TO ACKNOWLEDGE THIS TRIAL A SUCCESS.
GOSH, IT'S NIGHT ALREADY!
HIS MAJESTY'S OUT SO LATE...
GI (CREAK)
OH!
WELCOME BACK!

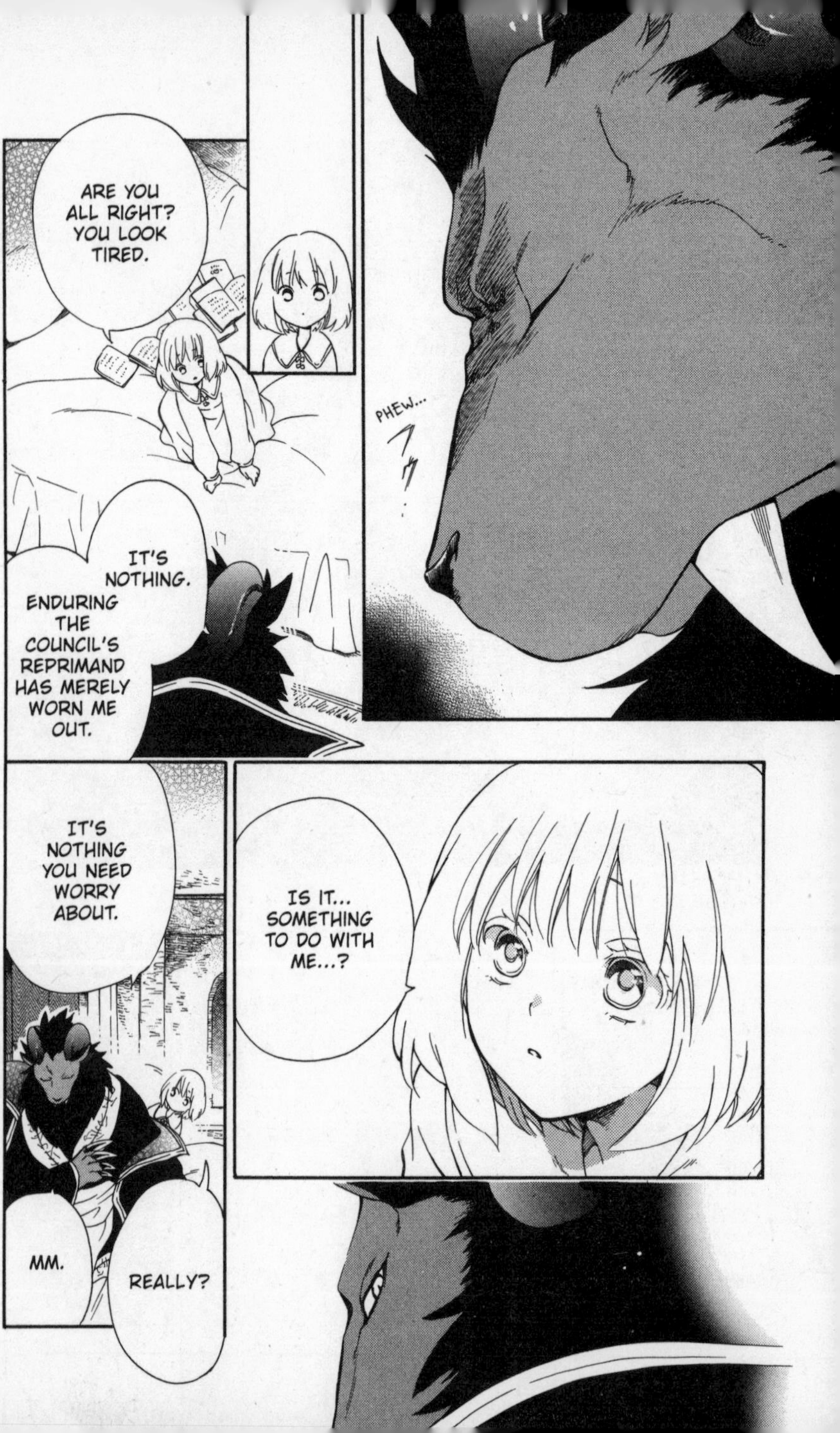
PHEW...
ARE YOU ALL RIGHT? YOU LOOK TIRED.
IT'S NOTHING.
ENDURING THE COUNCIL'S REPRIMAND HAS MERELY WORN ME OUT.
IS IT... SOMETHING TO DO WITH ME...?
IT'S NOTHING YOU NEED WORRY ABOUT.
REALLY?
MM.

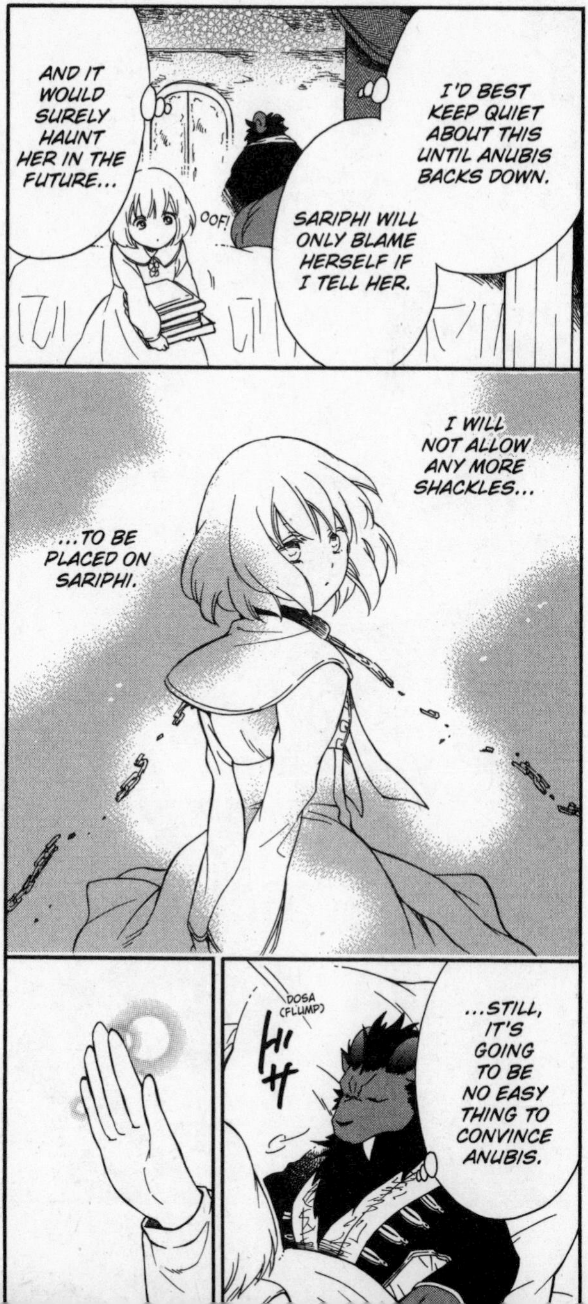
I'D BEST KEEP QUIET ABOUT THIS UNTIL ANUBIS BACKS DOWN.
SARIPHI WILL ONLY BLAME HERSELF IF I TELL HER.
OOF!
AND IT WOULD SURELY HAUNT HER IN THE FUTURE...
I WILL NOT ALLOW ANY MORE SHACKLES...
...TO BE PLACED ON SARIPHI.
...STILL, IT'S GOING TO BE NO EASY THING TO CONVINCE ANUBIS.
DOSA (FLUMP)
ドサ

GALOIS

I COBBLED HIM FROM ELEMENTS I LIKE— THE BATTLE-SCARRED OLD SOLDIER AND THE OLD-MAN WARRIOR. I WANTED TO DRAW MORE OF HIM WHEN HE WAS YOUNG, SO I'LL JUST LEAVE THIS HERE.

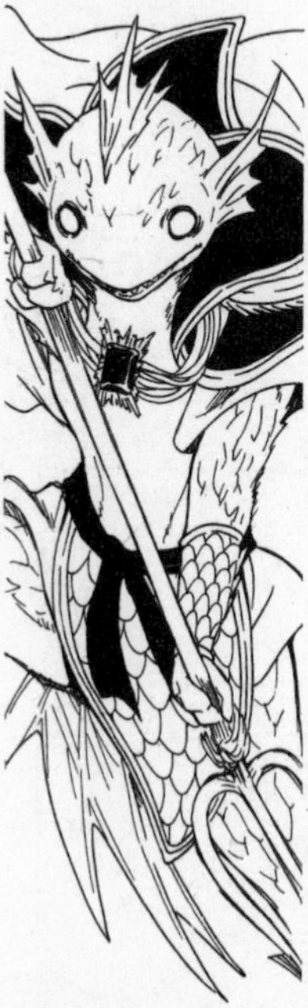

OLD AS HE IS, HE'S A SUPER-GRANDPA WHO CAN STILL FIGHT RINGS AROUND THE YOUNGSTERS. I HOPE I GET A CHANCE TO DRAW A FIGHT SCENE WITH HIM...

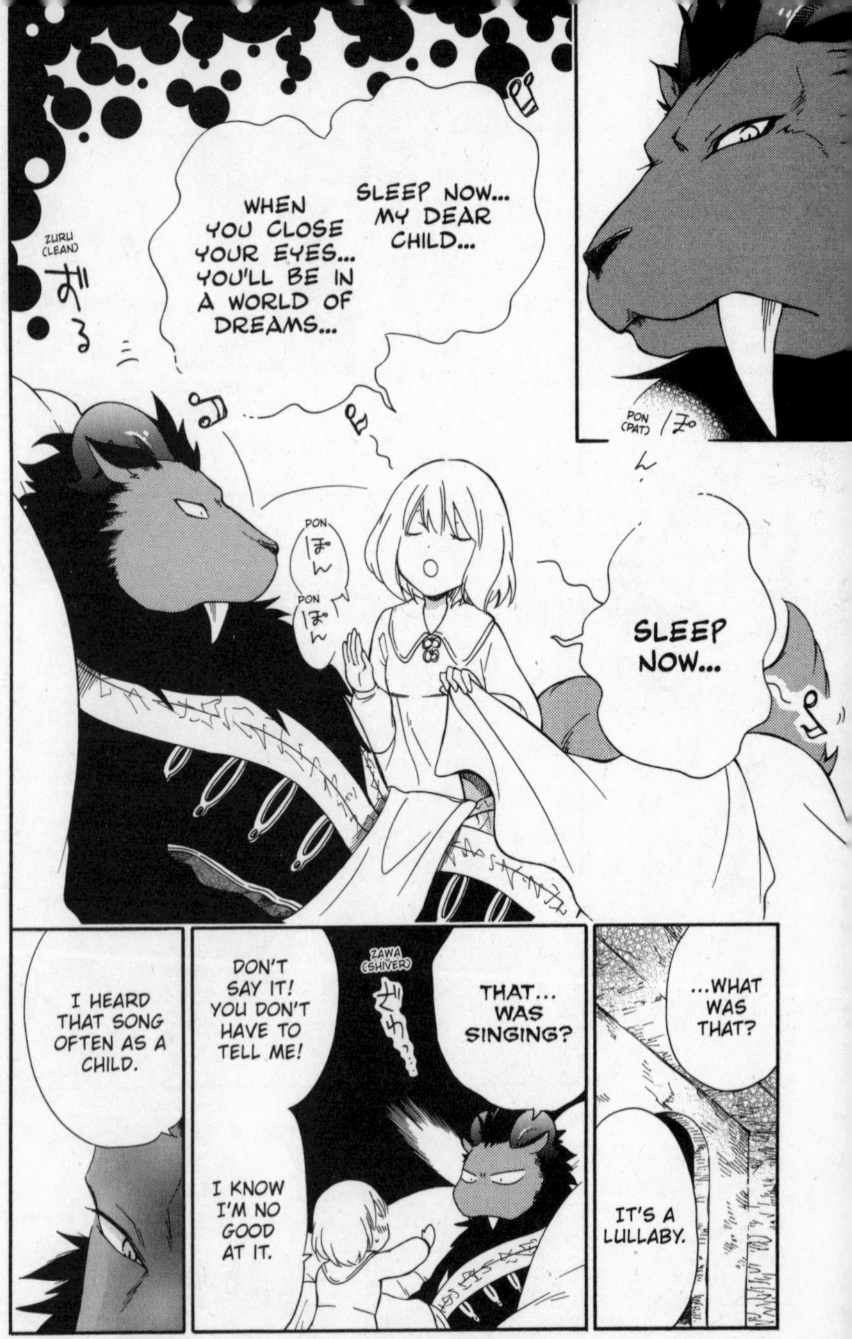
PON (PAT)
SLEEP NOW... MY DEAR CHILD...
WHEN YOU CLOSE YOUR EYES... YOU'LL BE IN A WORLD OF DREAMS...
ZURU (CLEAN)
SLEEP NOW...
PON
PON
...WHAT WAS THAT?
IT'S A LULLABY.
THAT... WAS SINGING?
ZAWA (SHIVER)
DON'T SAY IT! YOU DON'T HAVE TO TELL ME!
I KNOW I'M NO GOOD AT IT.
I HEARD THAT SONG OFTEN AS A CHILD.

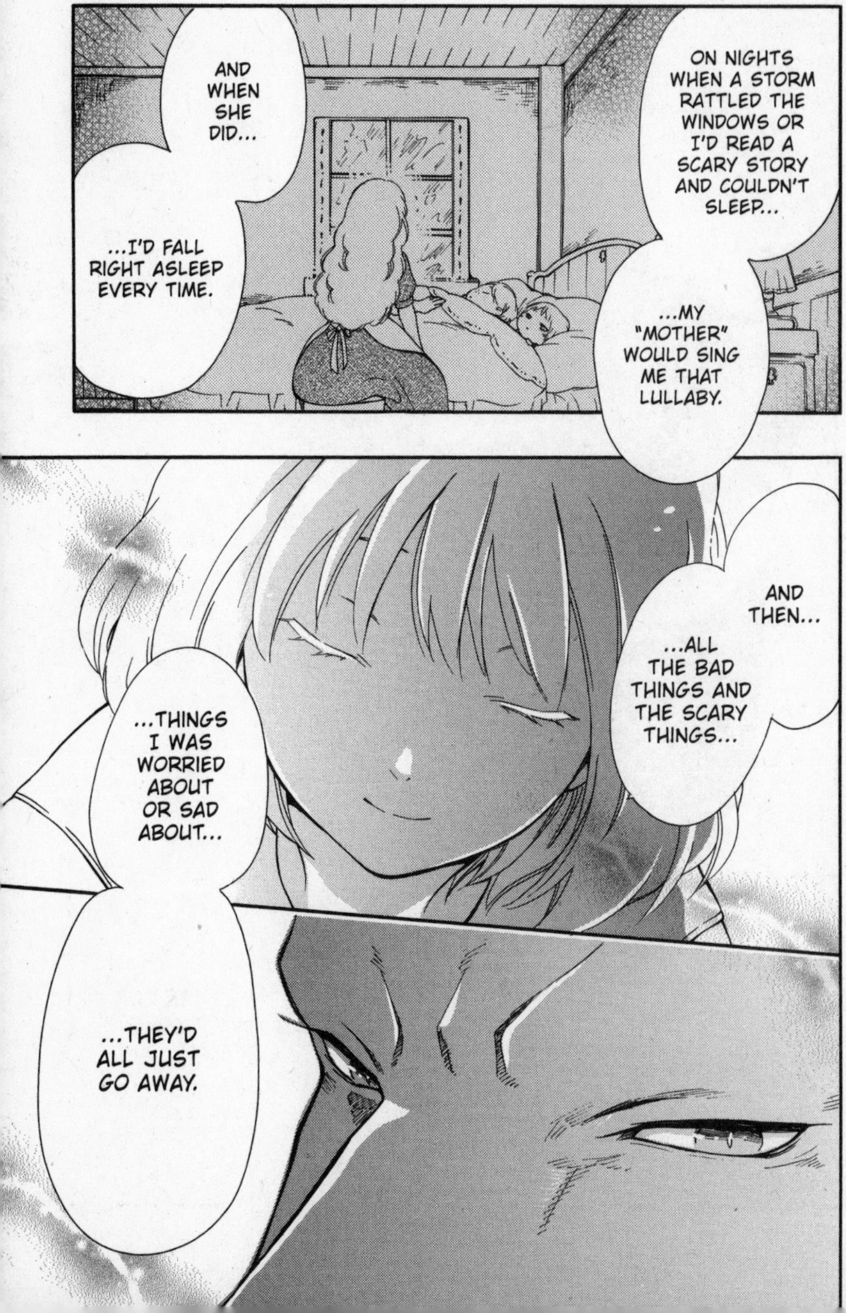
ON NIGHTS WHEN A STORM RATTLED THE WINDOWS OR I'D READ A SCARY STORY AND COULDN'T SLEEP...
...MY "MOTHER" WOULD SING ME THAT LULLABY.
AND WHEN SHE DID...
...I'D FALL RIGHT ASLEEP EVERY TIME.
AND THEN...
...ALL THE BAD THINGS AND THE SCARY THINGS...
...THINGS I WAS WORRIED ABOUT OR SAD ABOUT...
...THEY'D ALL JUST GO AWAY.

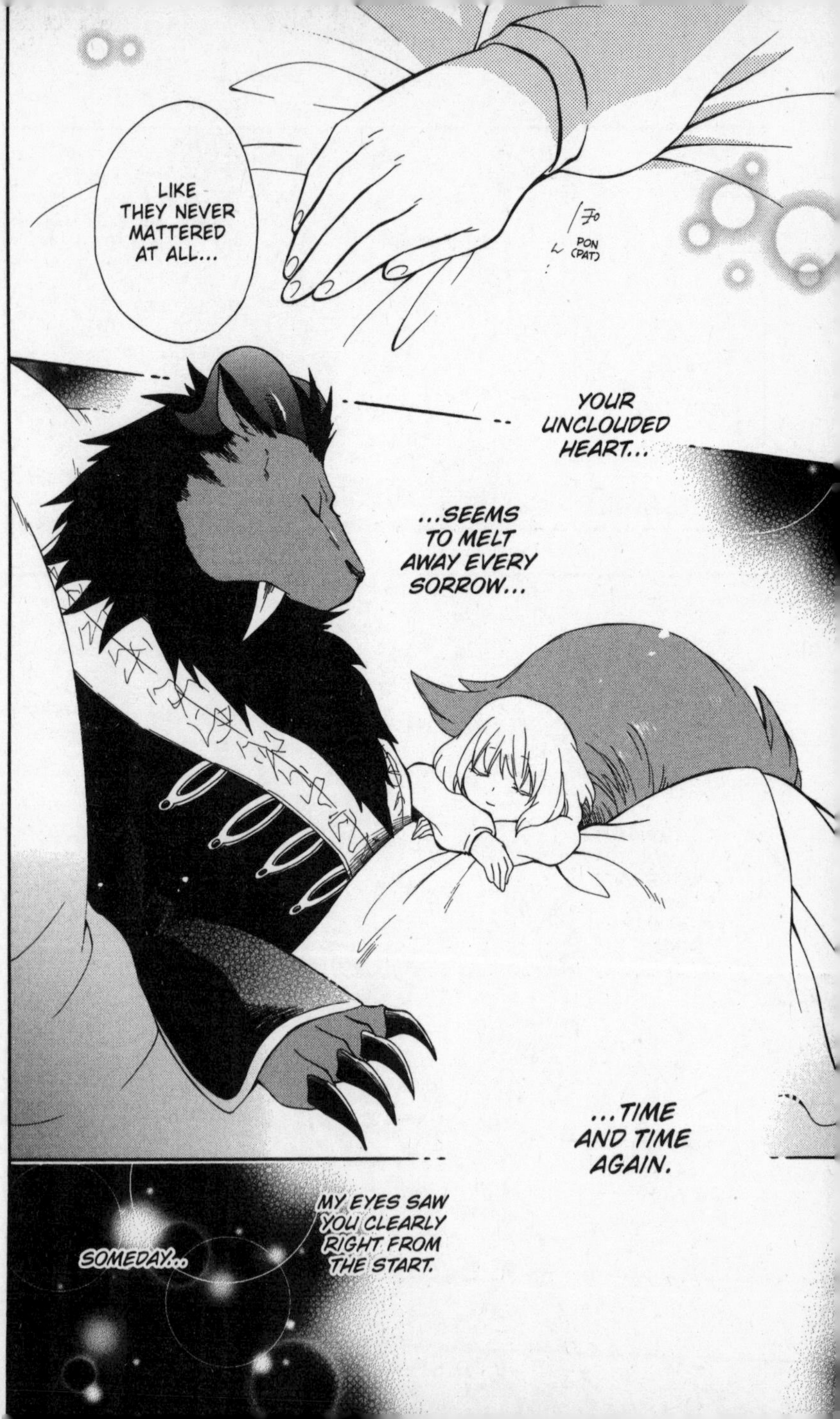
LIKE THEY NEVER MATTERED AT ALL...
PON (PAT)
YOUR UNCLOUDED HEART...
...SEEMS TO MELT AWAY EVERY SORROW...
...TIME AND TIME AGAIN.
MY EYES SAW YOU CLEARLY RIGHT FROM THE START.
SOMEDAY...

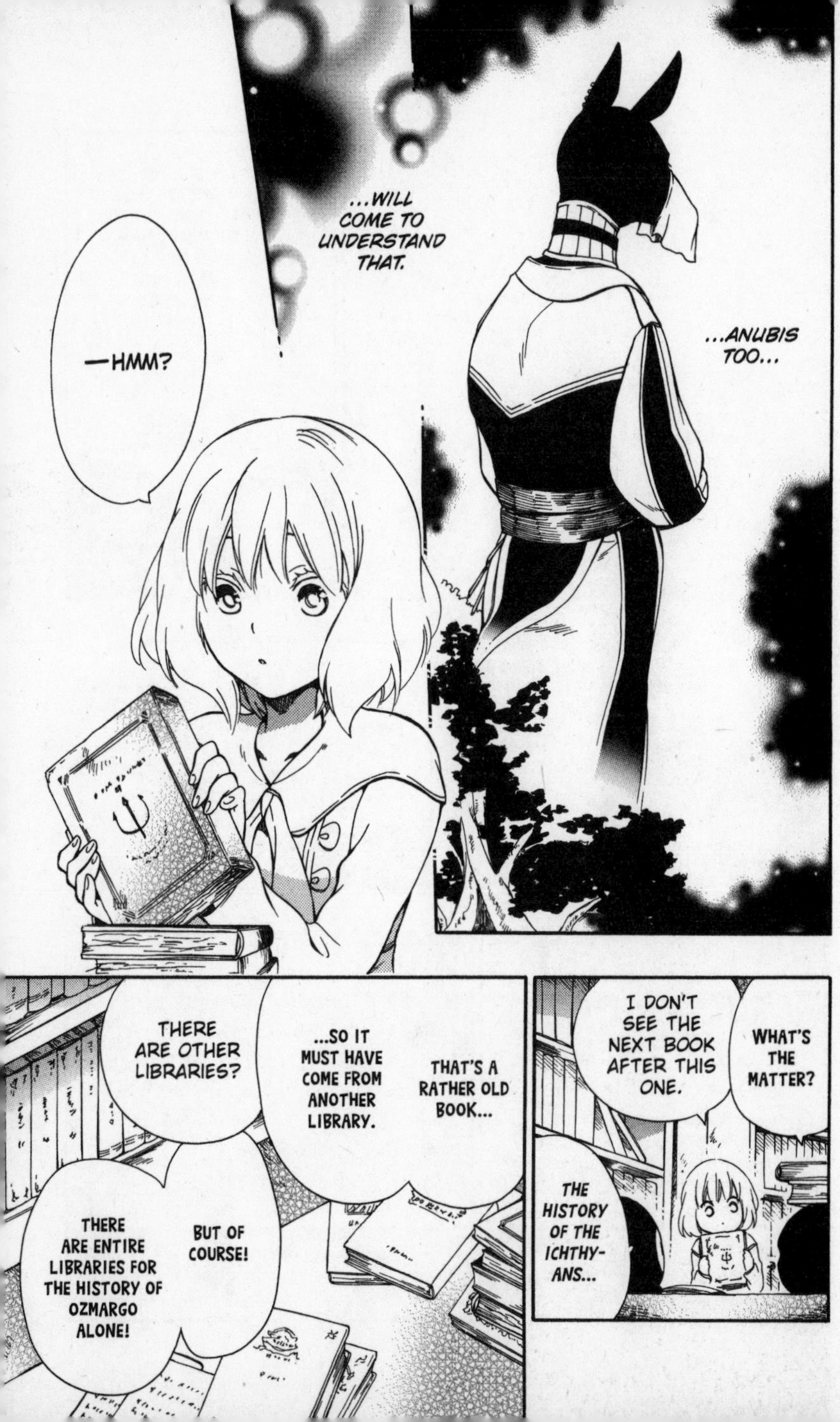

...ANUBIS TOO...
...WILL COME TO UNDERSTAND THAT.
—HMM?
WHAT'S THE MATTER?
I DON'T SEE THE NEXT BOOK AFTER THIS ONE.
THE HISTORY OF THE ICHTHY-ANS...
THAT'S A RATHER OLD BOOK...
...SO IT MUST HAVE COME FROM ANOTHER LIBRARY.
THERE ARE OTHER LIBRARIES?
BUT OF COURSE!
THERE ARE ENTIRE LIBRARIES FOR THE HISTORY OF OZMARGO ALONE!

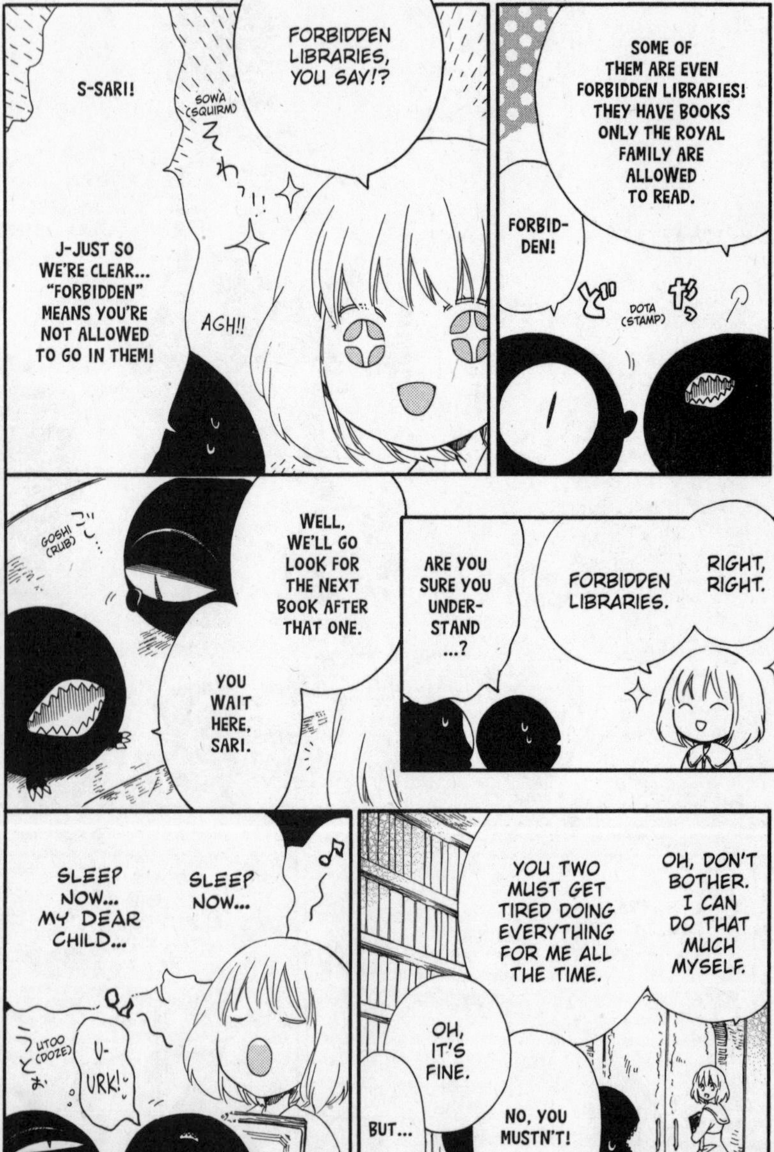
SOME OF THEM ARE EVEN FORBIDDEN LIBRARIES! THEY HAVE BOOKS ONLY THE ROYAL FAMILY ARE ALLOWED TO READ.
FORBID-DEN!
DOTA (STAMP)
FORBIDDEN LIBRARIES, YOU SAY!?
SOWA (SQUIRM)
S-SARI!
AGH!!
J-JUST SO WE'RE CLEAR... "FORBIDDEN" MEANS YOU'RE NOT ALLOWED TO GO IN THEM!
RIGHT, RIGHT.
FORBIDDEN LIBRARIES.
ARE YOU SURE YOU UNDER-STAND ...?
WELL, WE'LL GO LOOK FOR THE NEXT BOOK AFTER THAT ONE.
GOSHI (RUB)
YOU WAIT HERE, SARI.
OH, DON'T BOTHER. I CAN DO THAT MUCH MYSELF.
YOU TWO MUST GET TIRED DOING EVERYTHING FOR ME ALL THE TIME.
OH, IT'S FINE.
NO, YOU MUSTN'T!
BUT...
SLEEP NOW...
SLEEP NOW... MY DEAR CHILD...
UTOO (DOZE)
U-URK!

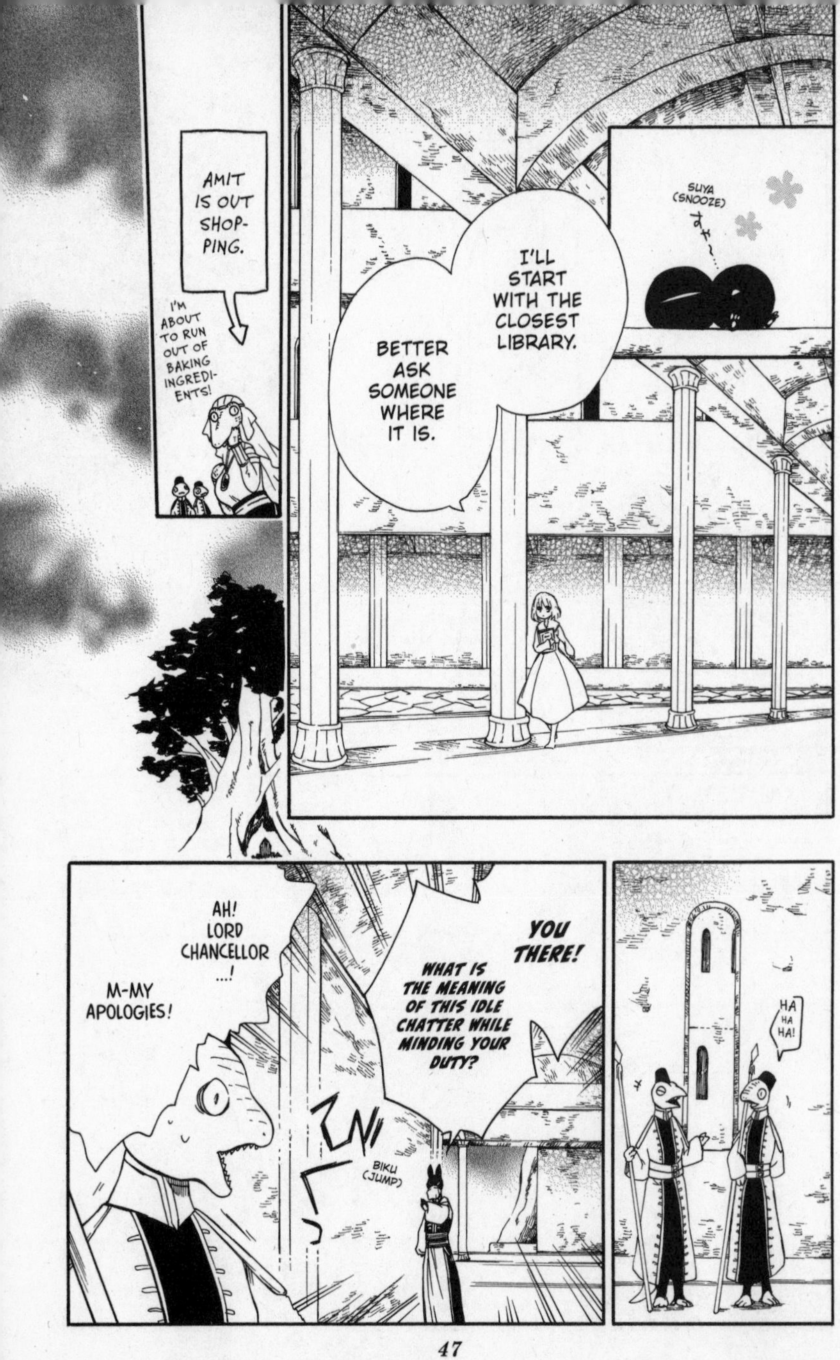
SUYA (SNOOZE)
すや~
I'LL START WITH THE CLOSEST LIBRARY.
BETTER ASK SOMEONE WHERE IT IS.
AMIT IS OUT SHOP-PING.
I'M ABOUT TO RUN OUT OF BAKING INGREDI-ENTS!
HA HA HA!
YOU THERE!
WHAT IS THE MEANING OF THIS IDLE CHATTER WHILE MINDING YOUR DUTY?
BIKU (JUMP)
AH! LORD CHANCELLOR ...!
M-MY APOLOGIES!

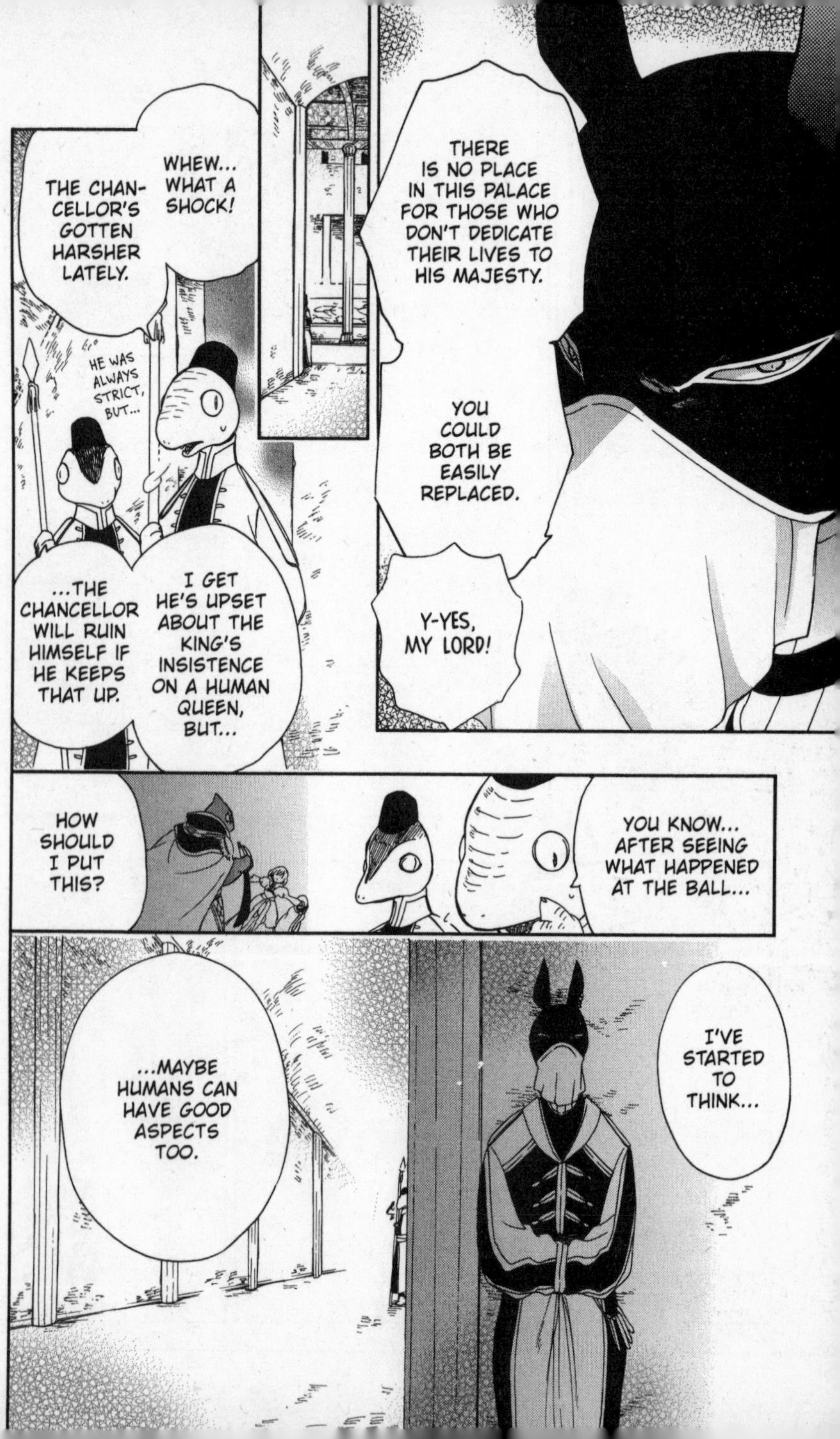
THERE IS NO PLACE IN THIS PALACE FOR THOSE WHO DON'T DEDICATE THEIR LIVES TO HIS MAJESTY.
YOU COULD BOTH BE EASILY REPLACED.
Y-YES, MY LORD!
WHEW... WHAT A SHOCK!
THE CHAN-CELLOR'S GOTTEN HARSHER LATELY.
HE WAS ALWAYS STRICT, BUT...
I GET HE'S UPSET ABOUT THE KING'S INSISTENCE ON A HUMAN QUEEN, BUT...
...THE CHANCELLOR WILL RUIN HIMSELF IF HE KEEPS THAT UP.
YOU KNOW... AFTER SEEING WHAT HAPPENED AT THE BALL...
HOW SHOULD I PUT THIS?
I'VE STARTED TO THINK...
...MAYBE HUMANS CAN HAVE GOOD ASPECTS TOO.

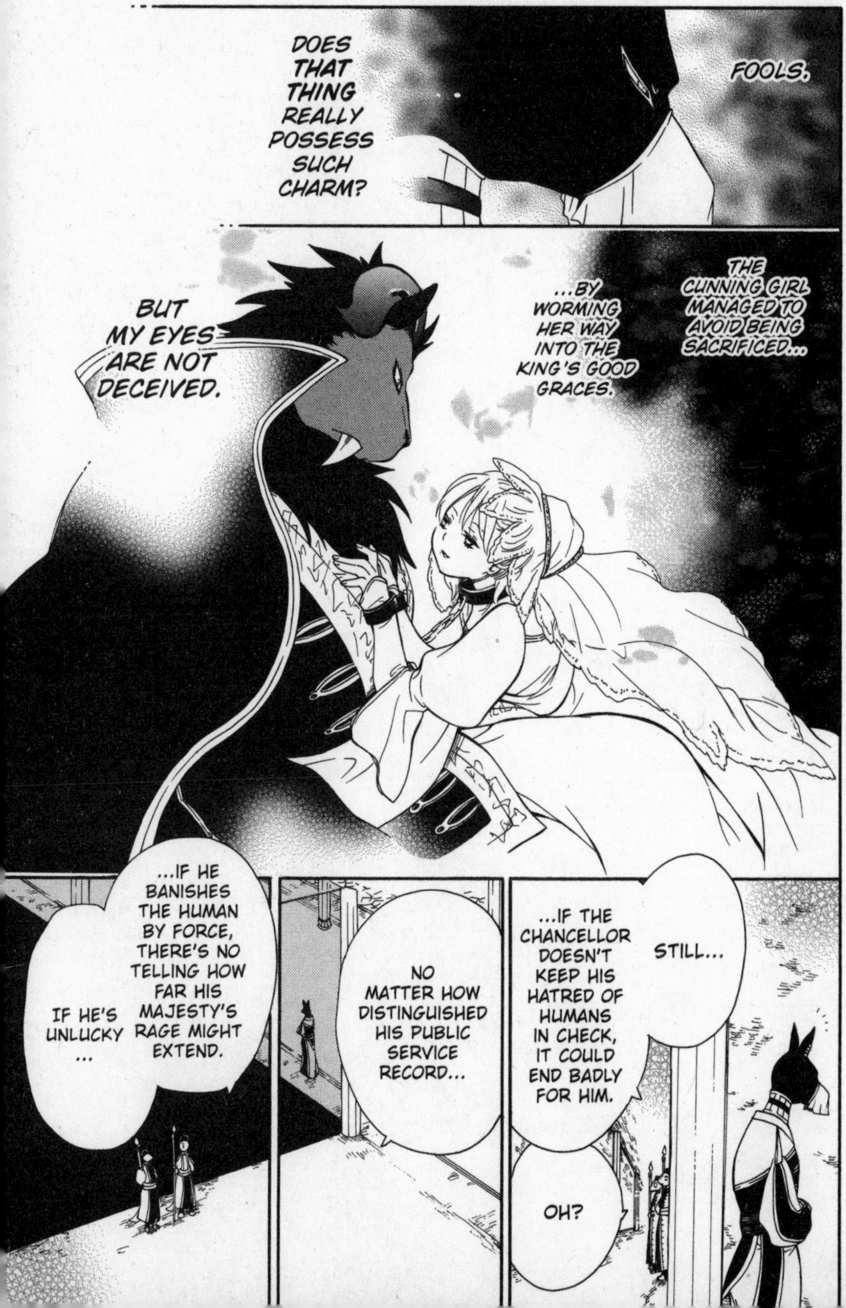
FOOLS.
DOES THAT THING REALLY POSSESS SUCH CHARM?
THE CUNNING GIRL MANAGED TO AVOID BEING SACRIFICED...
...BY WORMING HER WAY INTO THE KING'S GOOD GRACES.
BUT MY EYES ARE NOT DECEIVED.
STILL...
...IF THE CHANCELLOR DOESN'T KEEP HIS HATRED OF HUMANS IN CHECK, IT COULD END BADLY FOR HIM.
OH?
NO MATTER HOW DISTINGUISHED HIS PUBLIC SERVICE RECORD...
...IF HE BANISHES THE HUMAN BY FORCE, THERE'S NO TELLING HOW FAR HIS MAJESTY'S RAGE MIGHT EXTEND.
IF HE'S UNLUCKY...

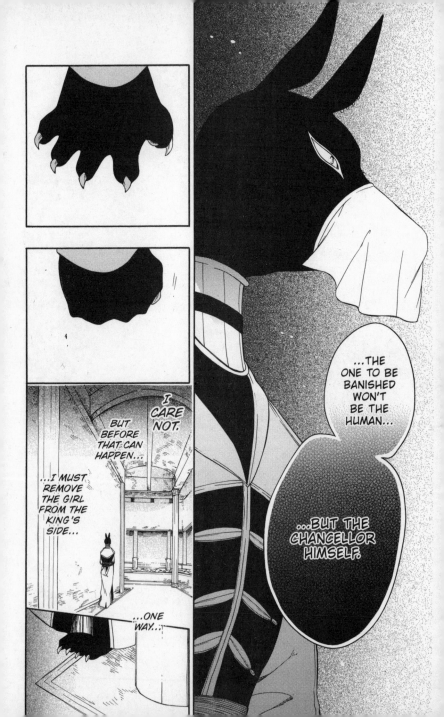

...THE ONE TO BE BANISHED WON'T BE THE HUMAN...

...BUT THE CHANCELLOR HIMSELF.

I CARE NOT.

BUT BEFORE THAT CAN HAPPEN...

...I MUST REMOVE THE GIRL FROM THE KING'S SIDE...

...ONE WAY...

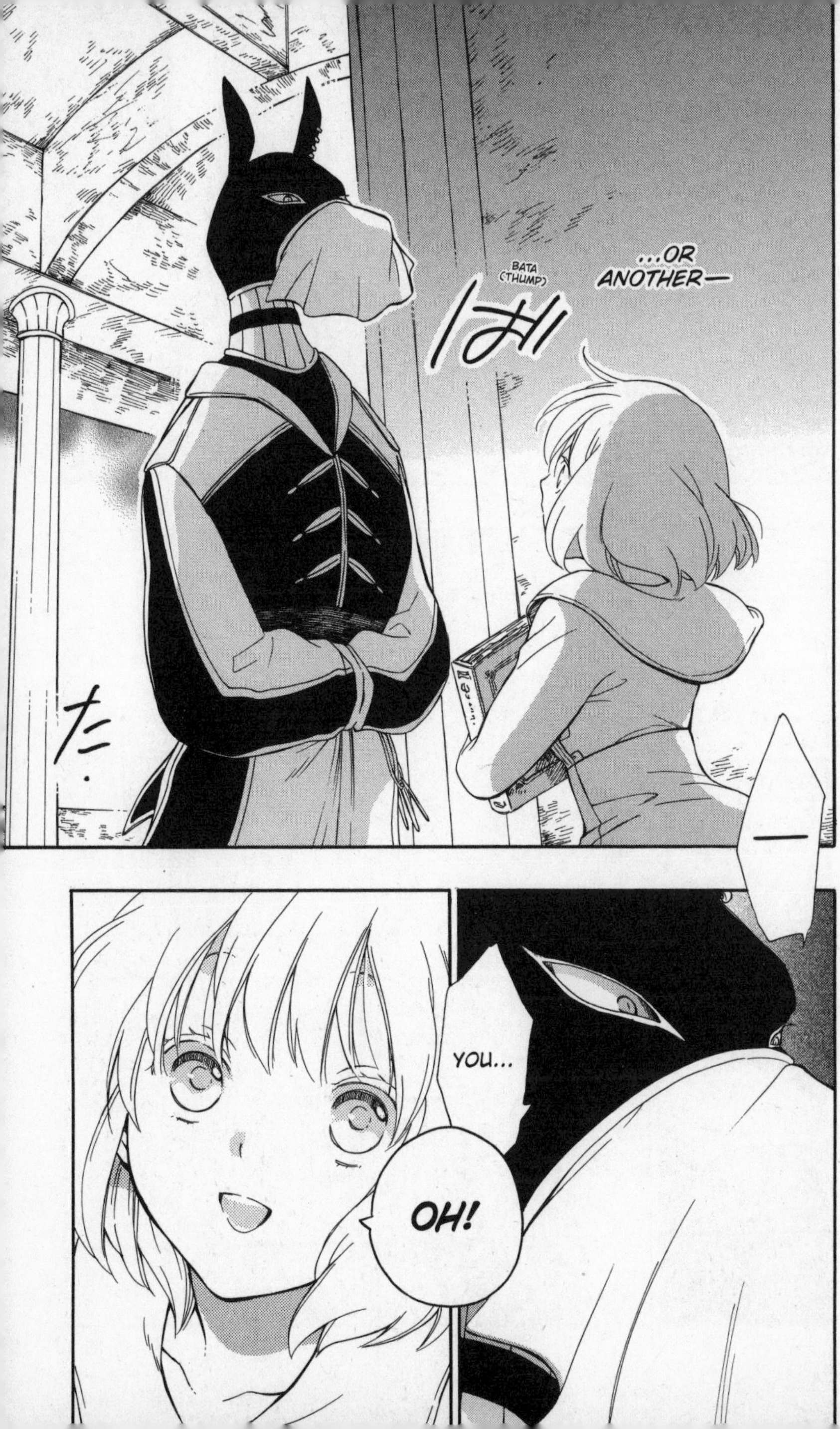
...OR ANOTHER—
BATA (THUMP)
た
—
YOU...
OH!

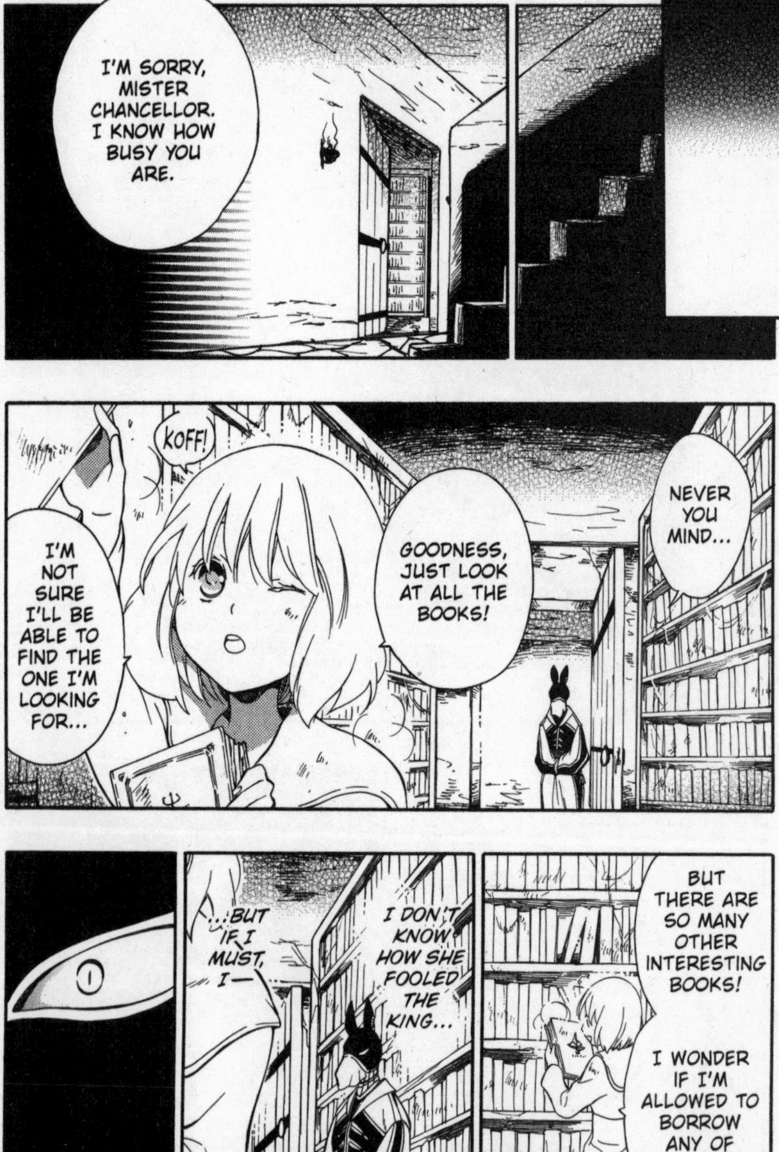
I'M SORRY, MISTER CHANCELLOR. I KNOW HOW BUSY YOU ARE.
NEVER YOU MIND...
GOODNESS, JUST LOOK AT ALL THE BOOKS!
KOFF!
I'M NOT SURE I'LL BE ABLE TO FIND THE ONE I'M LOOKING FOR...
BUT THERE ARE SO MANY OTHER INTERESTING BOOKS!
I WONDER IF I'M ALLOWED TO BORROW ANY OF THEM.
I DON'T KNOW HOW SHE FOOLED THE KING...
...BUT IF I MUST, I—

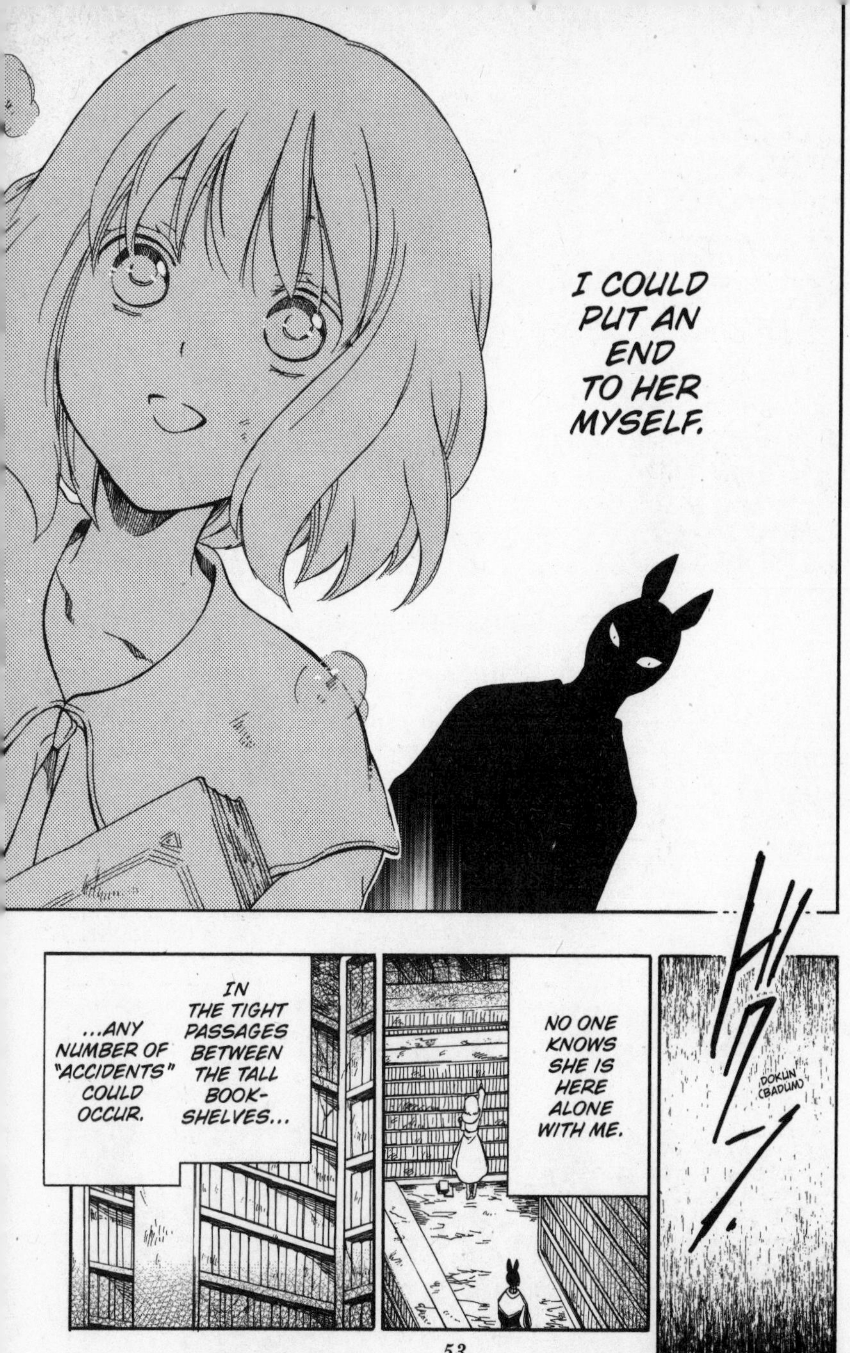
I COULD PUT AN END TO HER MYSELF.
DOKUN (BADUM)
NO ONE KNOWS SHE IS HERE ALONE WITH ME.
IN THE TIGHT PASSAGES BETWEEN THE TALL BOOK-SHELVES...
...ANY NUMBER OF "ACCIDENTS" COULD OCCUR.

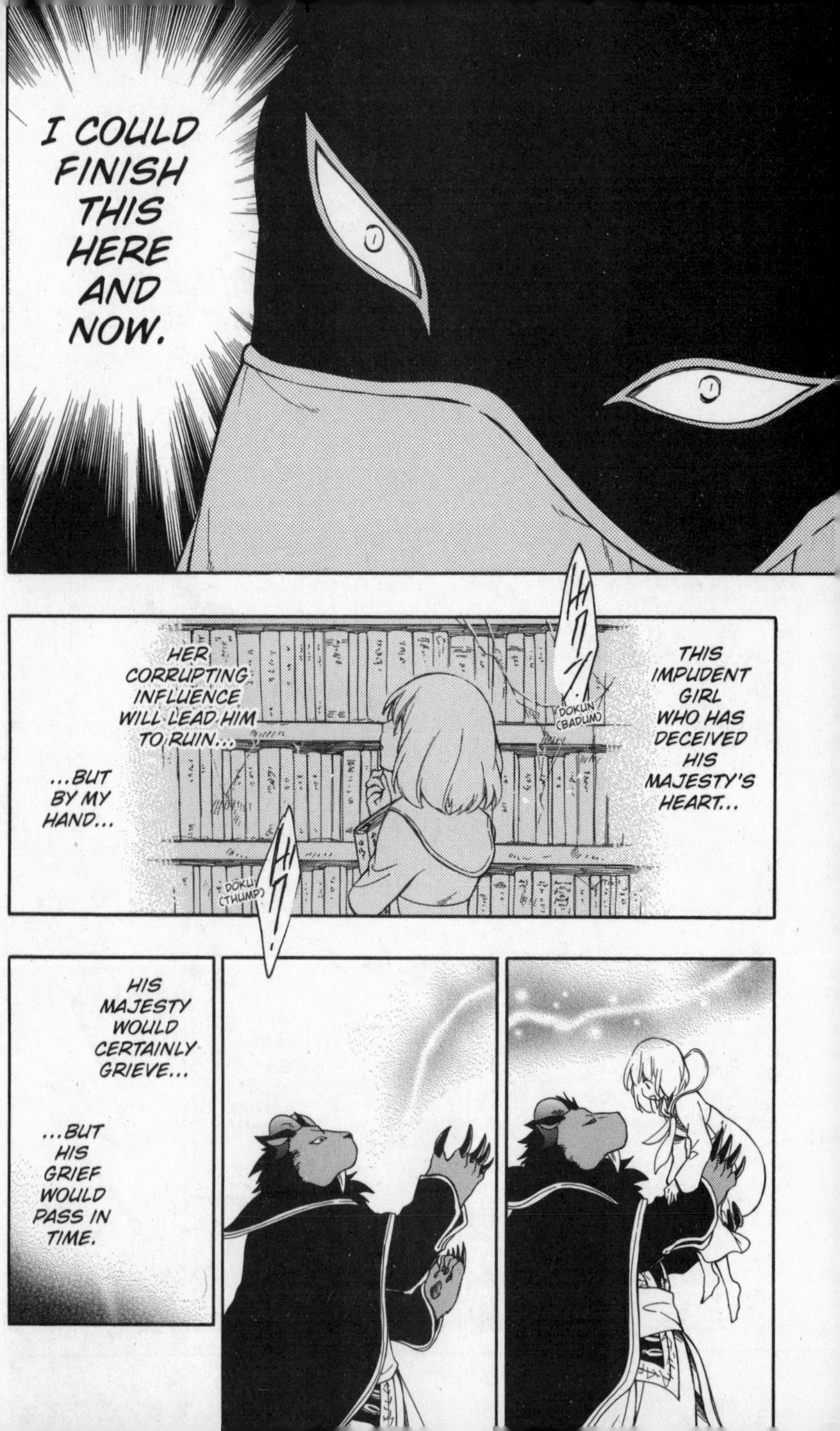
I COULD FINISH THIS HERE AND NOW.
THIS IMPUDENT GIRL WHO HAS DECEIVED HIS MAJESTY'S HEART...
DOKUN (BADUM)
HER CORRUPTING INFLUENCE WILL LEAD HIM TO RUIN...
...BUT BY MY HAND...
DOKU (THUMP)
HIS MAJESTY WOULD CERTAINLY GRIEVE...
...BUT HIS GRIEF WOULD PASS IN TIME.

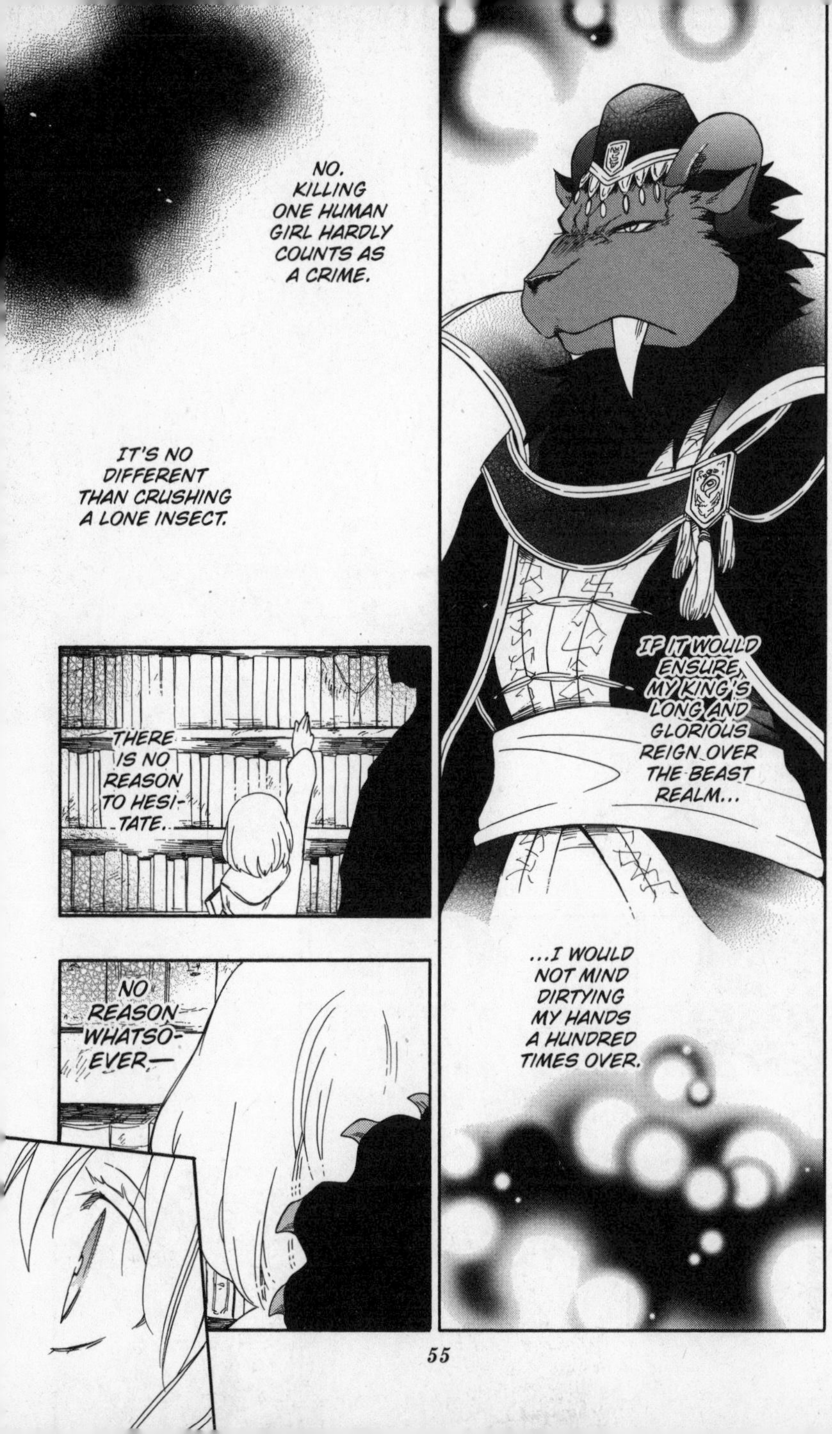
IF IT WOULD ENSURE MY KING'S LONG AND GLORIOUS REIGN OVER THE BEAST REALM...
...I WOULD NOT MIND DIRTYING MY HANDS A HUNDRED TIMES OVER.
NO. KILLING ONE HUMAN GIRL HARDLY COUNTS AS A CRIME.
IT'S NO DIFFERENT THAN CRUSHING A LONE INSECT.
THERE IS NO REASON TO HESI-TATE...
NO REASON WHATSO-EVER—

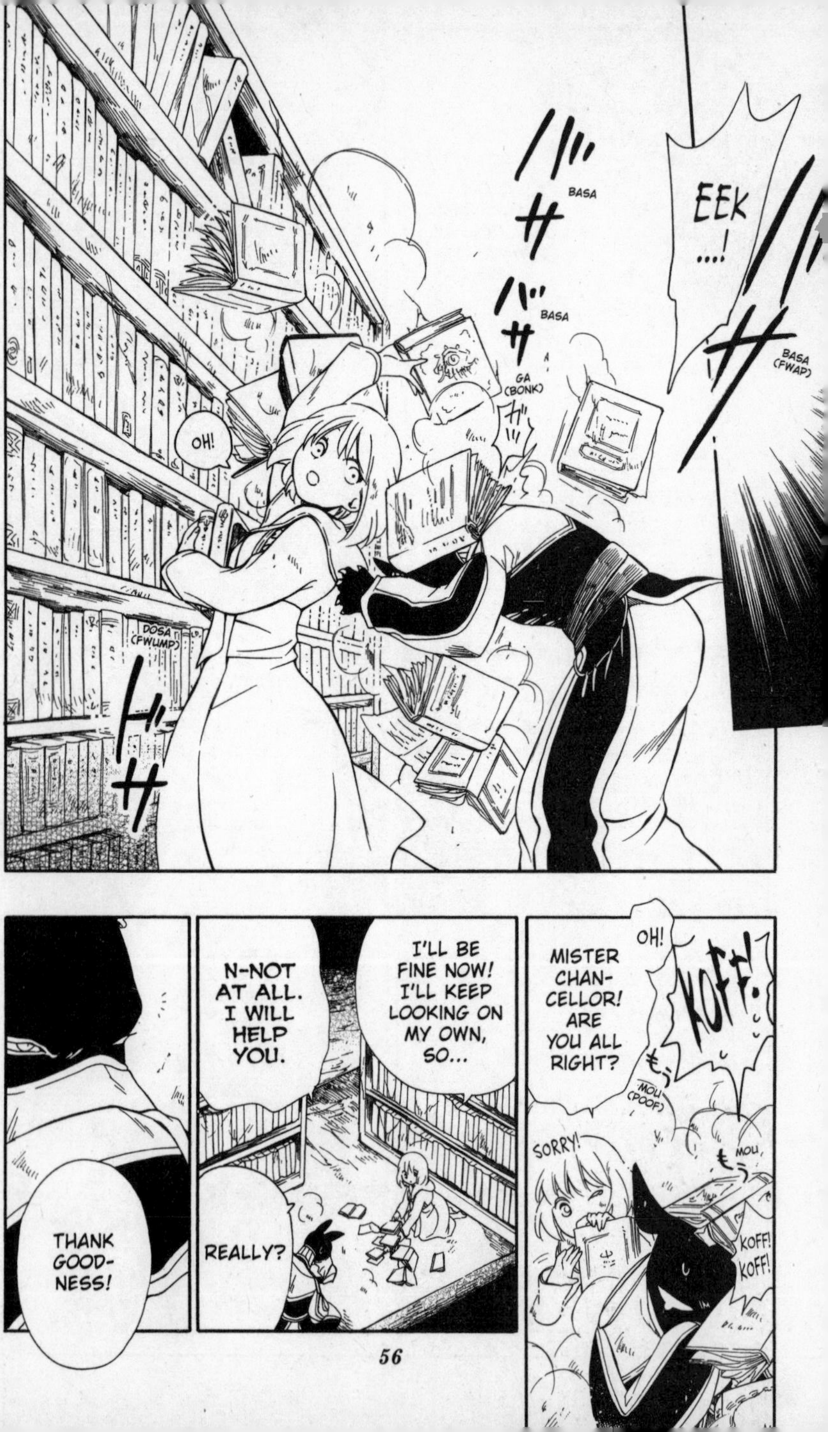
EEK ....!
BASA (FWAP)
BASA
BASA
GA (BONK)
OH!
DOSA (FWUMP)
KOFF!
OH!
MISTER CHAN-CELLOR! ARE YOU ALL RIGHT?
MOU (POOF)
MOU
SORRY!
KOFF! KOFF!
I'LL BE FINE NOW! I'LL KEEP LOOKING ON MY OWN, SO...
N-NOT AT ALL. I WILL HELP YOU.
REALLY?
THANK GOOD-NESS!

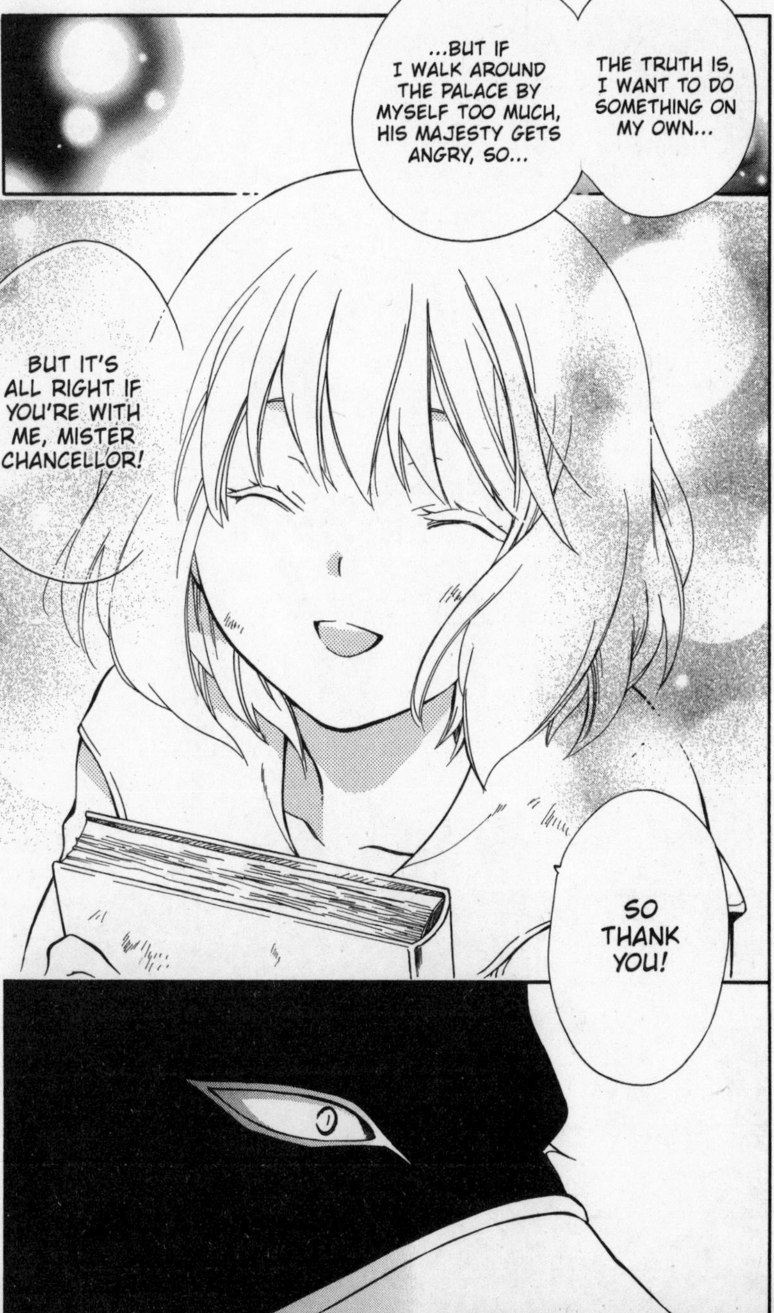
THE TRUTH IS, I WANT TO DO SOMETHING ON MY OWN...
...BUT IF I WALK AROUND THE PALACE BY MYSELF TOO MUCH, HIS MAJESTY GETS ANGRY, SO...
BUT IT'S ALL RIGHT IF YOU'RE WITH ME, MISTER CHANCELLOR!
SO THANK YOU!

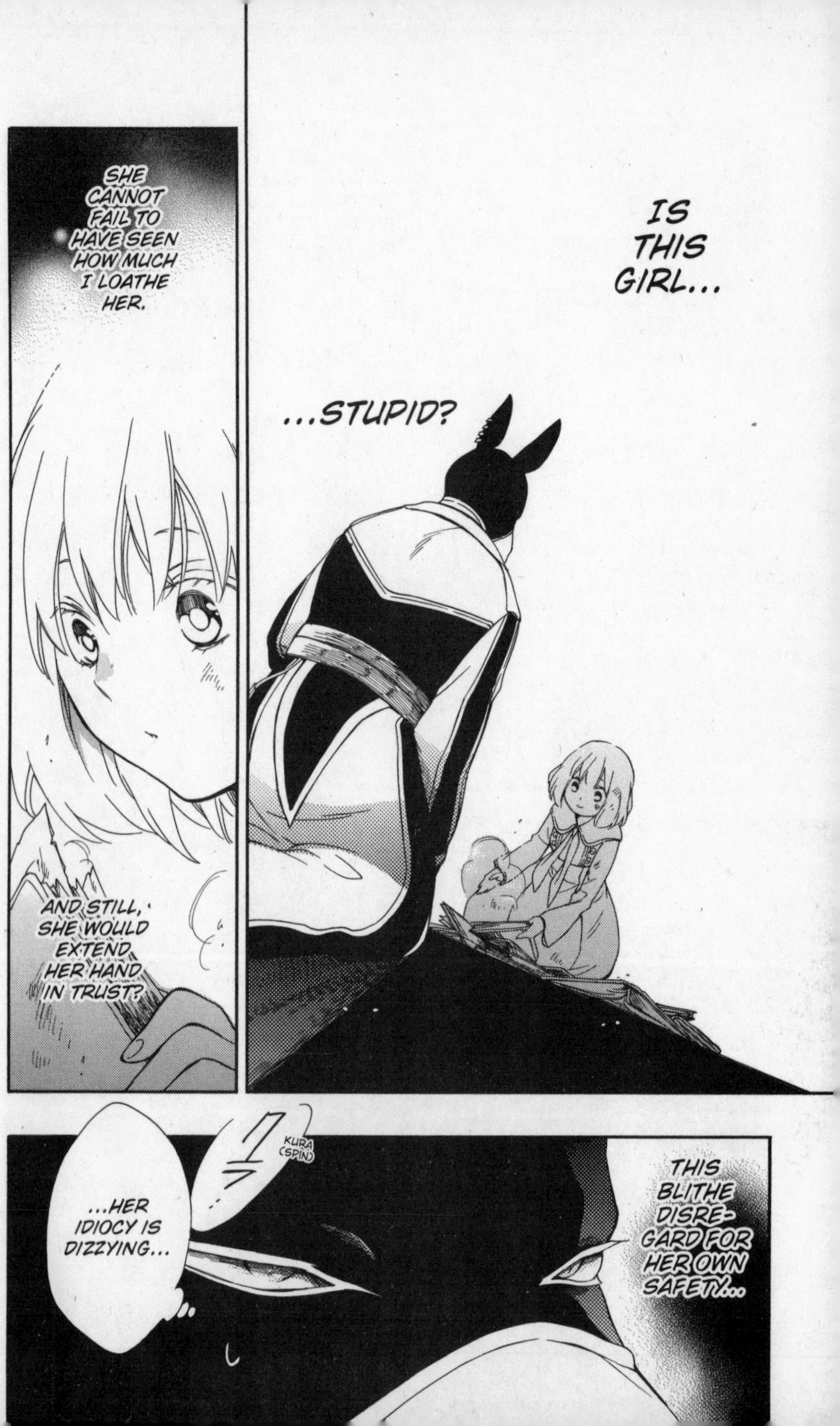
IS THIS GIRL...
...STUPID?
SHE CANNOT FAIL TO HAVE SEEN HOW MUCH I LOATHE HER.
AND STILL, SHE WOULD EXTEND HER HAND IN TRUST?
THIS BLITHE DISREGARD FOR HER OWN SAFETY...
KURA (SPIN)
...HER IDIOCY IS DIZZYING...

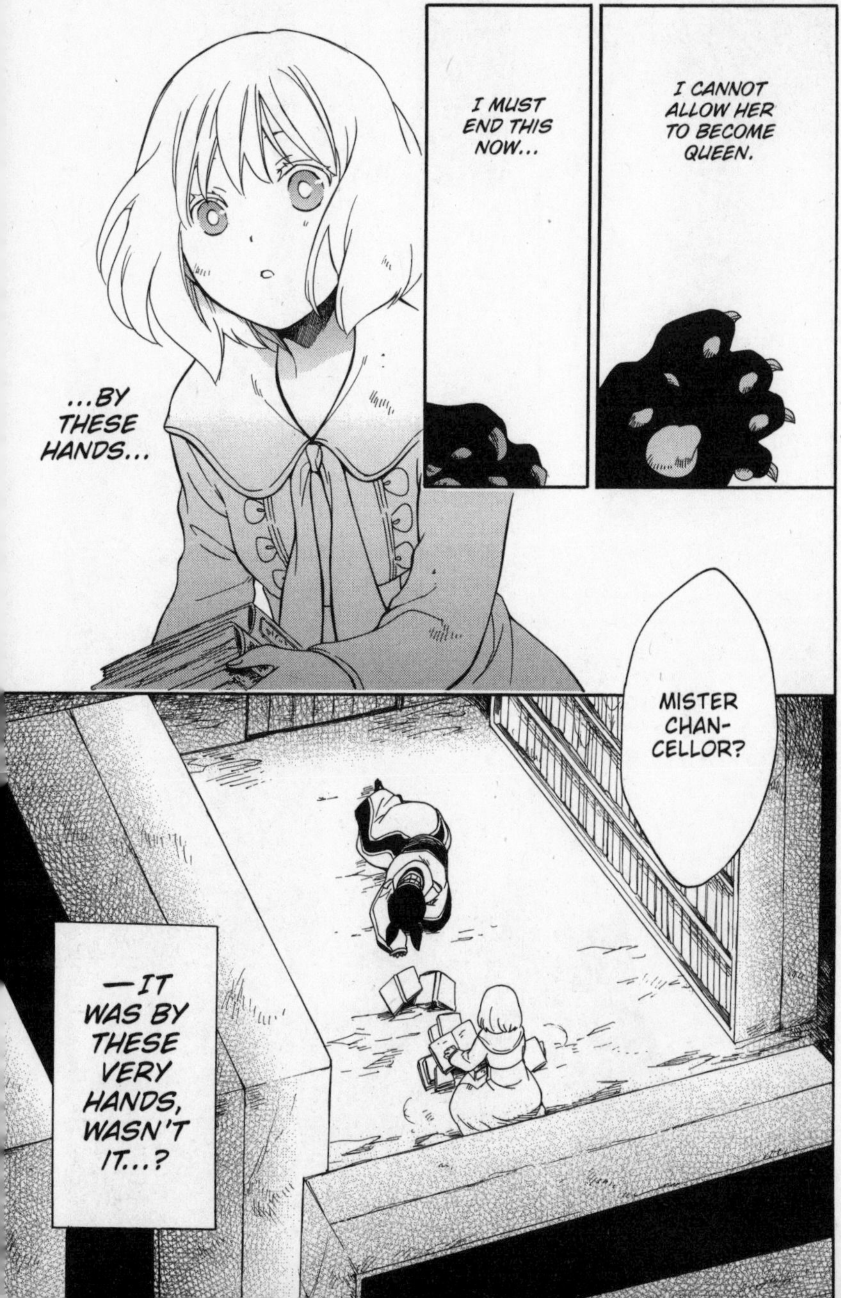
I CANNOT ALLOW HER TO BECOME QUEEN.
I MUST END THIS NOW...
...BY THESE HANDS...
MISTER CHAN-CELLOR?
—IT WAS BY THESE VERY HANDS, WASN'T IT...?

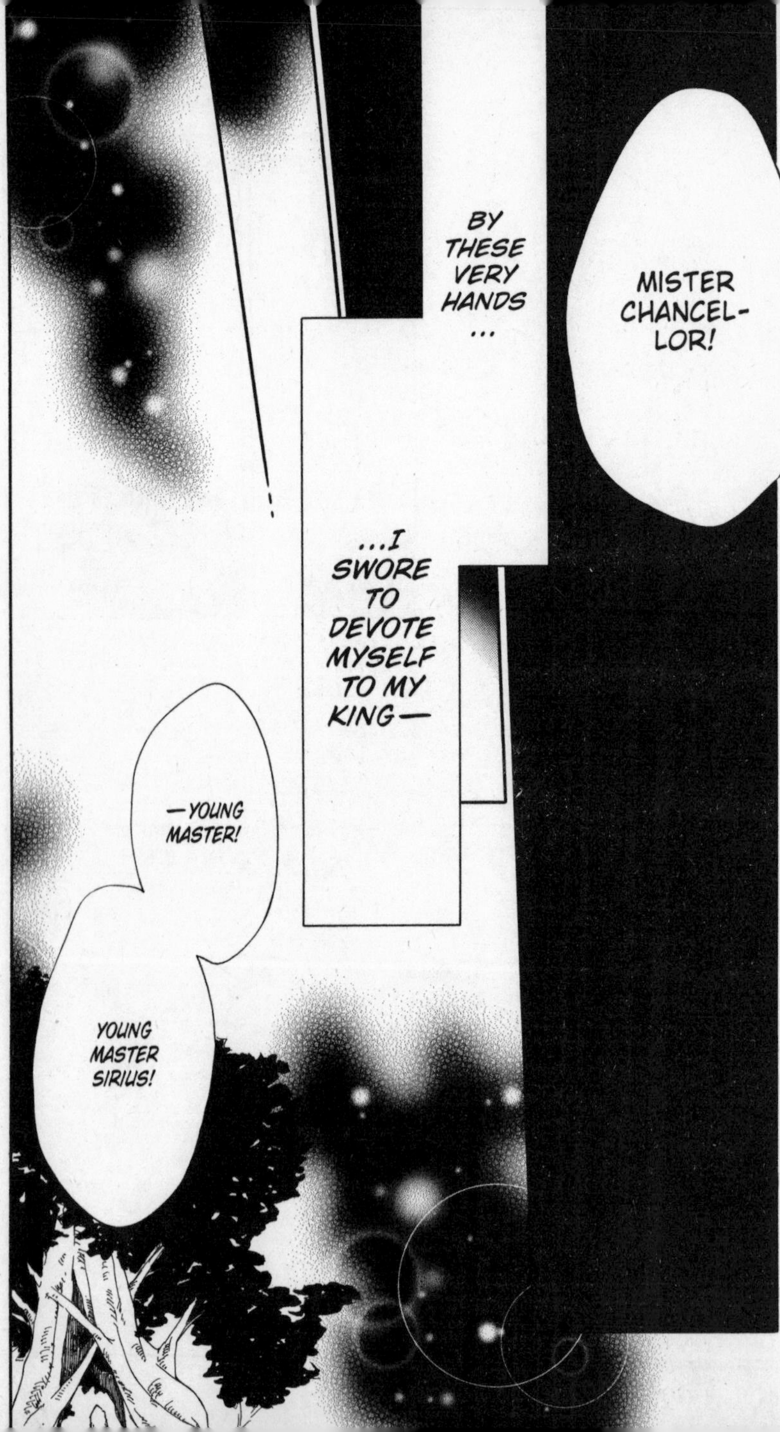
MISTER CHANCEL- LOR!
BY THESE VERY HANDS...
...I SWORE TO DEVOTE MYSELF TO MY KING—
—YOUNG MASTER!
YOUNG MASTER SIRIUS!

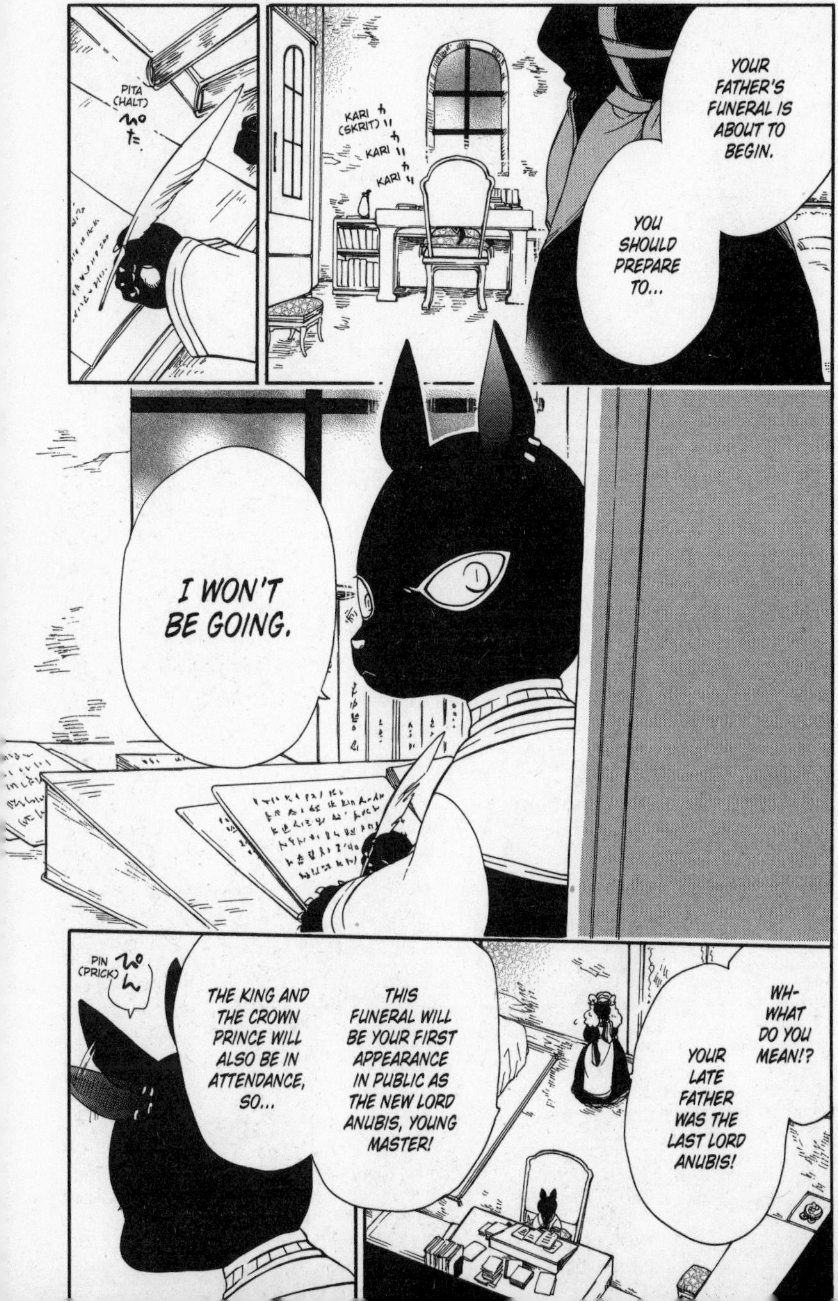
YOUR FATHER'S FUNERAL IS ABOUT TO BEGIN.
YOU SHOULD PREPARE TO...
KARI (SKRIT) KARI KARI
PITA (HALT)
I WON'T BE GOING.
WH- WHAT DO YOU MEAN!?
YOUR LATE FATHER WAS THE LAST LORD ANUBIS!
THIS FUNERAL WILL BE YOUR FIRST APPEARANCE IN PUBLIC AS THE NEW LORD ANUBIS, YOUNG MASTER!
THE KING AND THE CROWN PRINCE WILL ALSO BE IN ATTENDANCE, SO...
PIN (PRICK)

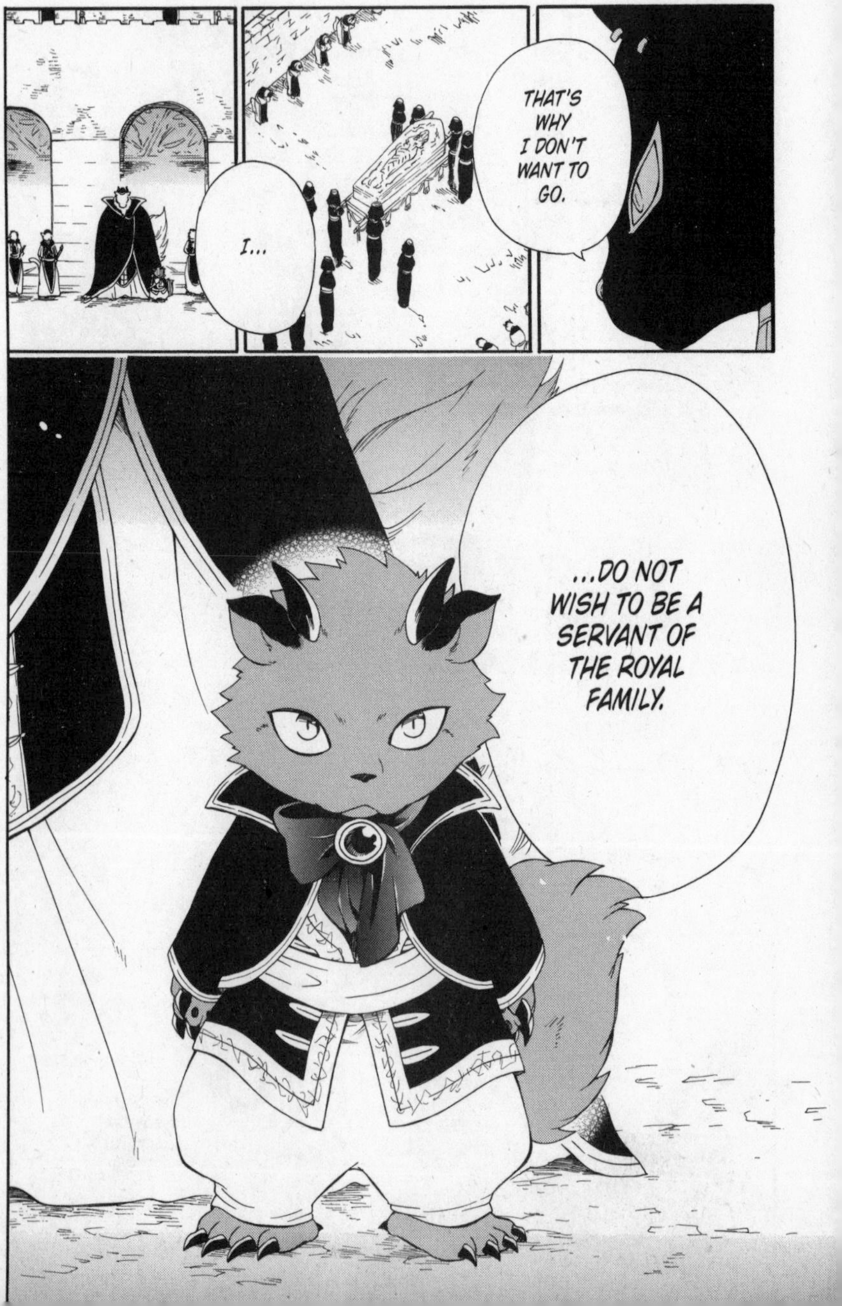
THAT'S WHY I DON'T WANT TO GO.
I...
...DO NOT WISH TO BE A SERVANT OF THE ROYAL FAMILY.

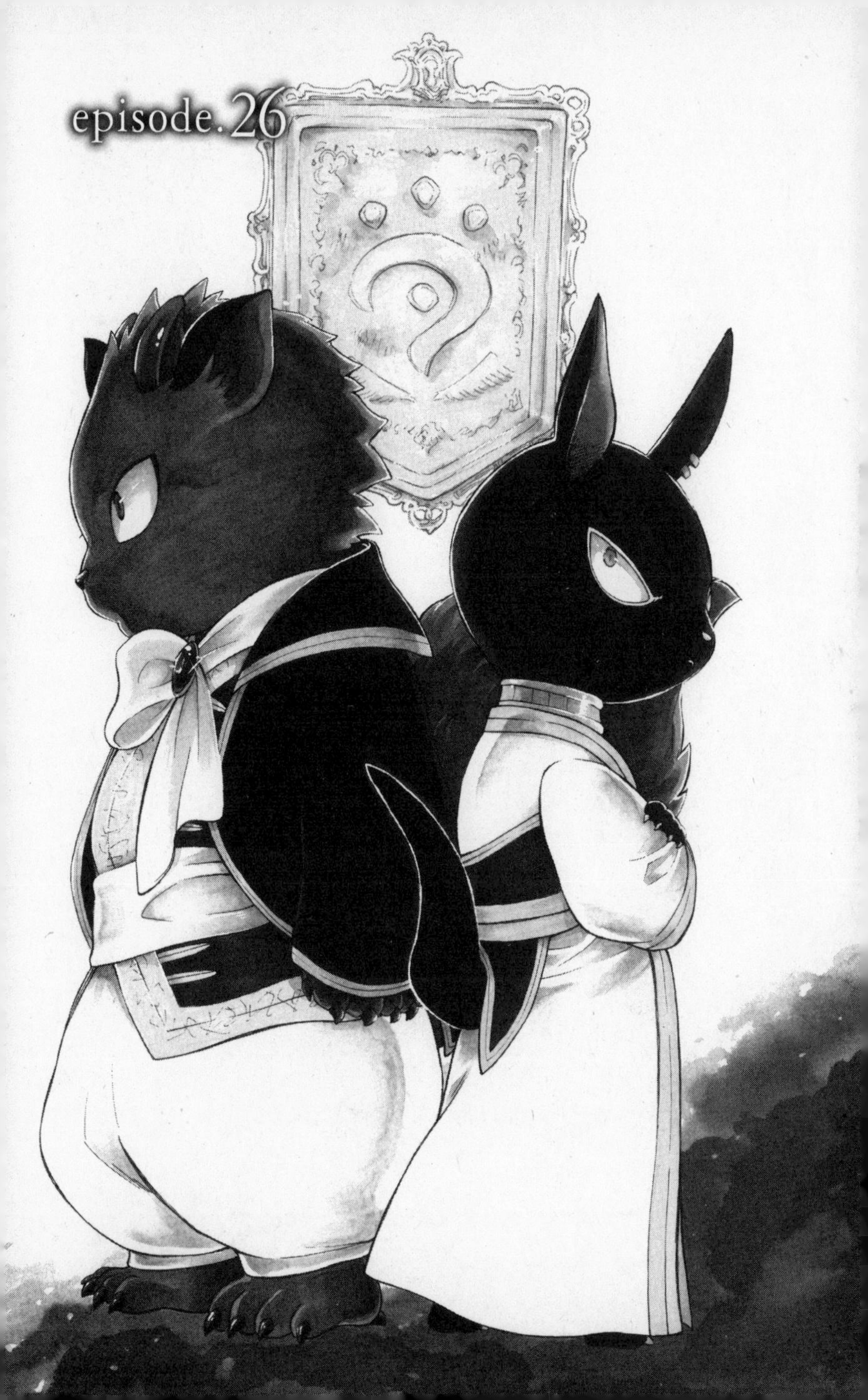
episode. 26

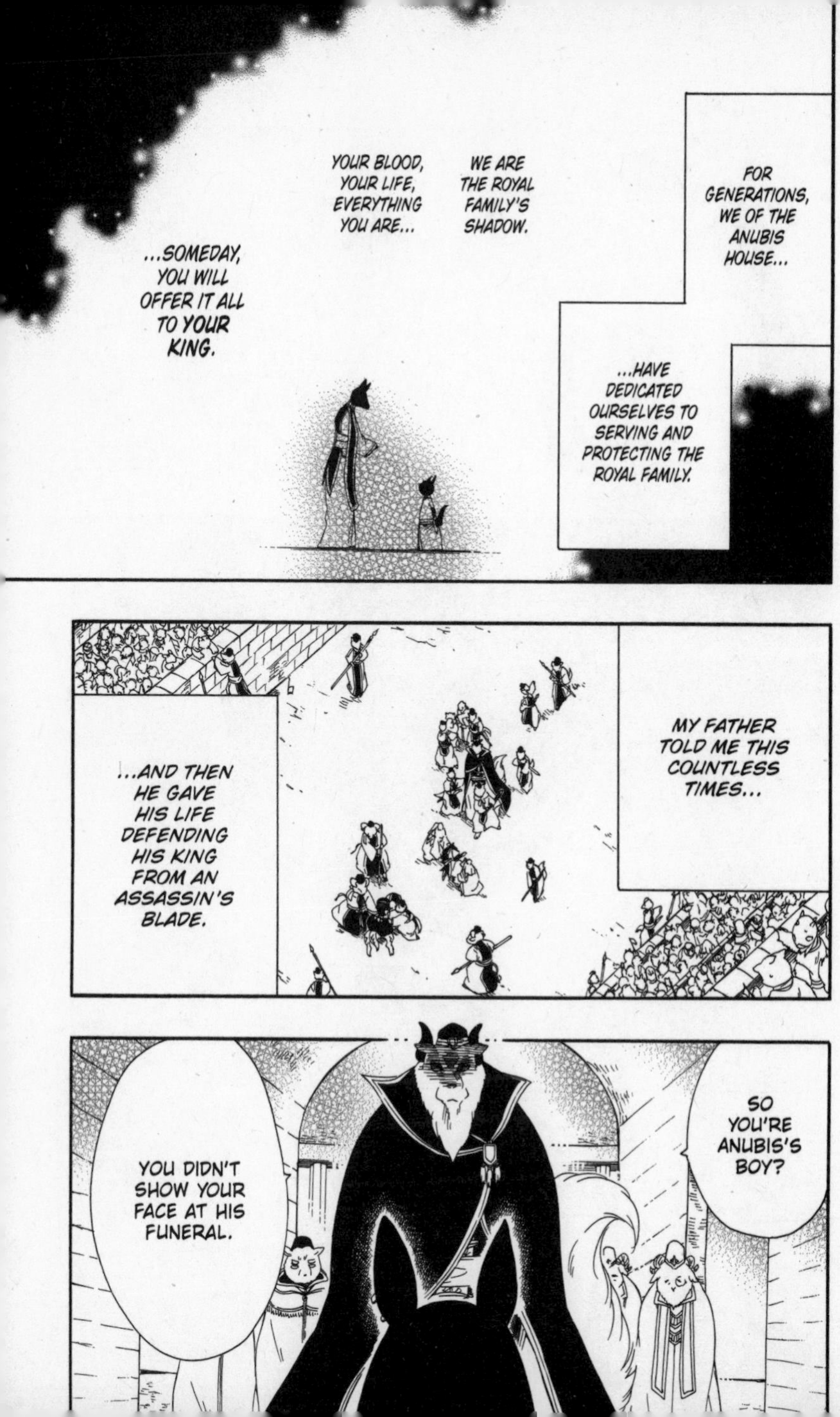
FOR GENERATIONS, WE OF THE ANUBIS HOUSE...
...HAVE DEDICATED OURSELVES TO SERVING AND PROTECTING THE ROYAL FAMILY.
WE ARE THE ROYAL FAMILY'S SHADOW.
YOUR BLOOD, YOUR LIFE, EVERYTHING YOU ARE...
...SOMEDAY, YOU WILL OFFER IT ALL TO YOUR KING.
MY FATHER TOLD ME THIS COUNTLESS TIMES...
...AND THEN HE GAVE HIS LIFE DEFENDING HIS KING FROM AN ASSASSIN'S BLADE.
SO YOU'RE ANUBIS'S BOY?
YOU DIDN'T SHOW YOUR FACE AT HIS FUNERAL.

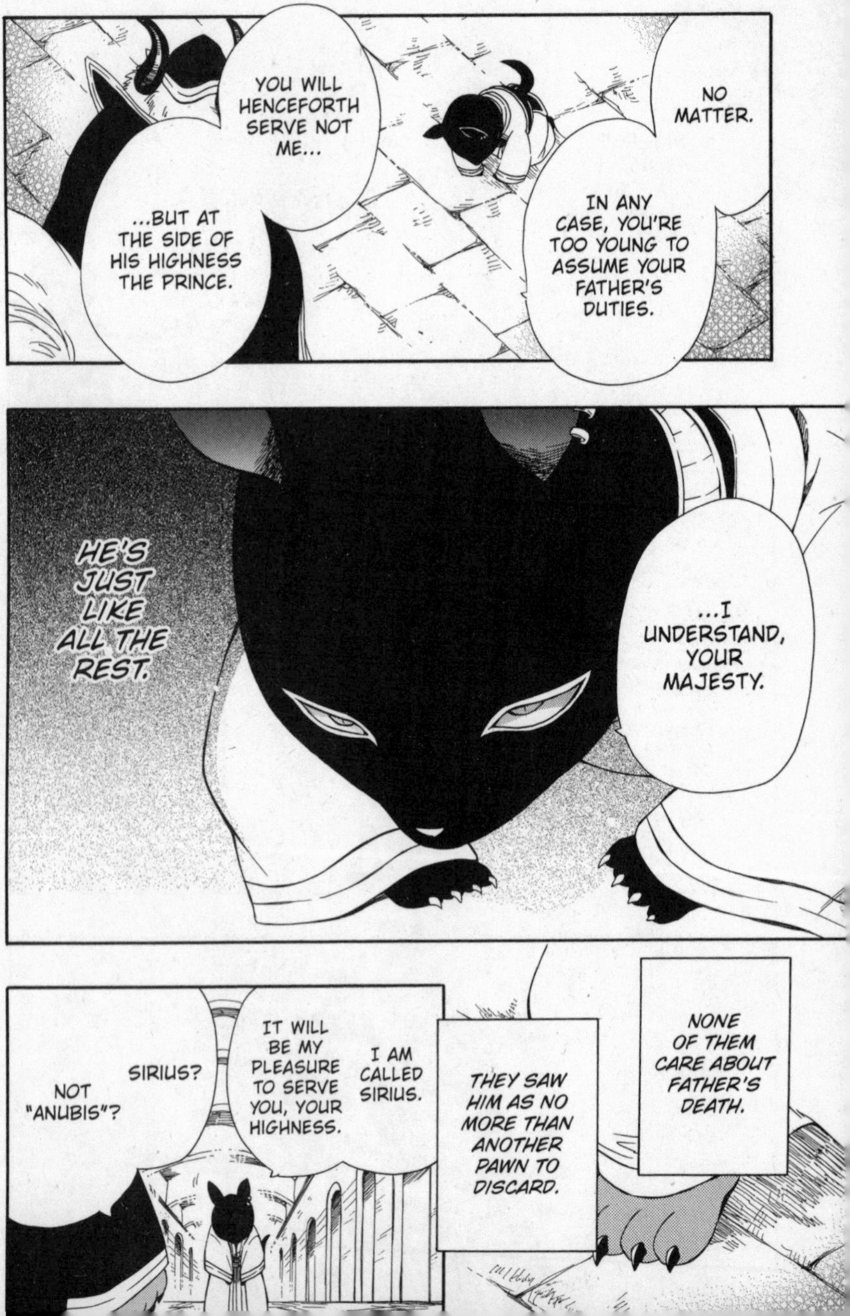
NO MATTER.
IN ANY CASE, YOU'RE TOO YOUNG TO ASSUME YOUR FATHER'S DUTIES.
YOU WILL HENCEFORTH SERVE NOT ME...
...BUT AT THE SIDE OF HIS HIGHNESS THE PRINCE.
...I UNDERSTAND, YOUR MAJESTY.
HE'S JUST LIKE ALL THE REST.
NONE OF THEM CARE ABOUT FATHER'S DEATH.
THEY SAW HIM AS NO MORE THAN ANOTHER PAWN TO DISCARD.
I AM CALLED SIRIUS.
IT WILL BE MY PLEASURE TO SERVE YOU, YOUR HIGHNESS.
SIRIUS?
NOT "ANUBIS"?

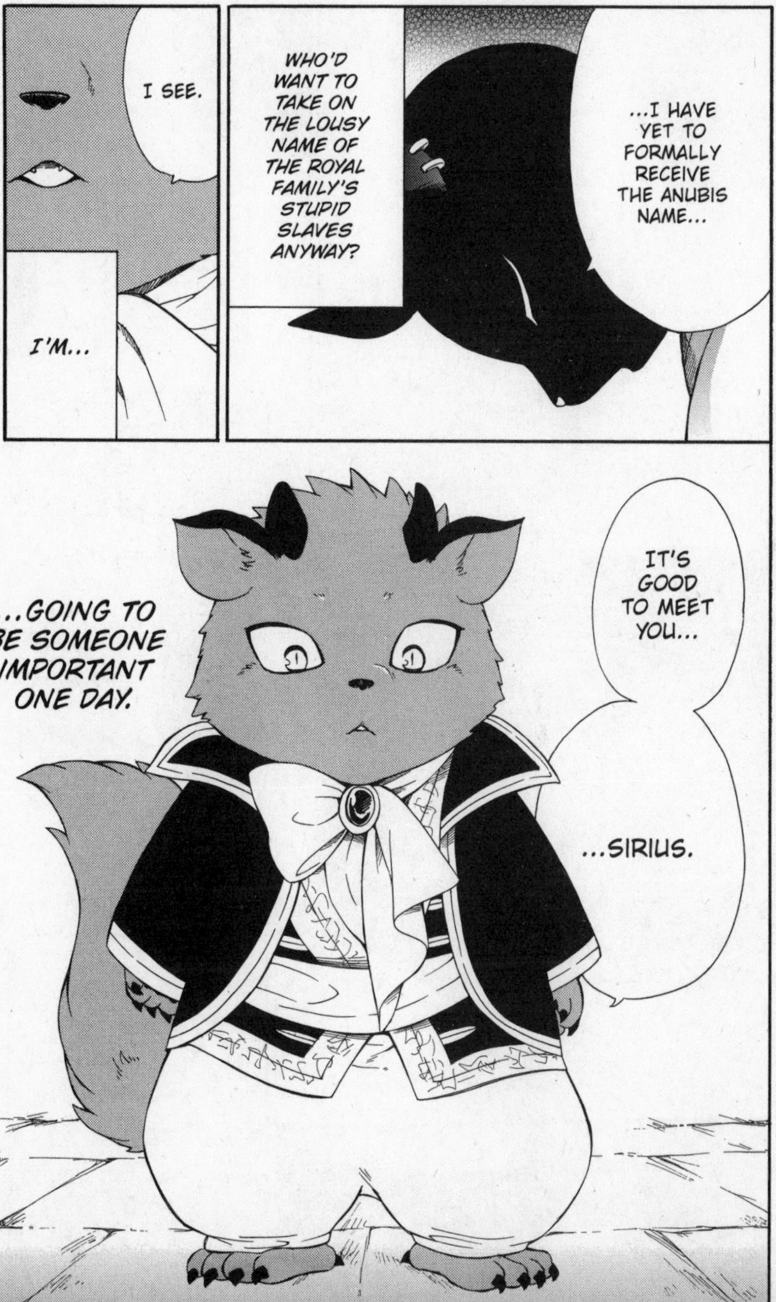
...I HAVE YET TO FORMALLY RECEIVE THE ANUBIS NAME...
WHO'D WANT TO TAKE ON THE LOUSY NAME OF THE ROYAL FAMILY'S STUPID SLAVES ANYWAY?
I SEE.
I'M...
IT'S GOOD TO MEET YOU...
...SIRIUS.
...GOING TO BE SOMEONE IMPORTANT ONE DAY.

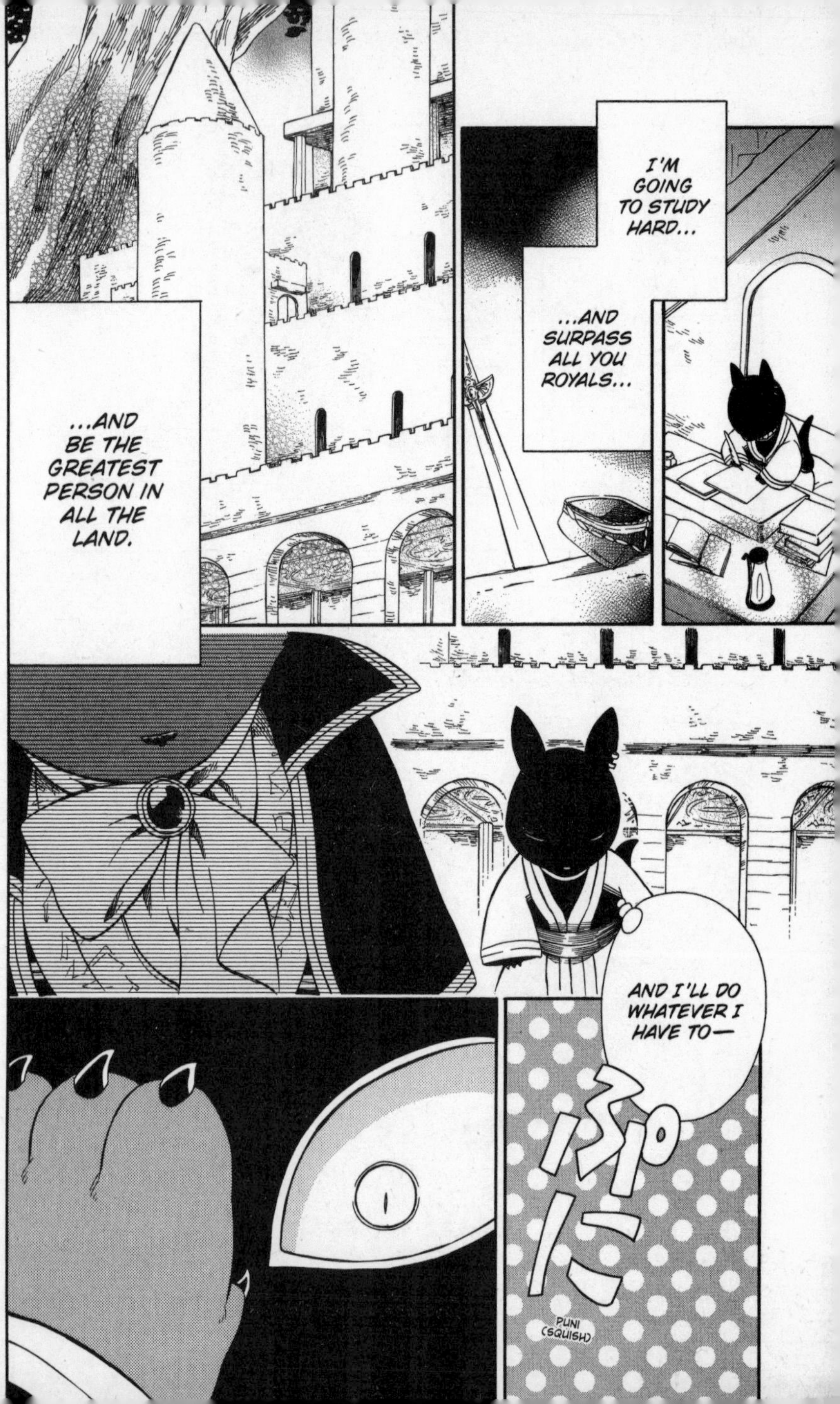
I'M GOING TO STUDY HARD...
...AND SURPASS ALL YOU ROYALS...
...AND BE THE GREATEST PERSON IN ALL THE LAND.
AND I'LL DO WHATEVER I HAVE TO—
ぷに
PUNI (SQUISH)

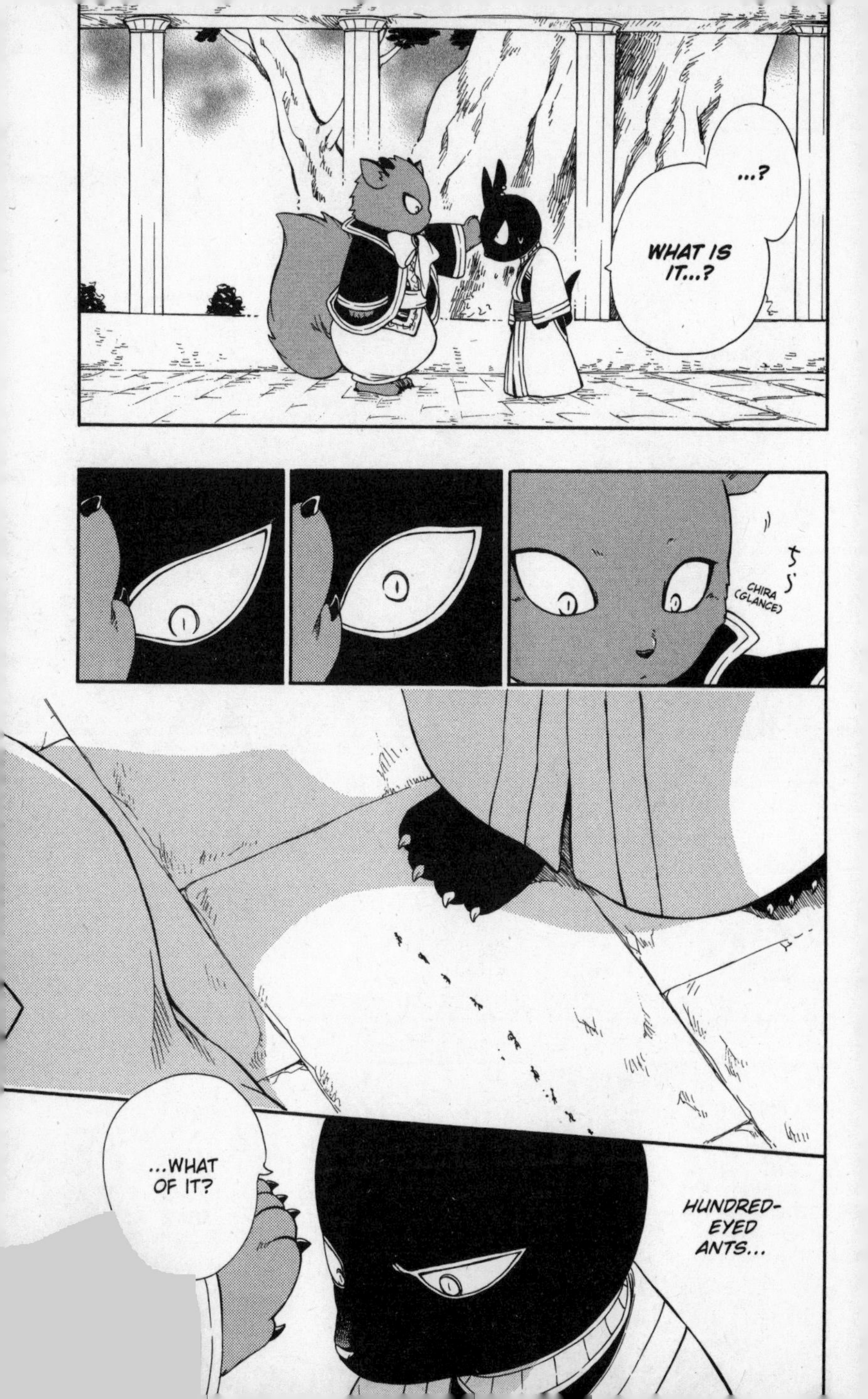
...?
WHAT IS IT...?
ちら
CHIRA (GLANCE)
HUNDRED-EYED ANTS...
...WHAT OF IT?

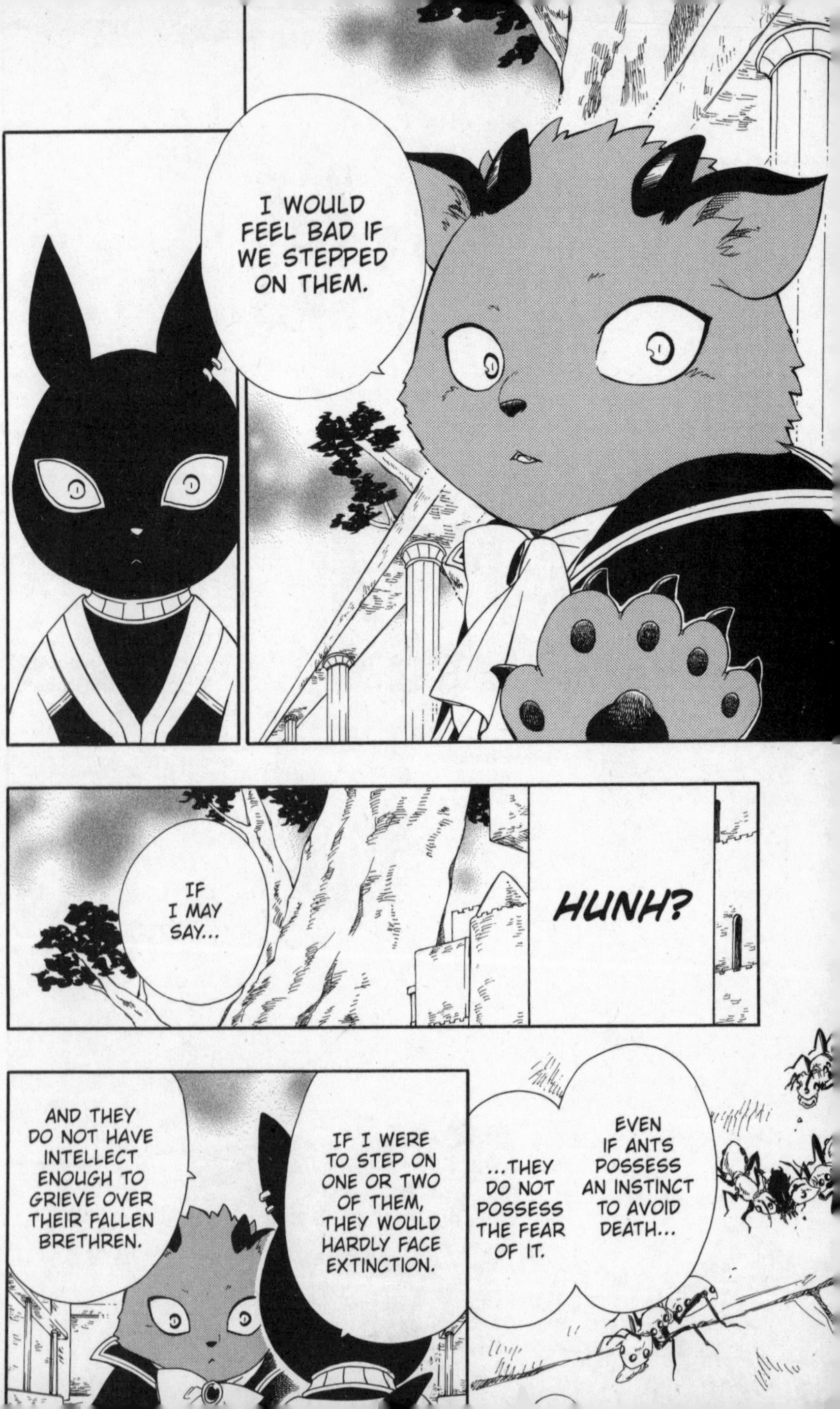
I WOULD FEEL BAD IF WE STEPPED ON THEM.
HUNH?
IF I MAY SAY...
EVEN IF ANTS POSSESS AN INSTINCT TO AVOID DEATH...
...THEY DO NOT POSSESS THE FEAR OF IT.
IF I WERE TO STEP ON ONE OR TWO OF THEM, THEY WOULD HARDLY FACE EXTINCTION.
AND THEY DO NOT HAVE INTELLECT ENOUGH TO GRIEVE OVER THEIR FALLEN BRETHREN.

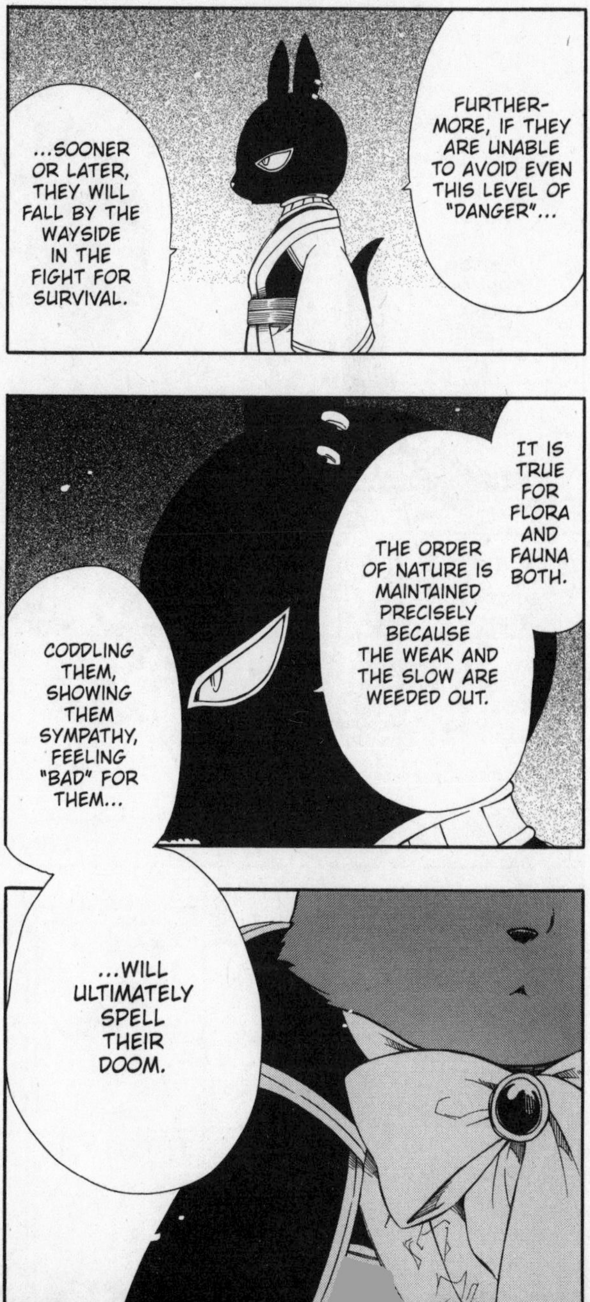
FURTHER-MORE, IF THEY ARE UNABLE TO AVOID EVEN THIS LEVEL OF "DANGER"...
...SOONER OR LATER, THEY WILL FALL BY THE WAYSIDE IN THE FIGHT FOR SURVIVAL.
IT IS TRUE FOR FLORA AND FAUNA BOTH.
THE ORDER OF NATURE IS MAINTAINED PRECISELY BECAUSE THE WEAK AND THE SLOW ARE WEEDED OUT.
CODDLING THEM, SHOWING THEM SYMPATHY, FEELING "BAD" FOR THEM...
...WILL ULTIMATELY SPELL THEIR DOOM.

JOZ

I KNEW FROM THE START THAT THERE WAS GOING TO BE A STAND-IN FOR GALOIS, SO HE GOT TO BE AS NASTY AS I COULD MAKE HIM. SINCE HE HAD TO PLAY THE VILLAIN, I MADE UP FOR IT BY MAKING HIS ACTUAL PERSONALITY UTTERLY CHARMING. HE'S SORT OF MY FAVORITE.

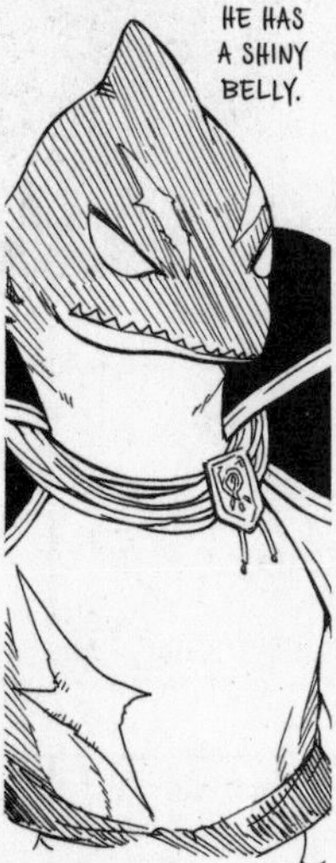
HE HAS A SHINY BELLY.

QUITE A FEW READERS THOUGHT HE WAS AN ORCA, BUT AS AN ICHTHYAN—FISH PEOPLE!—HE'S ACTUALLY A SHARK.

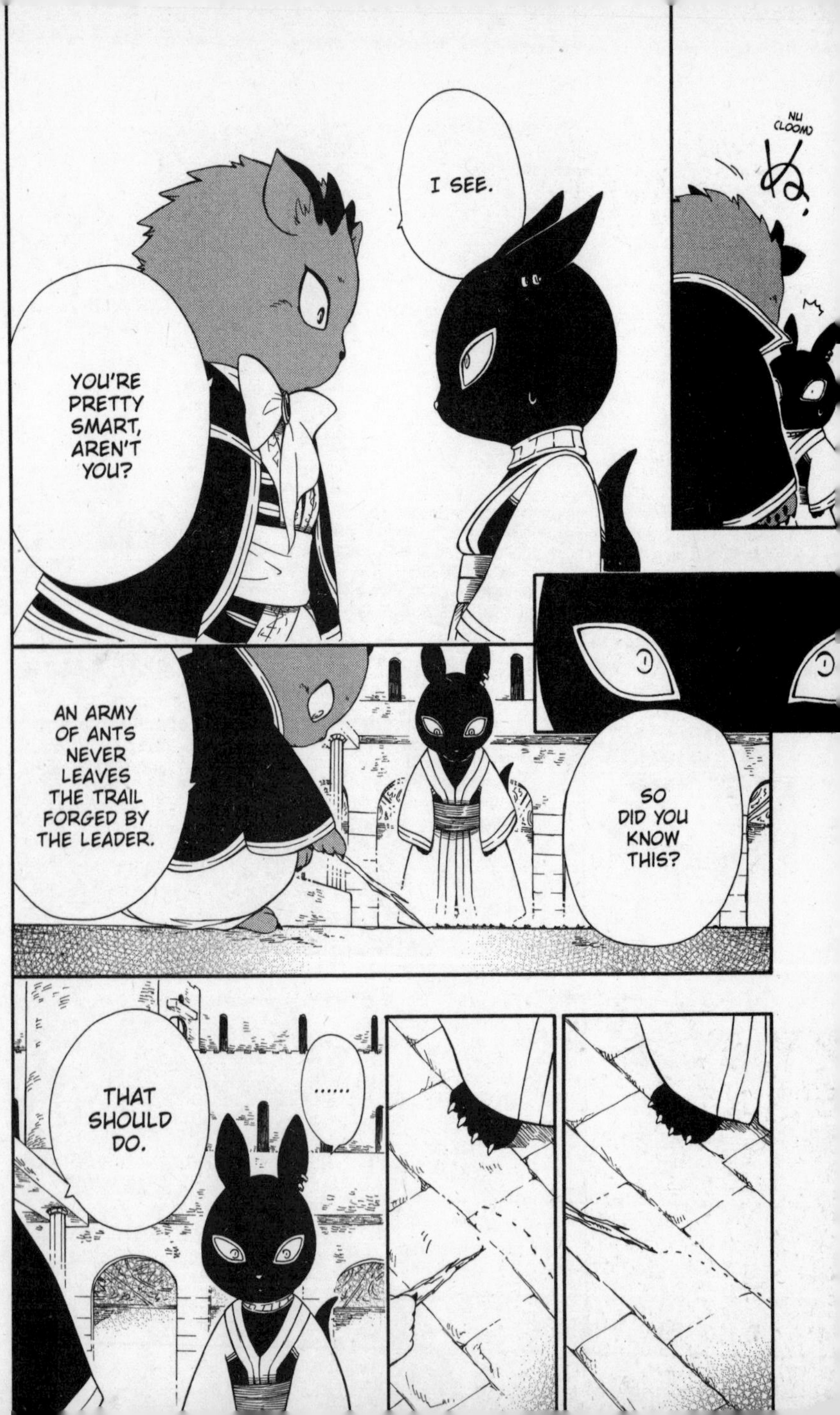

NU (LOOM)
ぬ
I SEE.
YOU'RE PRETTY SMART, AREN'T YOU?
SO DID YOU KNOW THIS?
AN ARMY OF ANTS NEVER LEAVES THE TRAIL FORGED BY THE LEADER.
......
THAT SHOULD DO.

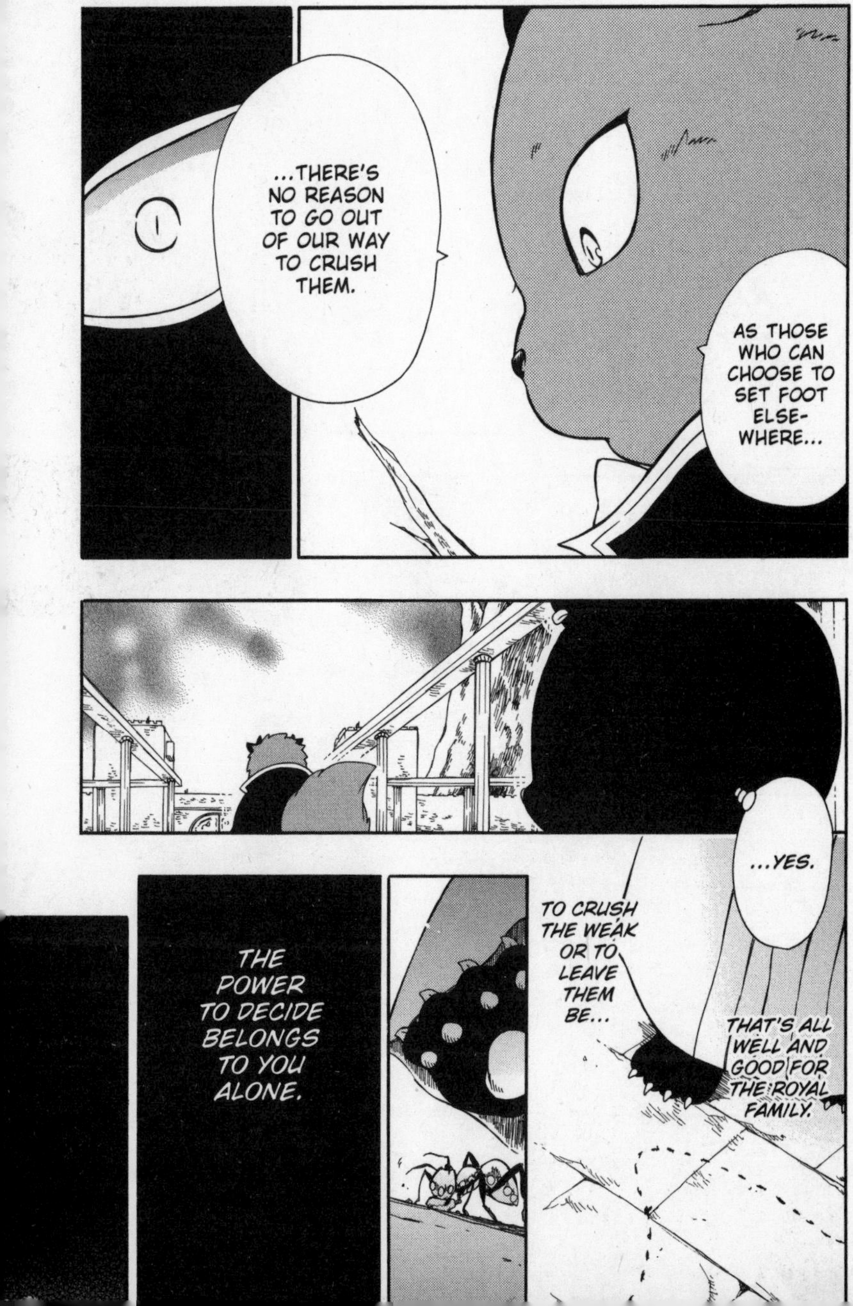
AS THOSE WHO CAN CHOOSE TO SET FOOT ELSE-WHERE...
...THERE'S NO REASON TO GO OUT OF OUR WAY TO CRUSH THEM.
...YES.
TO CRUSH THE WEAK OR TO LEAVE THEM BE...
THAT'S ALL WELL AND GOOD FOR THE ROYAL FAMILY.
THE POWER TO DECIDE BELONGS TO YOU ALONE.

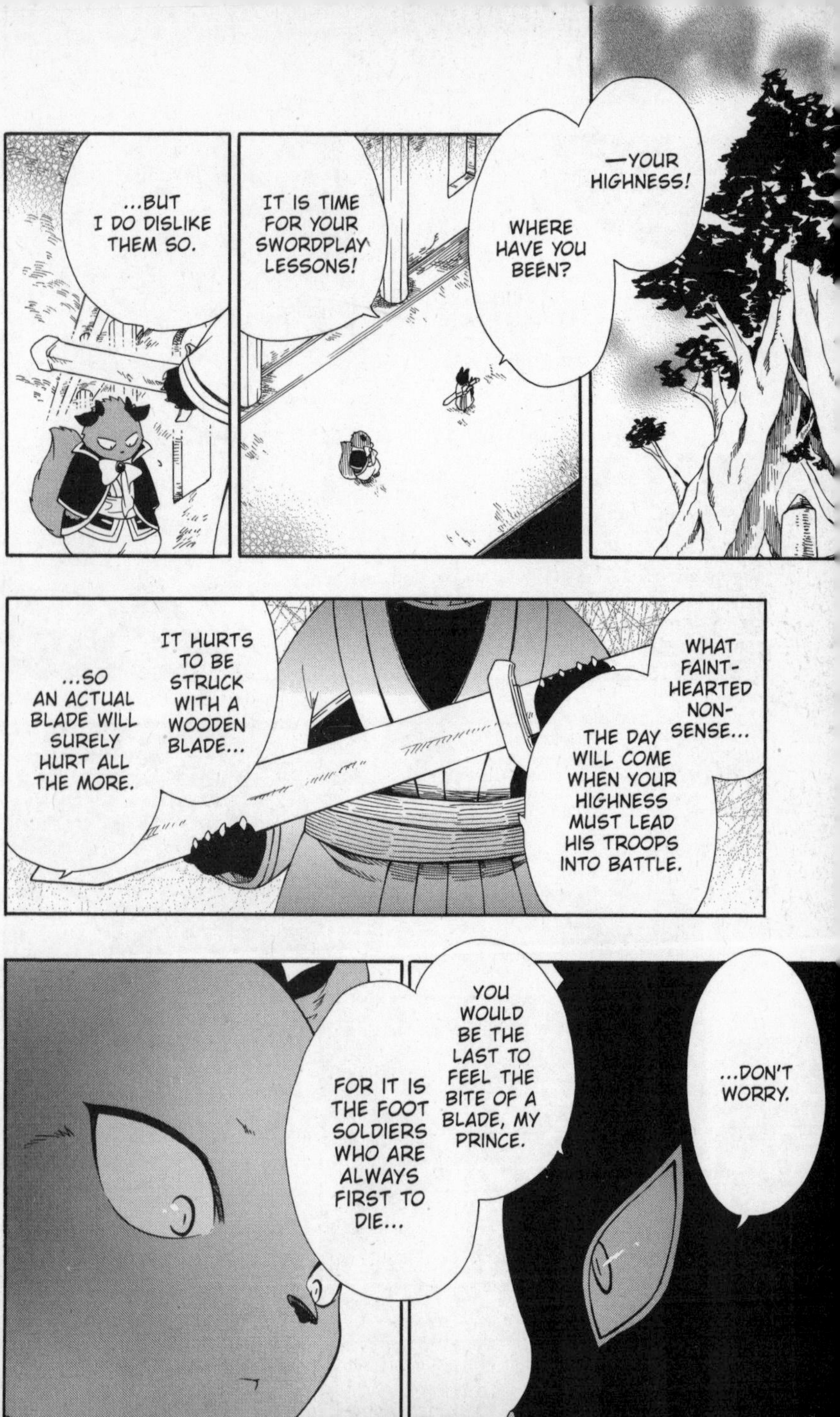
—YOUR HIGHNESS!
WHERE HAVE YOU BEEN?
IT IS TIME FOR YOUR SWORDPLAY LESSONS!
...BUT I DO DISLIKE THEM SO.
WHAT FAINT-HEARTED NON-SENSE...
THE DAY WILL COME WHEN YOUR HIGHNESS MUST LEAD HIS TROOPS INTO BATTLE.
IT HURTS TO BE STRUCK WITH A WOODEN BLADE...
...SO AN ACTUAL BLADE WILL SURELY HURT ALL THE MORE.
...DON'T WORRY.
YOU WOULD BE THE LAST TO FEEL THE BITE OF A BLADE, MY PRINCE.
FOR IT IS THE FOOT SOLDIERS WHO ARE ALWAYS FIRST TO DIE...

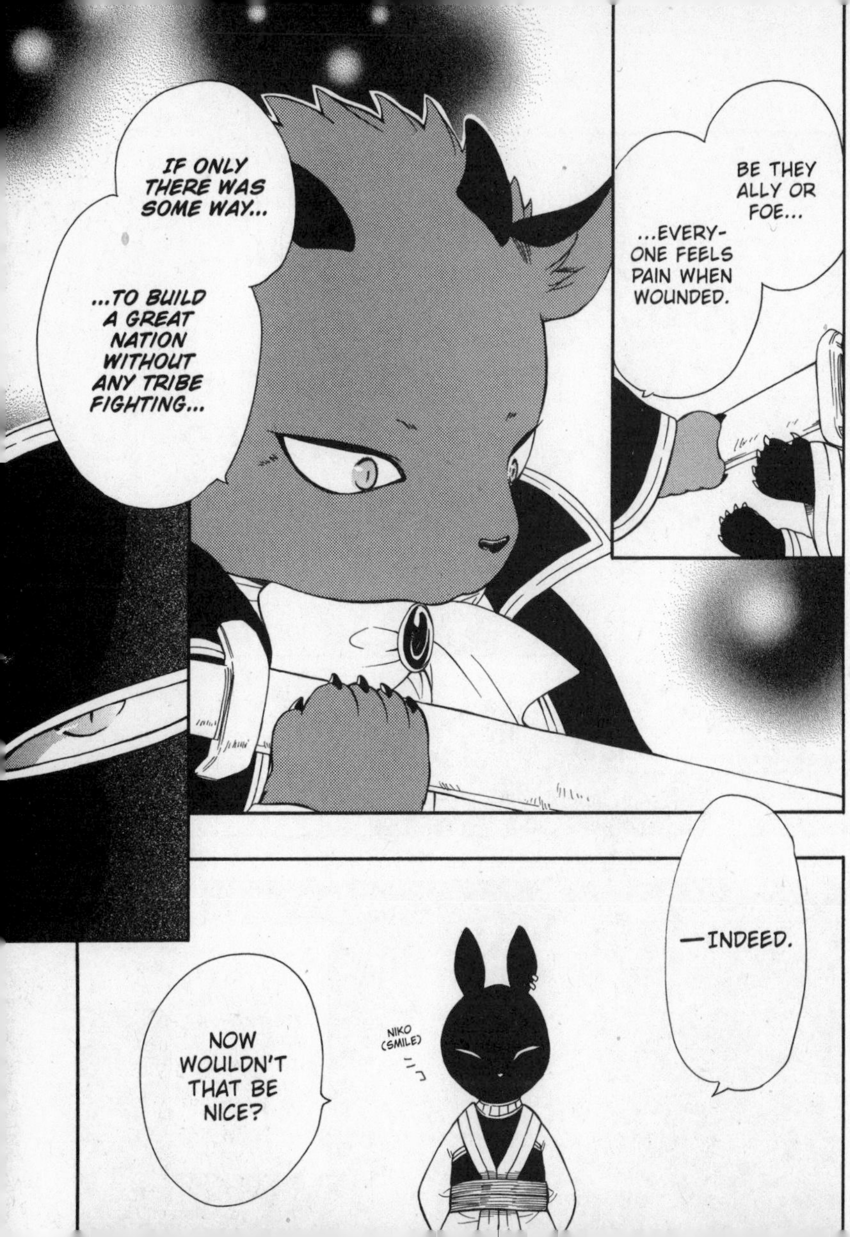
BE THEY ALLY OR FOE...
...EVERY-ONE FEELS PAIN WHEN WOUNDED.
IF ONLY THERE WAS SOME WAY...
...TO BUILD A GREAT NATION WITHOUT ANY TRIBE FIGHTING...
—INDEED.
NIKO (SMILE)
NOW WOULDN'T THAT BE NICE?

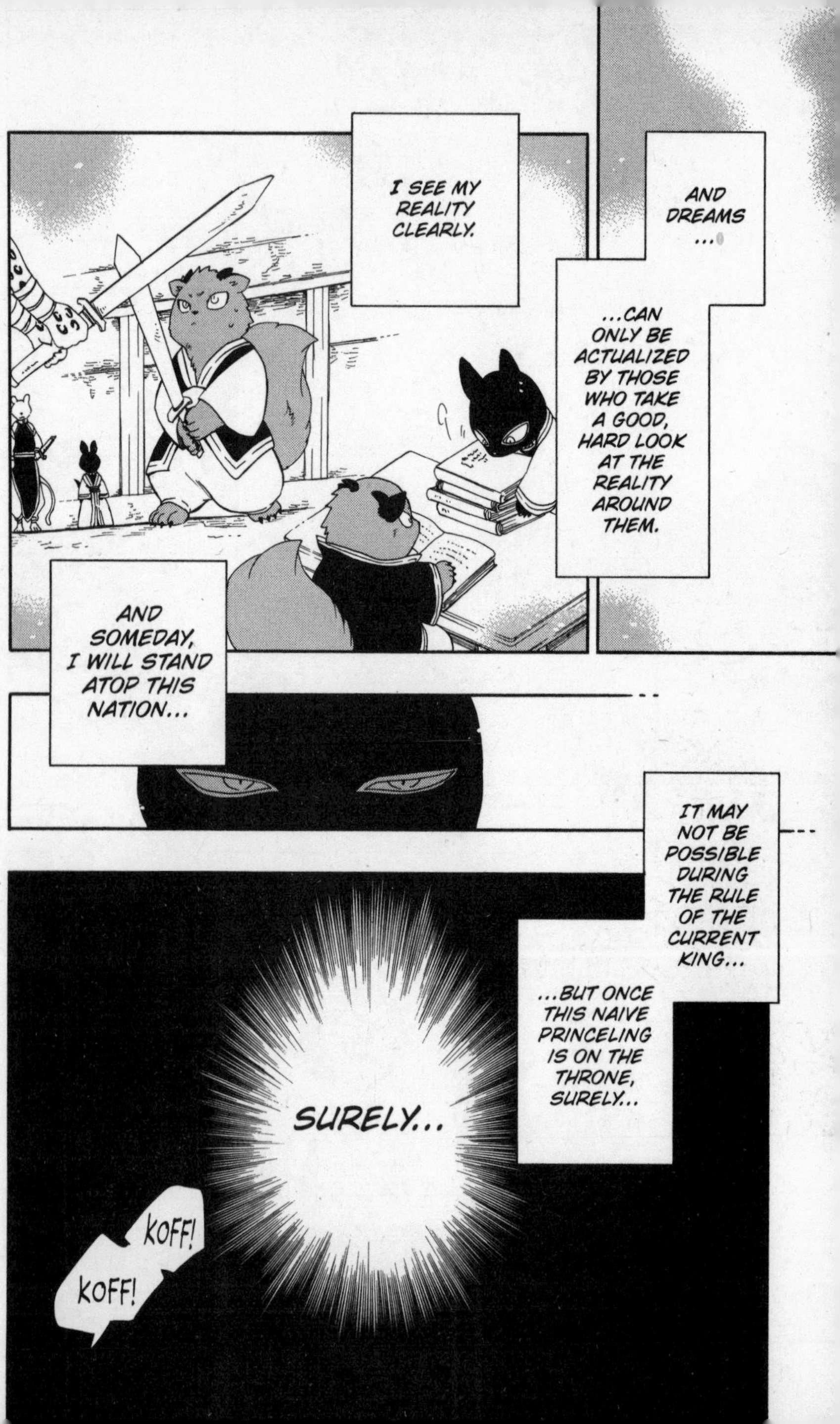
AND DREAMS...
...CAN ONLY BE ACTUALIZED BY THOSE WHO TAKE A GOOD, HARD LOOK AT THE REALITY AROUND THEM.
I SEE MY REALITY CLEARLY.
AND SOMEDAY, I WILL STAND ATOP THIS NATION...
IT MAY NOT BE POSSIBLE DURING THE RULE OF THE CURRENT KING...
...BUT ONCE THIS NAIVE PRINCELING IS ON THE THRONE, SURELY...
SURELY...
KOFF!
KOFF!

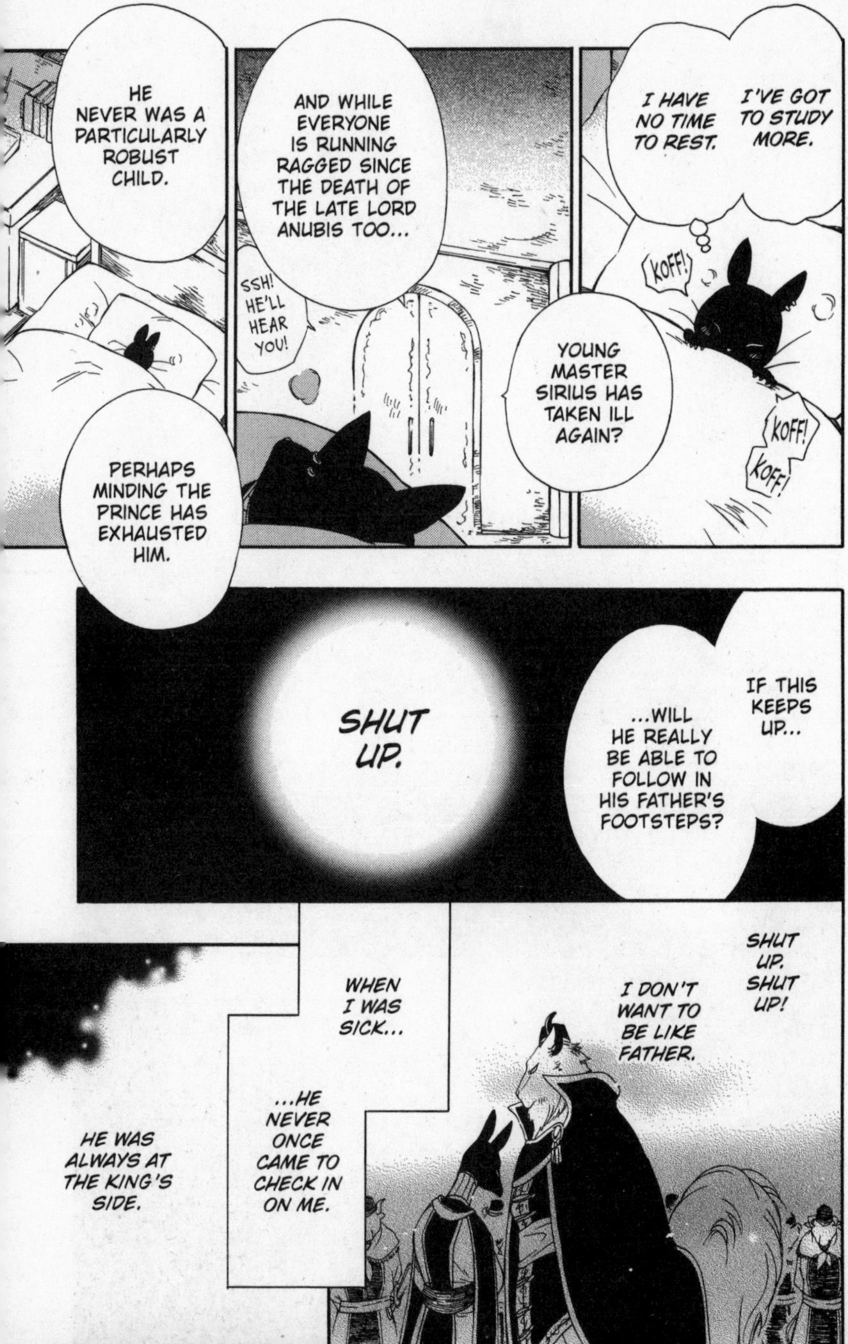
I'VE GOT TO STUDY MORE.
I HAVE NO TIME TO REST.
KOFF!
YOUNG MASTER SIRIUS HAS TAKEN ILL AGAIN?
KOFF! KOFF!
AND WHILE EVERYONE IS RUNNING RAGGED SINCE THE DEATH OF THE LATE LORD ANUBIS TOO...
SSH! HE'LL HEAR YOU!
HE NEVER WAS A PARTICULARLY ROBUST CHILD.
PERHAPS MINDING THE PRINCE HAS EXHAUSTED HIM.
IF THIS KEEPS UP...
...WILL HE REALLY BE ABLE TO FOLLOW IN HIS FATHER'S FOOTSTEPS?
SHUT UP.
SHUT UP. SHUT UP!
I DON'T WANT TO BE LIKE FATHER.
WHEN I WAS SICK...
...HE NEVER ONCE CAME TO CHECK IN ON ME.
HE WAS ALWAYS AT THE KING'S SIDE.

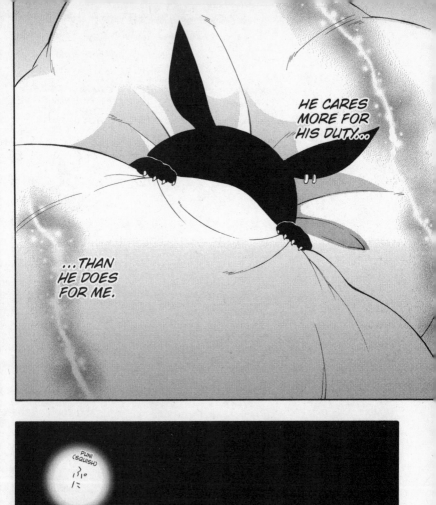

HE CARES MORE FOR HIS DUTY...

...THAN HE DOES FOR ME.

PUNI (SQUISH)

......?

WHAT WAS THAT ...?

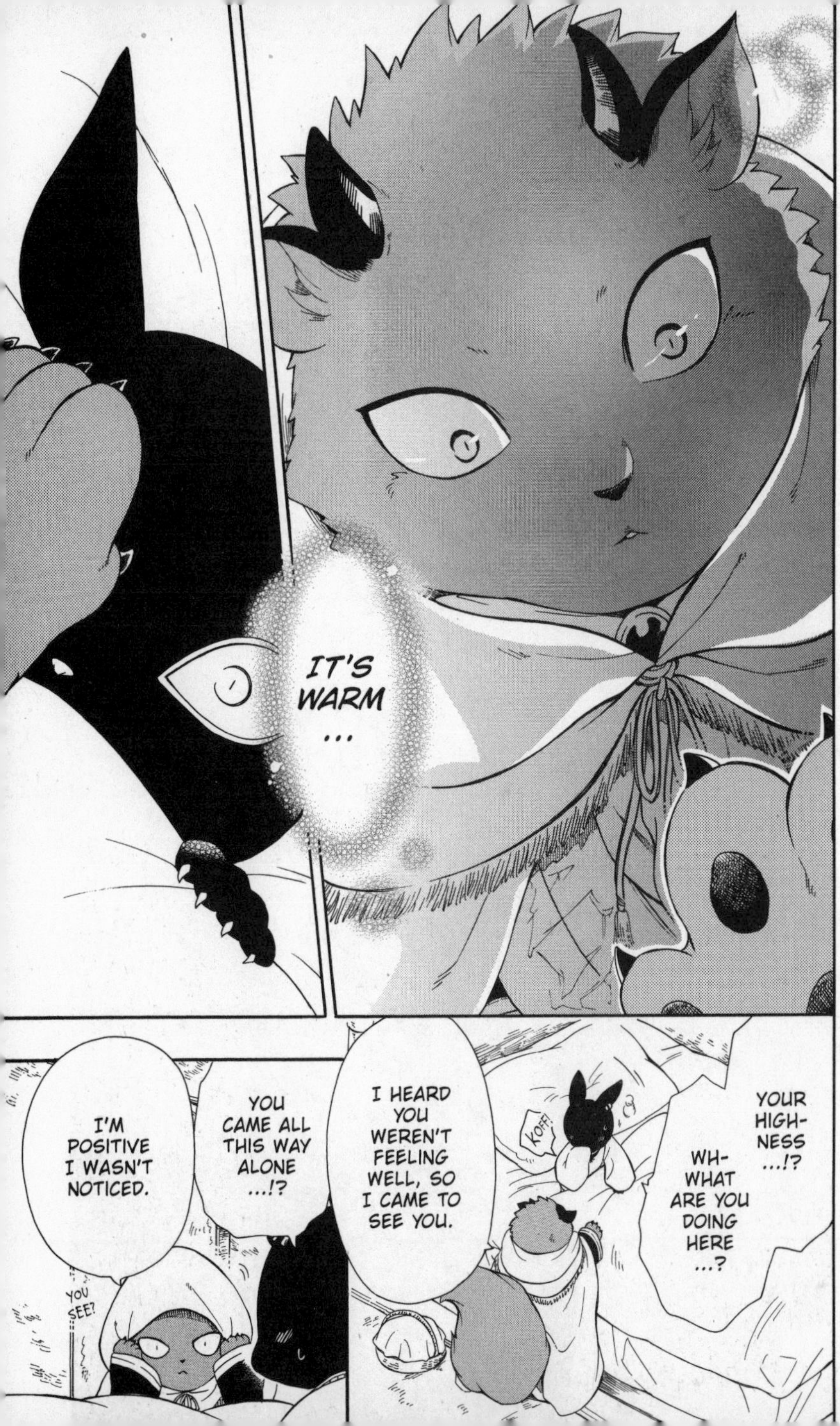
IT'S WARM ...
KOFF!
YOUR HIGHNESS ...!?
WH-WHAT ARE YOU DOING HERE ...?
I HEARD YOU WEREN'T FEELING WELL, SO I CAME TO SEE YOU.
YOU CAME ALL THIS WAY ALONE ...!?
I'M POSITIVE I WASN'T NOTICED.
YOU SEE?

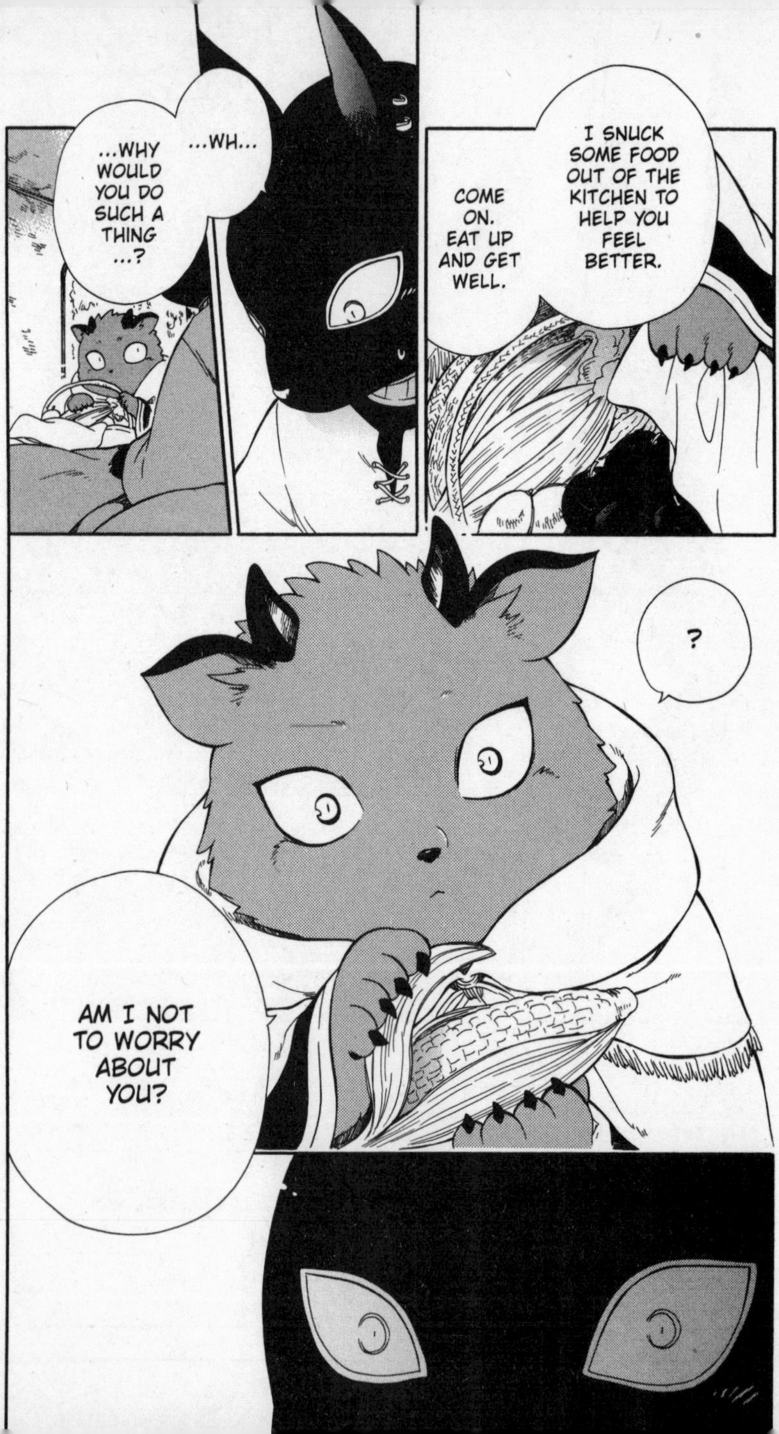
I SNUCK SOME FOOD OUT OF THE KITCHEN TO HELP YOU FEEL BETTER.
COME ON. EAT UP AND GET WELL.
...WH...
...WHY WOULD YOU DO SUCH A THING ...?
?
AM I NOT TO WORRY ABOUT YOU?

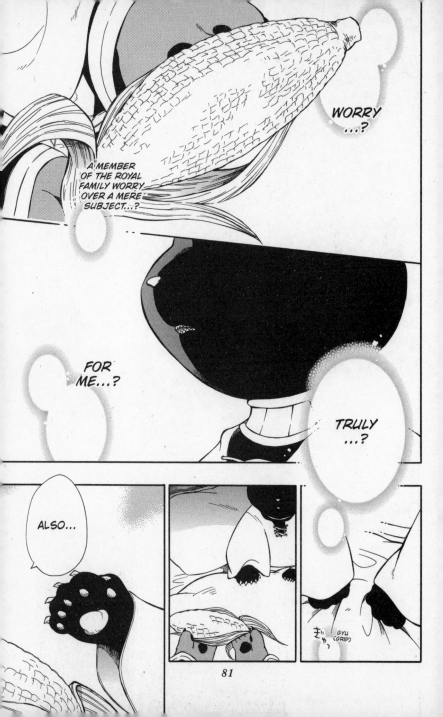

WORRY ...?

A MEMBER OF THE ROYAL FAMILY WORRY OVER A MERE SUBJECT...?

FOR ME...?

TRULY ...?

ALSO...

GYU (GRIP)

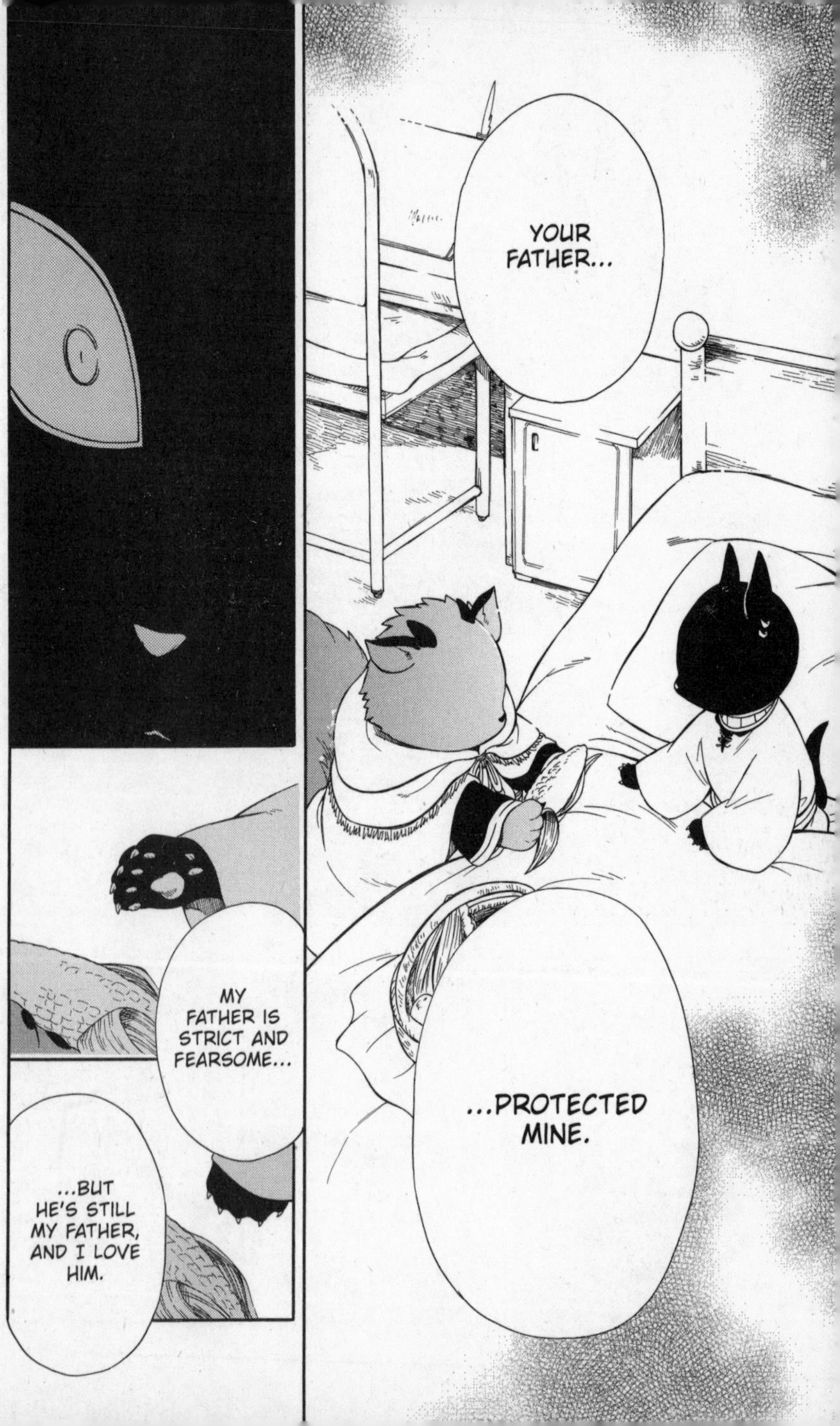
YOUR FATHER...
...PROTECTED MINE.
MY FATHER IS STRICT AND FEARSOME...
...BUT HE'S STILL MY FATHER, AND I LOVE HIM.

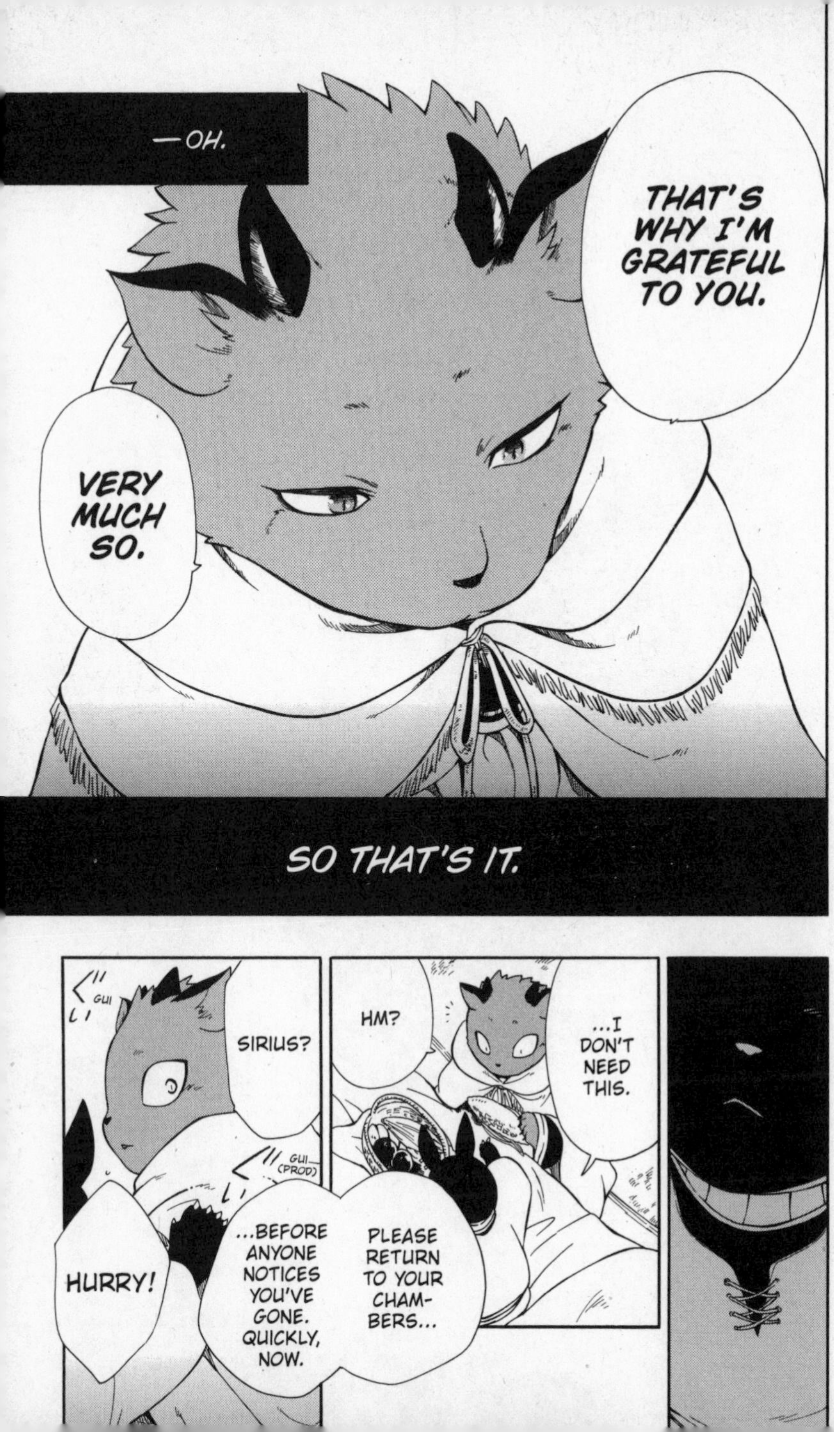
THAT'S WHY I'M GRATEFUL TO YOU.
—OH.
VERY MUCH SO.
SO THAT'S IT.
...I DON'T NEED THIS.
HM?
PLEASE RETURN TO YOUR CHAM-BERS...
...BEFORE ANYONE NOTICES YOU'VE GONE. QUICKLY, NOW.
SIRIUS?
GUI
GUI (PROD)
HURRY!

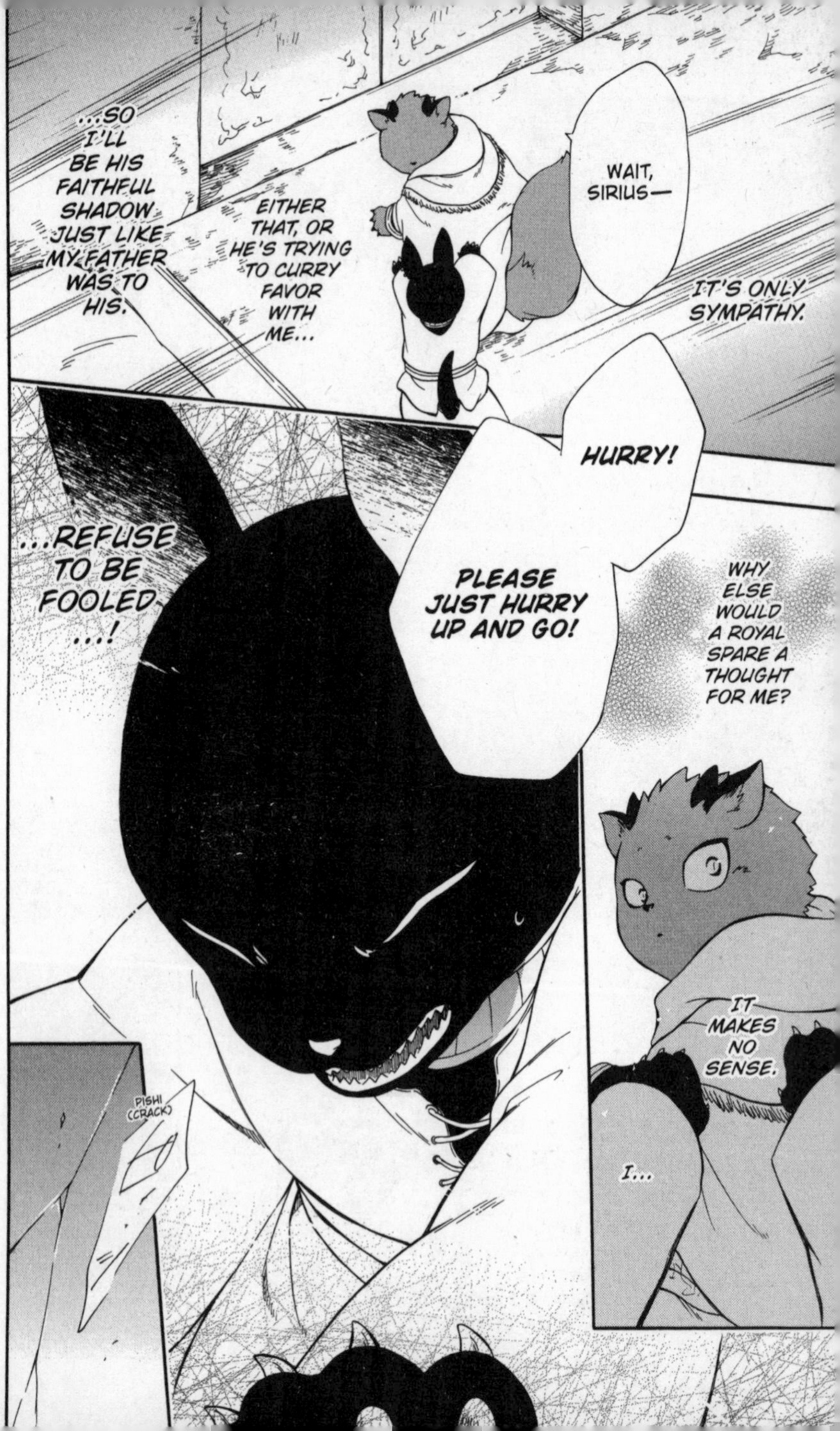
WAIT, SIRIUS—
IT'S ONLY SYMPATHY.
EITHER THAT, OR HE'S TRYING TO CURRY FAVOR WITH ME...
...SO I'LL BE HIS FAITHFUL SHADOW JUST LIKE MY FATHER WAS TO HIS.
HURRY!
PLEASE JUST HURRY UP AND GO!
WHY ELSE WOULD A ROYAL SPARE A THOUGHT FOR ME?
IT MAKES NO SENSE.
I...
...REFUSE TO BE FOOLED ...!
PISHI (CRACK)

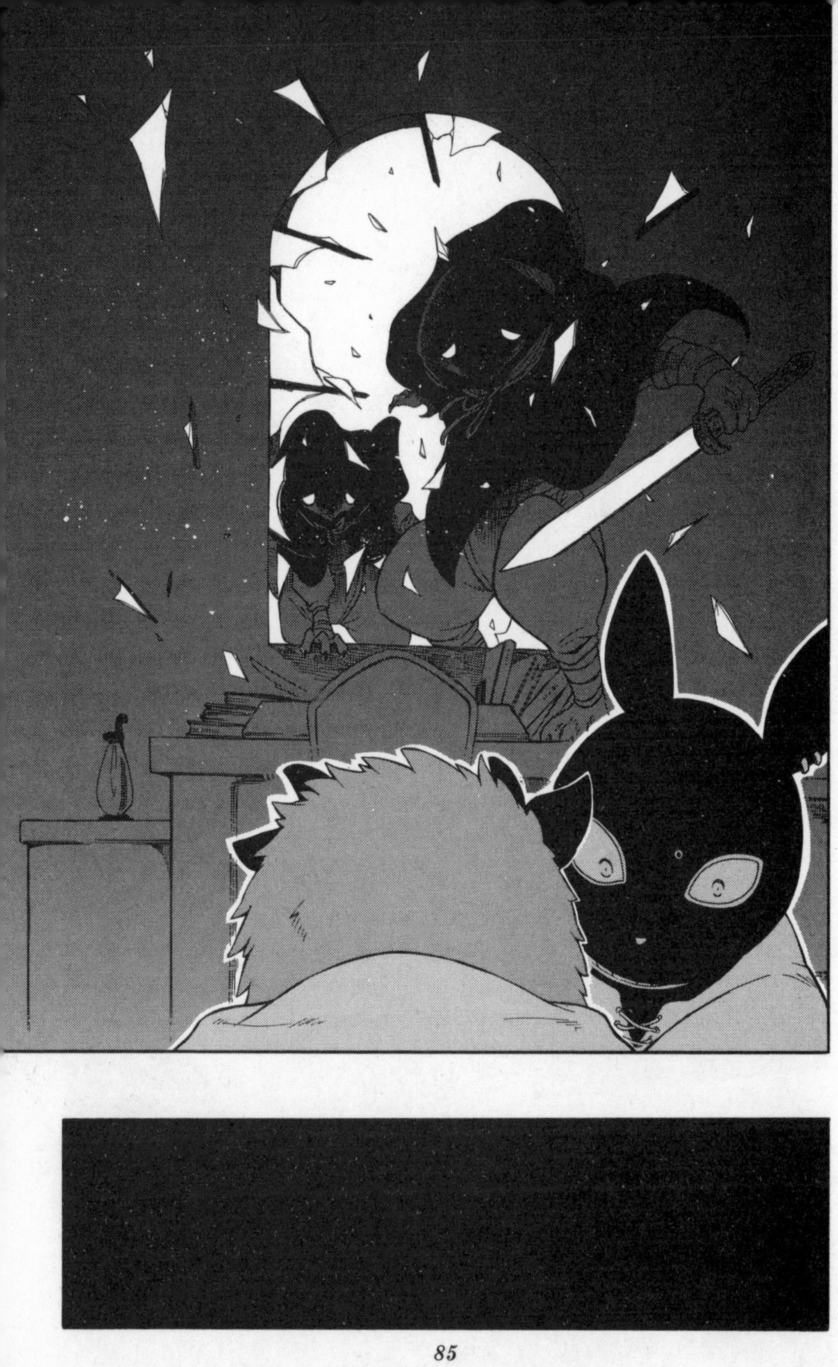

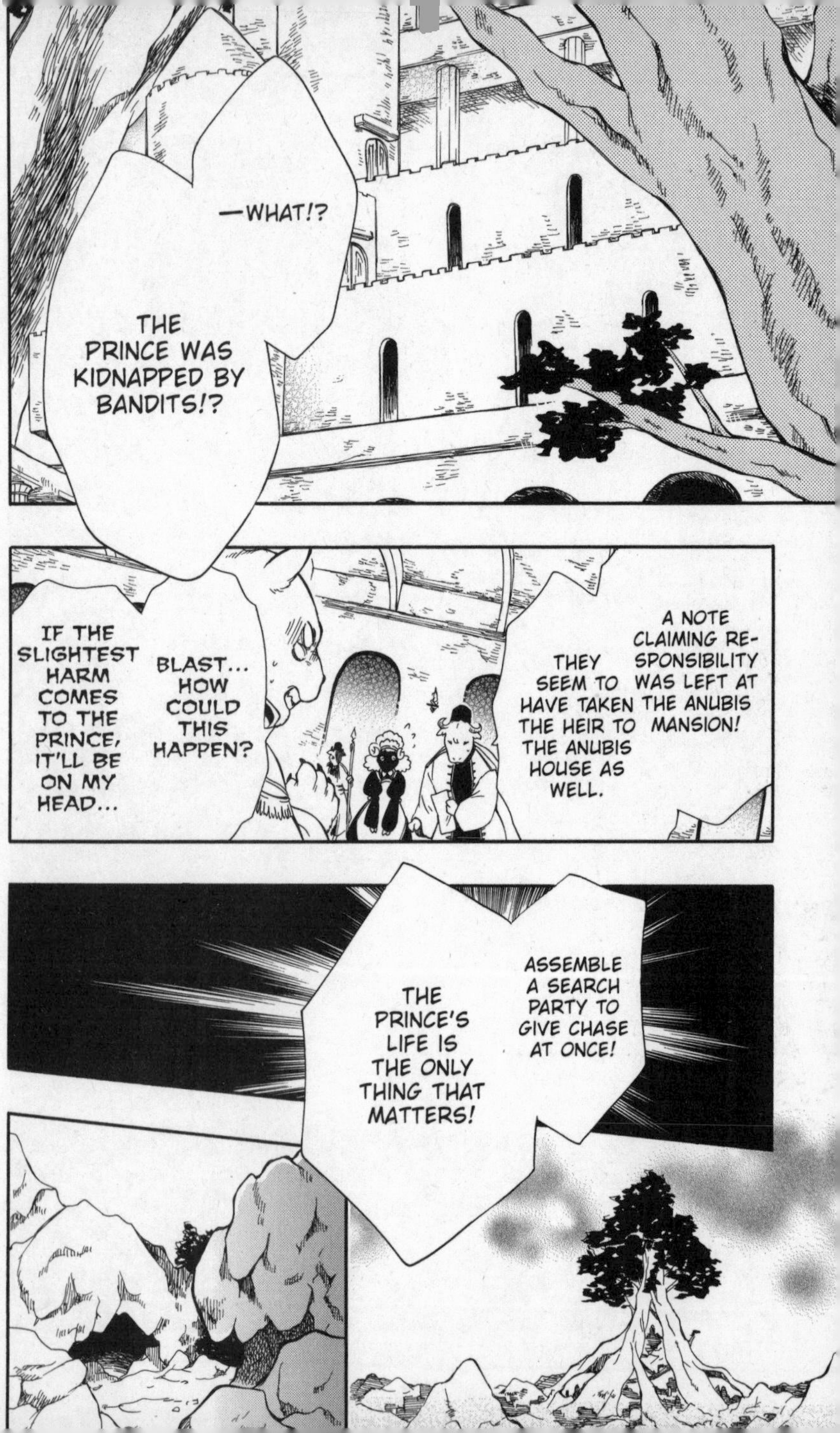
—WHAT!?
THE PRINCE WAS KIDNAPPED BY BANDITS!?
A NOTE CLAIMING RE-SPONSIBILITY WAS LEFT AT THE ANUBIS MANSION!
THEY SEEM TO HAVE TAKEN THE HEIR TO THE ANUBIS HOUSE AS WELL.
BLAST... HOW COULD THIS HAPPEN?
IF THE SLIGHTEST HARM COMES TO THE PRINCE, IT'LL BE ON MY HEAD...
ASSEMBLE A SEARCH PARTY TO GIVE CHASE AT ONCE!
THE PRINCE'S LIFE IS THE ONLY THING THAT MATTERS!

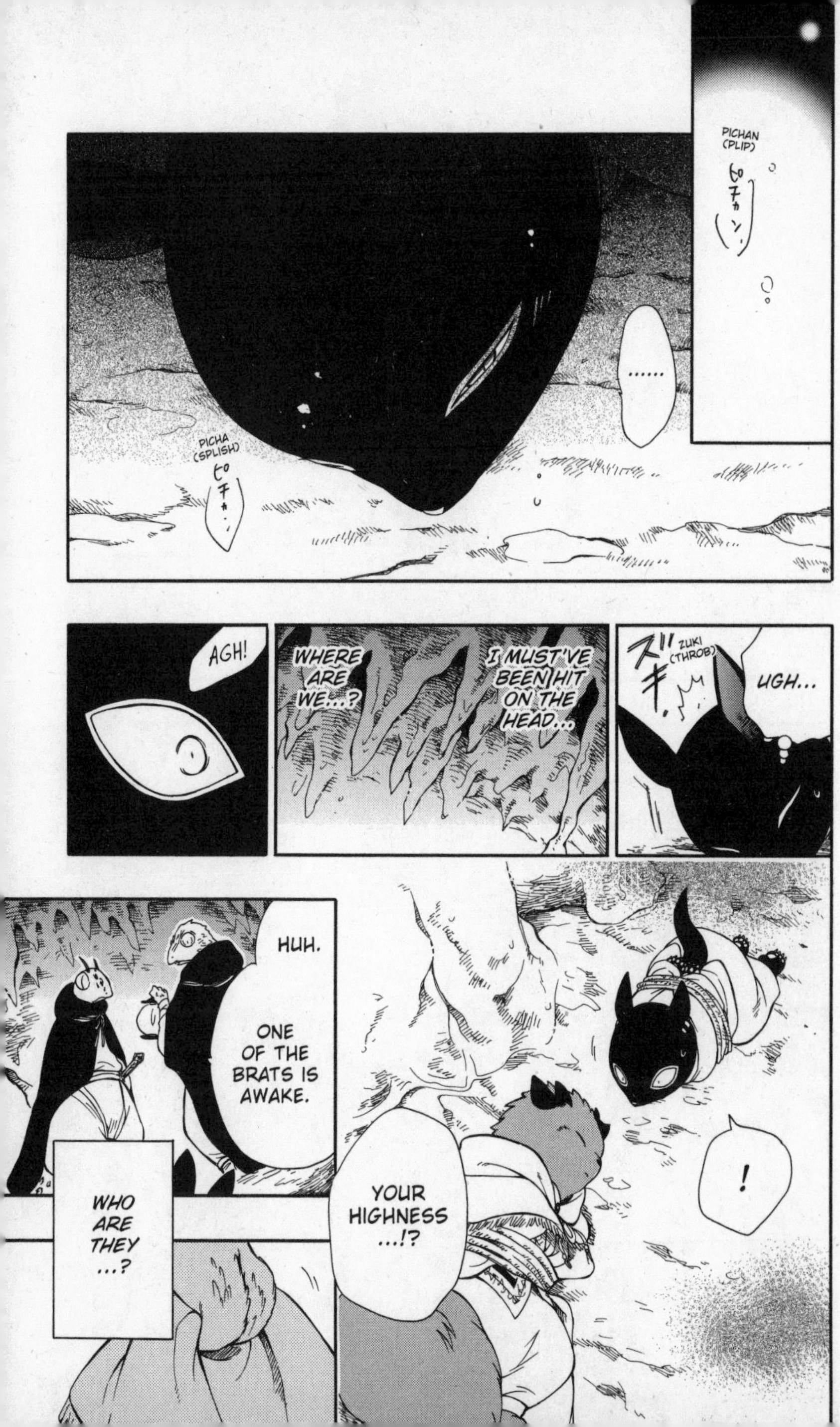
PICHAN (PLIP)
ピチャン
......
PICHA (SPLISH)
ピチャ
ZUKI (THROB)
ズキ
UGH...
I MUST'VE BEEN HIT ON THE HEAD...
WHERE ARE WE...?
AGH!
!
YOUR HIGHNESS ...!?
HUH.
ONE OF THE BRATS IS AWAKE.
WHO ARE THEY ...?

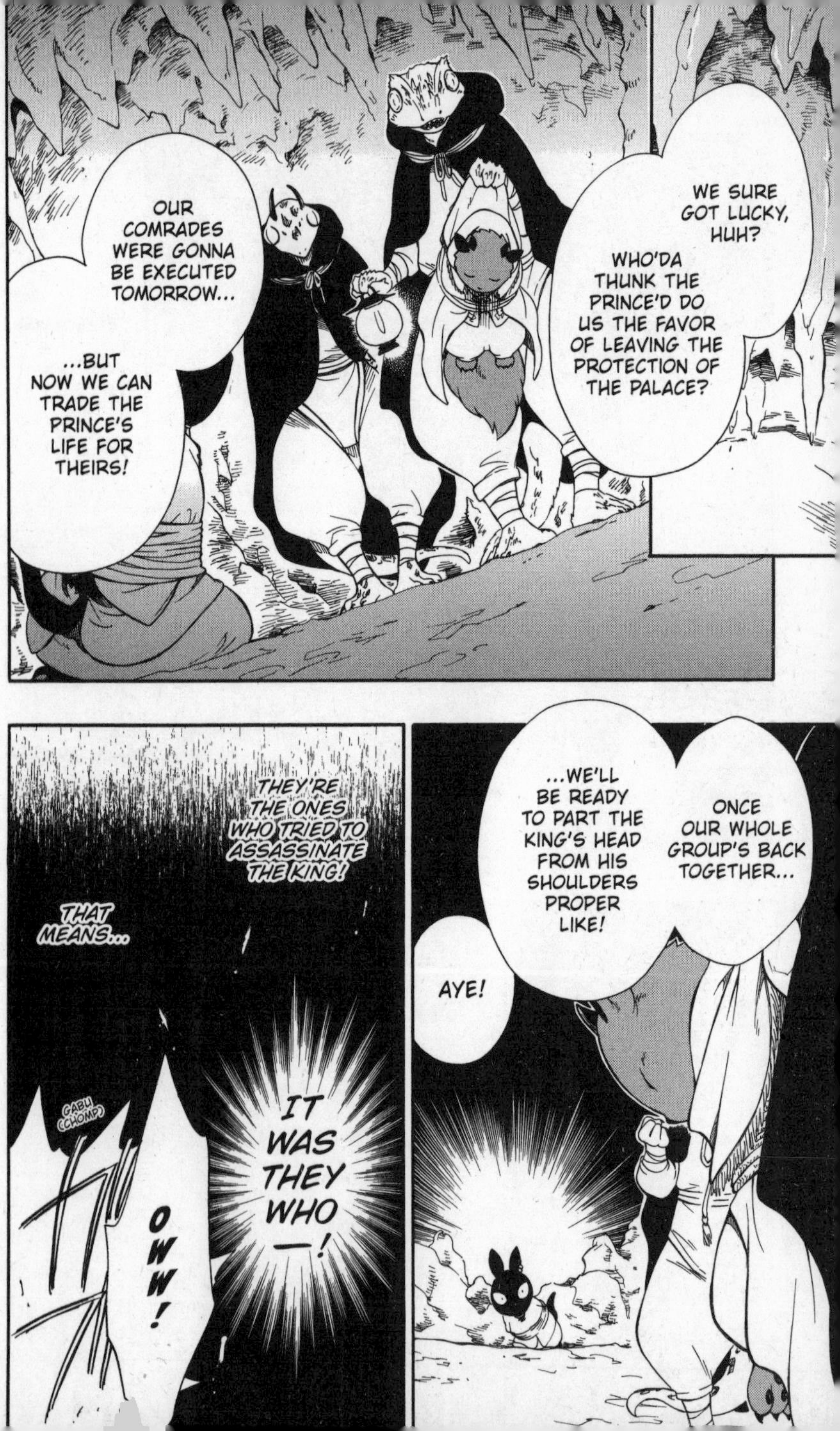
WE SURE GOT LUCKY, HUH?
WHO'DA THUNK THE PRINCE'D DO US THE FAVOR OF LEAVING THE PROTECTION OF THE PALACE?
OUR COMRADES WERE GONNA BE EXECUTED TOMORROW...
...BUT NOW WE CAN TRADE THE PRINCE'S LIFE FOR THEIRS!
ONCE OUR WHOLE GROUP'S BACK TOGETHER...
...WE'LL BE READY TO PART THE KING'S HEAD FROM HIS SHOULDERS PROPER LIKE!
AYE!
THEY'RE THE ONES WHO TRIED TO ASSASSINATE THE KING!
THAT MEANS...
IT WAS THEY WHO—!
GABU (CHOMP)
OWW!

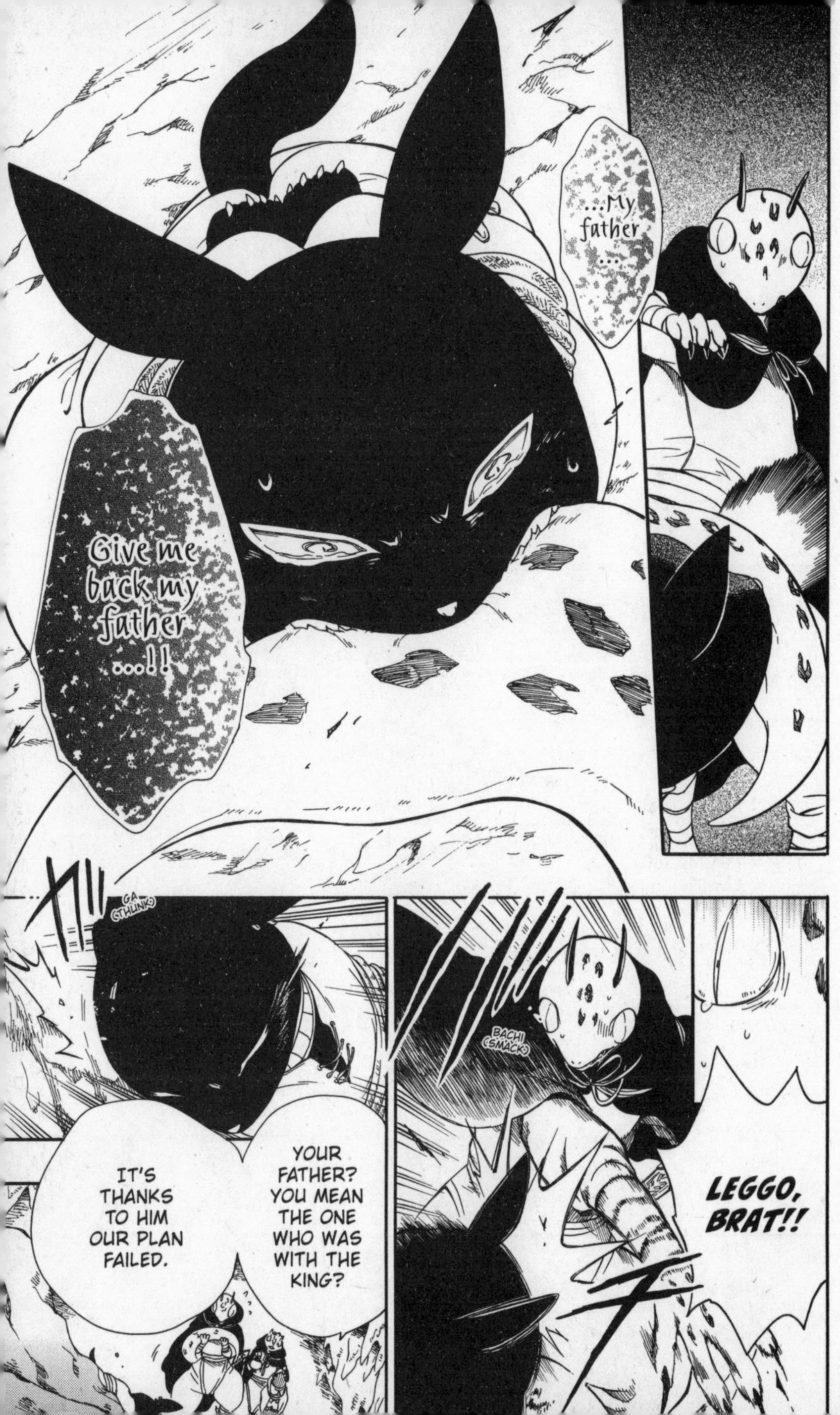
...My father...
Give me back my father...!!
LEGGO, BRAT!!
BACHI! (SMACK)
GA (THUNK)
YOUR FATHER? YOU MEAN THE ONE WHO WAS WITH THE KING?
IT'S THANKS TO HIM OUR PLAN FAILED.

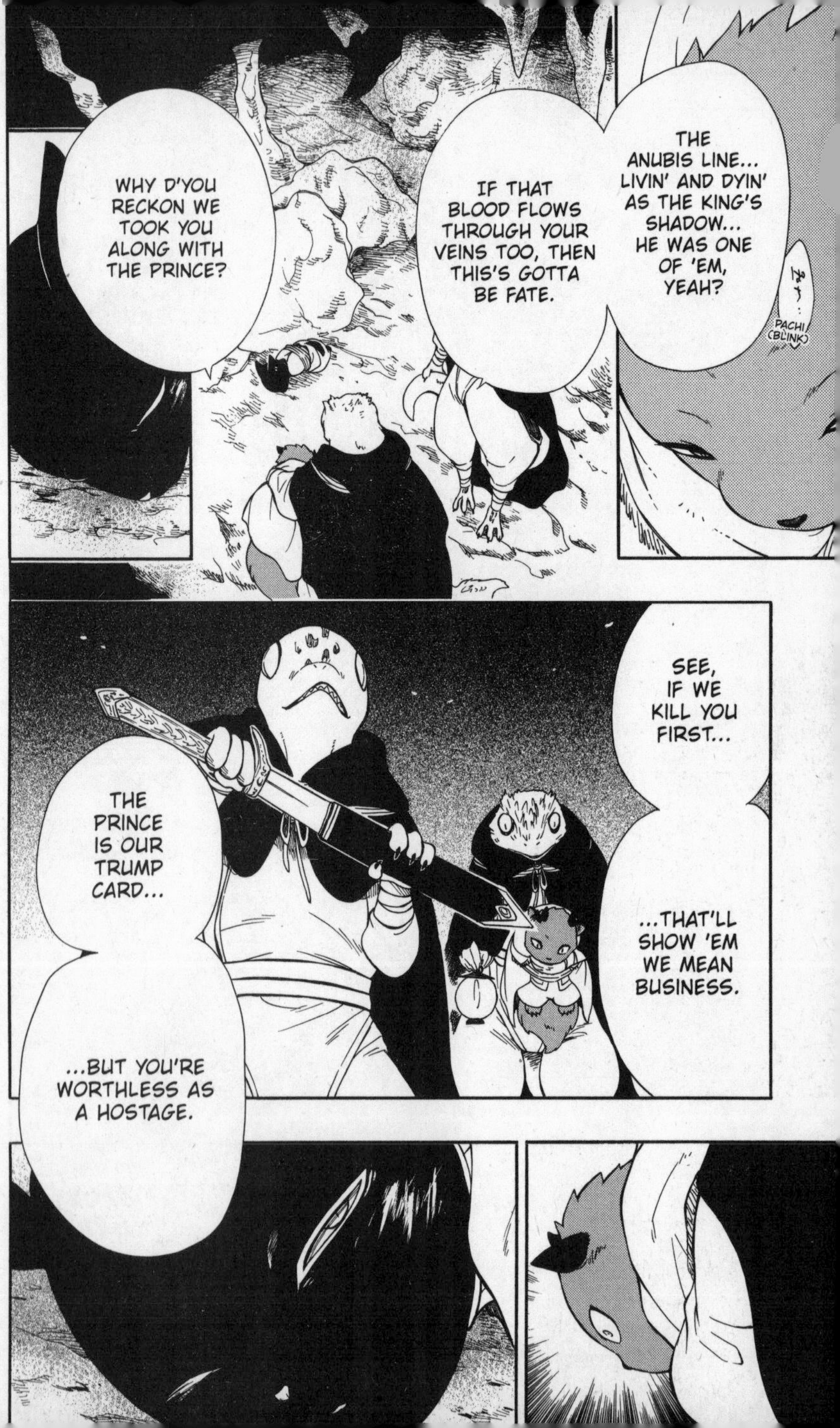
THE ANUBIS LINE... LIVIN' AND DYIN' AS THE KING'S SHADOW... HE WAS ONE OF 'EM, YEAH?
PACHI (BLINK)
IF THAT BLOOD FLOWS THROUGH YOUR VEINS TOO, THEN THIS'S GOTTA BE FATE.
WHY D'YOU RECKON WE TOOK YOU ALONG WITH THE PRINCE?
THE PRINCE IS OUR TRUMP CARD...
...BUT YOU'RE WORTHLESS AS A HOSTAGE.
SEE, IF WE KILL YOU FIRST...
...THAT'LL SHOW 'EM WE MEAN BUSINESS.

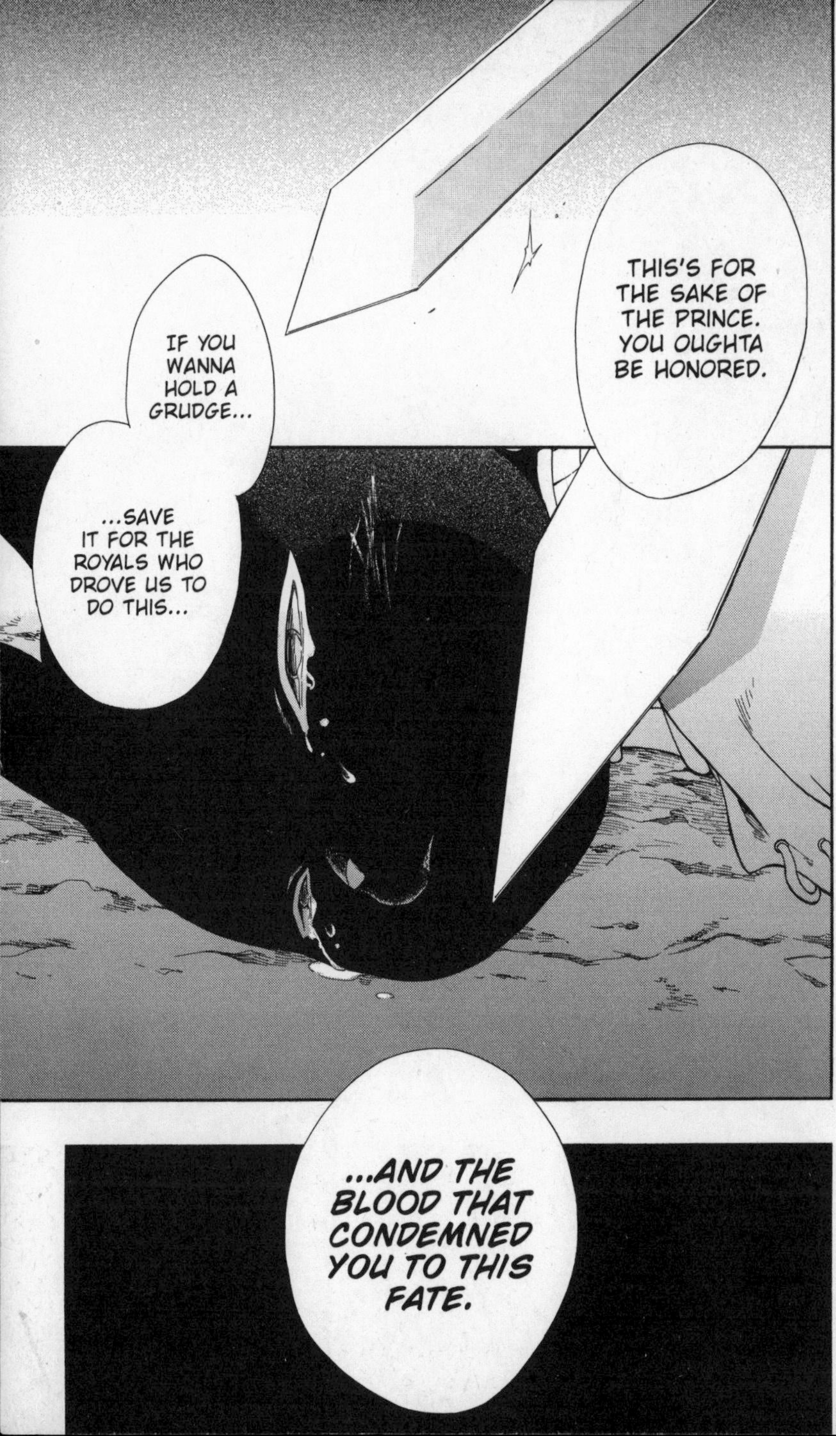
THIS'S FOR THE SAKE OF THE PRINCE. YOU OUGHTA BE HONORED.
IF YOU WANNA HOLD A GRUDGE...
...SAVE IT FOR THE ROYALS WHO DROVE US TO DO THIS...
...AND THE BLOOD THAT CONDEMNED YOU TO THIS FATE.

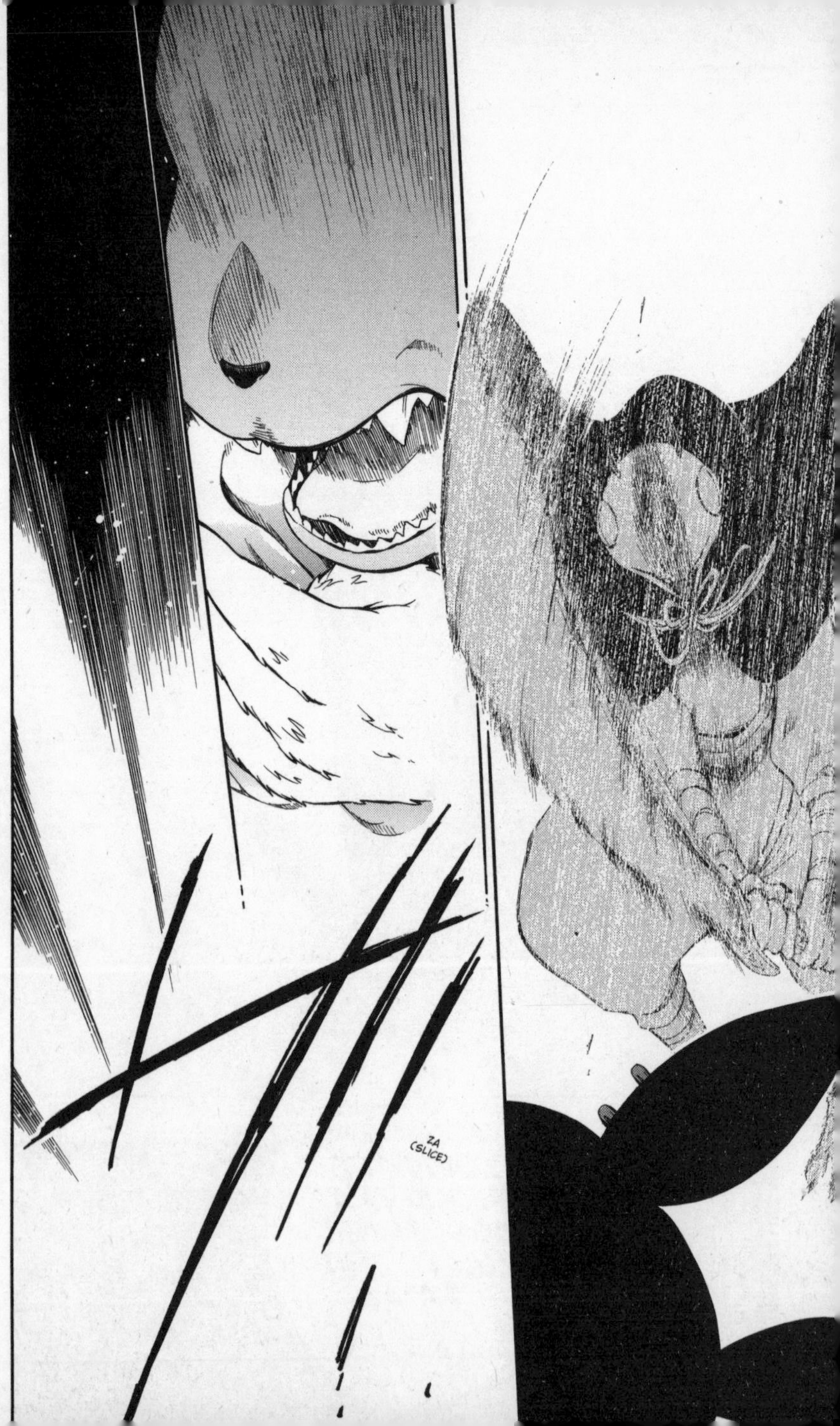
ZA (SLICE)

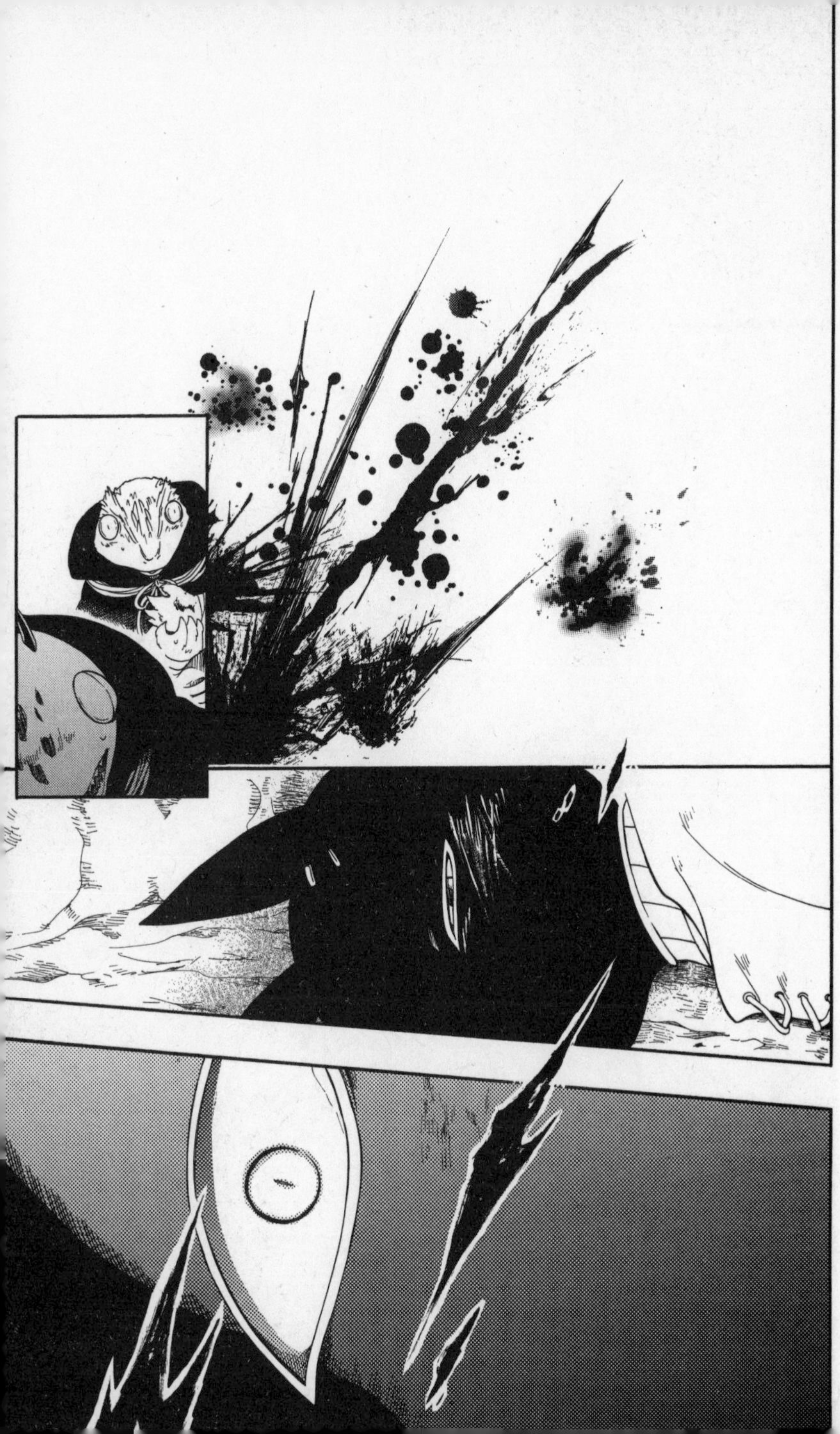

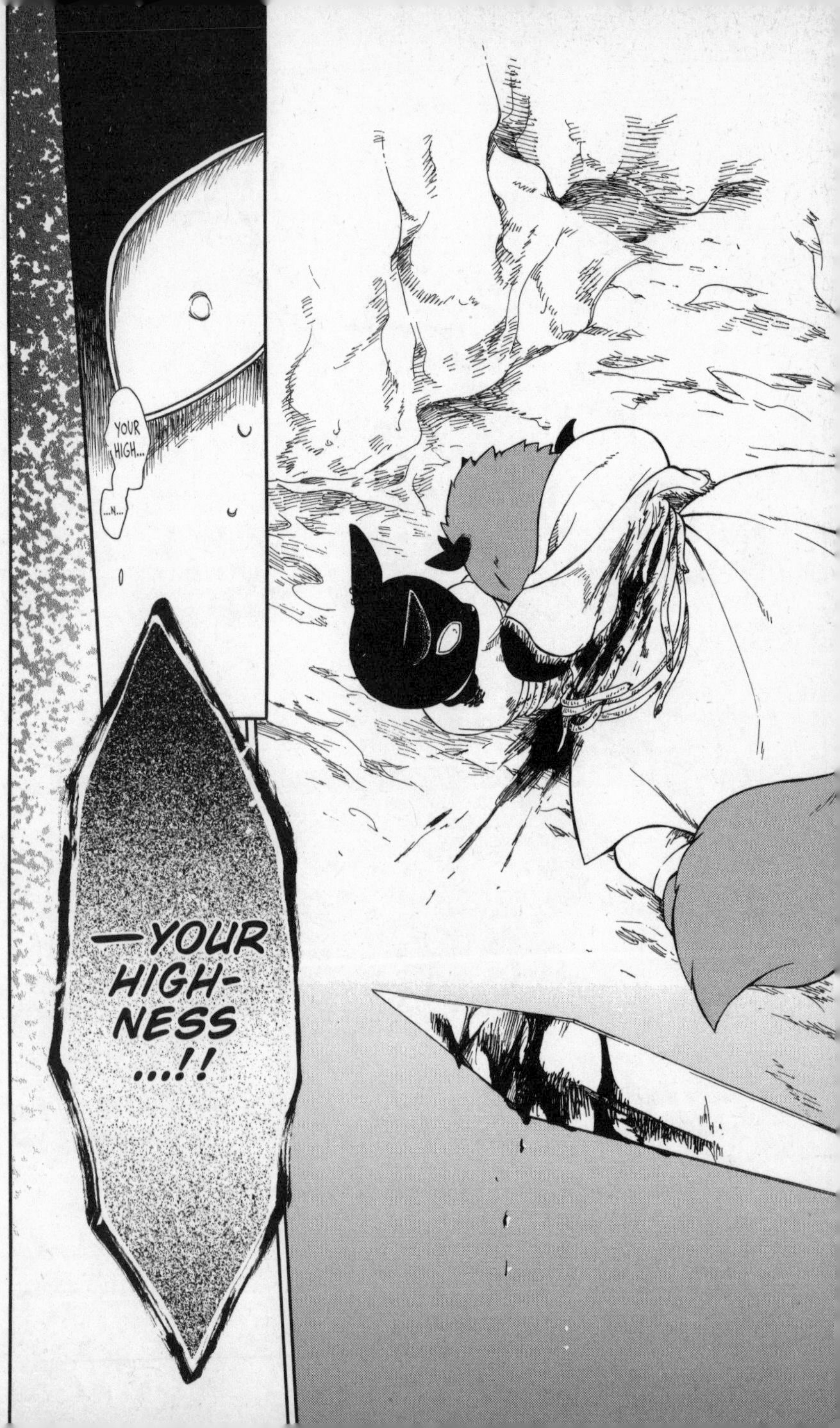
YOUR HIGH...
...N...
—YOUR HIGH-NESS ...!!

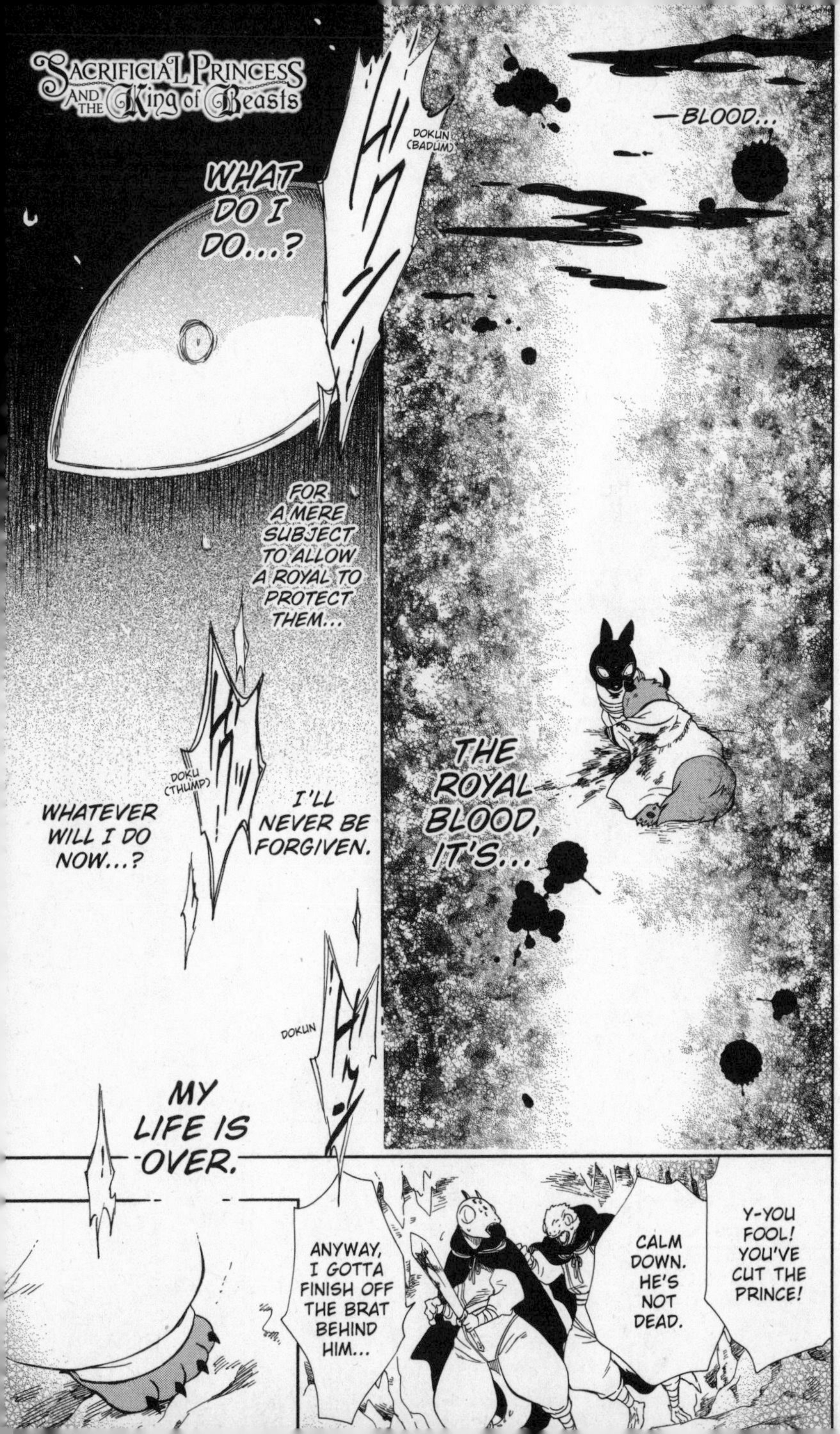
Sacrificial Princess and the King of Beasts
—BLOOD...
THE ROYAL BLOOD, IT'S...
DOKUN (BADUM)
WHAT DO I DO...?
FOR A MERE SUBJECT TO ALLOW A ROYAL TO PROTECT THEM...
I'LL NEVER BE FORGIVEN.
DOKU (THUMP)
WHATEVER WILL I DO NOW...?
DOKUN
MY LIFE IS OVER.
Y-YOU FOOL! YOU'VE CUT THE PRINCE!
CALM DOWN. HE'S NOT DEAD.
ANYWAY, I GOTTA FINISH OFF THE BRAT BEHIND HIM...

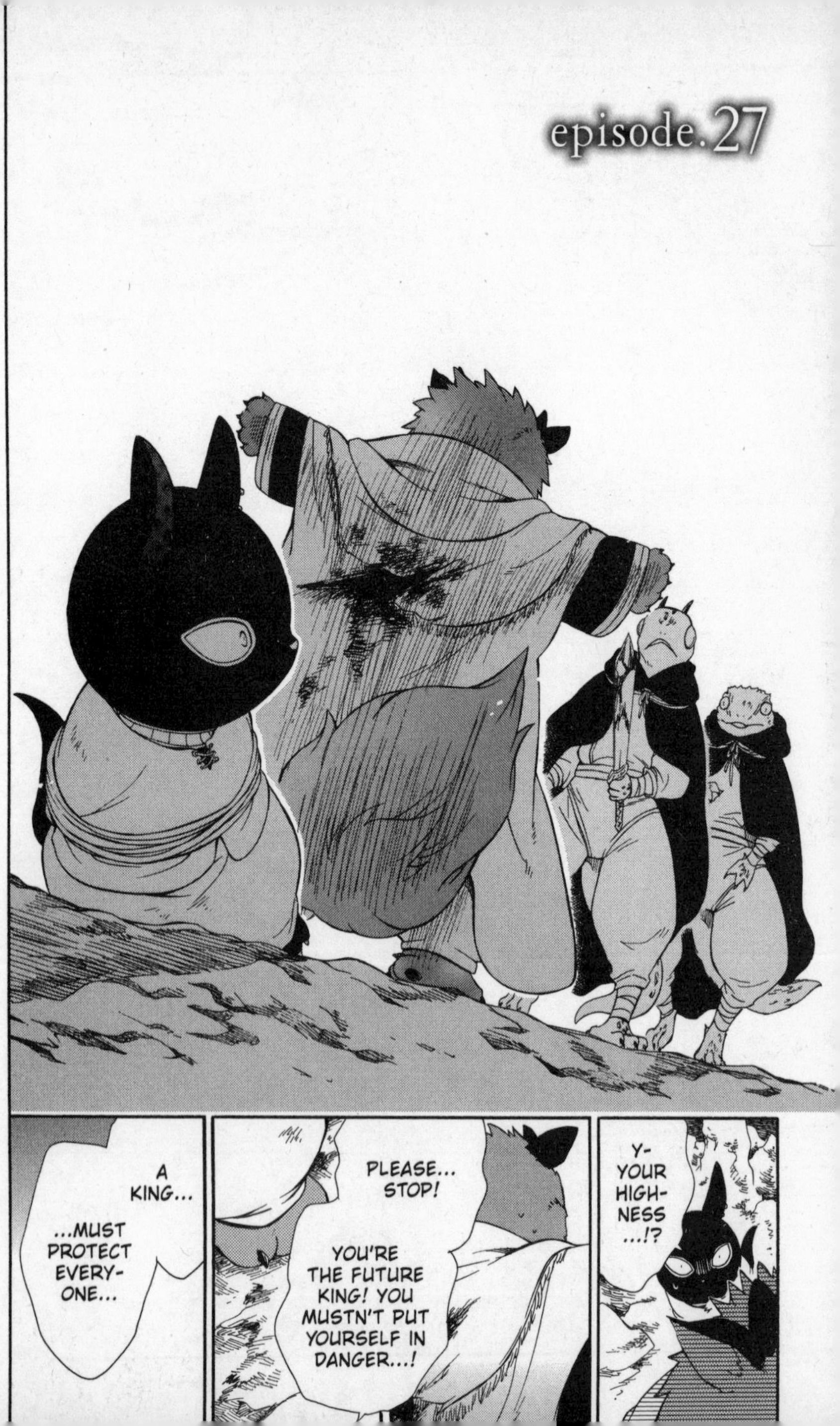
episode.27
Y- YOUR HIGHNESS ...!?
PLEASE... STOP!
YOU'RE THE FUTURE KING! YOU MUSTN'T PUT YOURSELF IN DANGER...!
A KING...
...MUST PROTECT EVERY-ONE...

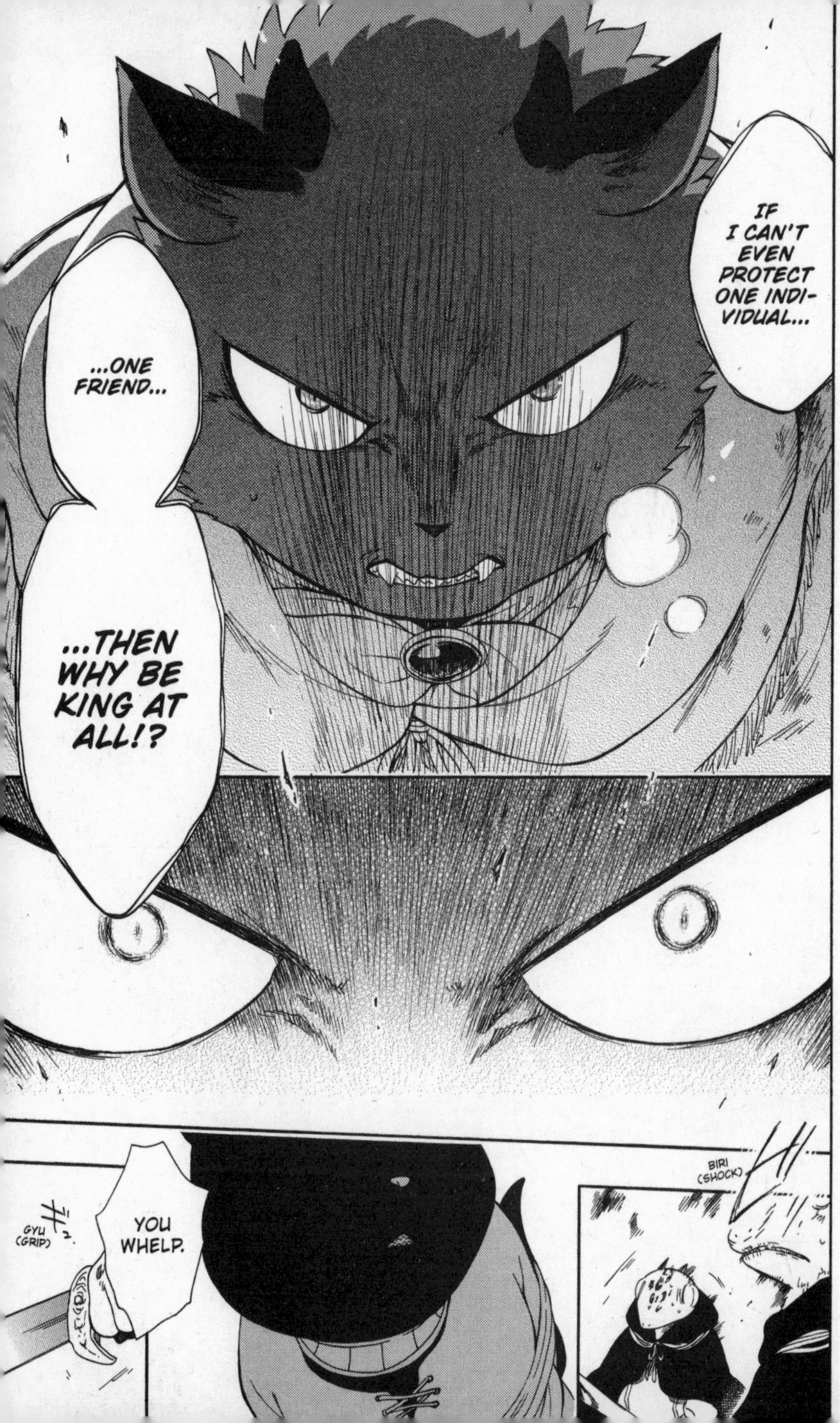
IF I CAN'T EVEN PROTECT ONE INDIVIDUAL...
...ONE FRIEND...
...THEN WHY BE KING AT ALL!?
BIRI (SHOCK)
GYU (GRIP)
YOU WHELP.

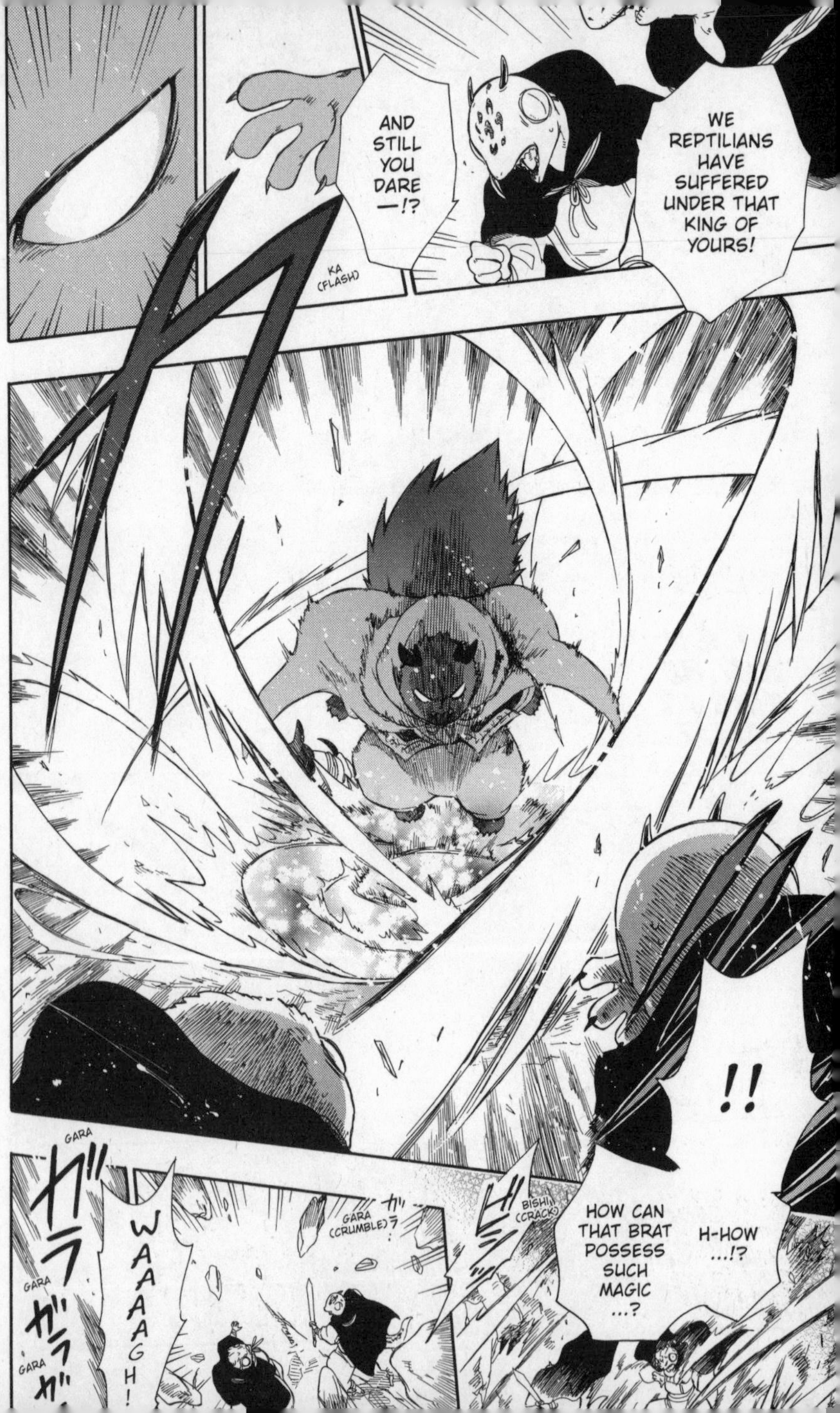
WE REPTILIANS HAVE SUFFERED UNDER THAT KING OF YOURS!
AND STILL YOU DARE—!?
KA (FLASH)
!!
H-HOW ...!?
HOW CAN THAT BRAT POSSESS SUCH MAGIC ...?
BISHI (CRACK)
GARA (CRUMBLE)
WAAAAAGH!
GARA
GARA
GARA

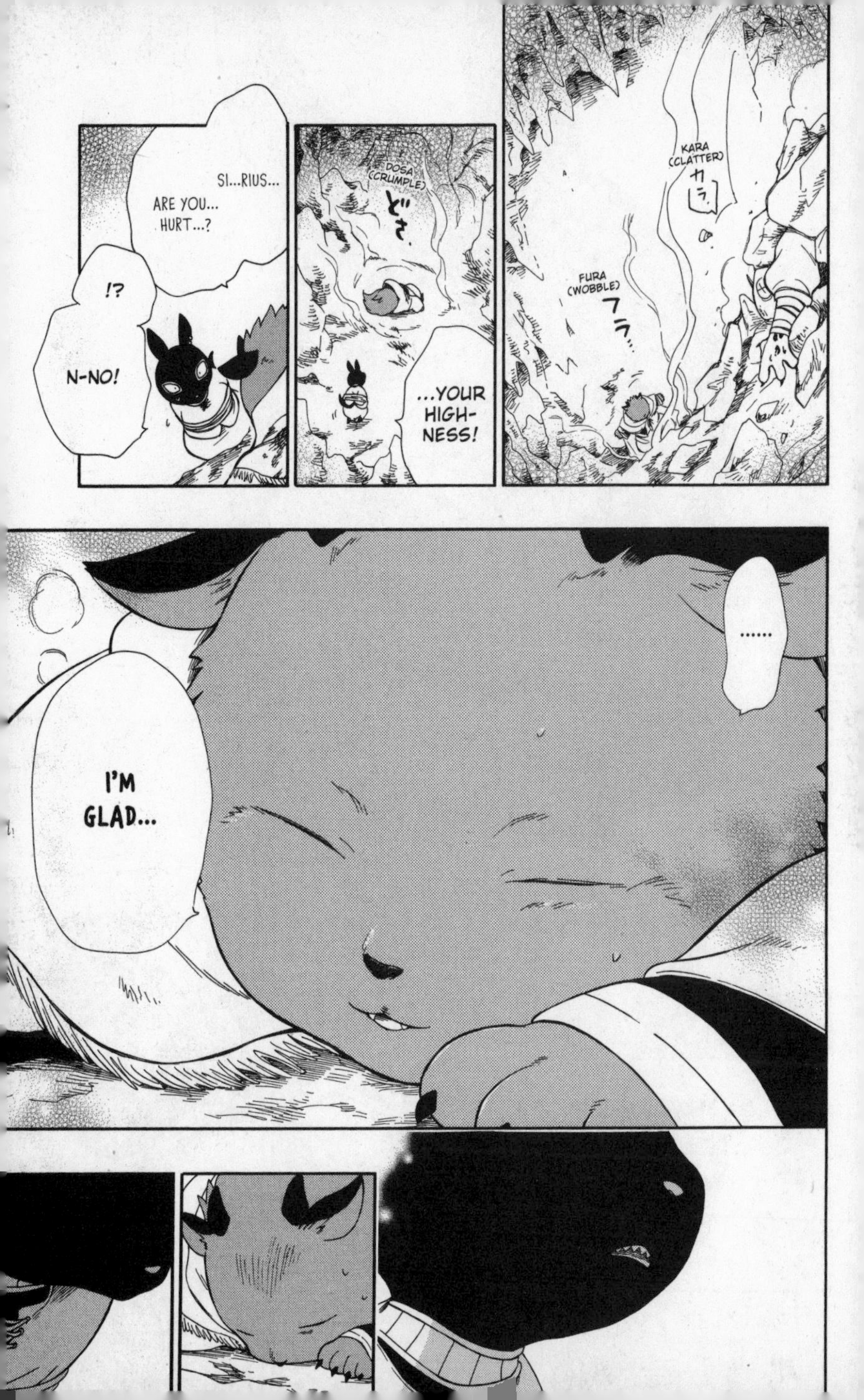
KARA (CLATTER)
カラ
FURA (WOBBLE)
フラ…
DOSA (CRUMPLE)
どさ
...YOUR HIGH-NESS!
SI...RIUS...
ARE YOU... HURT...?
!?
N-NO!
......
I'M GLAD...

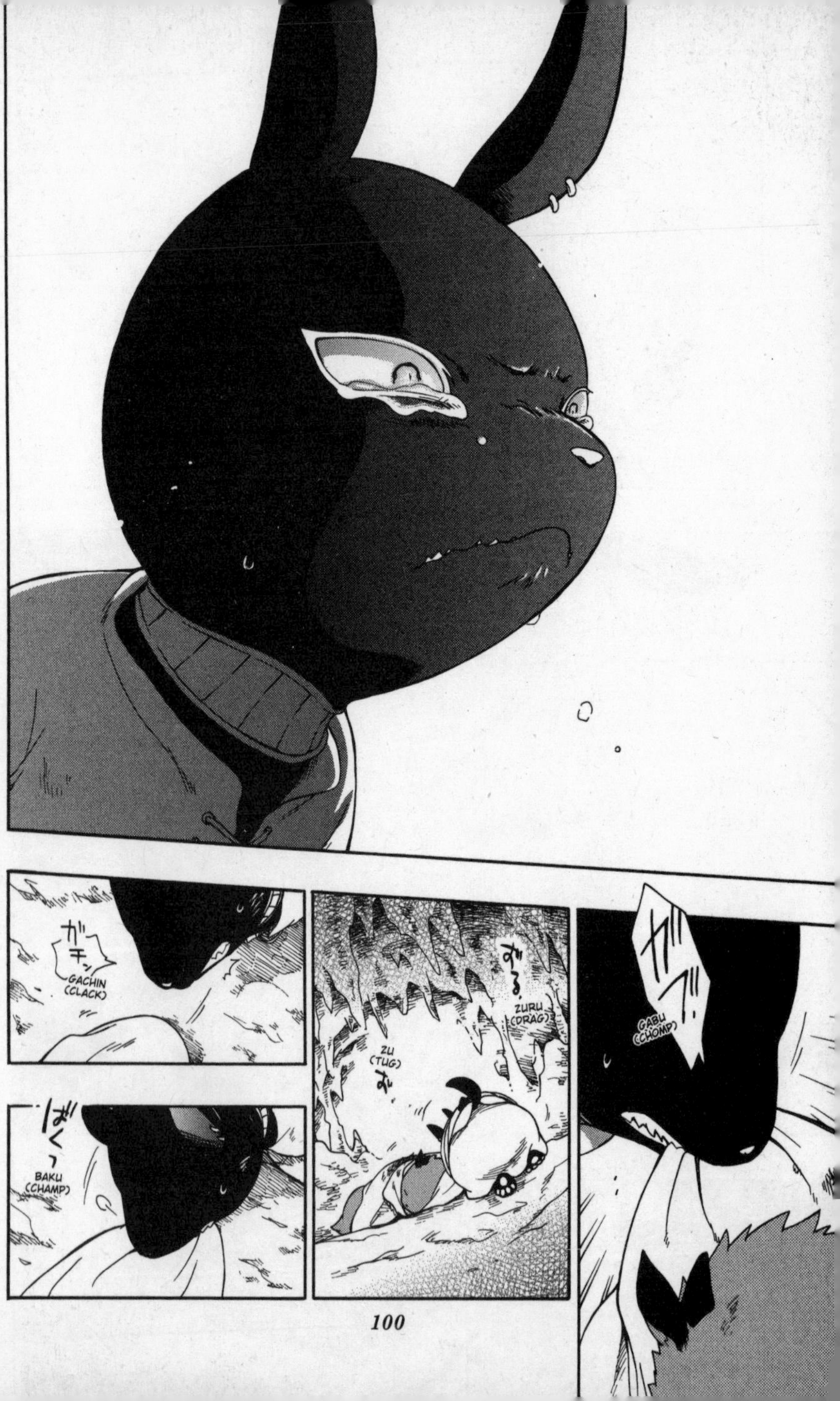
ガブッ
GABU (CHOMP)
ずる
ZURU (DRAG)
ず
ZU (TUG)
ガチッ
GACHIN (CLACK)
ばくっ
BAKU (CHAMP)

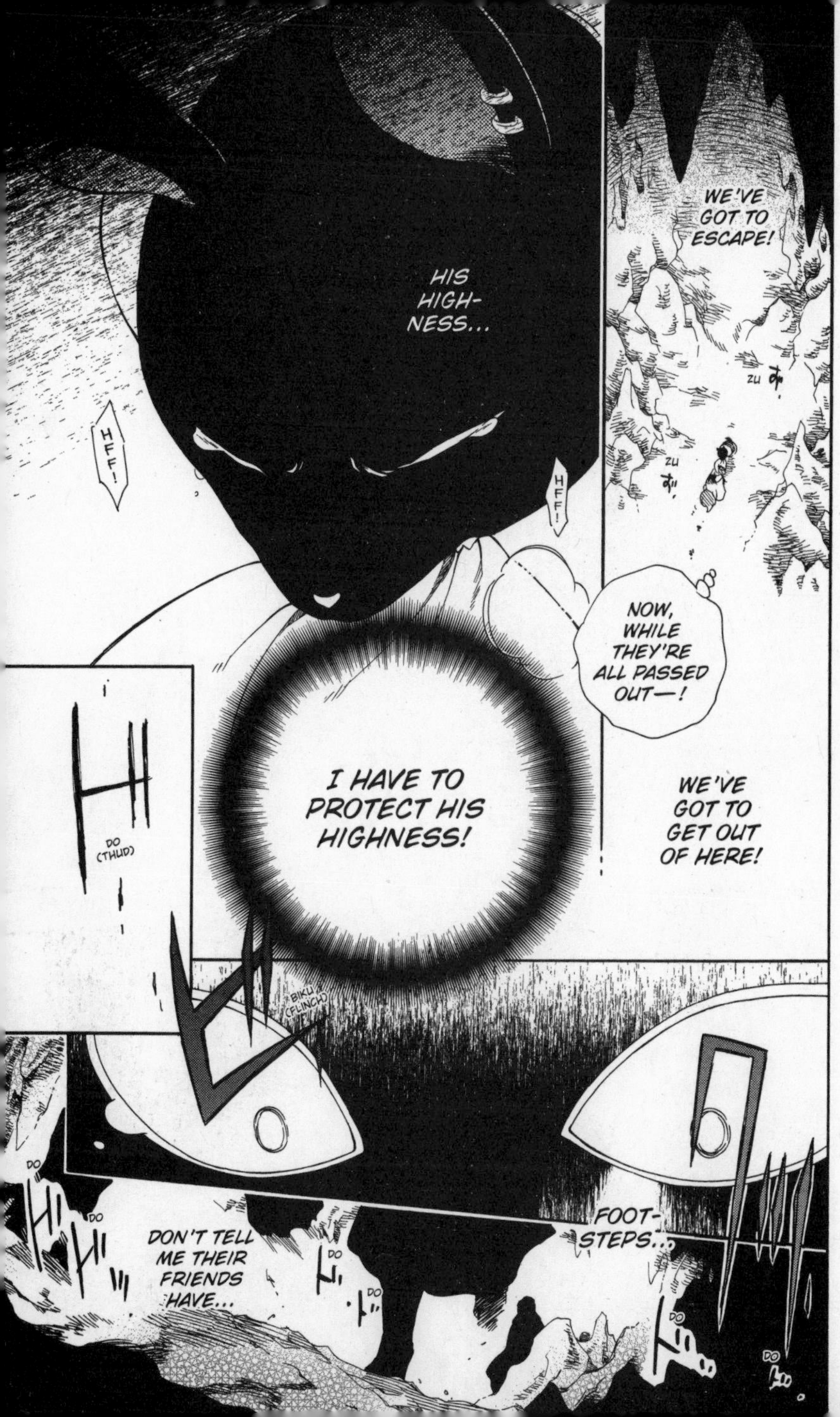
WE'VE GOT TO ESCAPE!
ZU
ZU
NOW, WHILE THEY'RE ALL PASSED OUT—!
WE'VE GOT TO GET OUT OF HERE!
HIS HIGH-NESS...
HFF!
HFF!
I HAVE TO PROTECT HIS HIGHNESS!
DO (THUD)
BIKU (FLINCH)
DO
DO
FOOT-STEPS...
DO
DO
DON'T TELL ME THEIR FRIENDS HAVE...
DO
DO

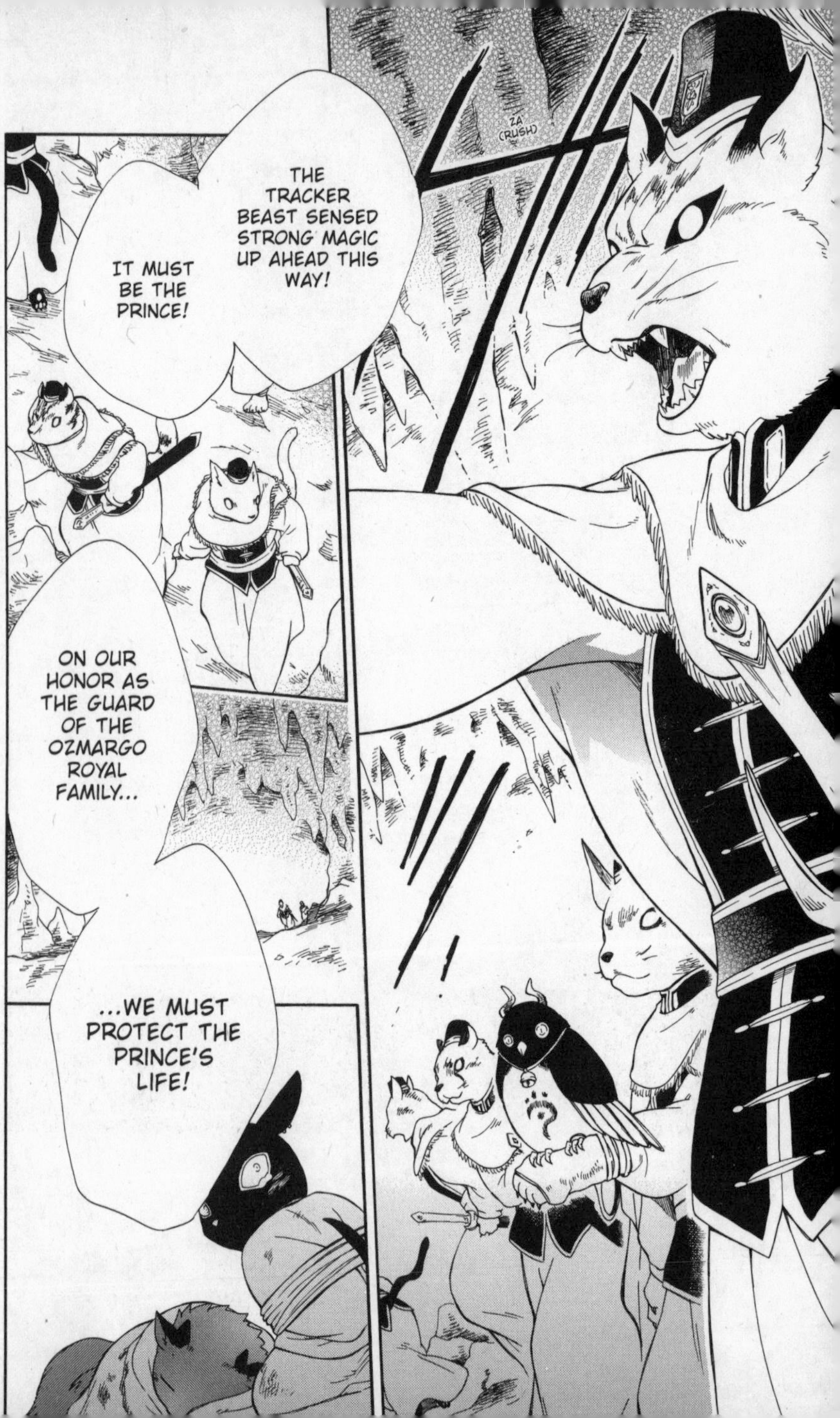
ZA (RUSH)
THE TRACKER BEAST SENSED STRONG MAGIC UP AHEAD THIS WAY!
IT MUST BE THE PRINCE!
ON OUR HONOR AS THE GUARD OF THE OZMARGO ROYAL FAMILY...
...WE MUST PROTECT THE PRINCE'S LIFE!

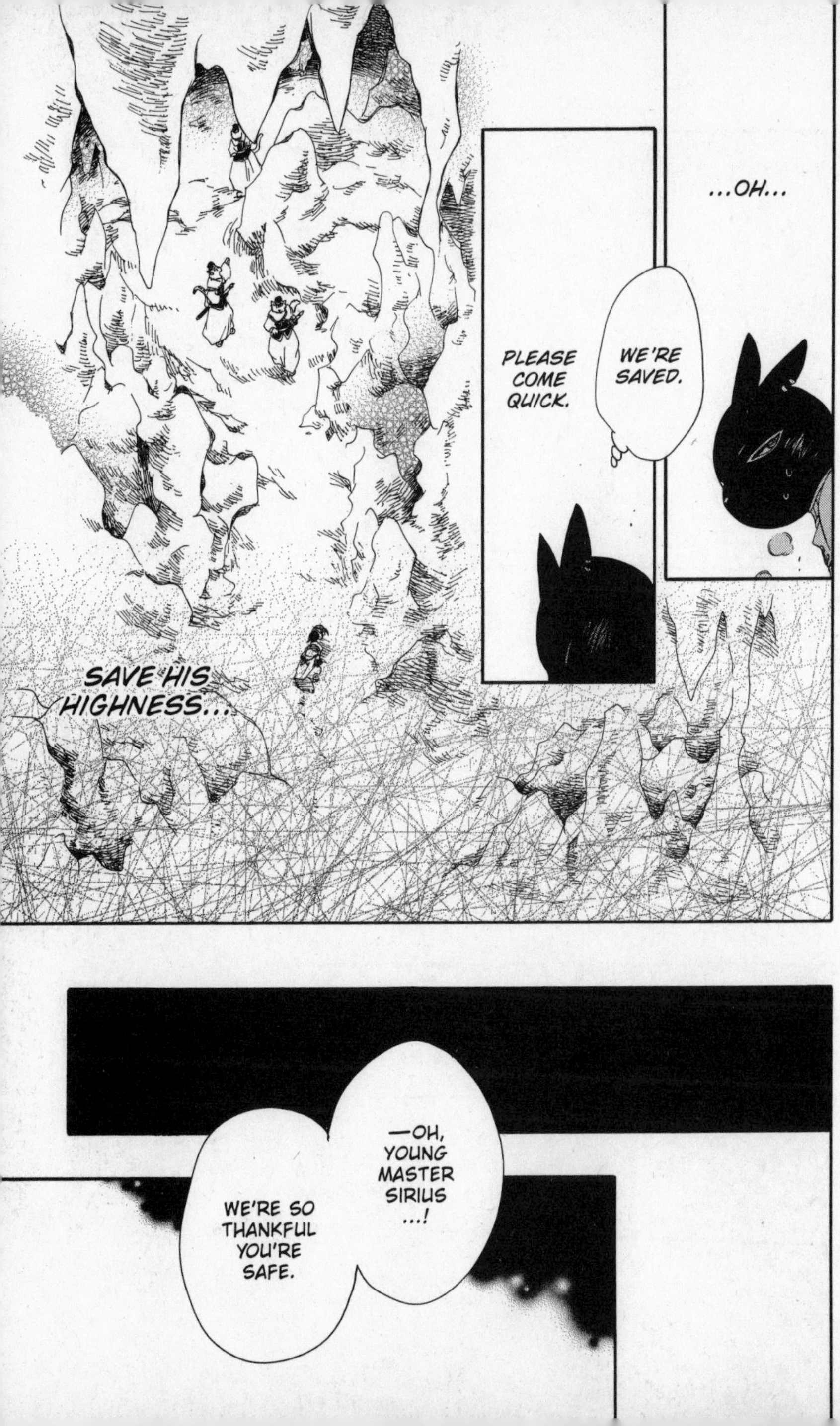
...OH...
WE'RE SAVED.
PLEASE COME QUICK.
SAVE HIS HIGHNESS...
—OH, YOUNG MASTER SIRIUS ...!
WE'RE SO THANKFUL YOU'RE SAFE.

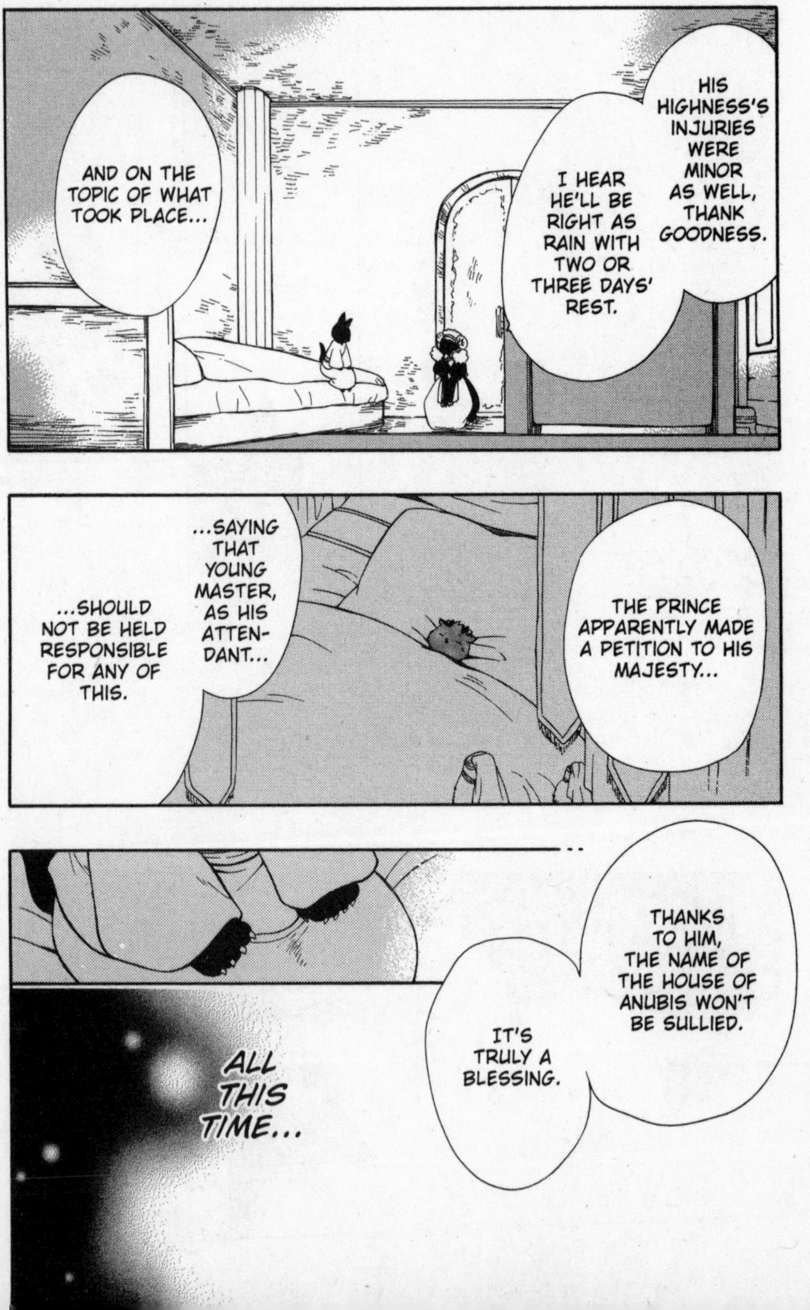
HIS HIGHNESS'S INJURIES WERE MINOR AS WELL, THANK GOODNESS.
I HEAR HE'LL BE RIGHT AS RAIN WITH TWO OR THREE DAYS' REST.
AND ON THE TOPIC OF WHAT TOOK PLACE...
THE PRINCE APPARENTLY MADE A PETITION TO HIS MAJESTY...
...SAYING THAT YOUNG MASTER, AS HIS ATTENDANT...
...SHOULD NOT BE HELD RESPONSIBLE FOR ANY OF THIS.
THANKS TO HIM, THE NAME OF THE HOUSE OF ANUBIS WON'T BE SULLIED.
IT'S TRULY A BLESSING.
ALL THIS TIME...

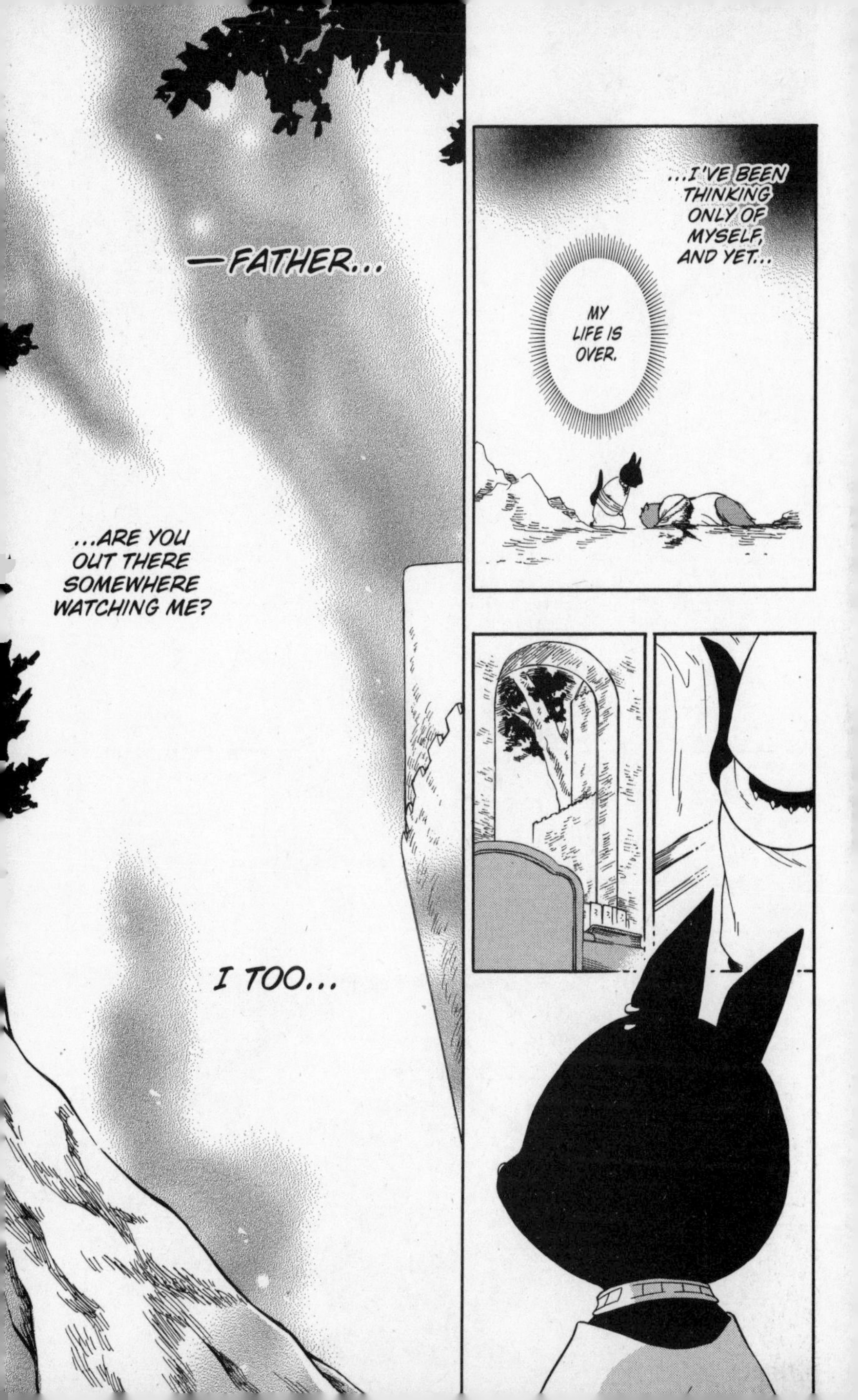
...I'VE BEEN THINKING ONLY OF MYSELF, AND YET...
MY LIFE IS OVER.
—FATHER...
...ARE YOU OUT THERE SOMEWHERE WATCHING ME?
I TOO...

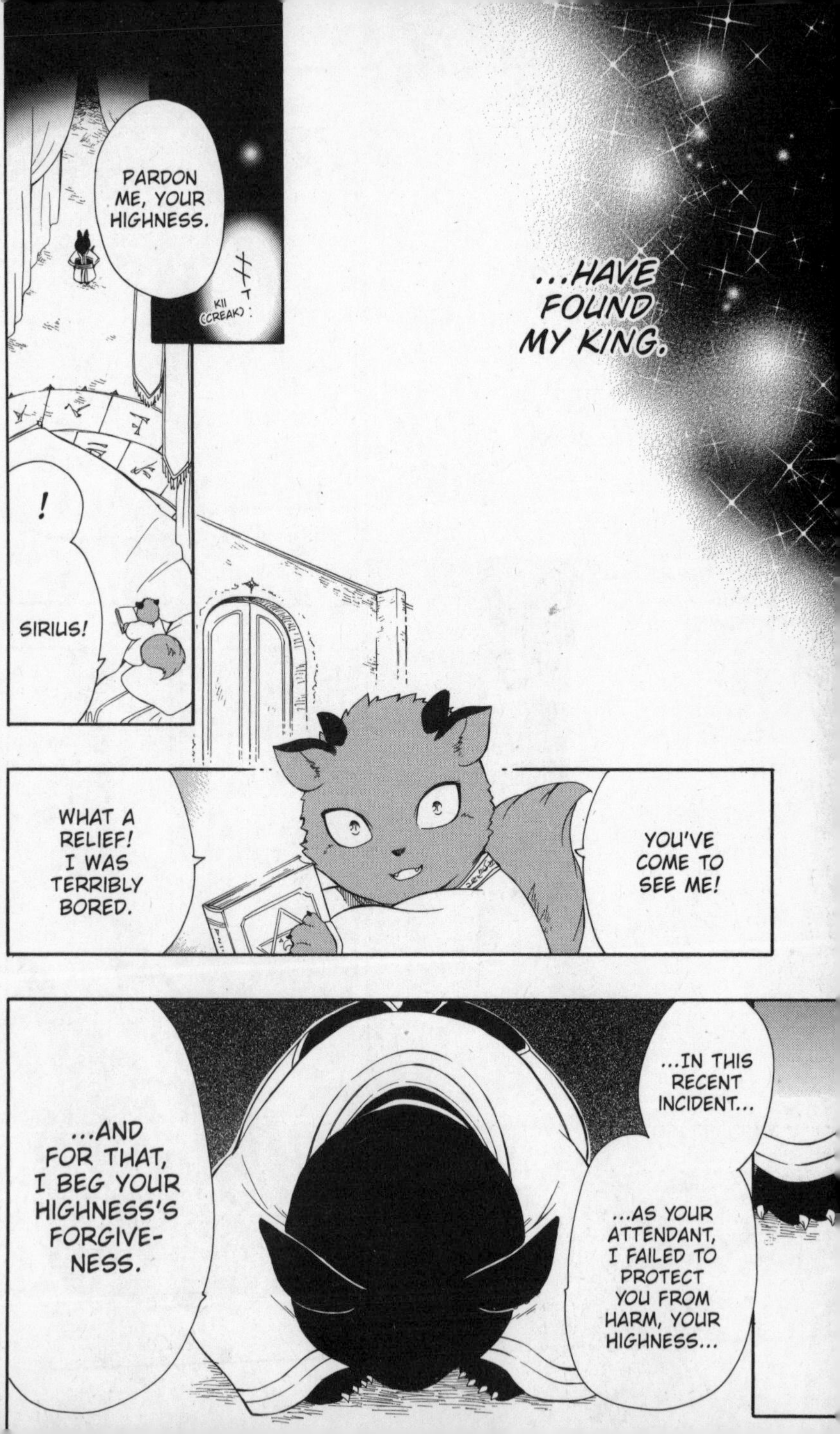
...HAVE FOUND MY KING.
PARDON ME, YOUR HIGHNESS.
KII (CREAK)
!
SIRIUS!
YOU'VE COME TO SEE ME!
WHAT A RELIEF! I WAS TERRIBLY BORED.
...IN THIS RECENT INCIDENT...
...AS YOUR ATTENDANT, I FAILED TO PROTECT YOU FROM HARM, YOUR HIGHNESS...
...AND FOR THAT, I BEG YOUR HIGHNESS'S FORGIVE-NESS.

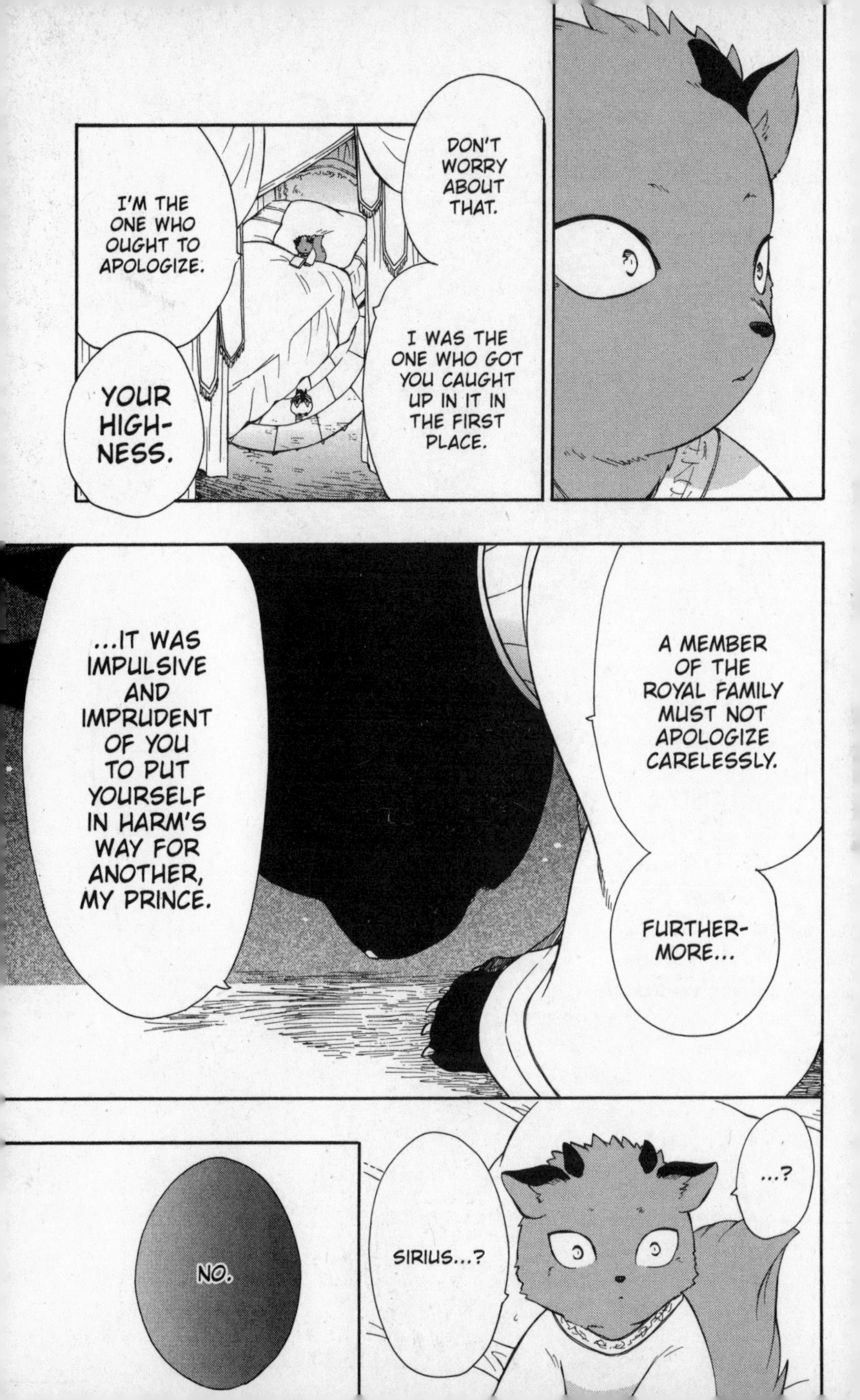
DON'T WORRY ABOUT THAT.
I WAS THE ONE WHO GOT YOU CAUGHT UP IN IT IN THE FIRST PLACE.
I'M THE ONE WHO OUGHT TO APOLOGIZE.
YOUR HIGHNESS.
A MEMBER OF THE ROYAL FAMILY MUST NOT APOLOGIZE CARELESSLY.
FURTHER-MORE...
...IT WAS IMPULSIVE AND IMPRUDENT OF YOU TO PUT YOURSELF IN HARM'S WAY FOR ANOTHER, MY PRINCE.
...?
SIRIUS...?
NO.

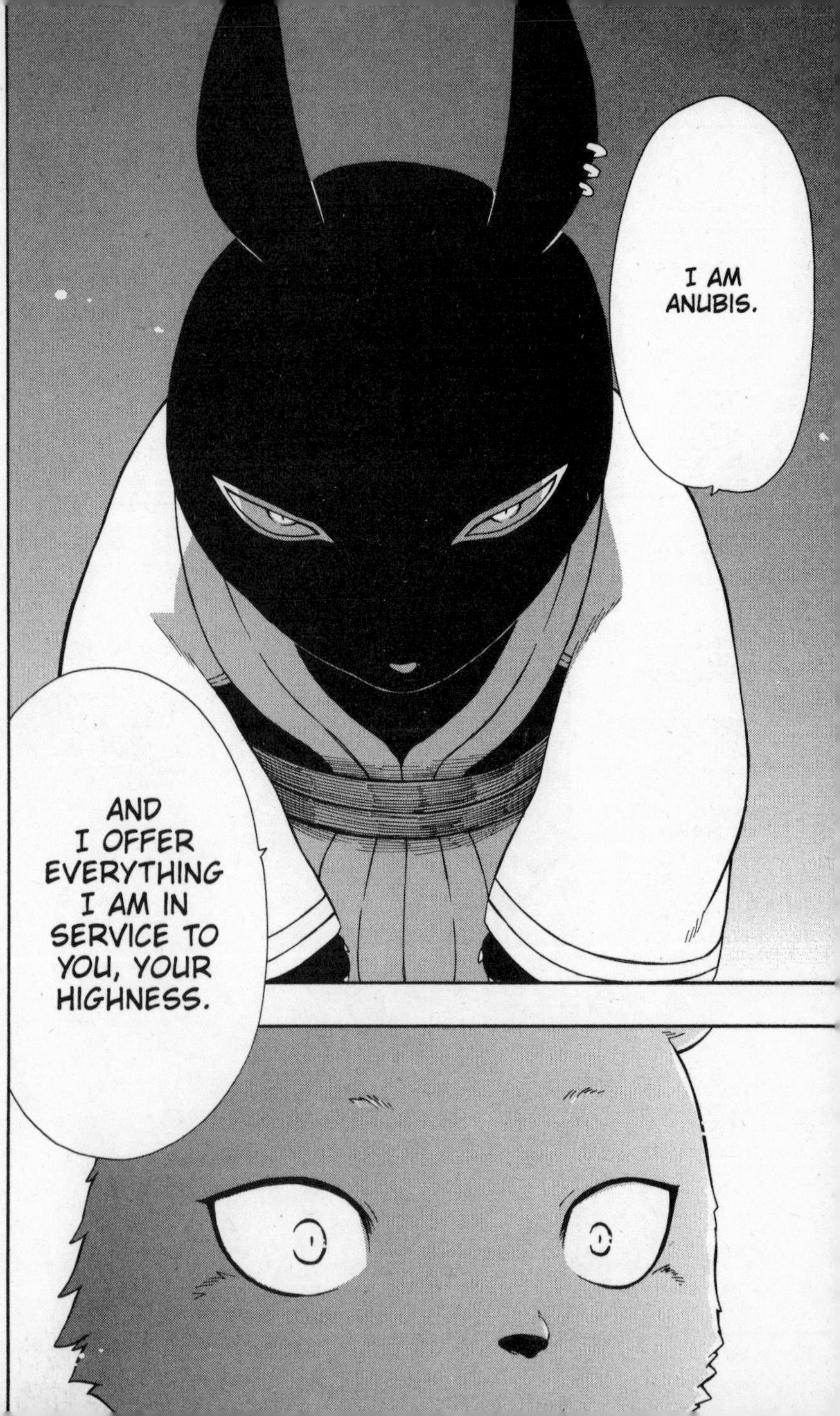
I AM ANUBIS.
AND I OFFER EVERYTHING I AM IN SERVICE TO YOU, YOUR HIGHNESS.

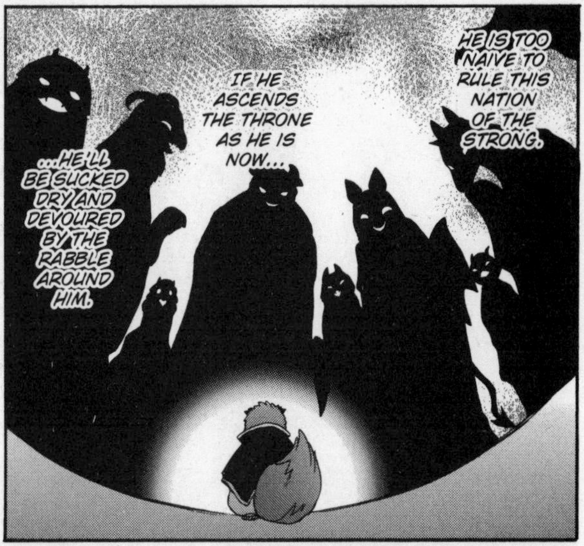
HE IS TOO NAIVE TO RULE THIS NATION OF THE STRONG.
IF HE ASCENDS THE THRONE AS HE IS NOW...
...HE'LL BE SUCKED DRY AND DEVOURED BY THE RABBLE AROUND HIM.

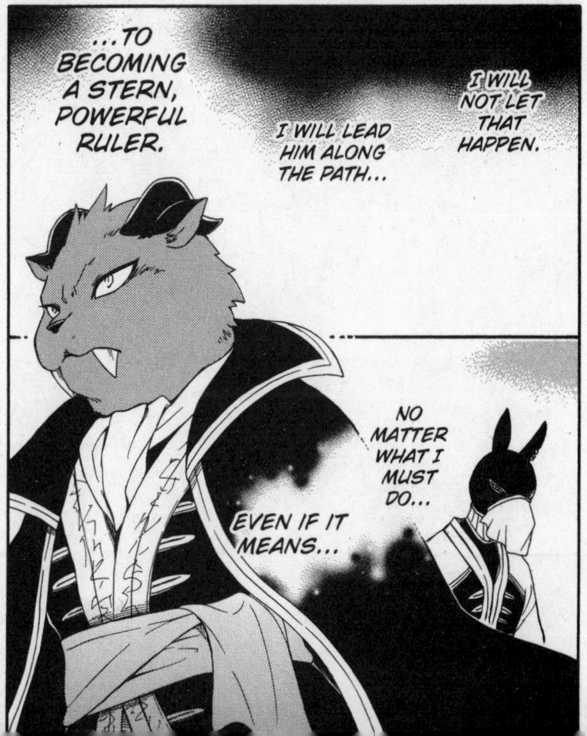
I WILL NOT LET THAT HAPPEN.
I WILL LEAD HIM ALONG THE PATH...
...TO BECOMING A STERN, POWERFUL RULER.
NO MATTER WHAT I MUST DO...
EVEN IF IT MEANS...

WHO EVEN CARES!? BACKGROUND NOTES

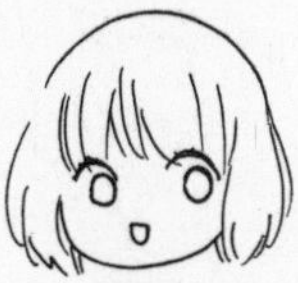

SARIPHI HAS A LOT OF HAIR. WHEN SHE WAKES UP IN THE MORNING, IT'S A TOTAL DISASTER.

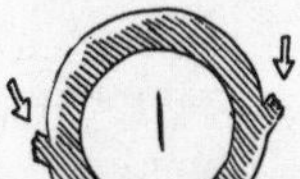

IN THE FIRST CHAPTER OF THIS MANGA, CY HAS LITTLE FINGERS.

THE FIRST CHAPTER WAS WRITTEN AS A ONE-SHOT, SO I GUESS I HAD YET TO FINALIZE SOME OF THE DETAILS.

INCIDENTALLY, ANUBIS'S NECK ORNAMENT IS DIFFERENT NOW. WHEN →  SACRIFICIAL PRINCESS BECAME A SERIES, I CHANGED IT INTO SOMETHING EASIER TO DRAW.

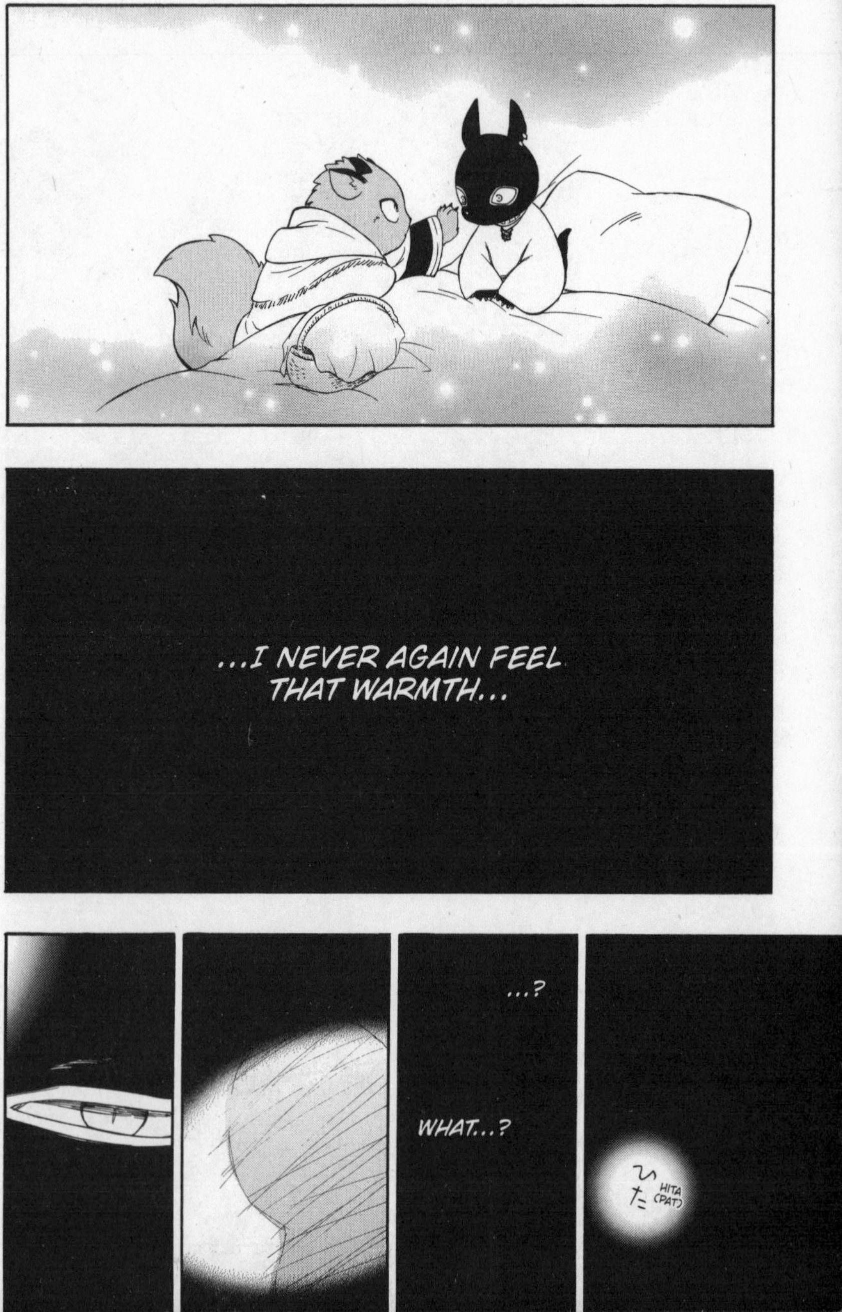
...I NEVER AGAIN FEEL THAT WARMTH...
ひた
HITA (PAT)
...?
WHAT...?

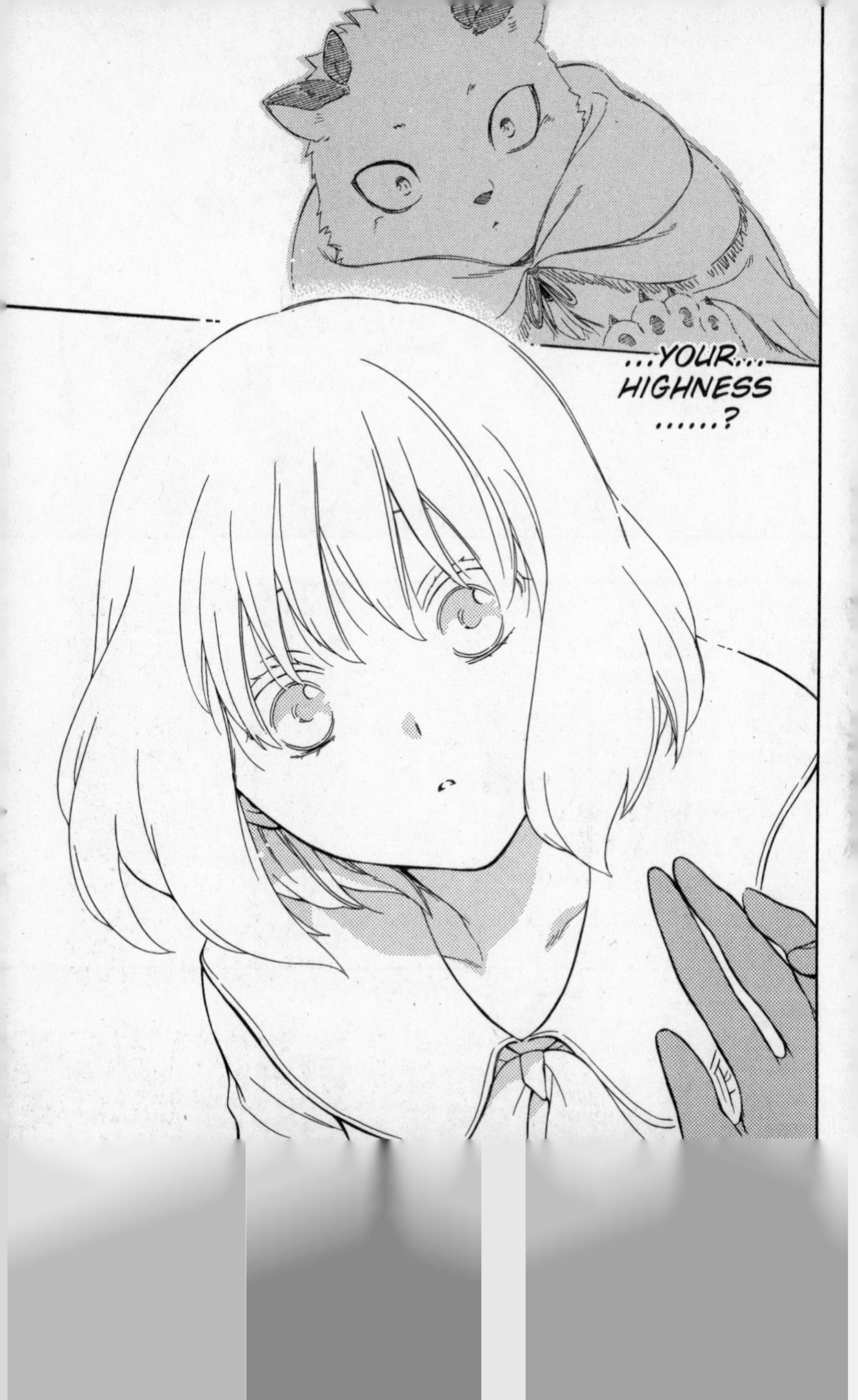
...YOUR... HIGHNESS ......?

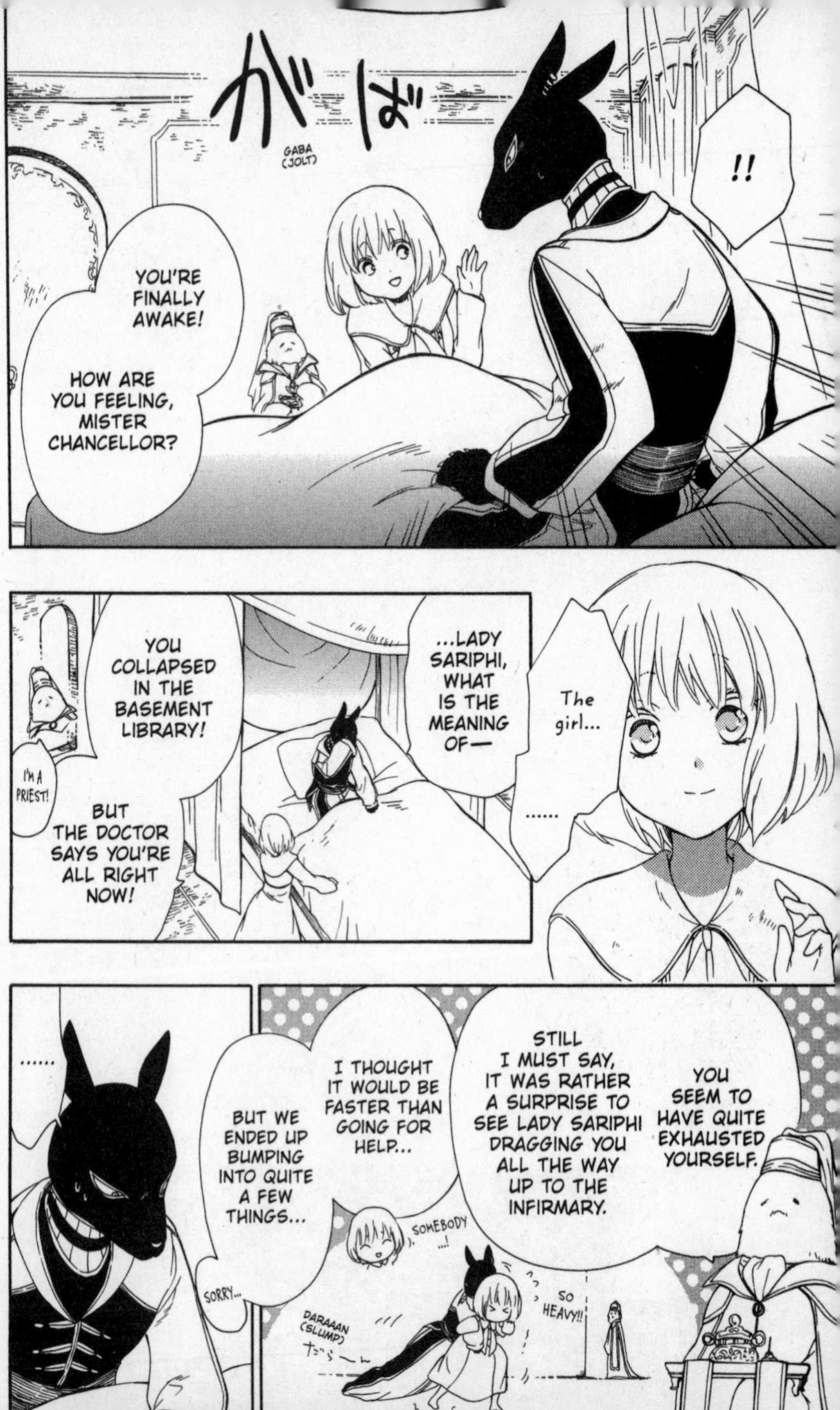
!!
GABA (JOLT)
YOU'RE FINALLY AWAKE!
HOW ARE YOU FEELING, MISTER CHANCELLOR?
The girl...
......
...LADY SARIPHI, WHAT IS THE MEANING OF—
YOU COLLAPSED IN THE BASEMENT LIBRARY!
I'M A PRIEST!
BUT THE DOCTOR SAYS YOU'RE ALL RIGHT NOW!
YOU SEEM TO HAVE QUITE EXHAUSTED YOURSELF.
STILL I MUST SAY, IT WAS RATHER A SURPRISE TO SEE LADY SARIPHI DRAGGING YOU ALL THE WAY UP TO THE INFIRMARY.
SO HEAVY!!
SOMEBODY ...!
DARAAAN (SLUMP)
I THOUGHT IT WOULD BE FASTER THAN GOING FOR HELP...
BUT WE ENDED UP BUMPING INTO QUITE A FEW THINGS...
SORRY...
......

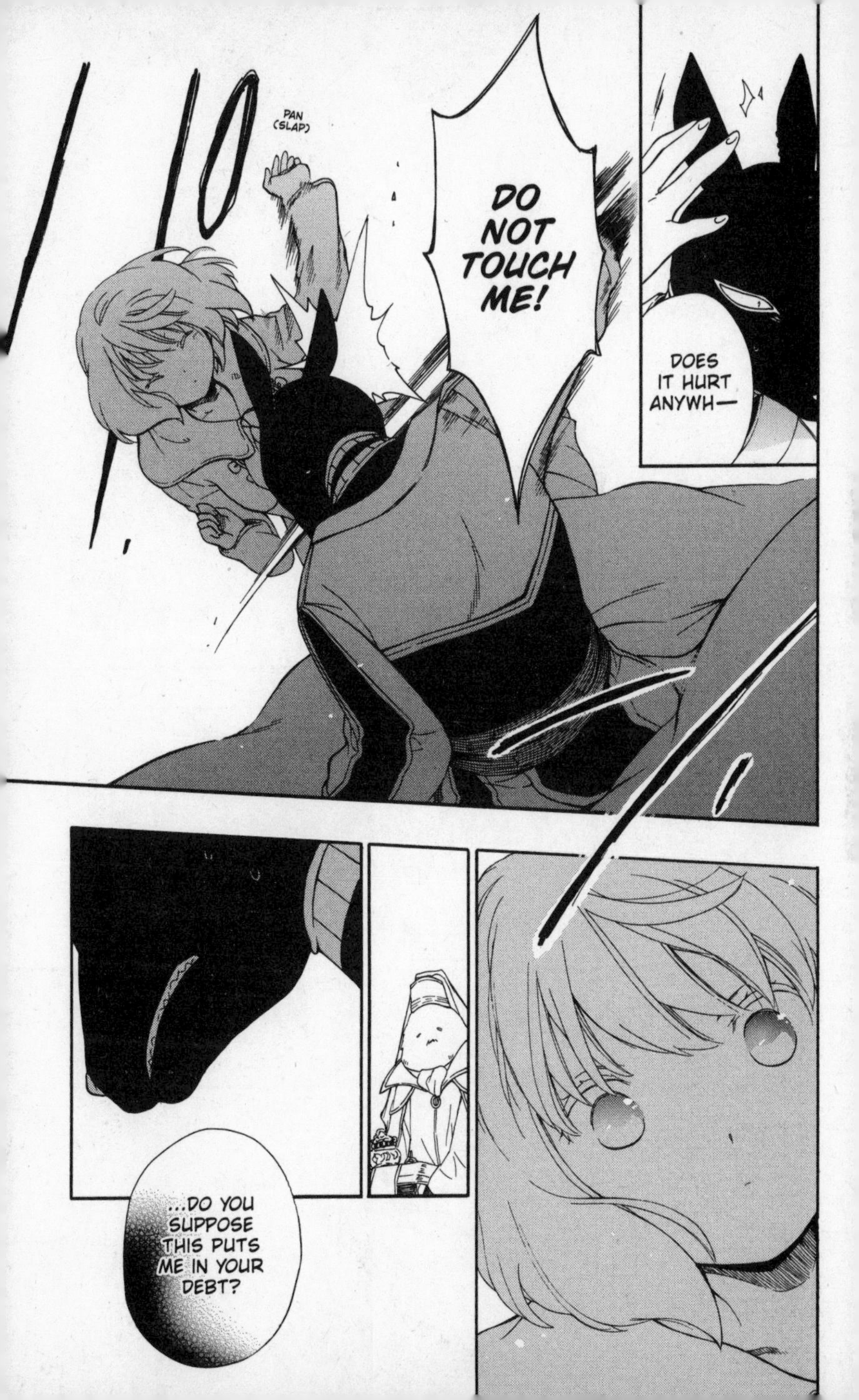
DOES IT HURT ANYWH—
DO NOT TOUCH ME!
PAN (SLAP)
...DO YOU SUPPOSE THIS PUTS ME IN YOUR DEBT?

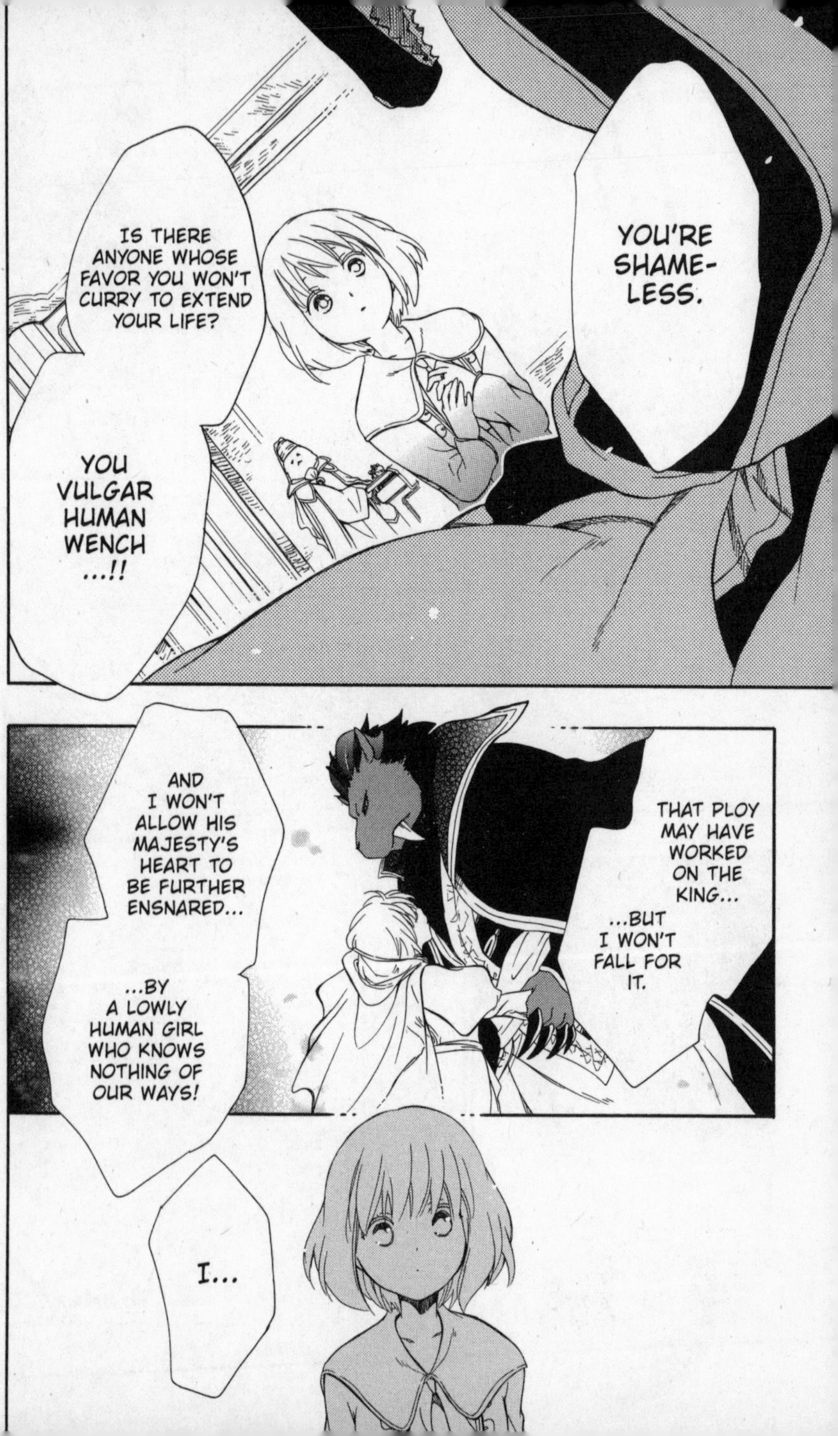
YOU'RE SHAME-LESS.
IS THERE ANYONE WHOSE FAVOR YOU WON'T CURRY TO EXTEND YOUR LIFE?
YOU VULGAR HUMAN WENCH ...!!
THAT PLOY MAY HAVE WORKED ON THE KING...
...BUT I WON'T FALL FOR IT.
AND I WON'T ALLOW HIS MAJESTY'S HEART TO BE FURTHER ENSNARED...
...BY A LOWLY HUMAN GIRL WHO KNOWS NOTHING OF OUR WAYS!
I...

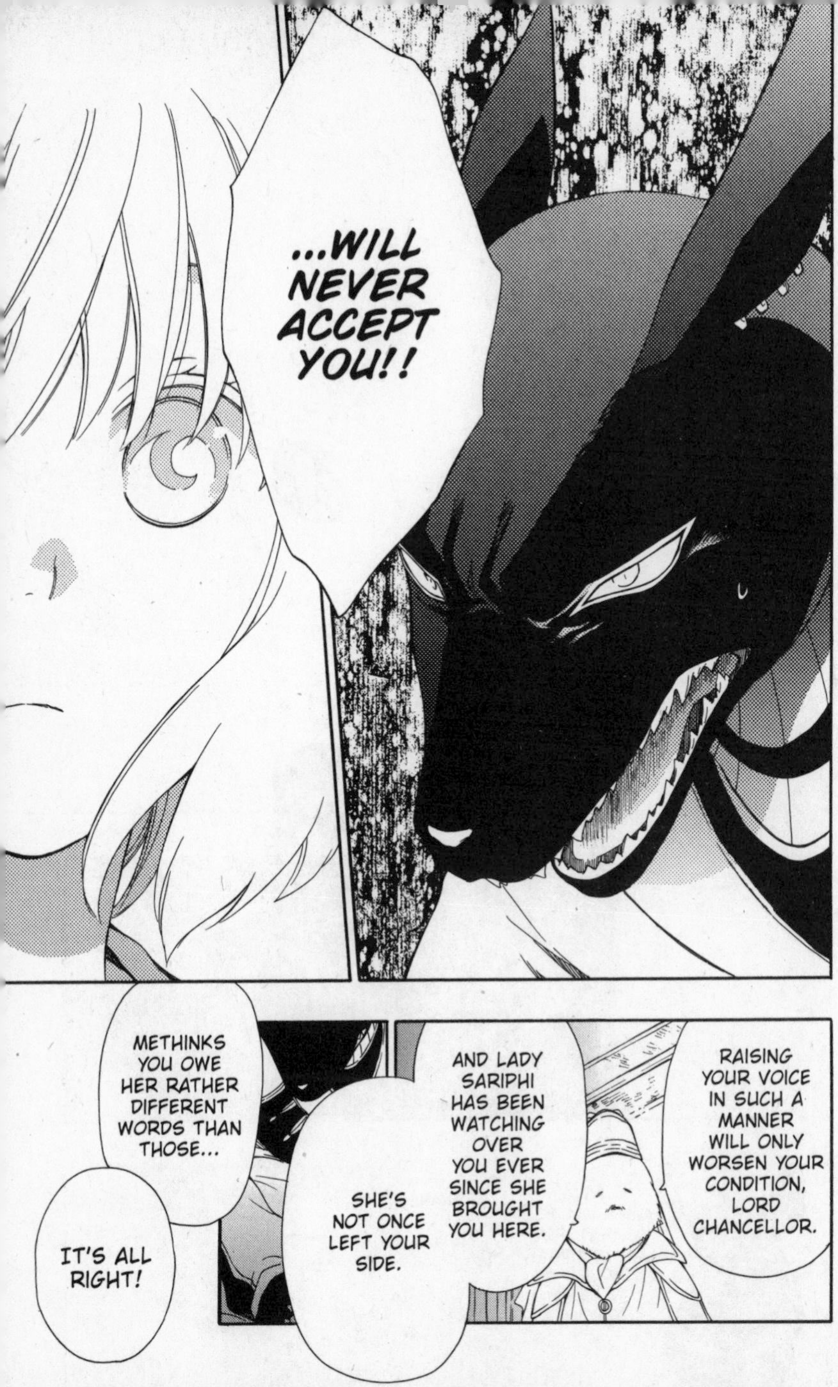
...WILL NEVER ACCEPT YOU!!
RAISING YOUR VOICE IN SUCH A MANNER WILL ONLY WORSEN YOUR CONDITION, LORD CHANCELLOR.
AND LADY SARIPHI HAS BEEN WATCHING OVER YOU EVER SINCE SHE BROUGHT YOU HERE.
SHE'S NOT ONCE LEFT YOUR SIDE.
METHINKS YOU OWE HER RATHER DIFFERENT WORDS THAN THOSE...
IT'S ALL RIGHT!

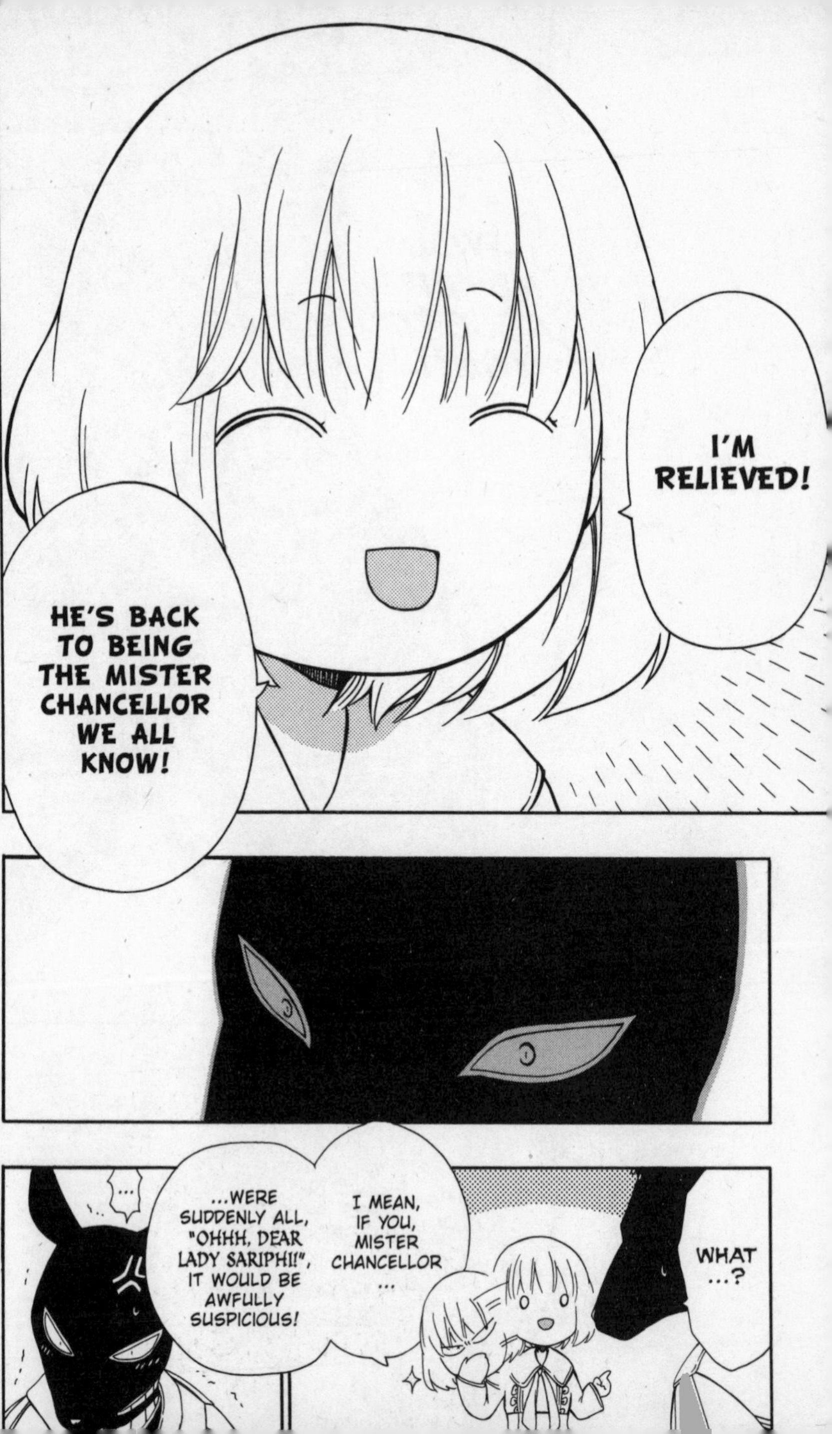
I'M RELIEVED!
HE'S BACK TO BEING THE MISTER CHANCELLOR WE ALL KNOW!
WHAT ...?
I MEAN, IF YOU, MISTER CHANCELLOR ...
...WERE SUDDENLY ALL, "OHHH, DEAR LADY SARIPHI!", IT WOULD BE AWFULLY SUSPICIOUS!
...

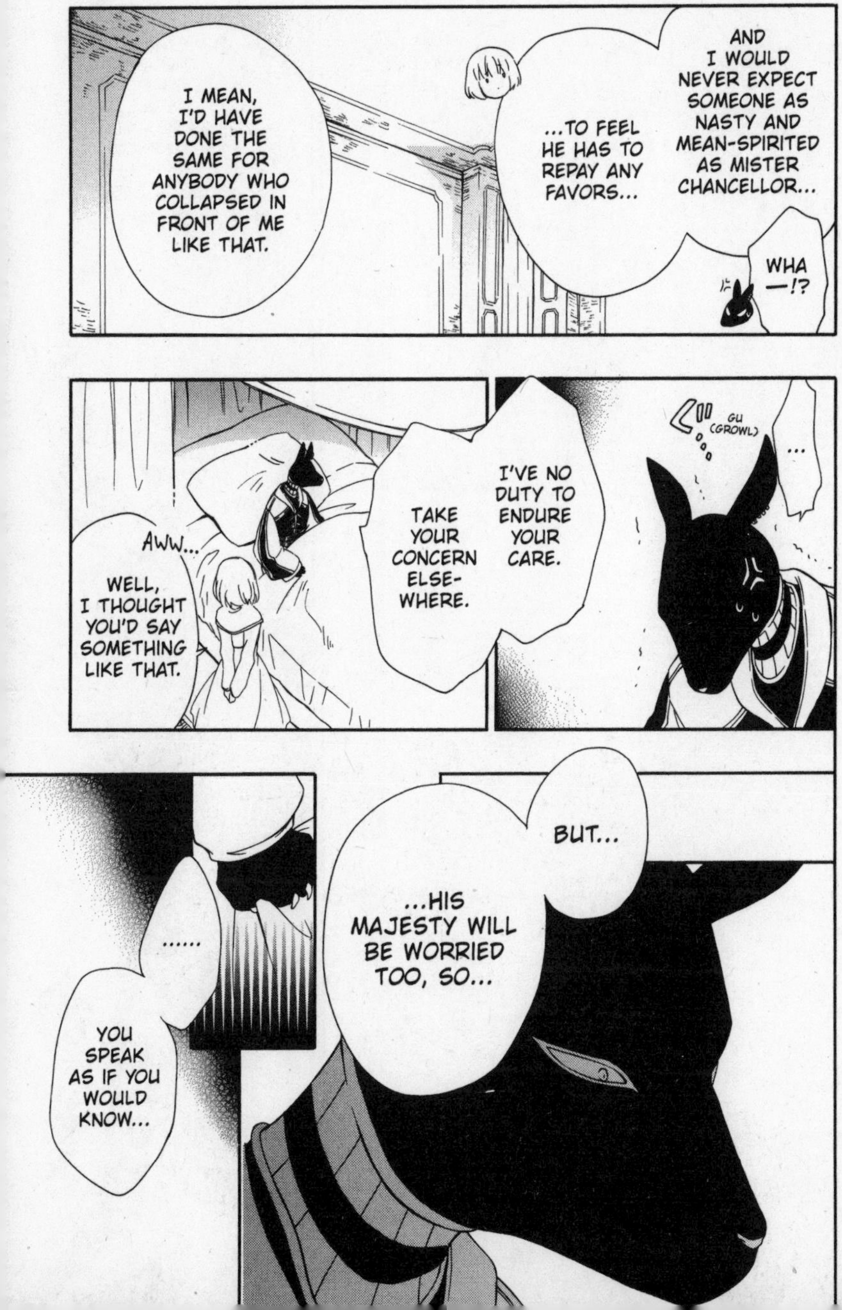
AND I WOULD NEVER EXPECT SOMEONE AS NASTY AND MEAN-SPIRITED AS MISTER CHANCELLOR...
...TO FEEL HE HAS TO REPAY ANY FAVORS...
WHA—!?
I MEAN, I'D HAVE DONE THE SAME FOR ANYBODY WHO COLLAPSED IN FRONT OF ME LIKE THAT.
GU (GROWL)
...
I'VE NO DUTY TO ENDURE YOUR CARE.
TAKE YOUR CONCERN ELSE-WHERE.
AWW...
WELL, I THOUGHT YOU'D SAY SOMETHING LIKE THAT.
BUT...
...HIS MAJESTY WILL BE WORRIED TOO, SO...
......
YOU SPEAK AS IF YOU WOULD KNOW...

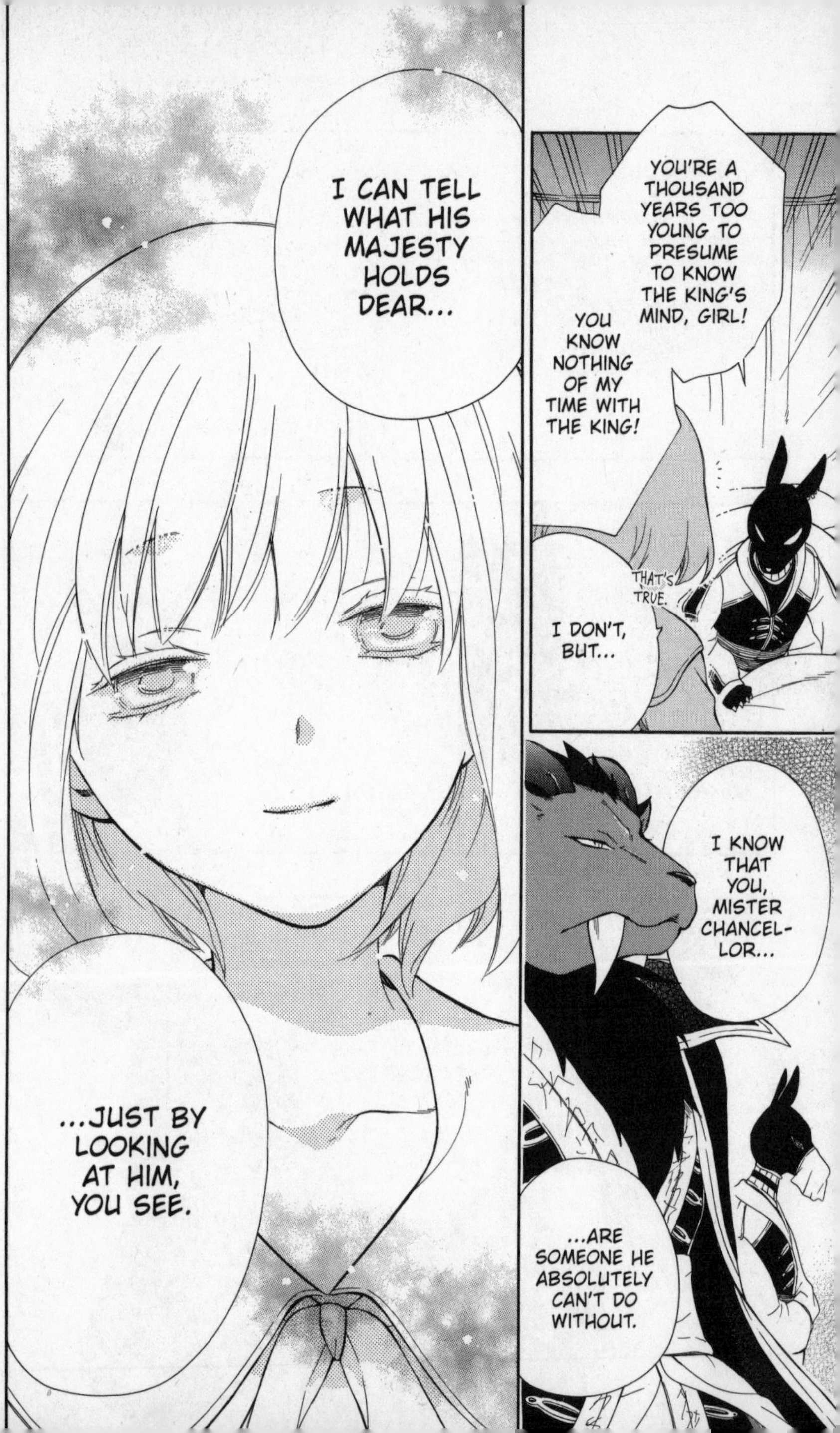
YOU'RE A THOUSAND YEARS TOO YOUNG TO PRESUME TO KNOW THE KING'S MIND, GIRL!
YOU KNOW NOTHING OF MY TIME WITH THE KING!
THAT'S TRUE.
I DON'T, BUT...
I KNOW THAT YOU, MISTER CHANCEL-LOR...
...ARE SOMEONE HE ABSOLUTELY CAN'T DO WITHOUT.
I CAN TELL WHAT HIS MAJESTY HOLDS DEAR...
...JUST BY LOOKING AT HIM, YOU SEE.

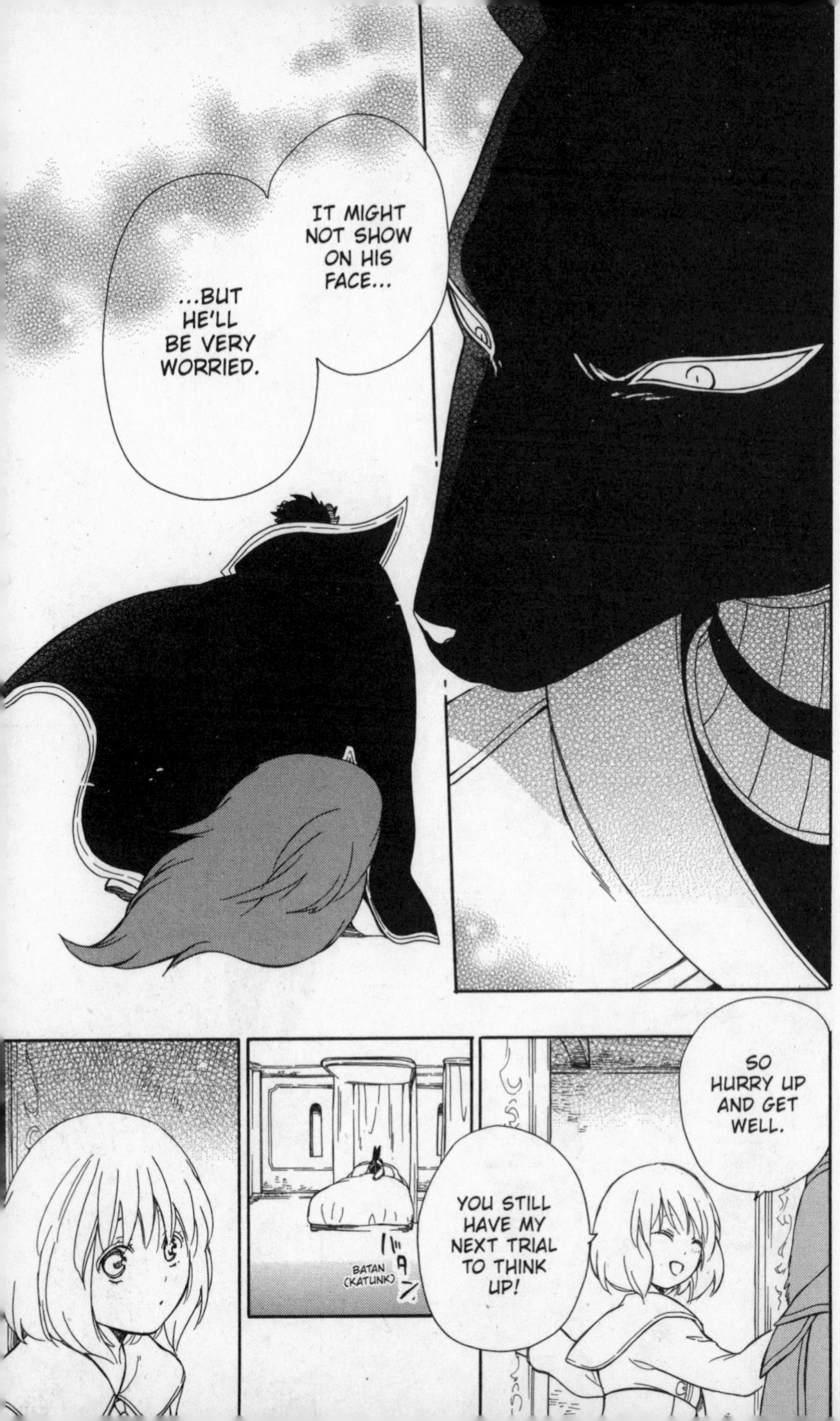
IT MIGHT NOT SHOW ON HIS FACE...
...BUT HE'LL BE VERY WORRIED.
SO HURRY UP AND GET WELL.
YOU STILL HAVE MY NEXT TRIAL TO THINK UP!
BATAN (KATUNK)

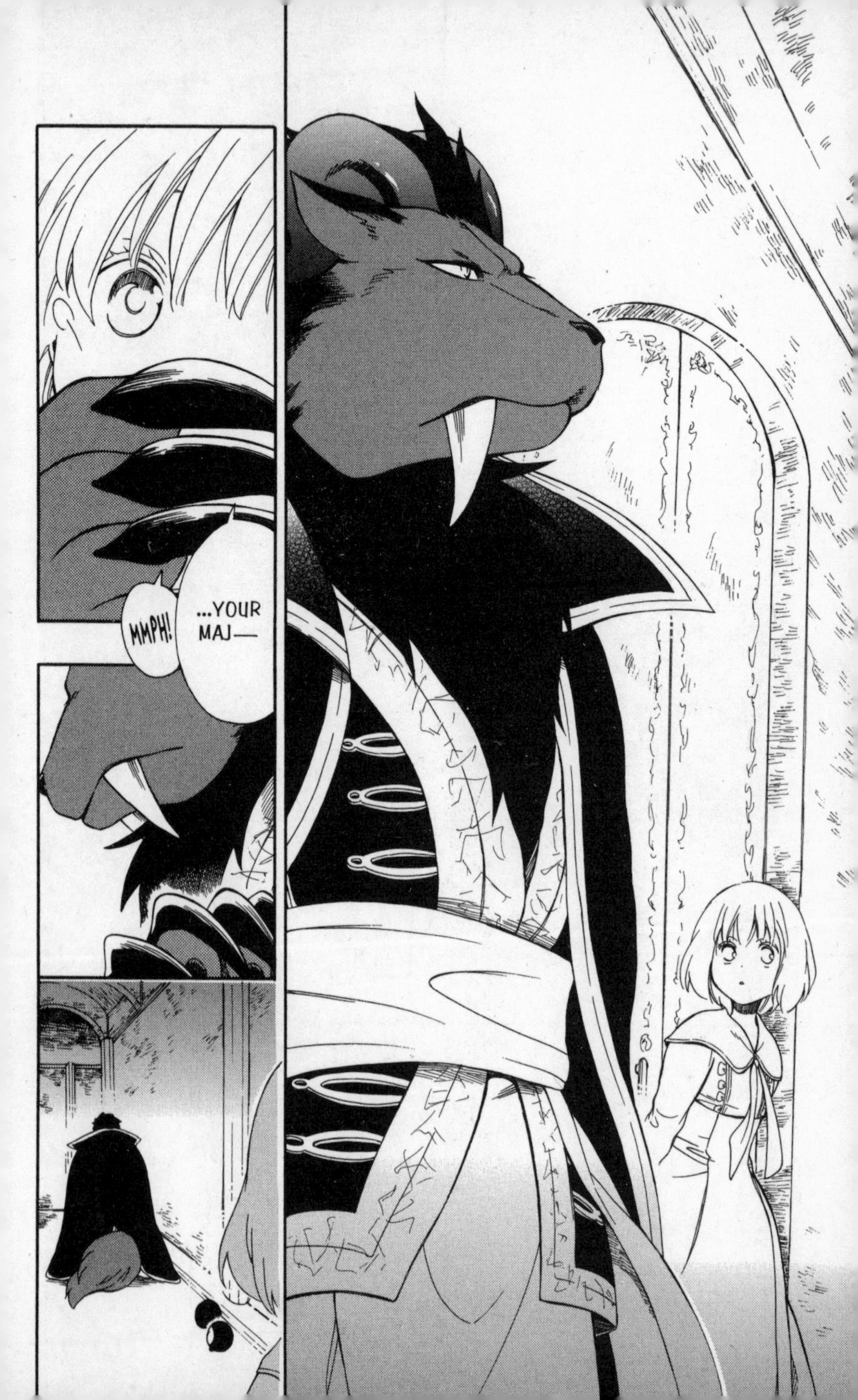
...YOUR MAJ—
MMPH!

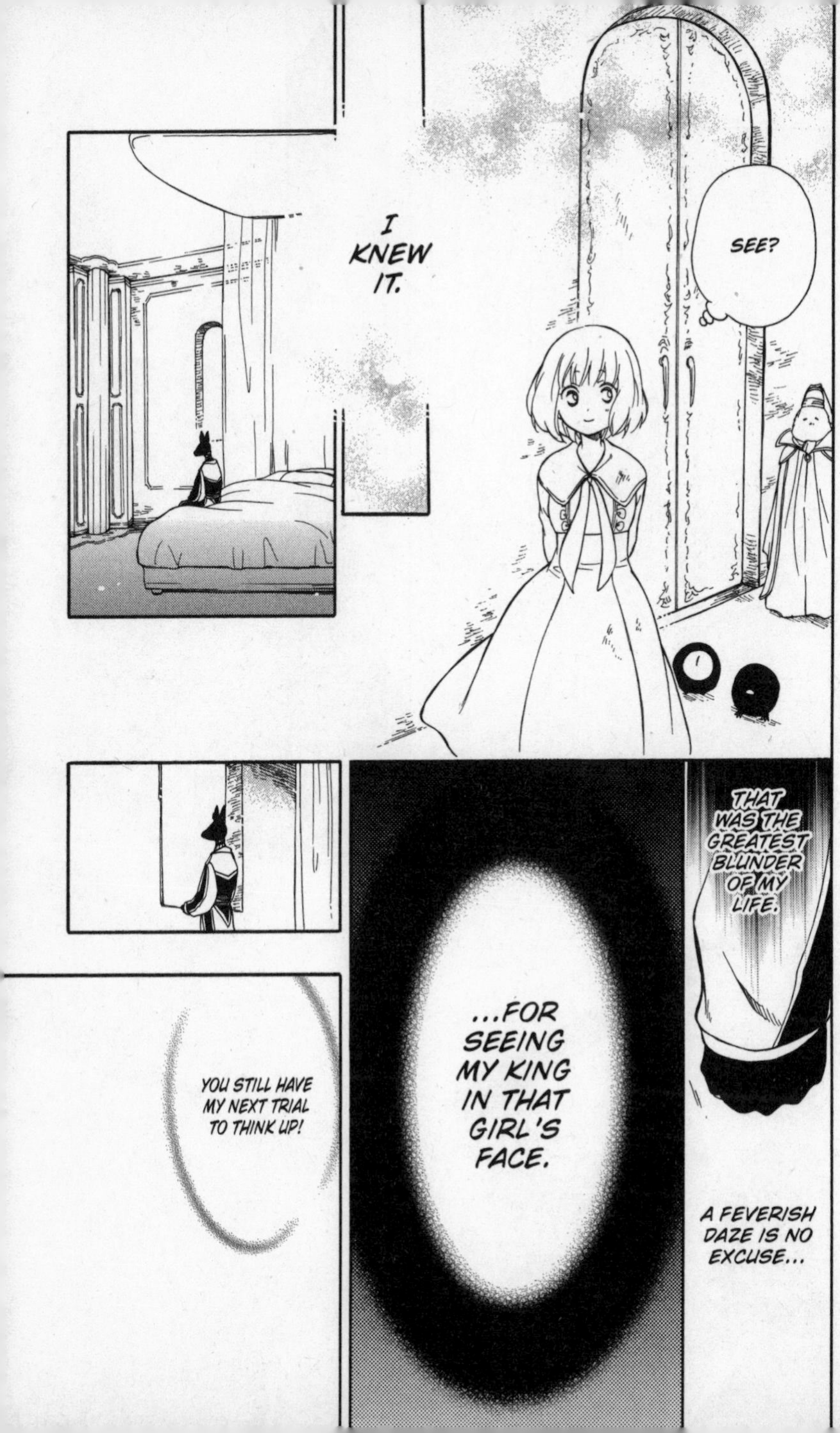
SEE?
I KNEW IT.
THAT WAS THE GREATEST BLUNDER OF MY LIFE.
A FEVERISH DAZE IS NO EXCUSE...
...FOR SEEING MY KING IN THAT GIRL'S FACE.
YOU STILL HAVE MY NEXT TRIAL TO THINK UP!

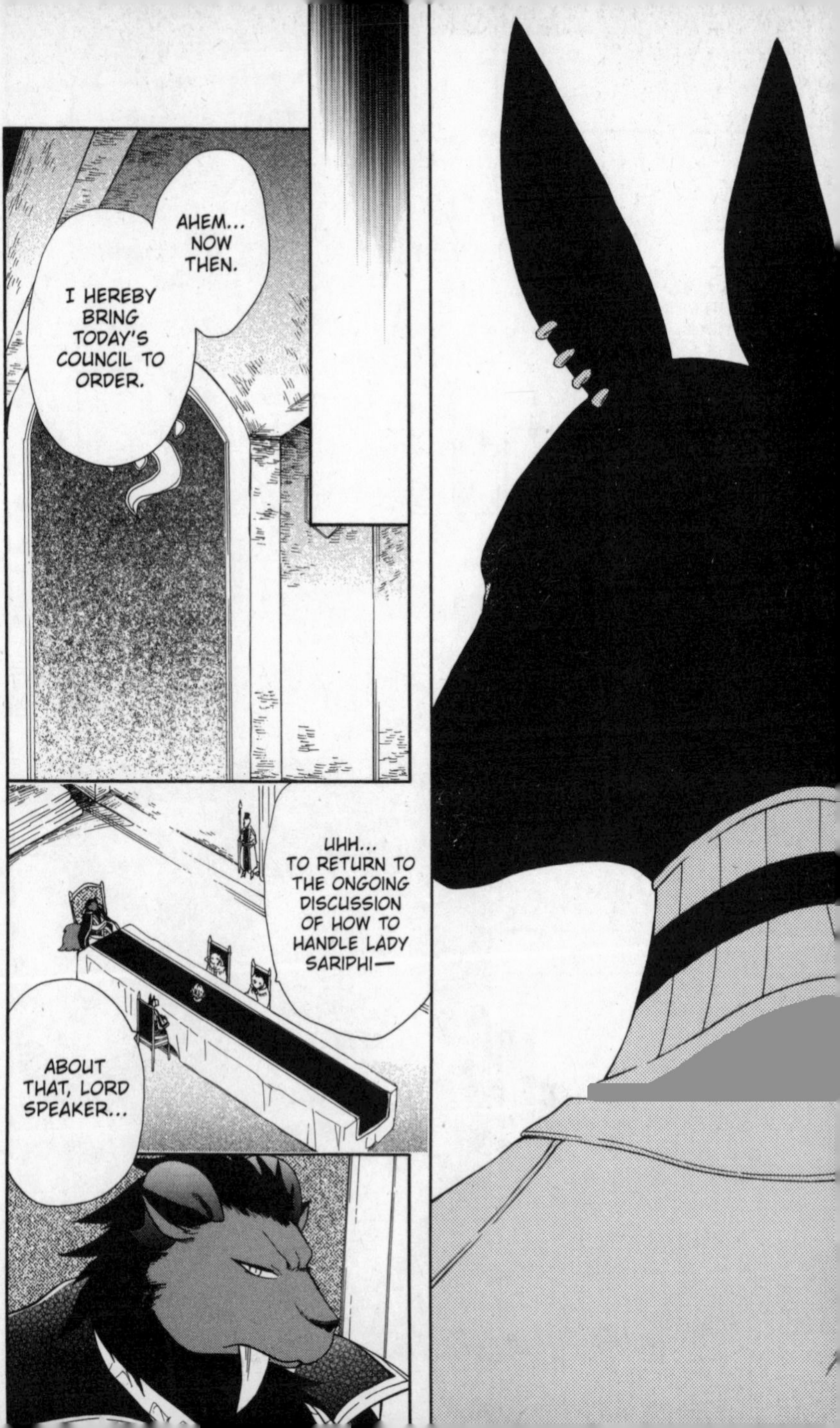
AHEM... NOW THEN.
I HEREBY BRING TODAY'S COUNCIL TO ORDER.
UHH... TO RETURN TO THE ONGOING DISCUSSION OF HOW TO HANDLE LADY SARIPHI—
ABOUT THAT, LORD SPEAKER...

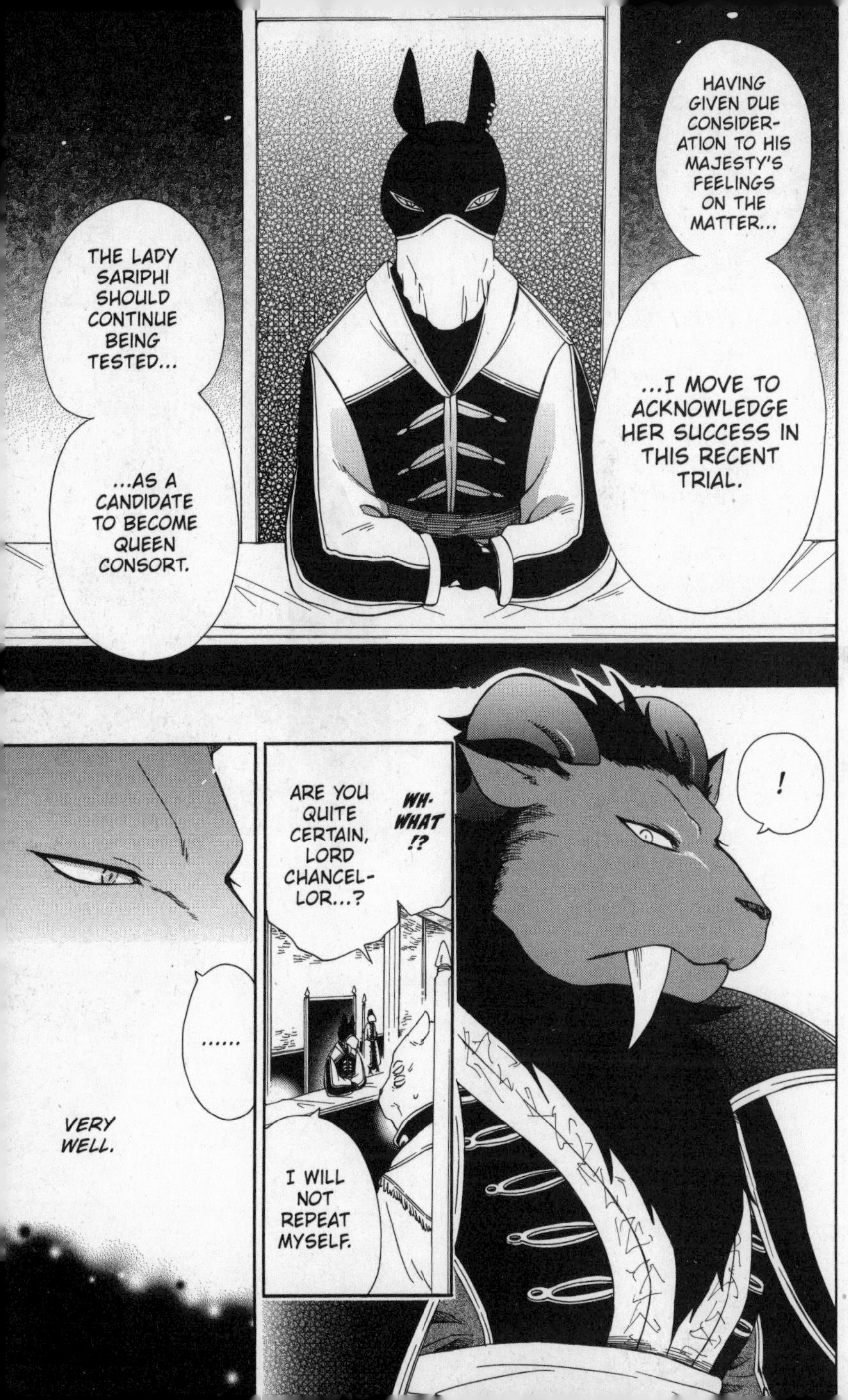
HAVING GIVEN DUE CONSIDERATION TO HIS MAJESTY'S FEELINGS ON THE MATTER...
...I MOVE TO ACKNOWLEDGE HER SUCCESS IN THIS RECENT TRIAL.
THE LADY SARIPHI SHOULD CONTINUE BEING TESTED...
...AS A CANDIDATE TO BECOME QUEEN CONSORT.
!
WH-WHAT!?
ARE YOU QUITE CERTAIN, LORD CHANCELLOR...?
I WILL NOT REPEAT MYSELF.
......
VERY WELL.

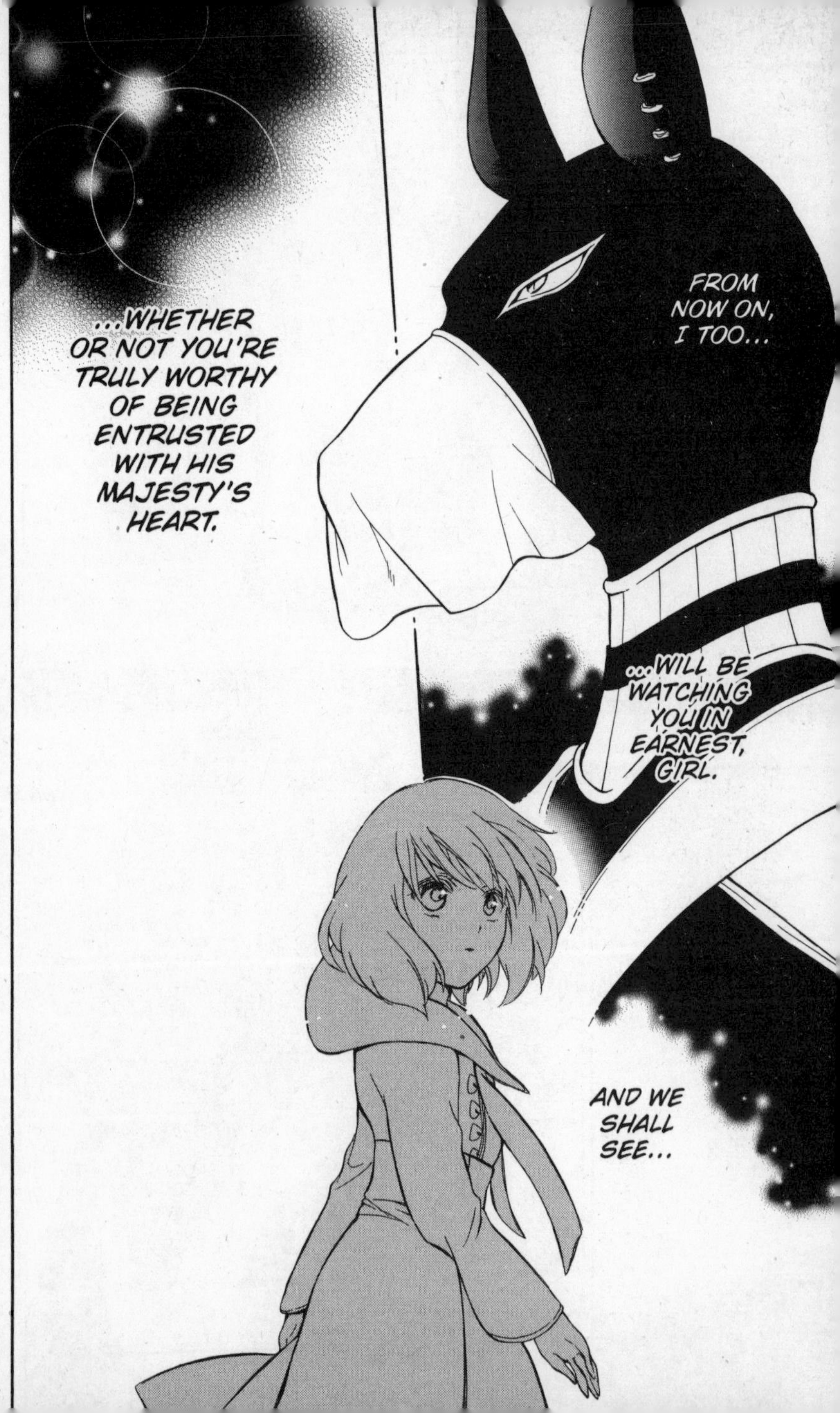
FROM NOW ON, I TOO...
...WILL BE WATCHING YOU IN EARNEST, GIRL.
AND WE SHALL SEE...
...WHETHER OR NOT YOU'RE TRULY WORTHY OF BEING ENTRUSTED WITH HIS MAJESTY'S HEART.

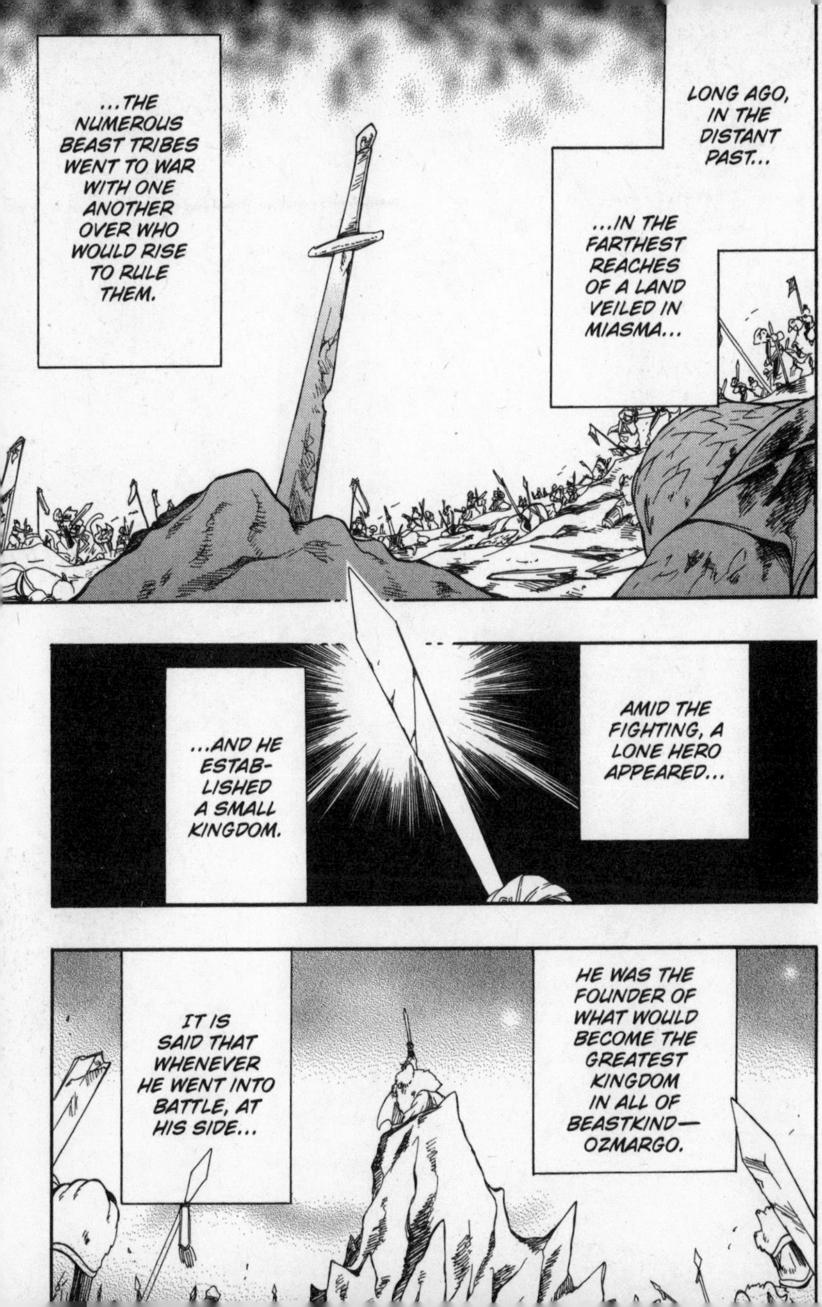
LONG AGO, IN THE DISTANT PAST...
...IN THE FARTHEST REACHES OF A LAND VEILED IN MIASMA...
...THE NUMEROUS BEAST TRIBES WENT TO WAR WITH ONE ANOTHER OVER WHO WOULD RISE TO RULE THEM.
AMID THE FIGHTING, A LONE HERO APPEARED...
...AND HE ESTAB-LISHED A SMALL KINGDOM.
HE WAS THE FOUNDER OF WHAT WOULD BECOME THE GREATEST KINGDOM IN ALL OF BEASTKIND—OZMARGO.
IT IS SAID THAT WHENEVER HE WENT INTO BATTLE, AT HIS SIDE...

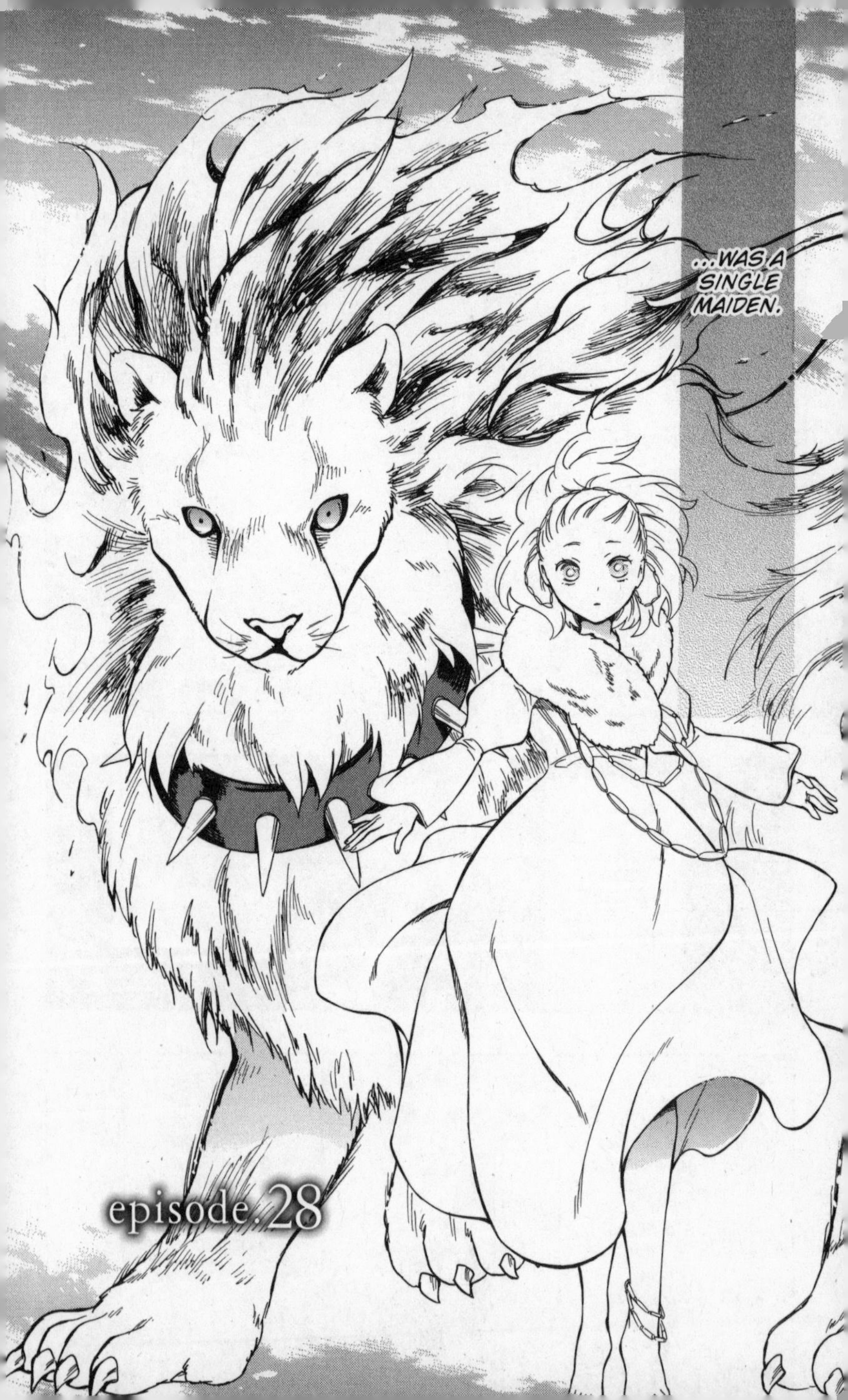
...WAS A SINGLE MAIDEN.
episode.28

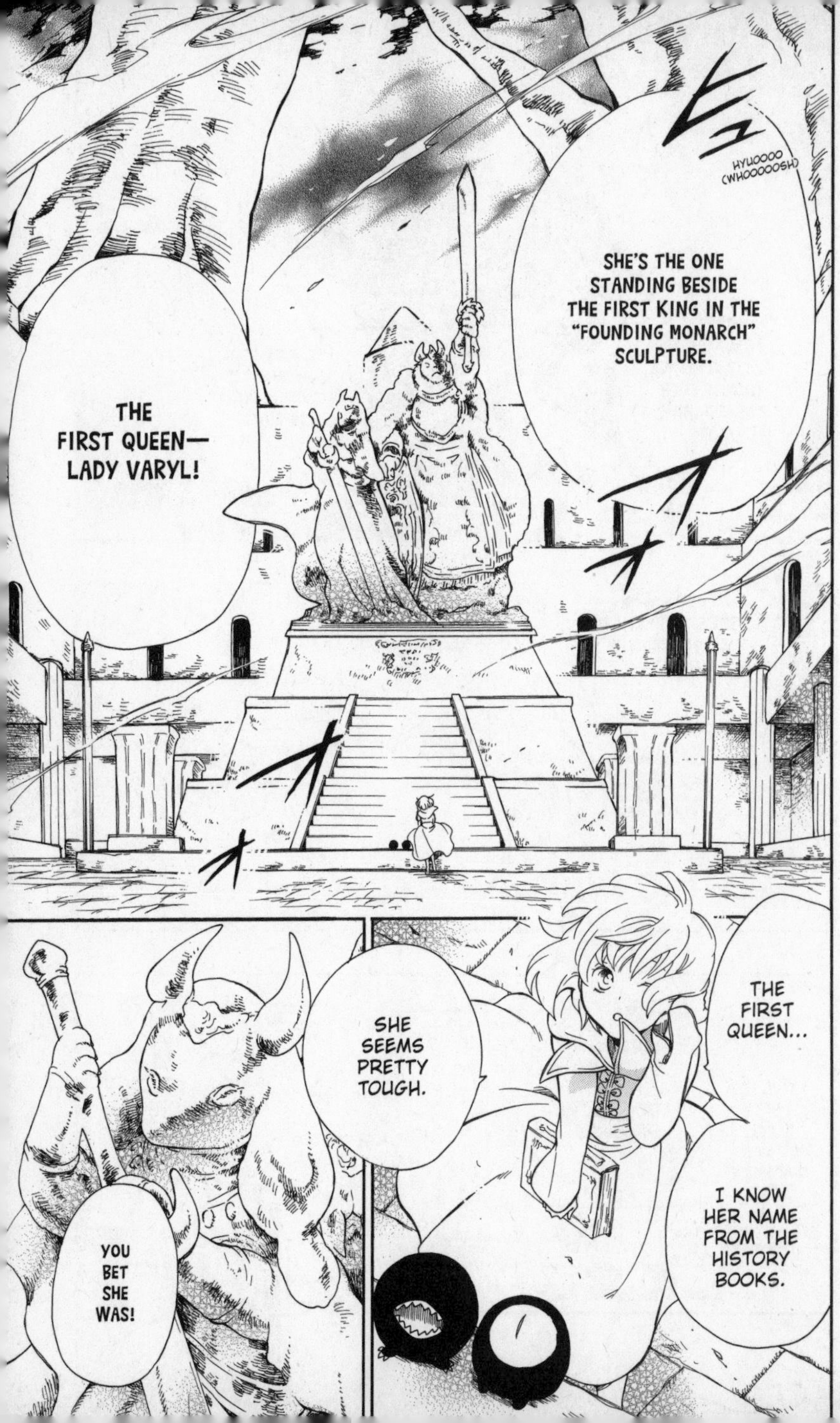
HYUOOO (WHOOOOOSH)
SHE'S THE ONE STANDING BESIDE THE FIRST KING IN THE "FOUNDING MONARCH" SCULPTURE.
THE FIRST QUEEN—LADY VARYL!
THE FIRST QUEEN...
I KNOW HER NAME FROM THE HISTORY BOOKS.
SHE SEEMS PRETTY TOUGH.
YOU BET SHE WAS!

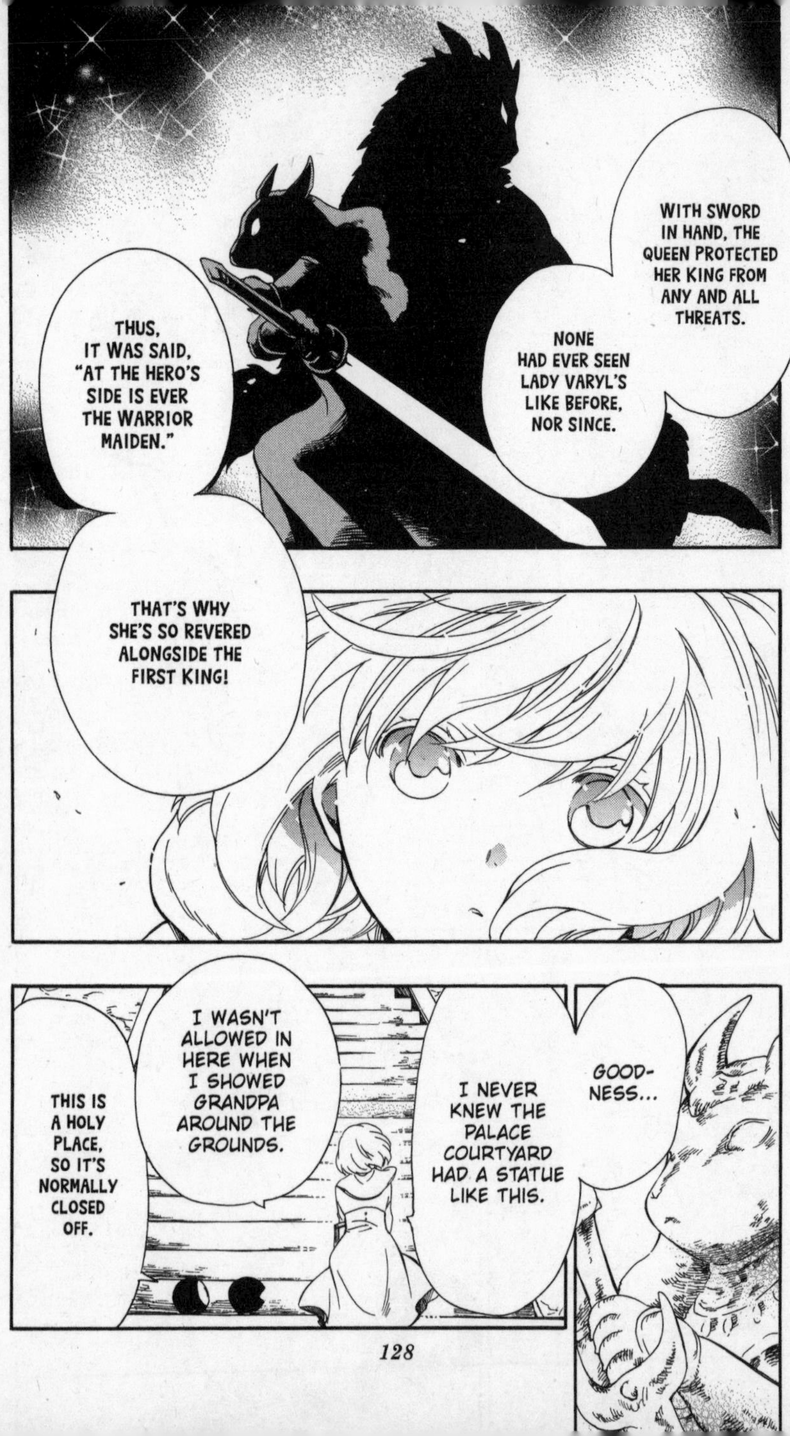
WITH SWORD IN HAND, THE QUEEN PROTECTED HER KING FROM ANY AND ALL THREATS.
NONE HAD EVER SEEN LADY VARYL'S LIKE BEFORE, NOR SINCE.
THUS, IT WAS SAID, "AT THE HERO'S SIDE IS EVER THE WARRIOR MAIDEN."
THAT'S WHY SHE'S SO REVERED ALONGSIDE THE FIRST KING!
GOOD-NESS...
I NEVER KNEW THE PALACE COURTYARD HAD A STATUE LIKE THIS.
I WASN'T ALLOWED IN HERE WHEN I SHOWED GRANDPA AROUND THE GROUNDS.
THIS IS A HOLY PLACE, SO IT'S NORMALLY CLOSED OFF.

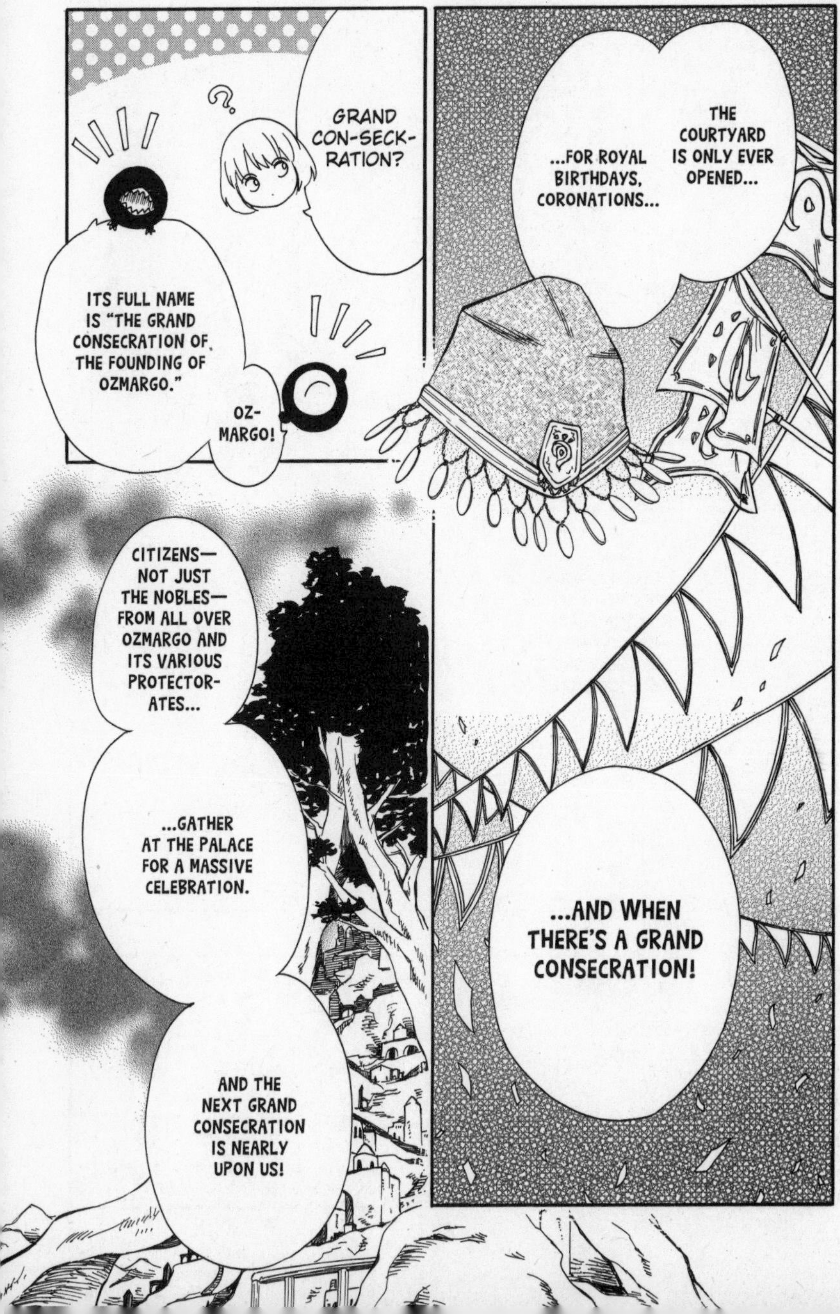
THE COURTYARD IS ONLY EVER OPENED...
...FOR ROYAL BIRTHDAYS, CORONATIONS...
...AND WHEN THERE'S A GRAND CONSECRATION!
GRAND CON-SECK-RATION?
ITS FULL NAME IS "THE GRAND CONSECRATION OF THE FOUNDING OF OZMARGO."
OZ-MARGO!
CITIZENS—NOT JUST THE NOBLES—FROM ALL OVER OZMARGO AND ITS VARIOUS PROTECTOR-ATES...
...GATHER AT THE PALACE FOR A MASSIVE CELEBRATION.
AND THE NEXT GRAND CONSECRATION IS NEARLY UPON US!

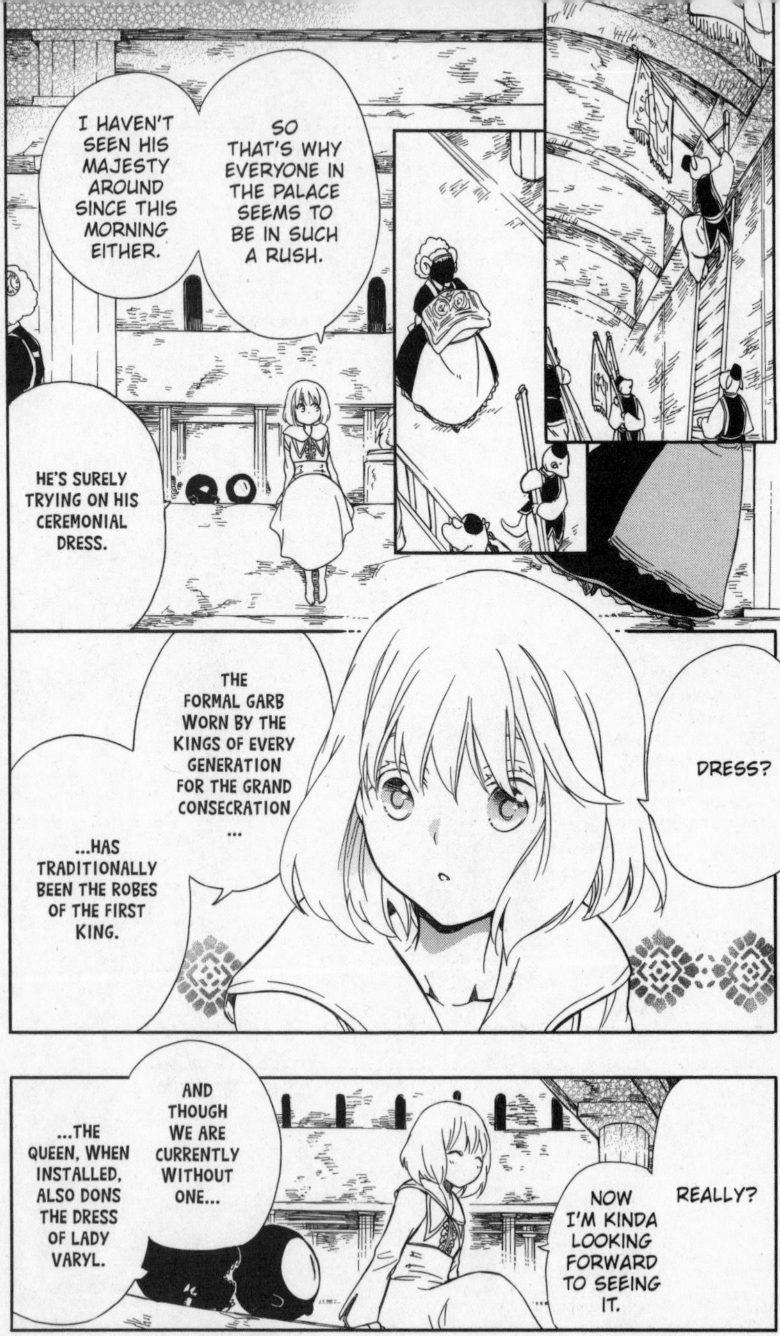
SO THAT'S WHY EVERYONE IN THE PALACE SEEMS TO BE IN SUCH A RUSH.
I HAVEN'T SEEN HIS MAJESTY AROUND SINCE THIS MORNING EITHER.
HE'S SURELY TRYING ON HIS CEREMONIAL DRESS.
DRESS?
THE FORMAL GARB WORN BY THE KINGS OF EVERY GENERATION FOR THE GRAND CONSECRATION...
...HAS TRADITIONALLY BEEN THE ROBES OF THE FIRST KING.
REALLY?
NOW I'M KINDA LOOKING FORWARD TO SEEING IT.
AND THOUGH WE ARE CURRENTLY WITHOUT ONE...
...THE QUEEN, WHEN INSTALLED, ALSO DONS THE DRESS OF LADY VARYL.

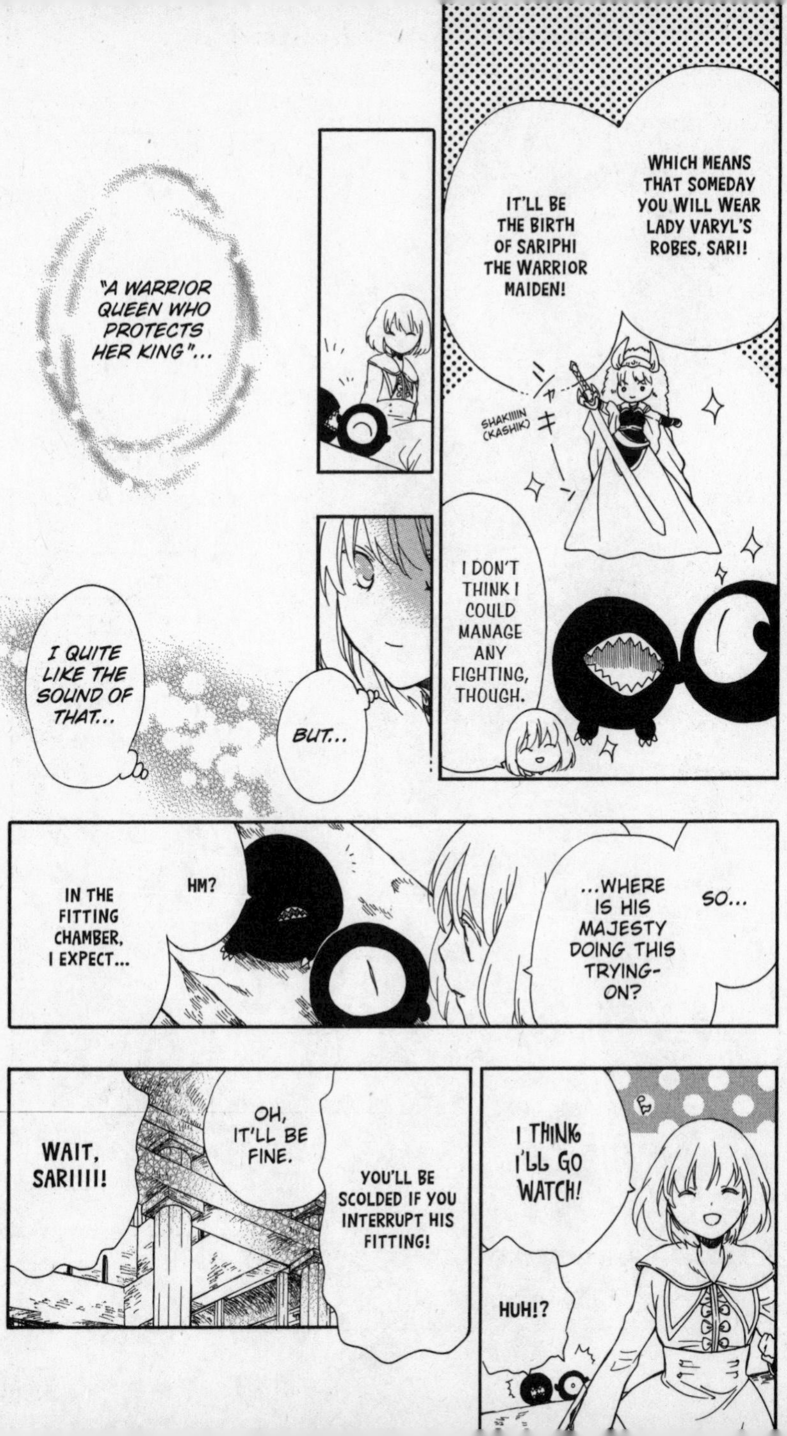
WHICH MEANS THAT SOMEDAY YOU WILL WEAR LADY VARYL'S ROBES, SARI!
IT'LL BE THE BIRTH OF SARIPHI THE WARRIOR MAIDEN!
SHAKIIIN (KASHIK)
I DON'T THINK I COULD MANAGE ANY FIGHTING, THOUGH.
BUT...
"A WARRIOR QUEEN WHO PROTECTS HER KING"...
I QUITE LIKE THE SOUND OF THAT...
SO...
...WHERE IS HIS MAJESTY DOING THIS TRYING-ON?
HM?
IN THE FITTING CHAMBER, I EXPECT...
I THINK I'LL GO WATCH!
HUH!?
YOU'LL BE SCOLDED IF YOU INTERRUPT HIS FITTING!
OH, IT'LL BE FINE.
WAIT, SARIIII!

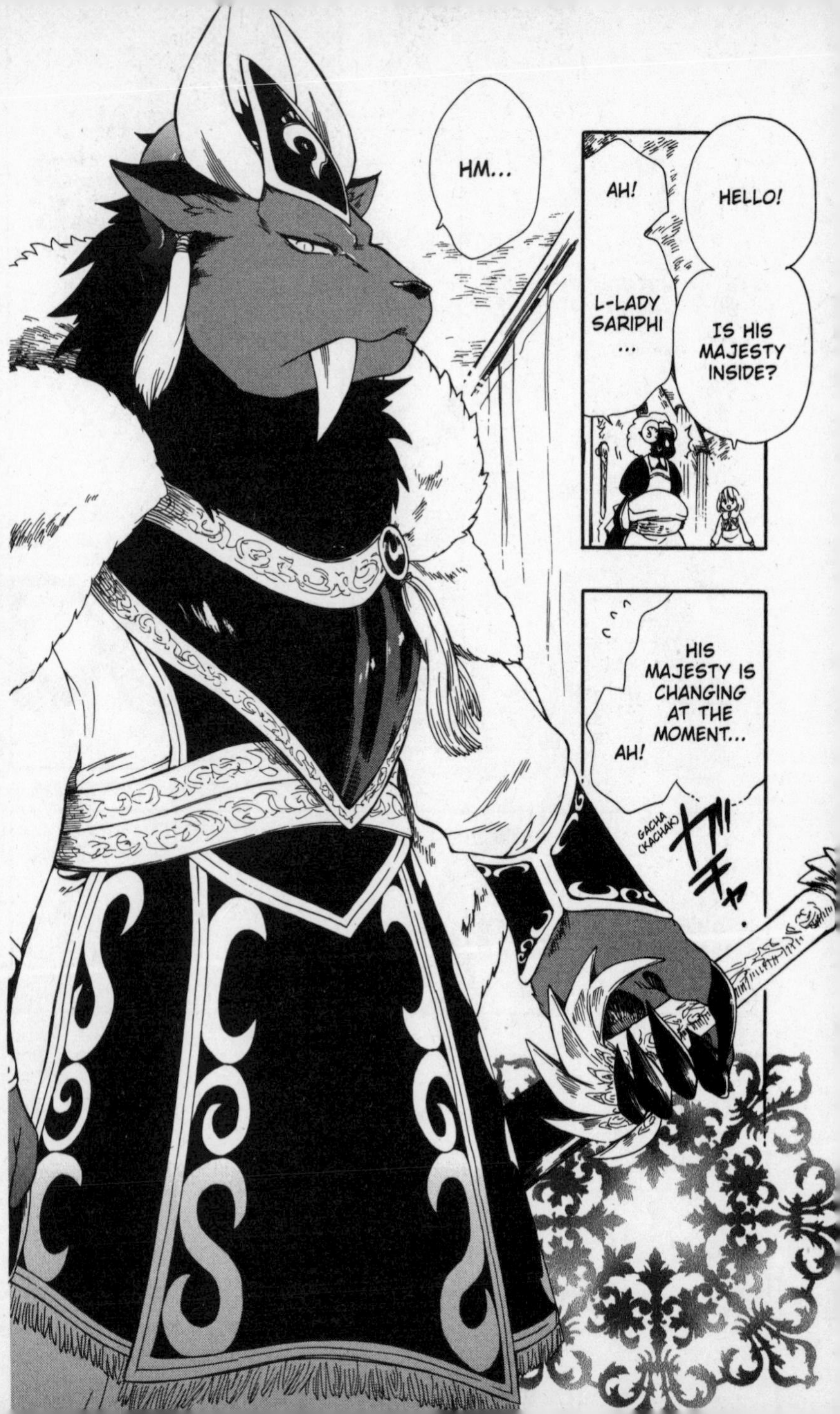
HELLO!
IS HIS MAJESTY INSIDE?
AH!
L-LADY SARIPHI ...
HIS MAJESTY IS CHANGING AT THE MOMENT...
AH!
GACHA (KACHAK)
HM...

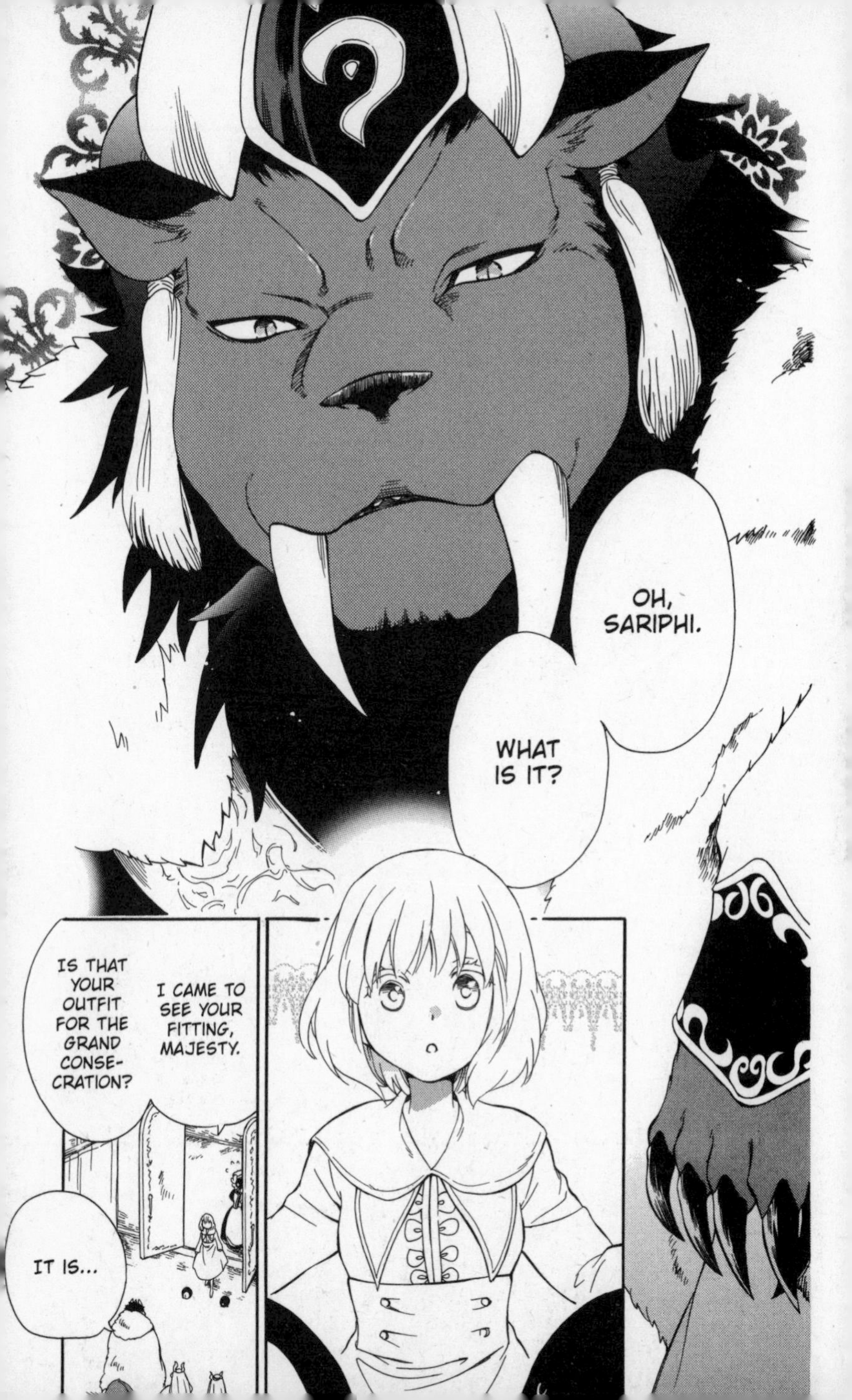
OH, SARIPHI.
WHAT IS IT?
I CAME TO SEE YOUR FITTING, MAJESTY.
IS THAT YOUR OUTFIT FOR THE GRAND CONSE-CRATION?
IT IS...

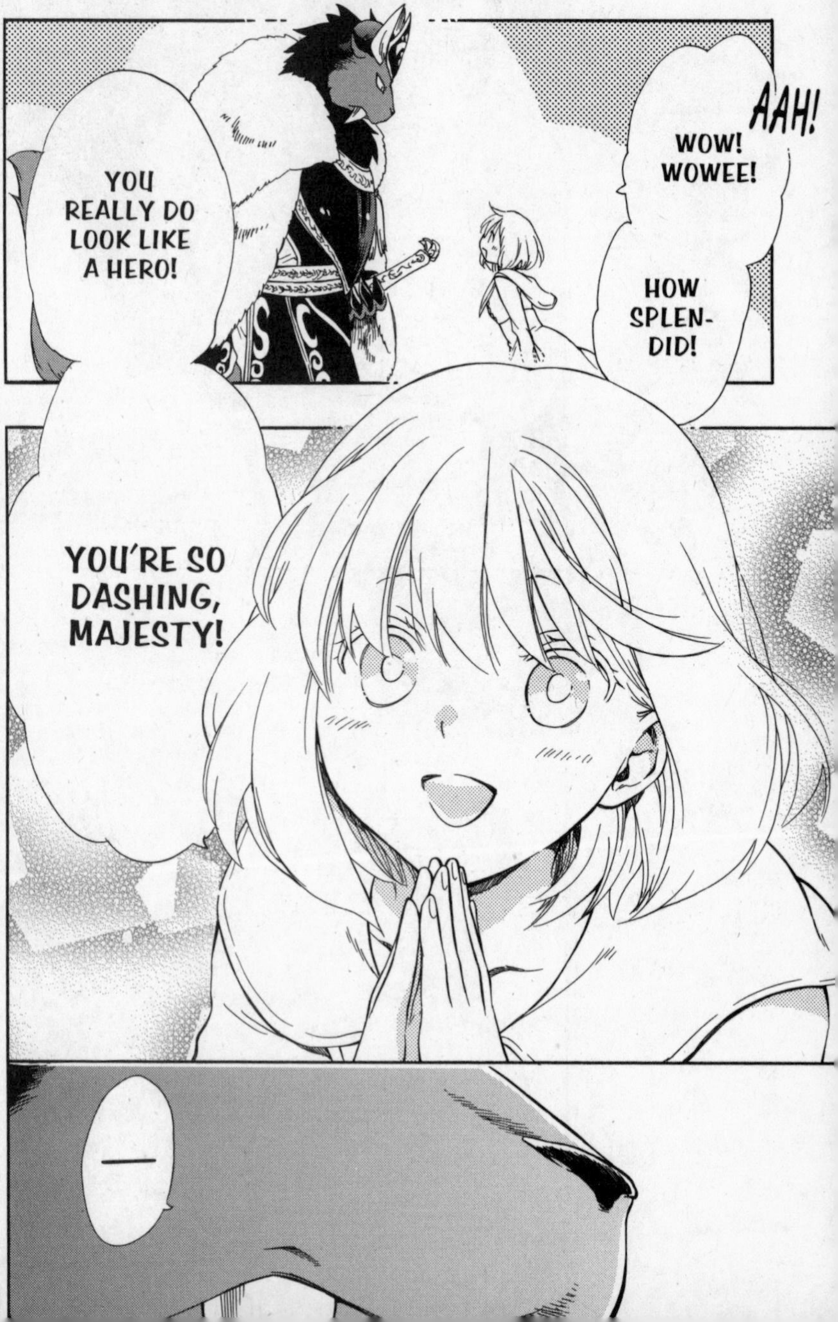
AAH!
WOW! WOWEE!
HOW SPLEN-DID!
YOU REALLY DO LOOK LIKE A HERO!
YOU'RE SO DASHING, MAJESTY!
—

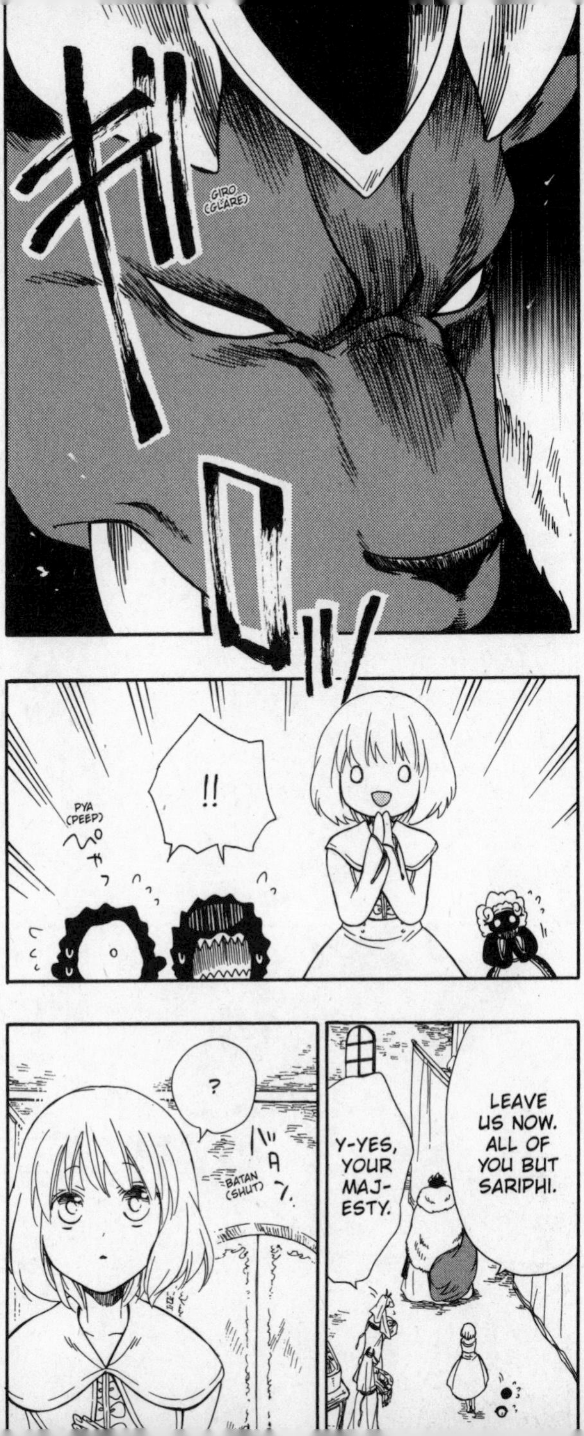
GIRO (GLARE)
PYA (PEEP)
!!
LEAVE US NOW. ALL OF YOU BUT SARIPHI.
Y-YES, YOUR MAJ-ESTY.
BATAN (SHUT)
?

WHO EVEN CARES!? BACKGROUND NOTES

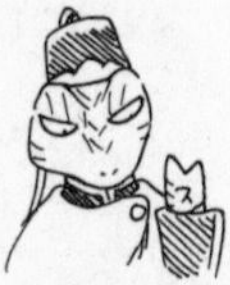

JORMUNGAND HAS THREE FINGERS. HE'S SUPPOSED TO LOOK SORT OF LIKE A SNAKE (THEY DON'T HAVE FINGERS), BUT FOR SOME REASON, I JUST...

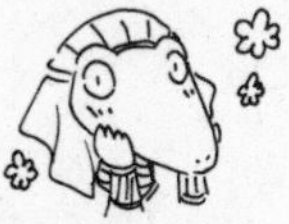

PRINCESS AMIT SMELLS NICE.

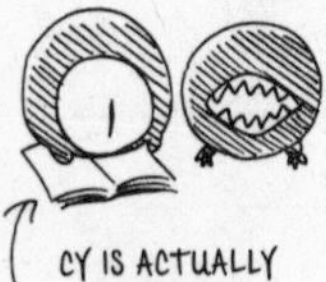

CY IS ACTUALLY A LITTLE BIT SMARTER THAN CLOPS, BUT HE HAS A HARDER TIME SPEAKING, SO CLOPS DOES IT FOR HIM. CLOPS IS ALSO THE MORE PRECOCIOUS ONE.

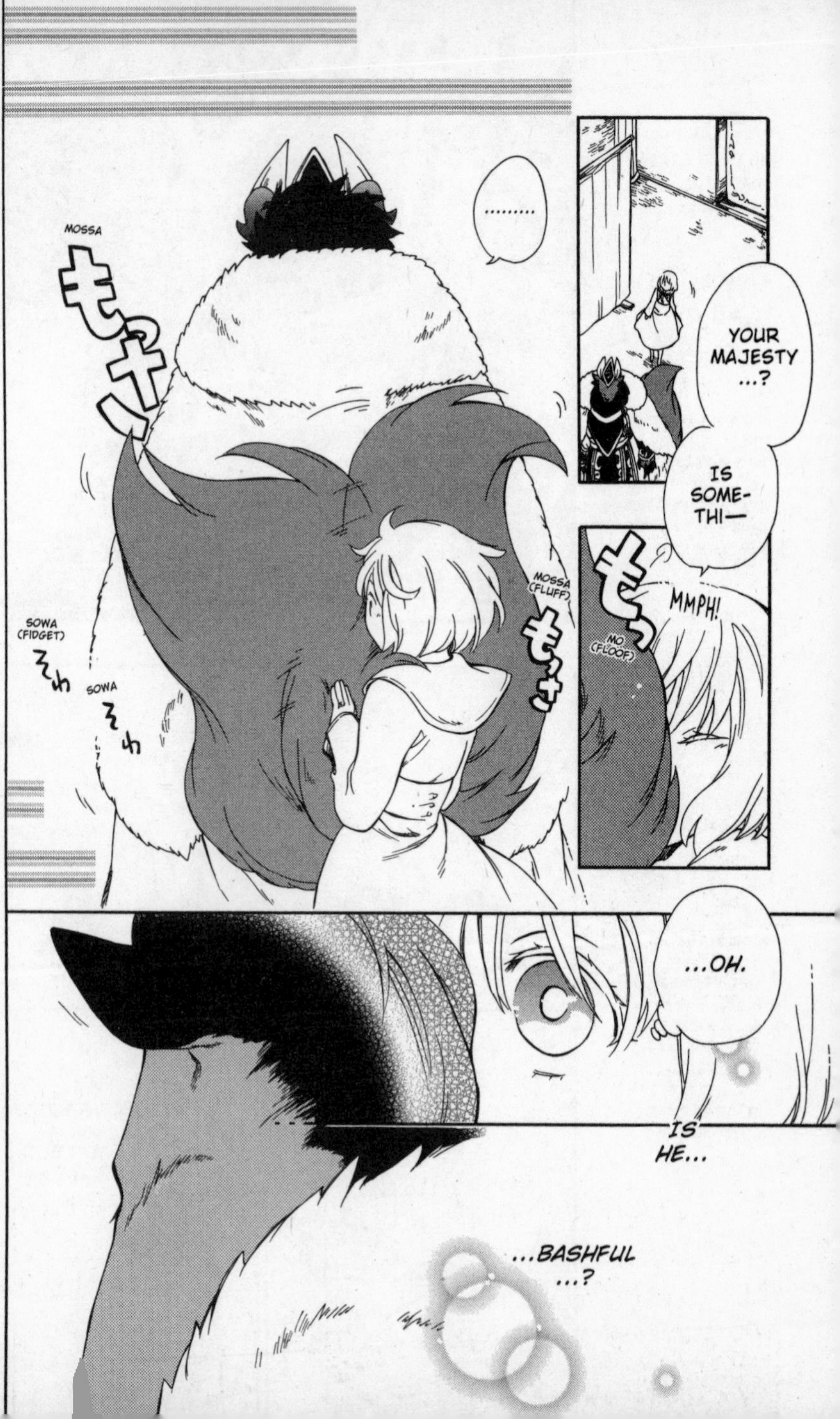

YOUR MAJESTY ...?
IS SOME-THI—
MMPH!
もっ
MO (FLOOF)
....
MOSSA
もっさ
MOSSA (FLUFF)
もっさ
SOWA (FIDGET)
そわ
SOWA
そわ
...OH.
IS HE...
...BASHFUL ...?

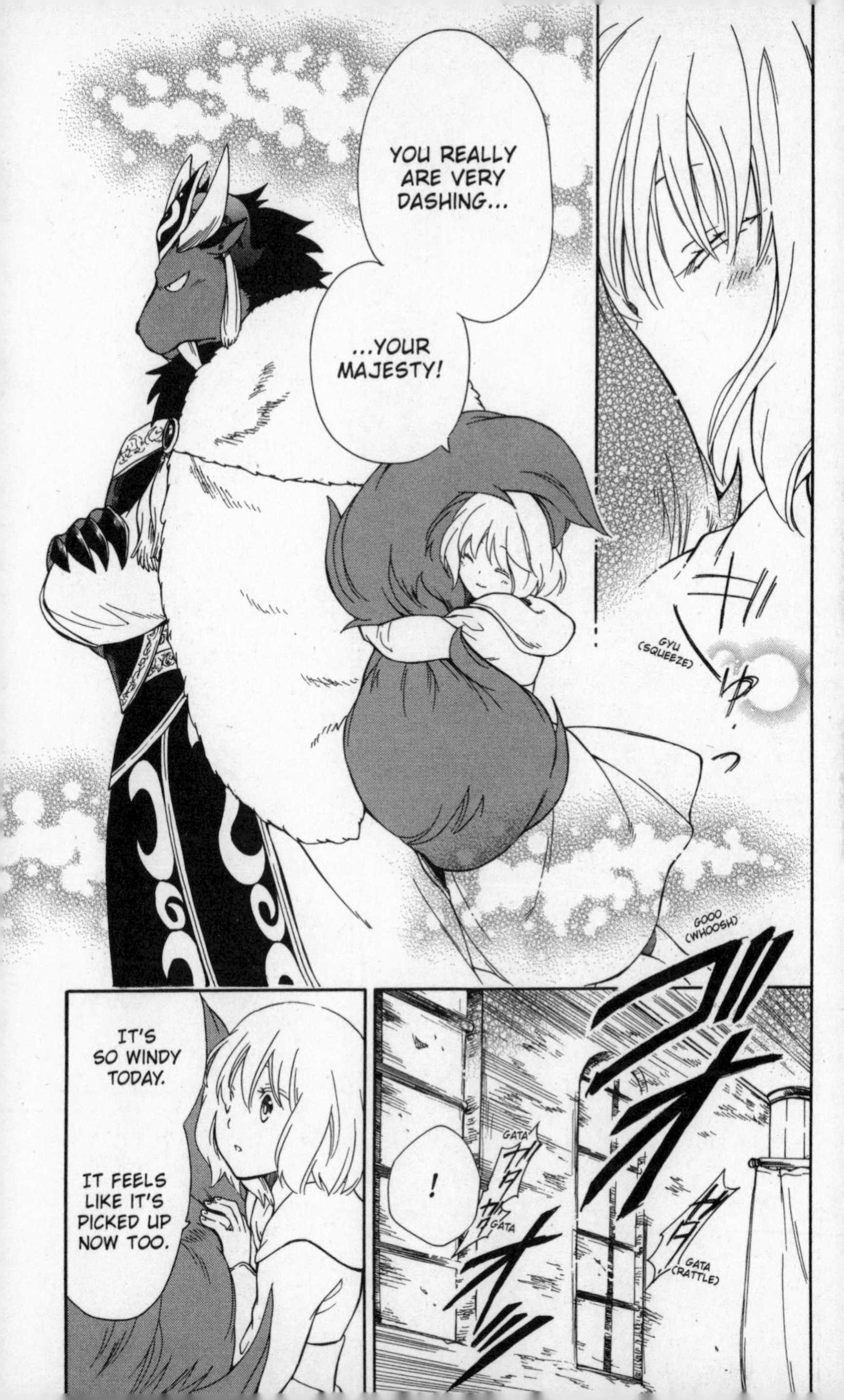
GYU (SQUEEZE)
YOU REALLY ARE VERY DASHING...
...YOUR MAJESTY!
GOOO (WHOOSH)
GATA
GATA
!
GATA (RATTLE)
IT'S SO WINDY TODAY.
IT FEELS LIKE IT'S PICKED UP NOW TOO.

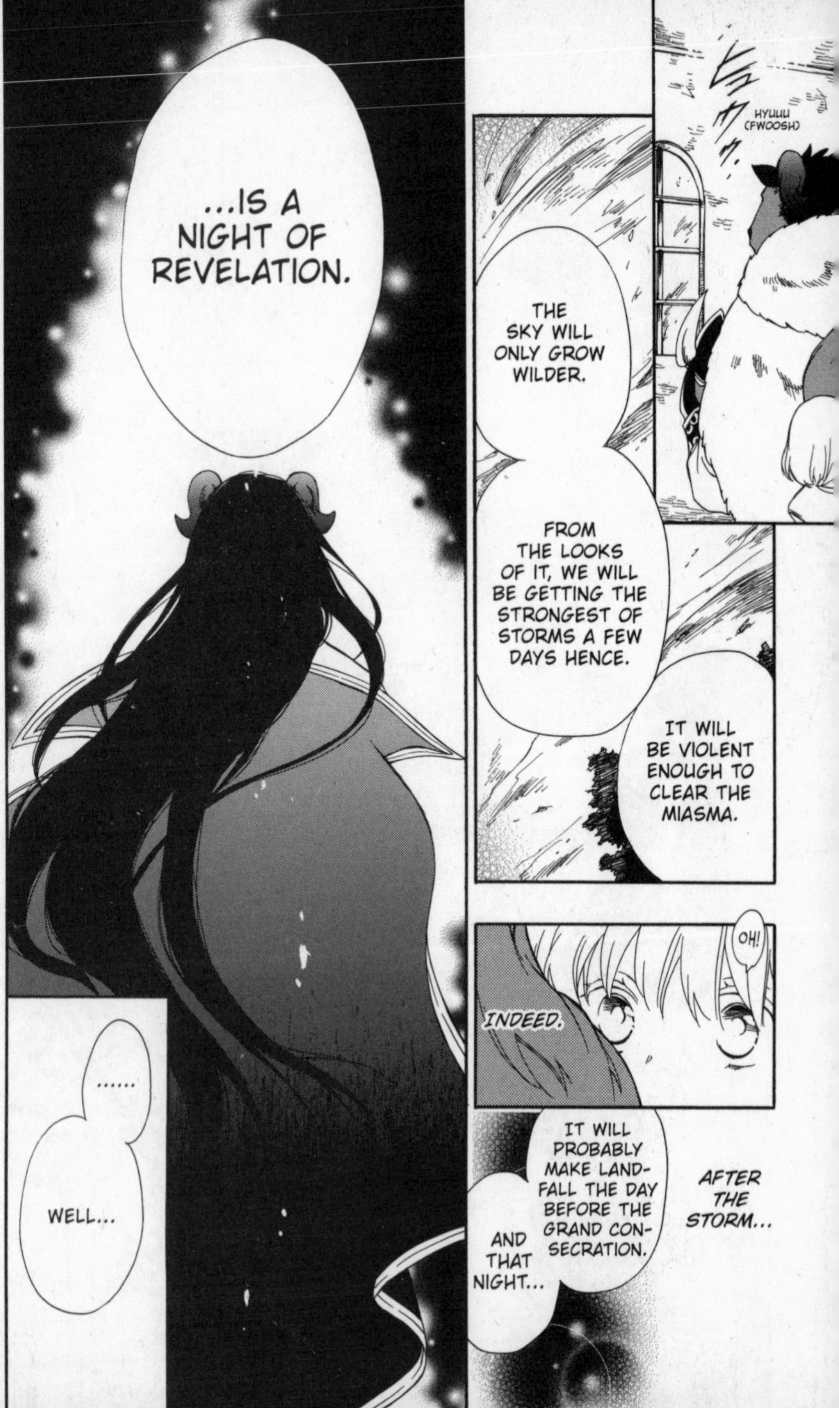
HYUUU (FWOOSH)
THE SKY WILL ONLY GROW WILDER.
FROM THE LOOKS OF IT, WE WILL BE GETTING THE STRONGEST OF STORMS A FEW DAYS HENCE.
IT WILL BE VIOLENT ENOUGH TO CLEAR THE MIASMA.
OH!
INDEED.
AFTER THE STORM...
IT WILL PROBABLY MAKE LANDFALL THE DAY BEFORE THE GRAND CONSECRATION.
AND THAT NIGHT...
...IS A NIGHT OF REVELATION.
......
WELL...

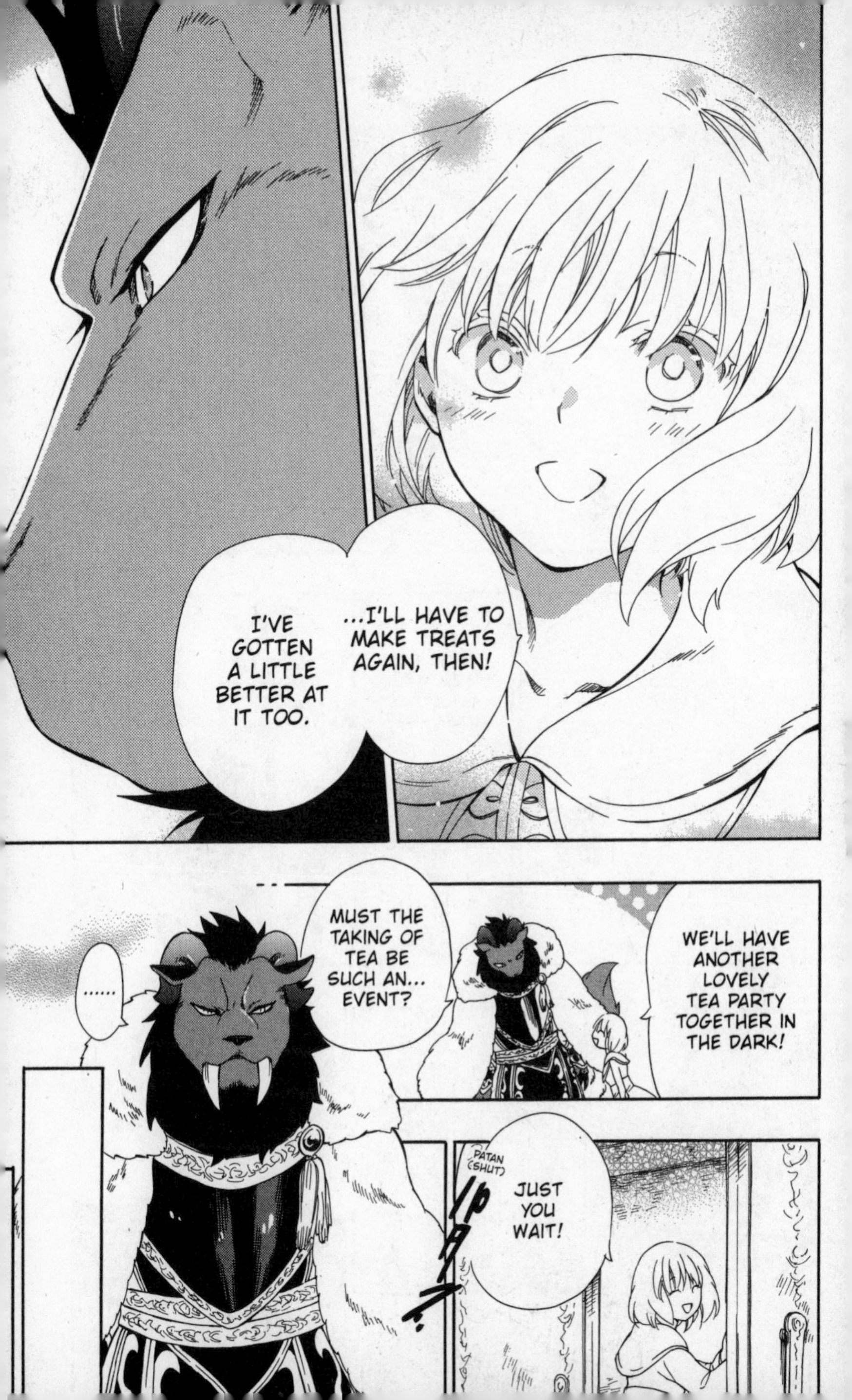

...I'LL HAVE TO MAKE TREATS AGAIN, THEN!
I'VE GOTTEN A LITTLE BETTER AT IT TOO.
WE'LL HAVE ANOTHER LOVELY TEA PARTY TOGETHER IN THE DARK!
JUST YOU WAIT!
PATAN (SHUT)
MUST THE TAKING OF TEA BE SUCH AN... EVENT?
......

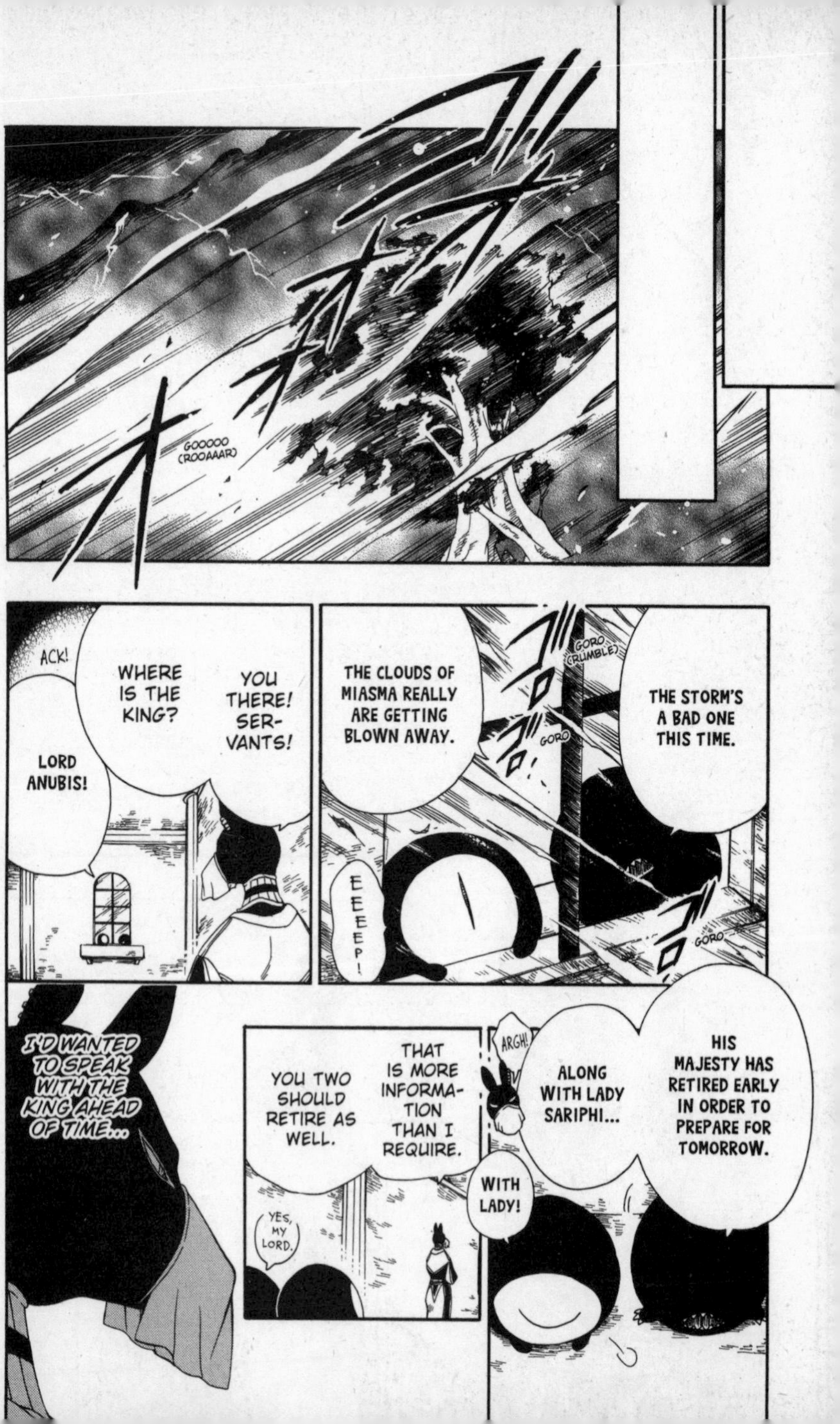
GOOOOO (ROOAAAR)
GORO (RUMBLE)
GORO
THE STORM'S A BAD ONE THIS TIME.
GORO
THE CLOUDS OF MIASMA REALLY ARE GETTING BLOWN AWAY.
EEEEEP!
YOU THERE! SERVANTS!
WHERE IS THE KING?
ACK!
LORD ANUBIS!
HIS MAJESTY HAS RETIRED EARLY IN ORDER TO PREPARE FOR TOMORROW.
ALONG WITH LADY SARIPHI...
ARGH!
WITH LADY!
THAT IS MORE INFORMATION THAN I REQUIRE.
YOU TWO SHOULD RETIRE AS WELL.
YES, MY LORD.
I'D WANTED TO SPEAK WITH THE KING AHEAD OF TIME...

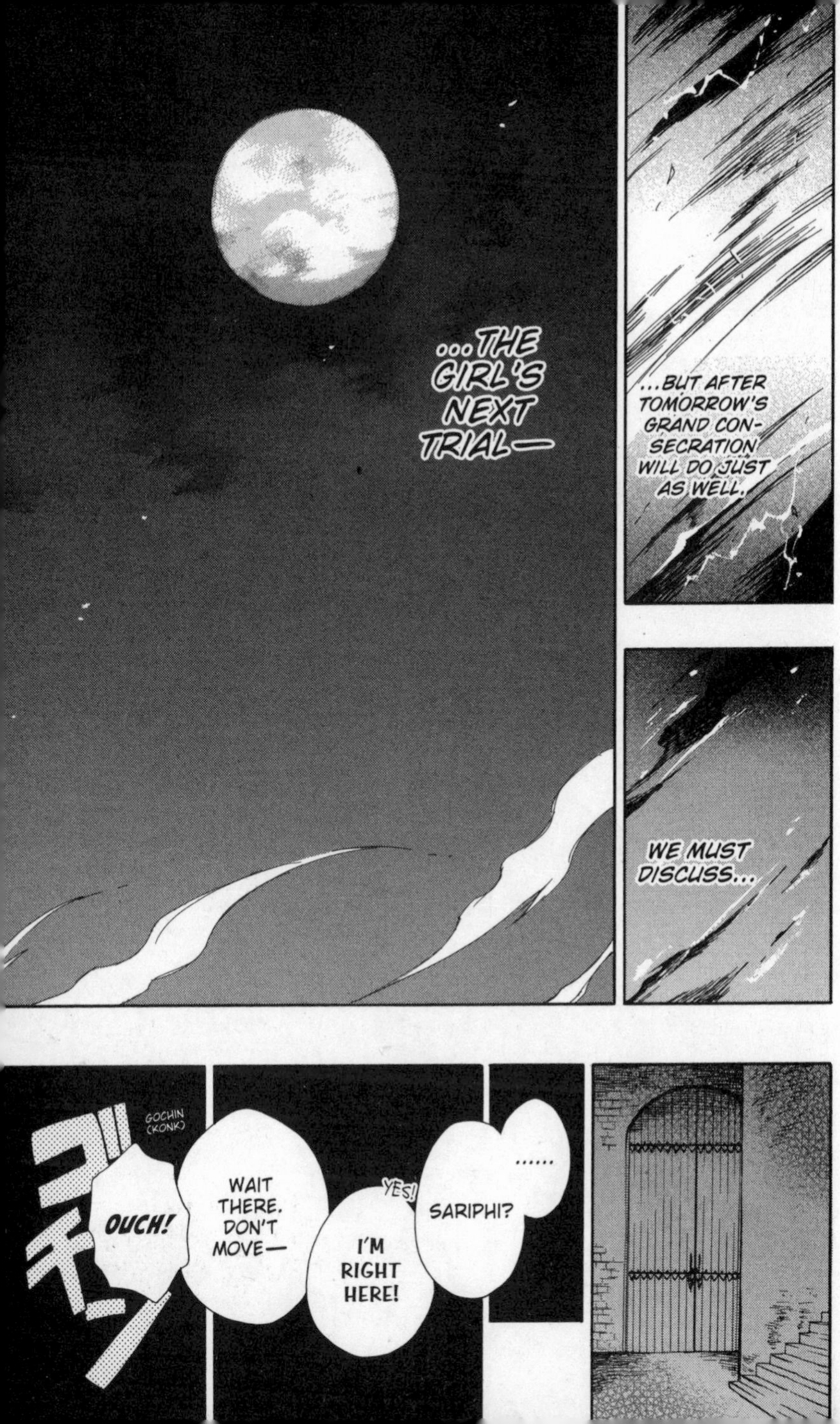
...BUT AFTER TOMORROW'S GRAND CON-SECRATION WILL DO JUST AS WELL.
WE MUST DISCUSS...
...THE GIRL'S NEXT TRIAL—
......
SARIPHI?
YES!
I'M RIGHT HERE!
WAIT THERE. DON'T MOVE—
GOCHIN (KONK)
OUCH!

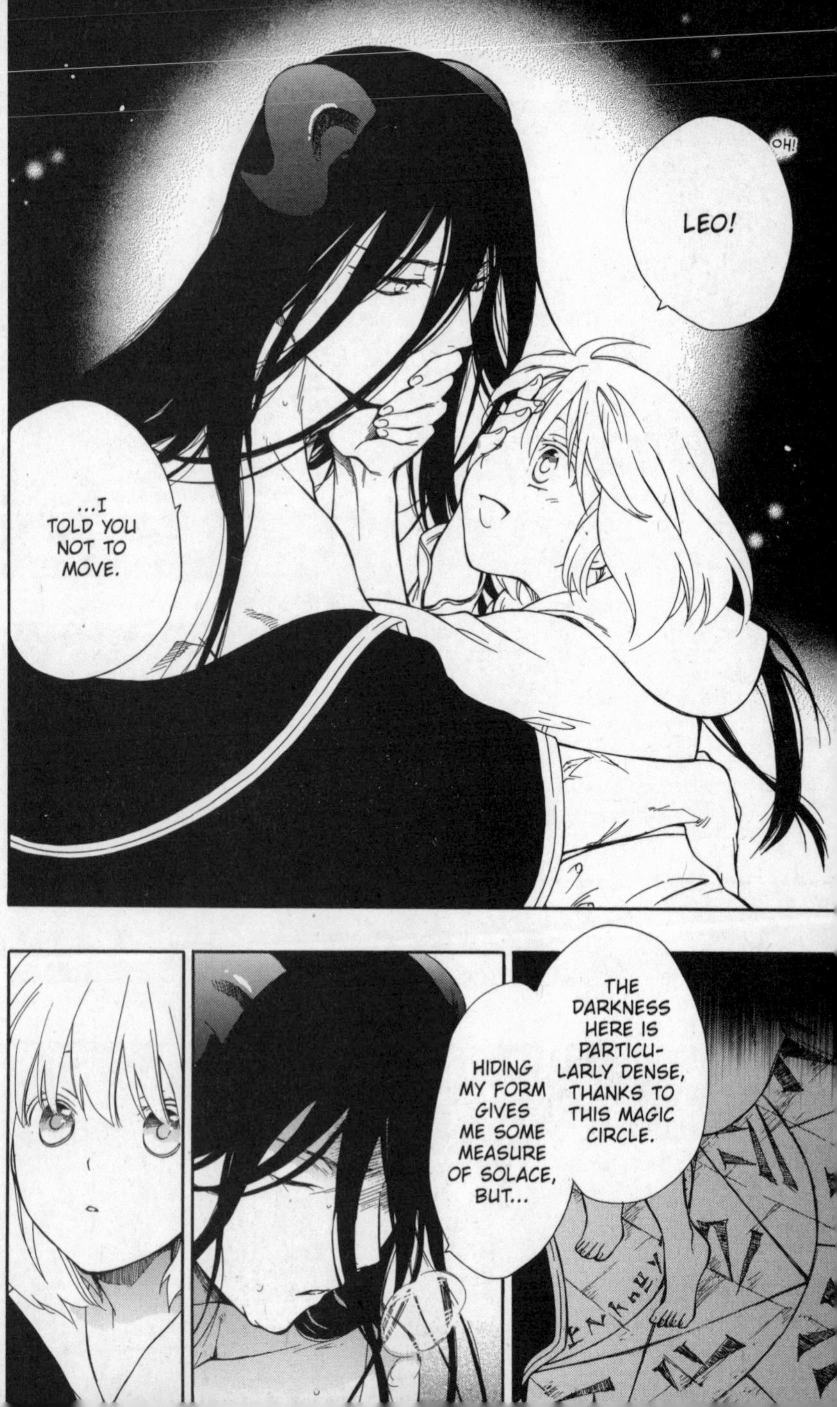
OH!
LEO!
...I TOLD YOU NOT TO MOVE.
THE DARKNESS HERE IS PARTICU-LARLY DENSE, THANKS TO THIS MAGIC CIRCLE.
HIDING MY FORM GIVES ME SOME MEASURE OF SOLACE, BUT...

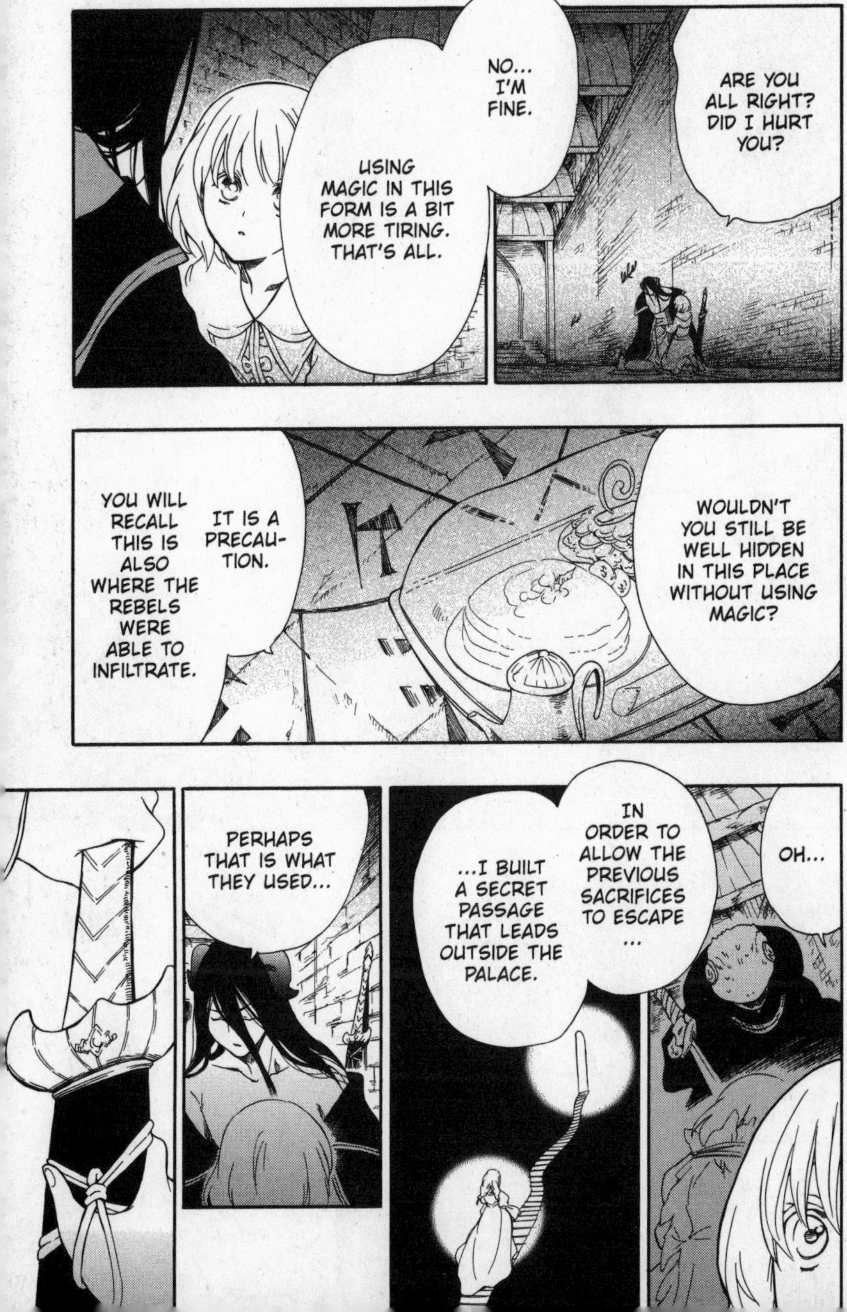
ARE YOU ALL RIGHT? DID I HURT YOU?
NO... I'M FINE.
USING MAGIC IN THIS FORM IS A BIT MORE TIRING. THAT'S ALL.
WOULDN'T YOU STILL BE WELL HIDDEN IN THIS PLACE WITHOUT USING MAGIC?
IT IS A PRECAU-TION.
YOU WILL RECALL THIS IS ALSO WHERE THE REBELS WERE ABLE TO INFILTRATE.
OH...
IN ORDER TO ALLOW THE PREVIOUS SACRIFICES TO ESCAPE...
...I BUILT A SECRET PASSAGE THAT LEADS OUTSIDE THE PALACE.
PERHAPS THAT IS WHAT THEY USED...

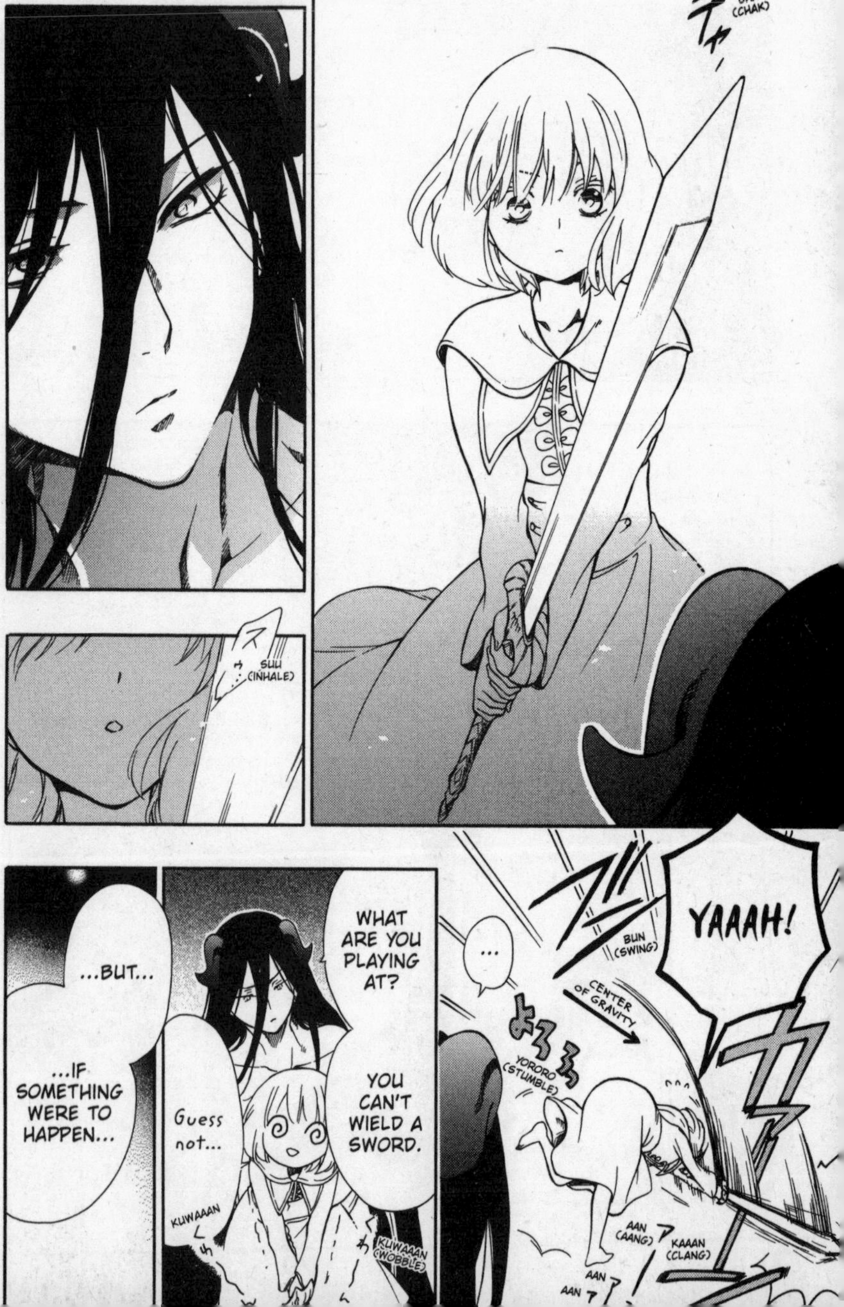
CHA (CHAK)
SUU (INHALE)
YAAAH!
BUN (SWING)
...
CENTER OF GRAVITY
YORORO (STUMBLE)
KAAAN (CLANG)
AAN (AANG)
AAN
AAN
WHAT ARE YOU PLAYING AT?
YOU CAN'T WIELD A SWORD.
Guess not...
KUWAAAN
KUWAAAN (WOBBLE)
...BUT...
...IF SOMETHING WERE TO HAPPEN...

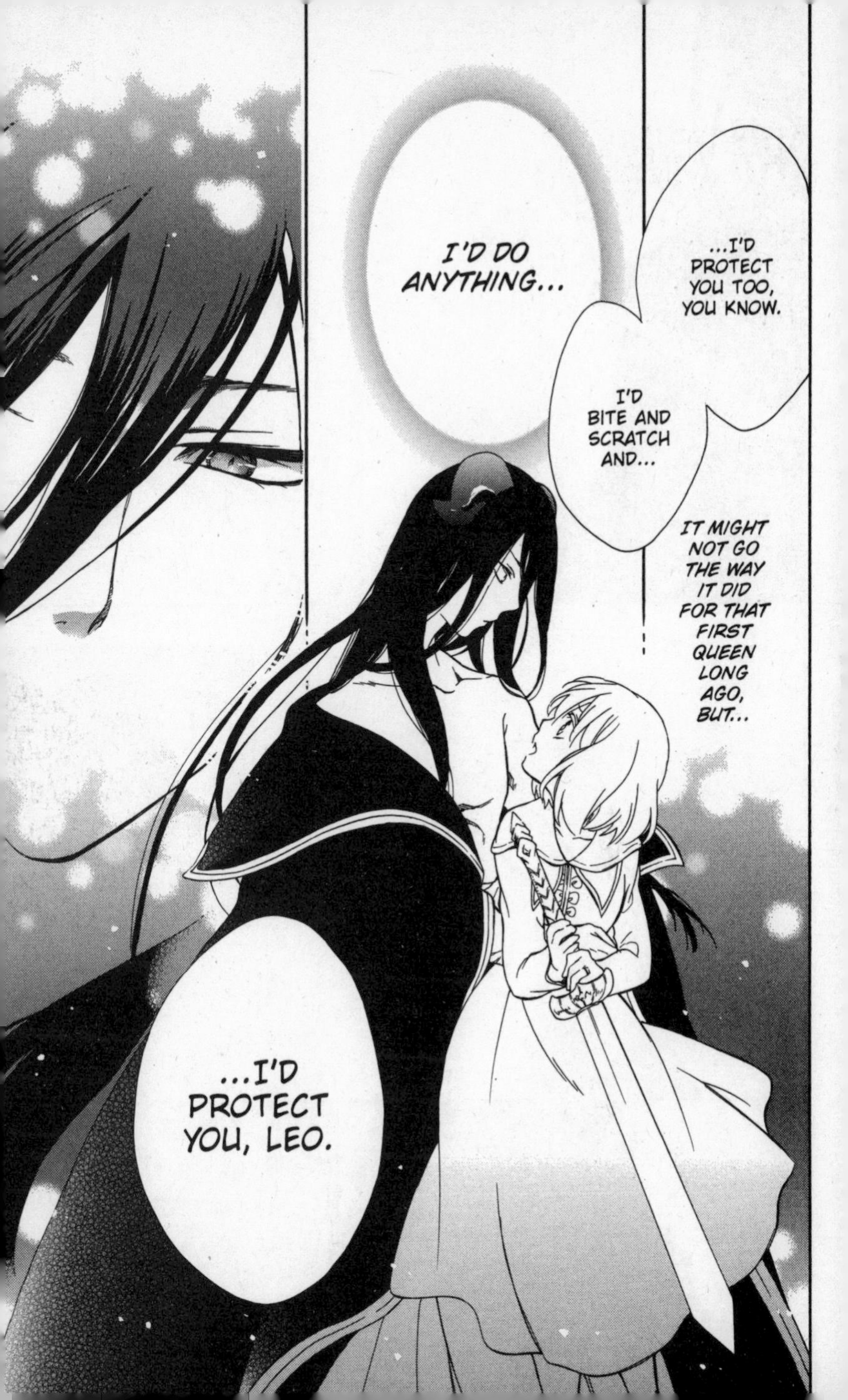
...I'D PROTECT YOU TOO, YOU KNOW.
I'D BITE AND SCRATCH AND...
IT MIGHT NOT GO THE WAY IT DID FOR THAT FIRST QUEEN LONG AGO, BUT...
I'D DO ANYTHING...
...I'D PROTECT YOU, LEO.

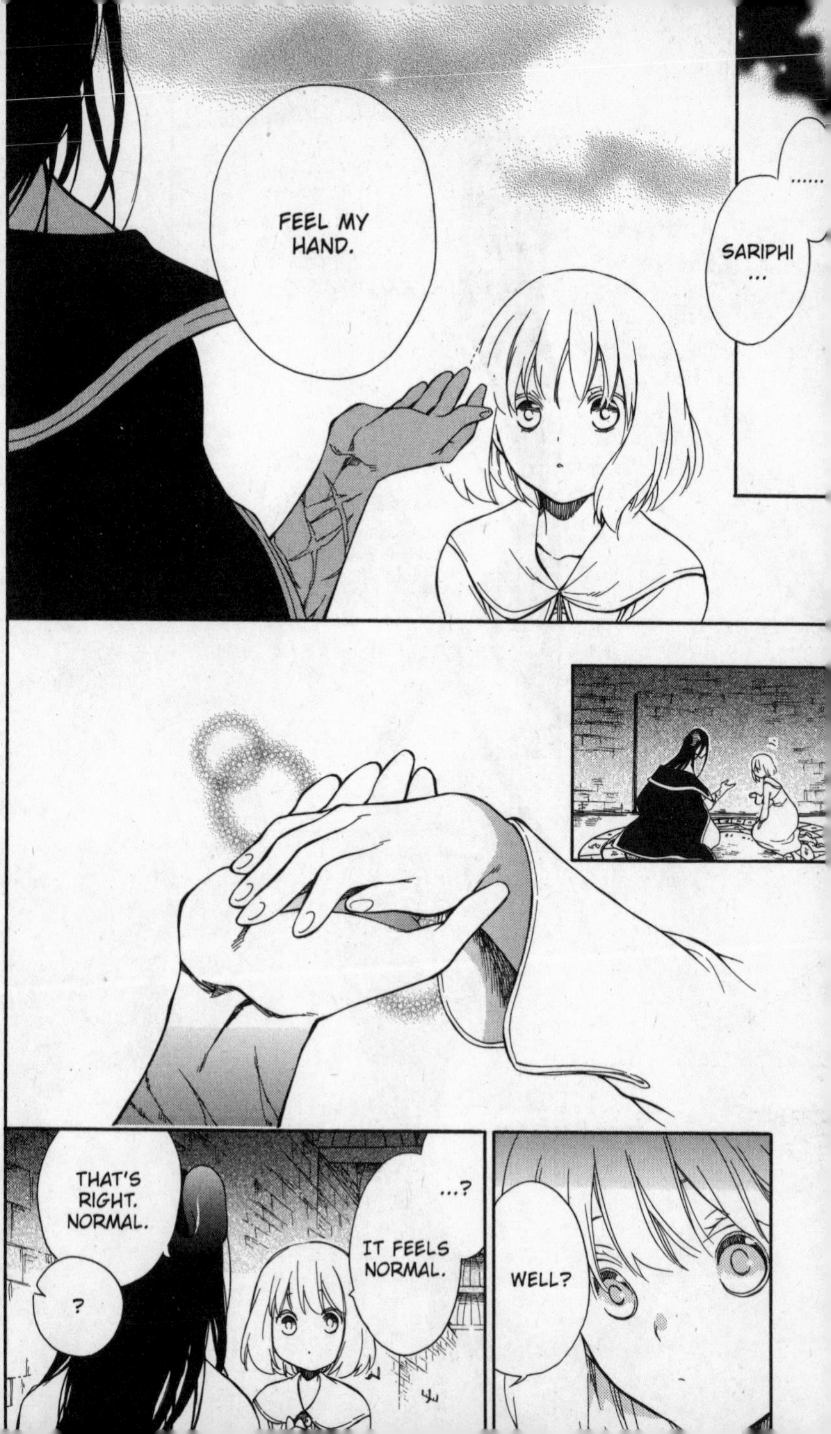
......
SARIPHI ...
FEEL MY HAND.
WELL?
...?
IT FEELS NORMAL.
THAT'S RIGHT. NORMAL.
?

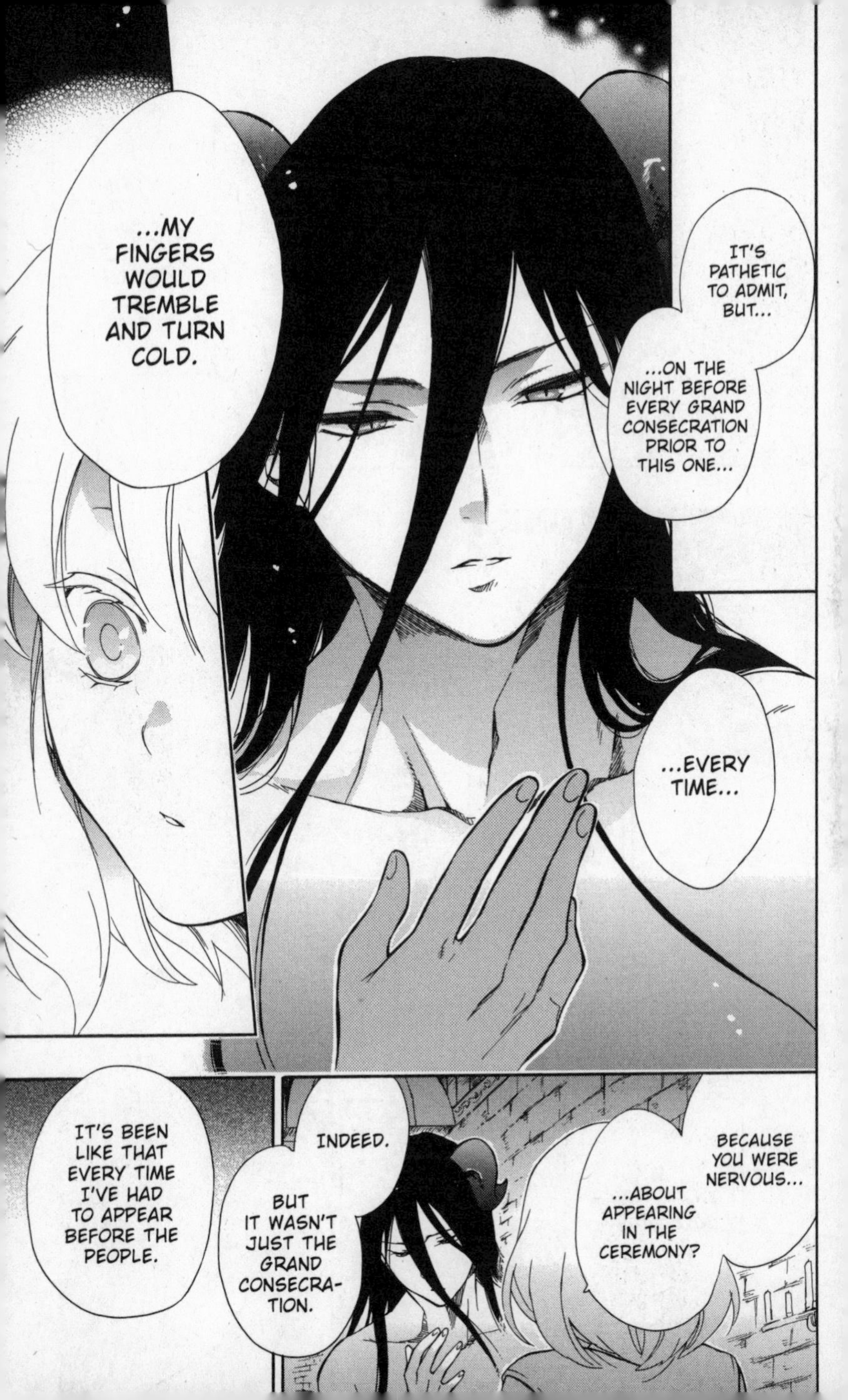
IT'S PATHETIC TO ADMIT, BUT...
...ON THE NIGHT BEFORE EVERY GRAND CONSECRATION PRIOR TO THIS ONE...
...EVERY TIME...
...MY FINGERS WOULD TREMBLE AND TURN COLD.
BECAUSE YOU WERE NERVOUS...
...ABOUT APPEARING IN THE CEREMONY?
INDEED.
BUT IT WASN'T JUST THE GRAND CONSECRATION.
IT'S BEEN LIKE THAT EVERY TIME I'VE HAD TO APPEAR BEFORE THE PEOPLE.

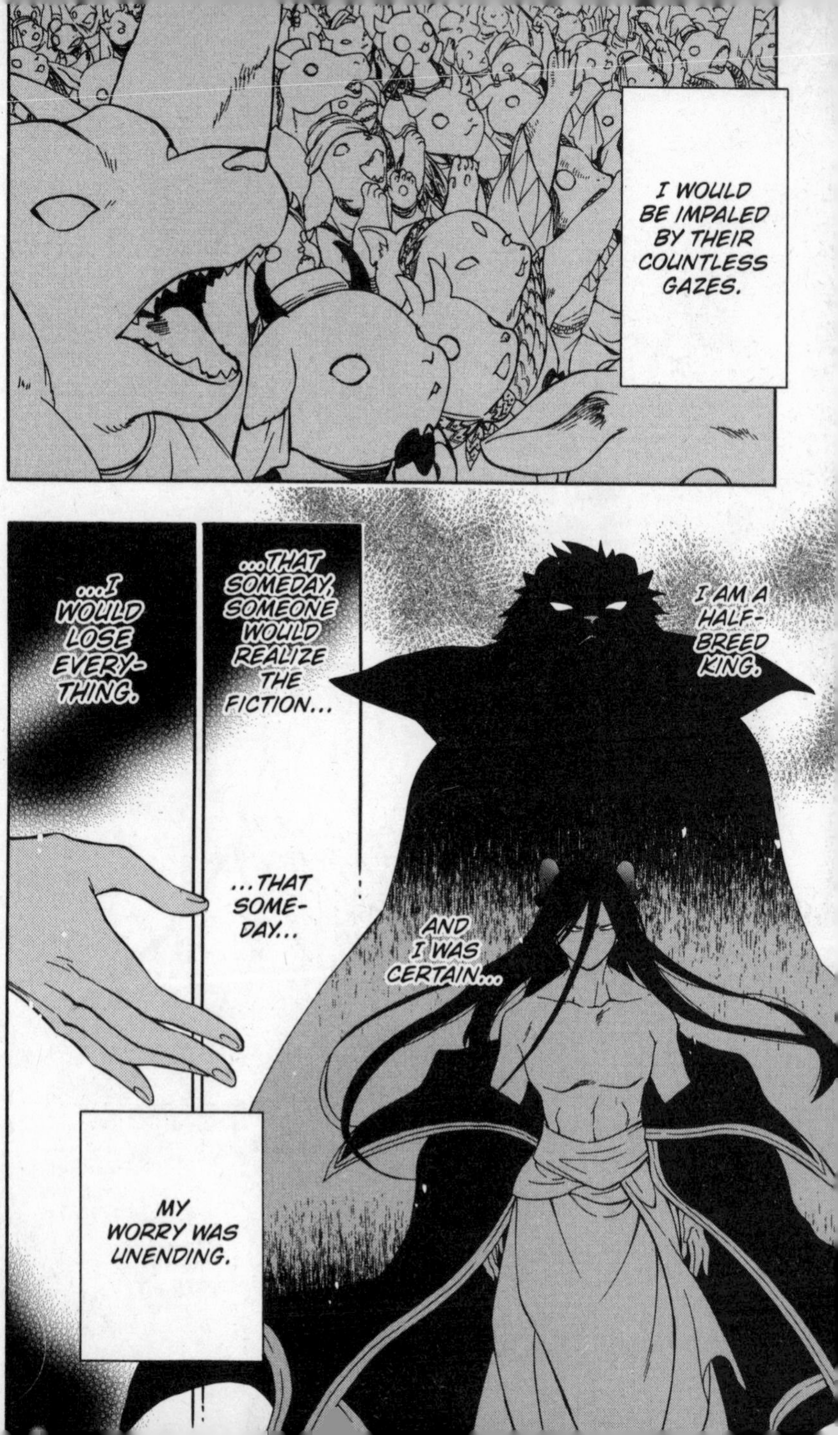
I WOULD BE IMPALED BY THEIR COUNTLESS GAZES.
I AM A HALF-BREED KING.
AND I WAS CERTAIN...
...THAT SOME-DAY...
...THAT SOMEDAY, SOMEONE WOULD REALIZE THE FICTION...
...I WOULD LOSE EVERY-THING.
MY WORRY WAS UNENDING.

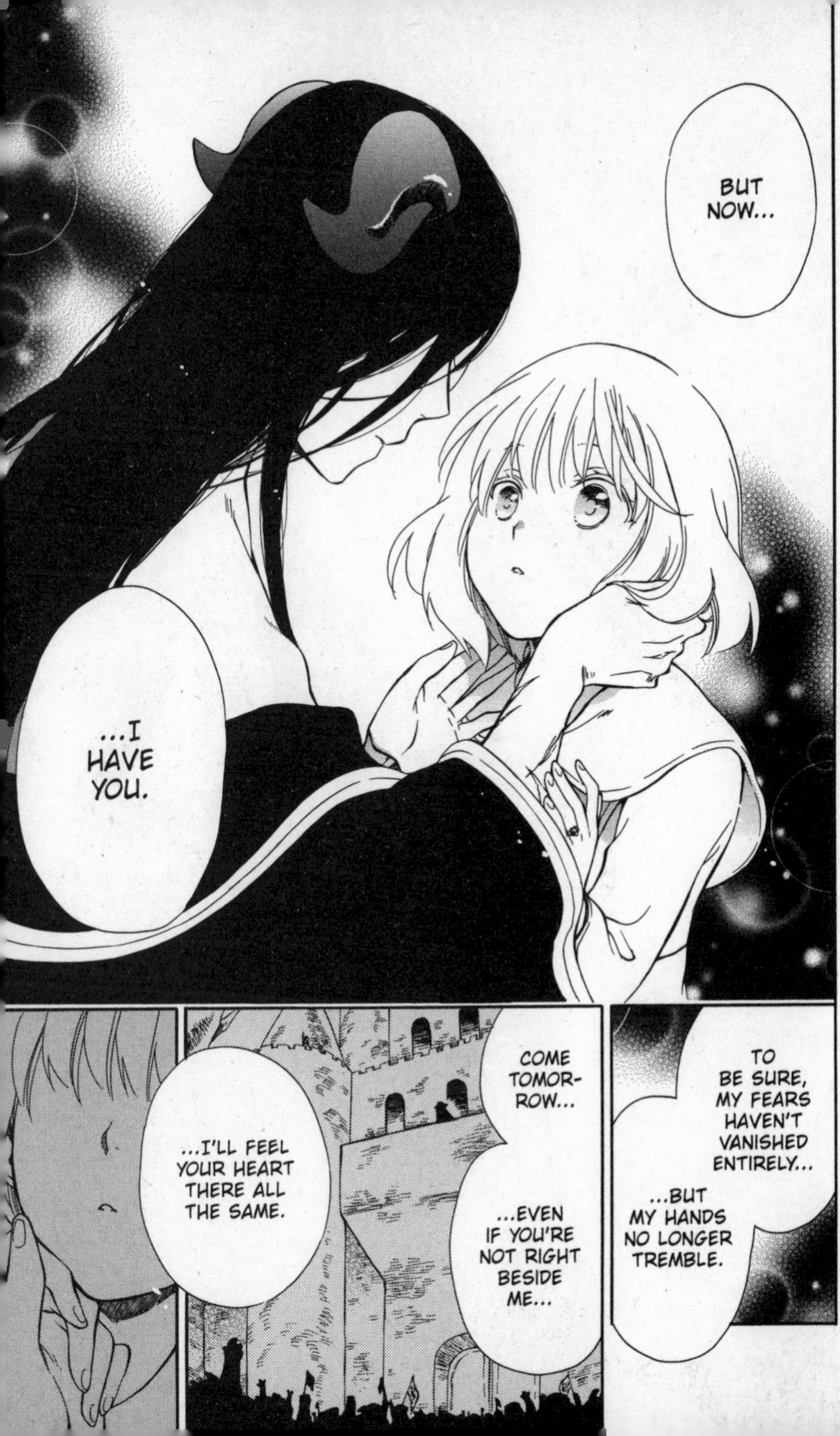
BUT NOW...
...I HAVE YOU.
TO BE SURE, MY FEARS HAVEN'T VANISHED ENTIRELY...
...BUT MY HANDS NO LONGER TREMBLE.
COME TOMOR-ROW...
...EVEN IF YOU'RE NOT RIGHT BESIDE ME...
...I'LL FEEL YOUR HEART THERE ALL THE SAME.

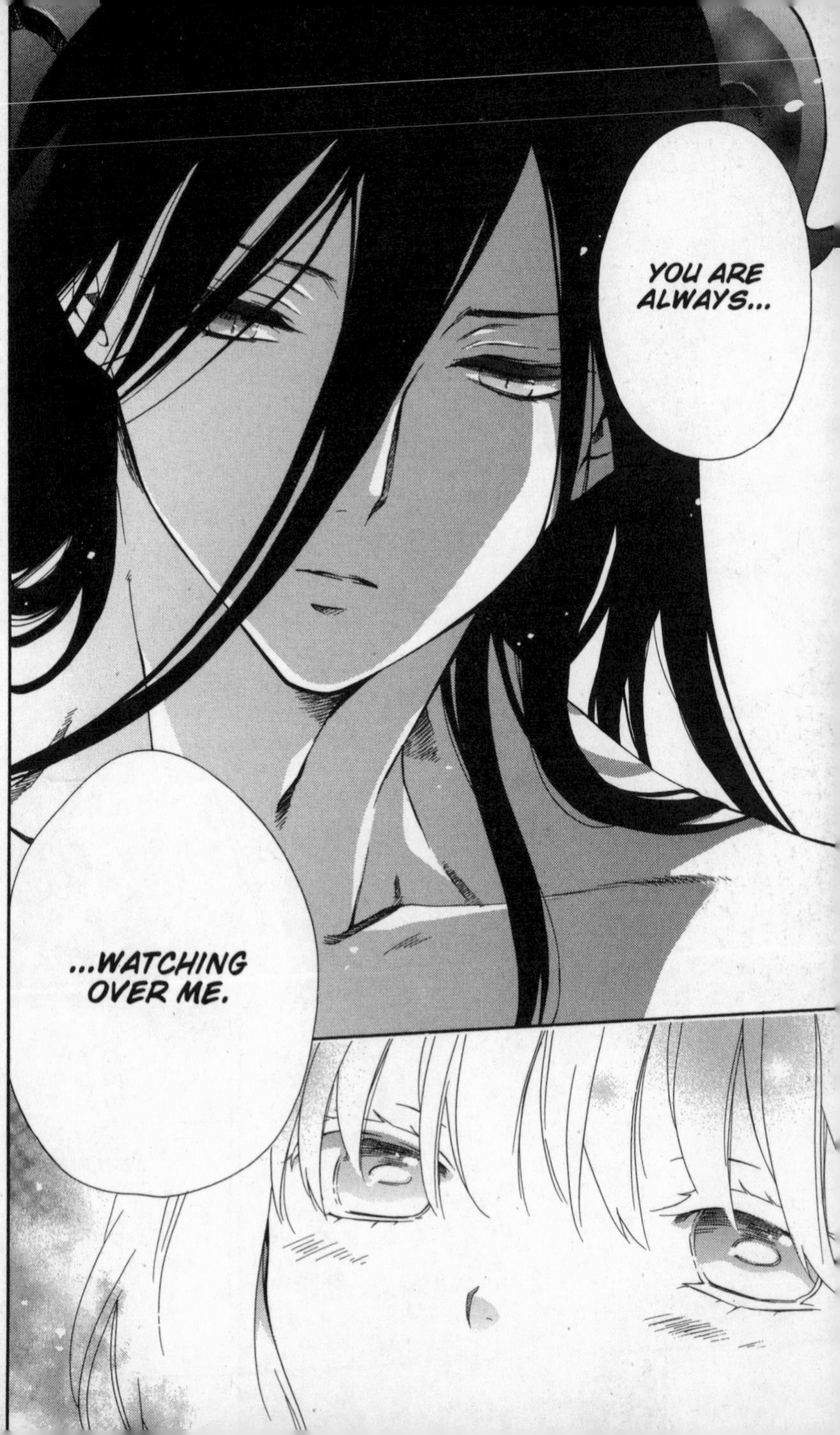
YOU ARE ALWAYS...
...WATCHING OVER ME.

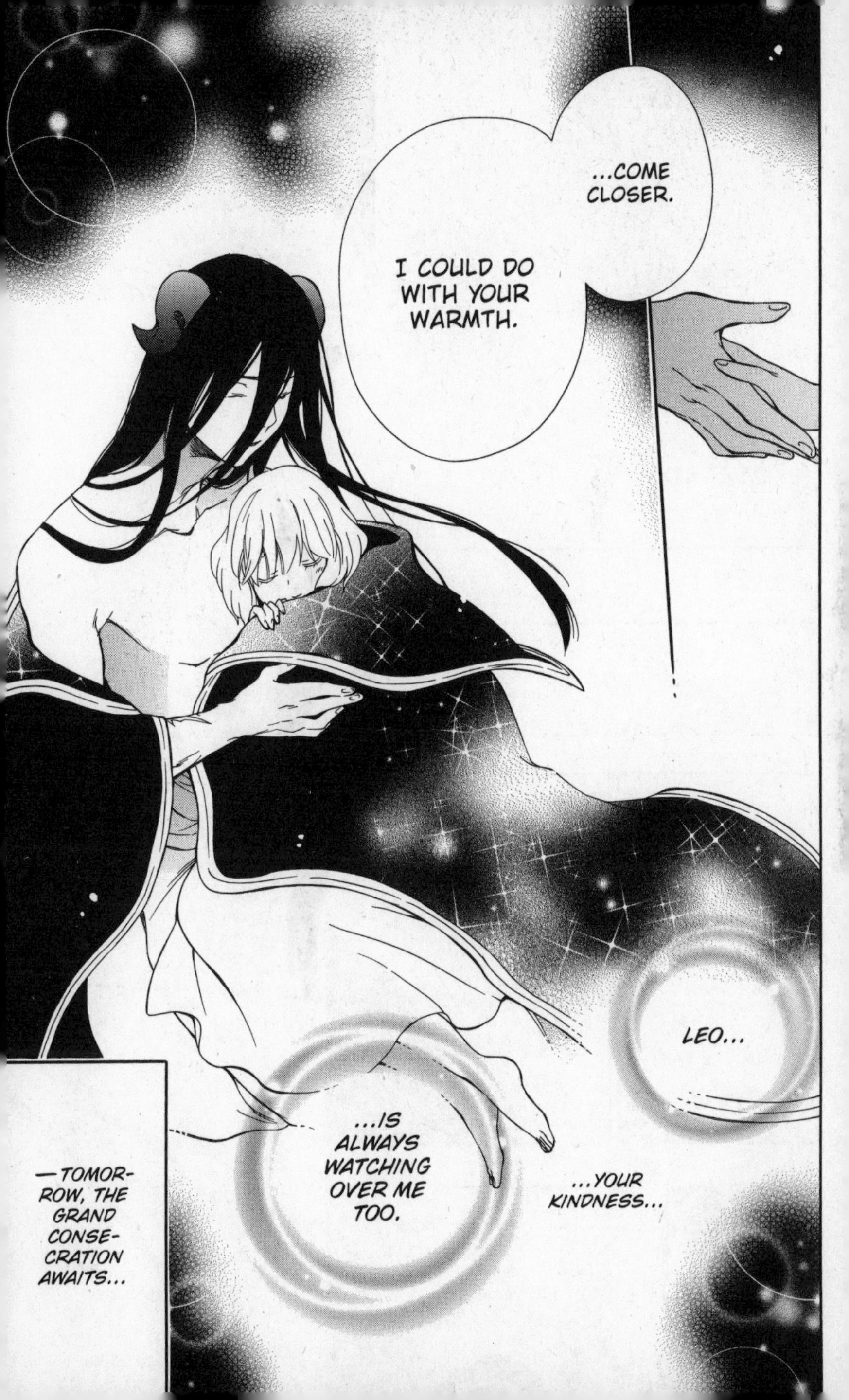
...COME CLOSER.
I COULD DO WITH YOUR WARMTH.
LEO...
...YOUR KINDNESS...
...IS ALWAYS WATCHING OVER ME TOO.
—TOMOR-ROW, THE GRAND CONSE-CRATION AWAITS...

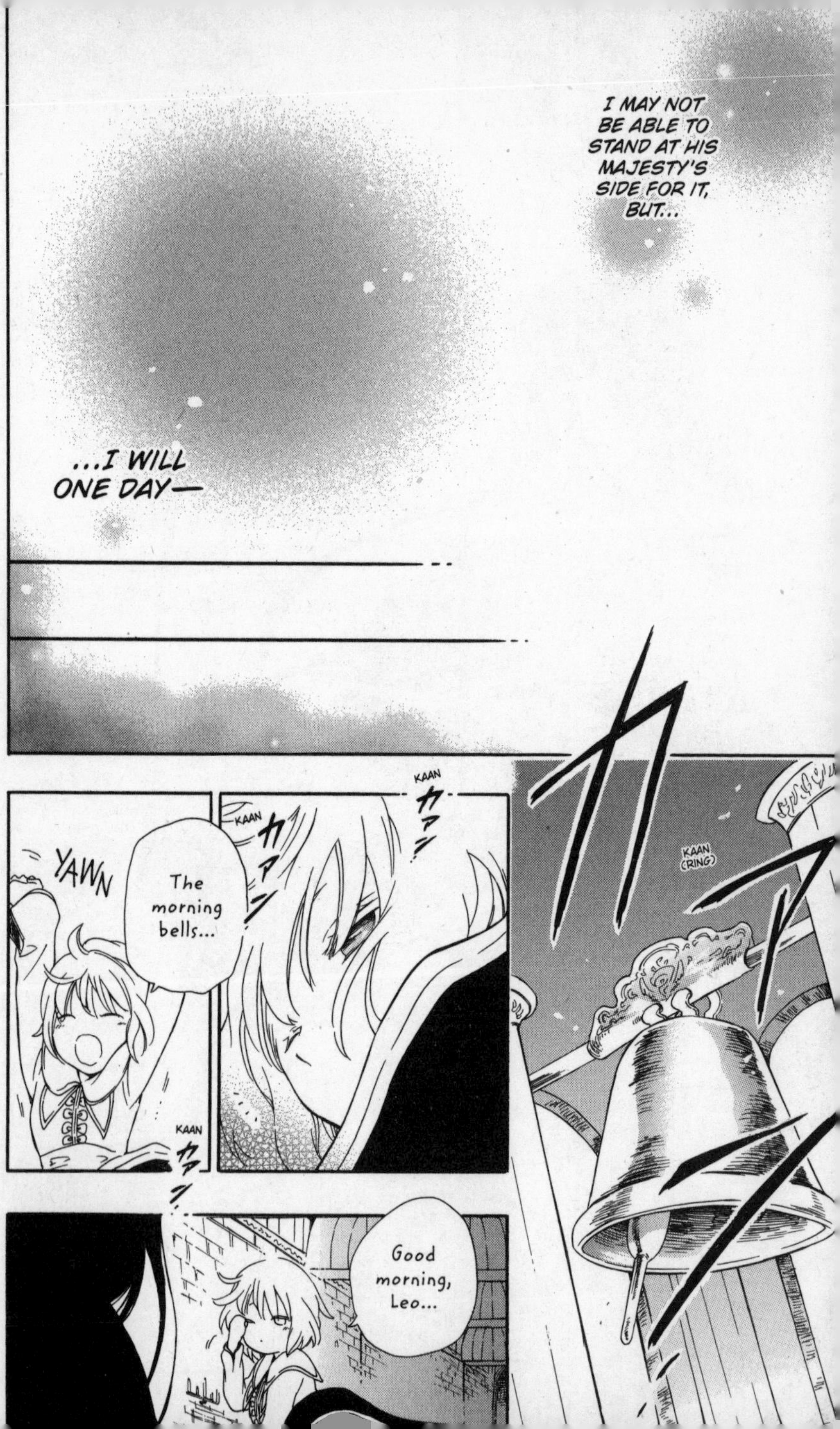
I MAY NOT BE ABLE TO STAND AT HIS MAJESTY'S SIDE FOR IT, BUT...
...I WILL ONE DAY—
KAAN (RING)
KAAN
KAAN
The morning bells...
YAWN
KAAN
Good morning, Leo...

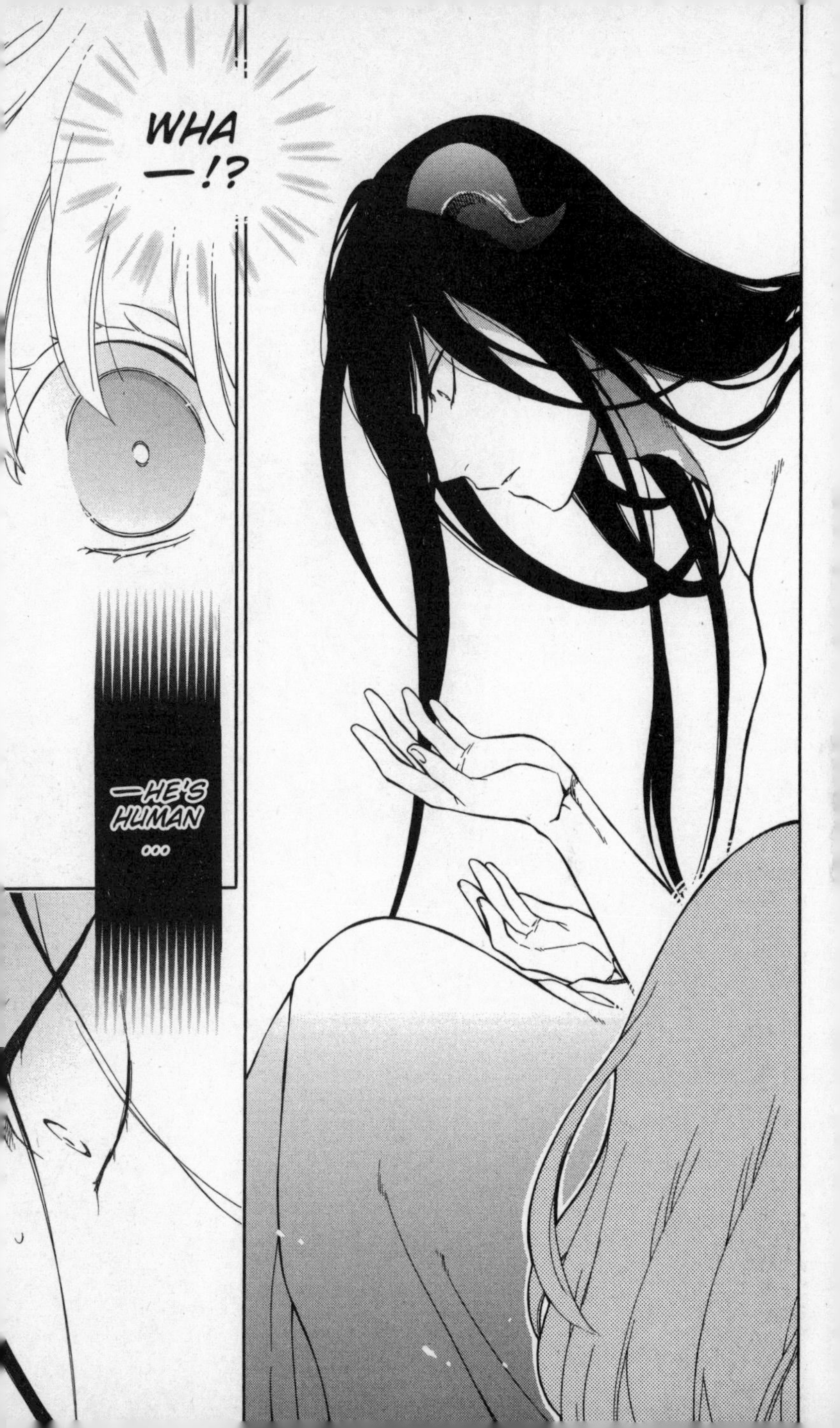
WHA—!?
—HE'S HUMAN...

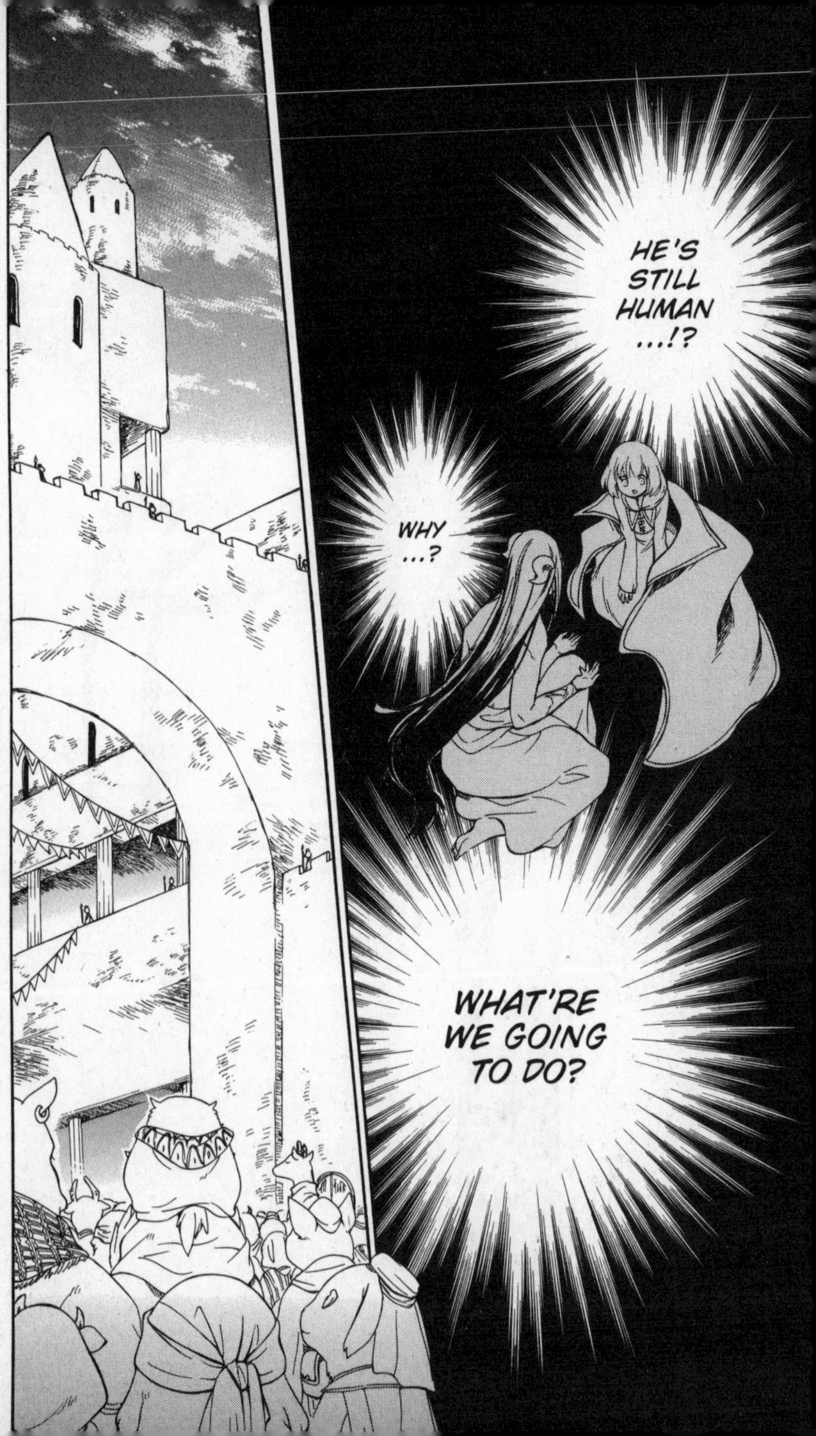
HE'S STILL HUMAN ...!?
WHY ...?
WHAT'RE WE GOING TO DO?

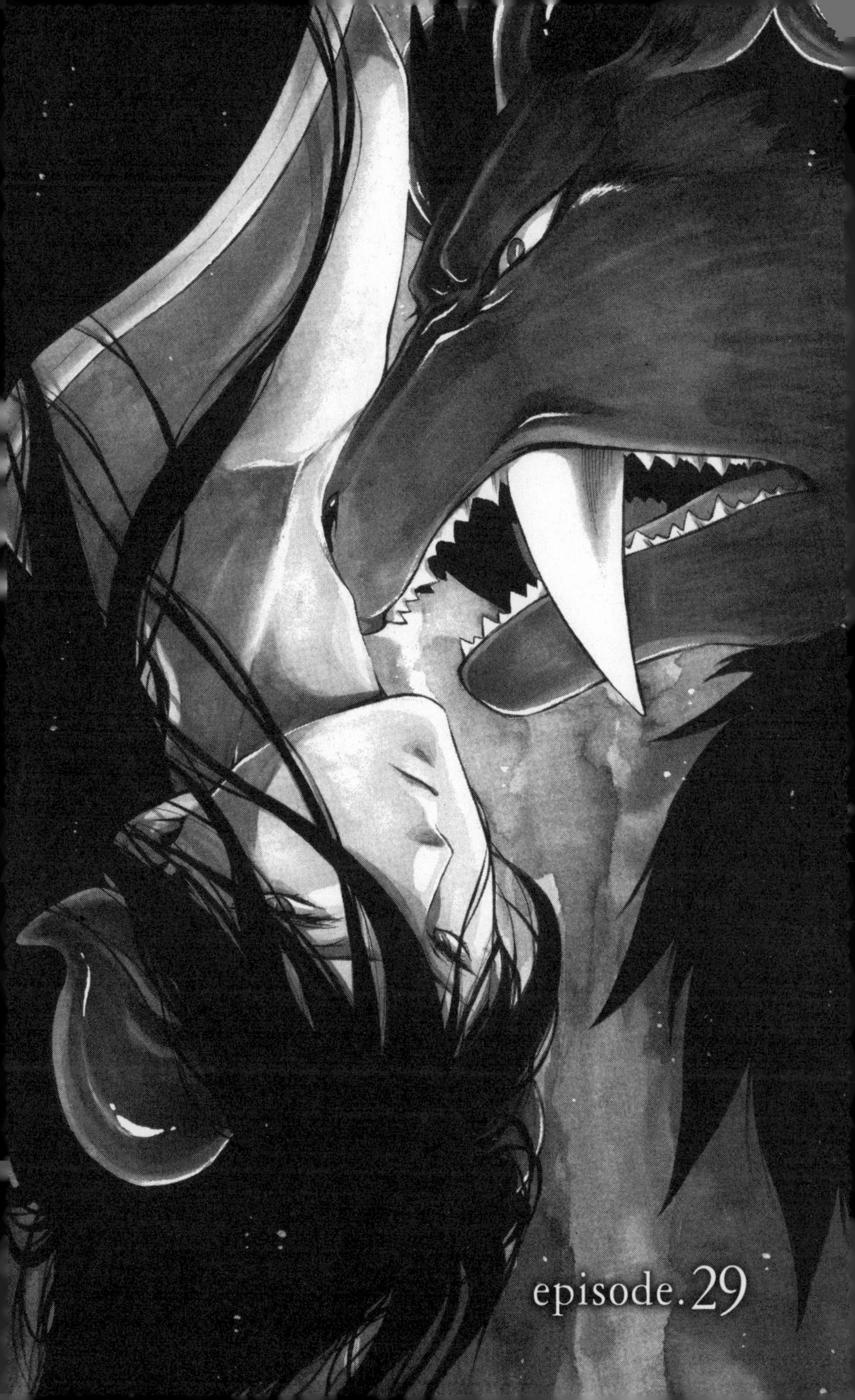
episode. 29

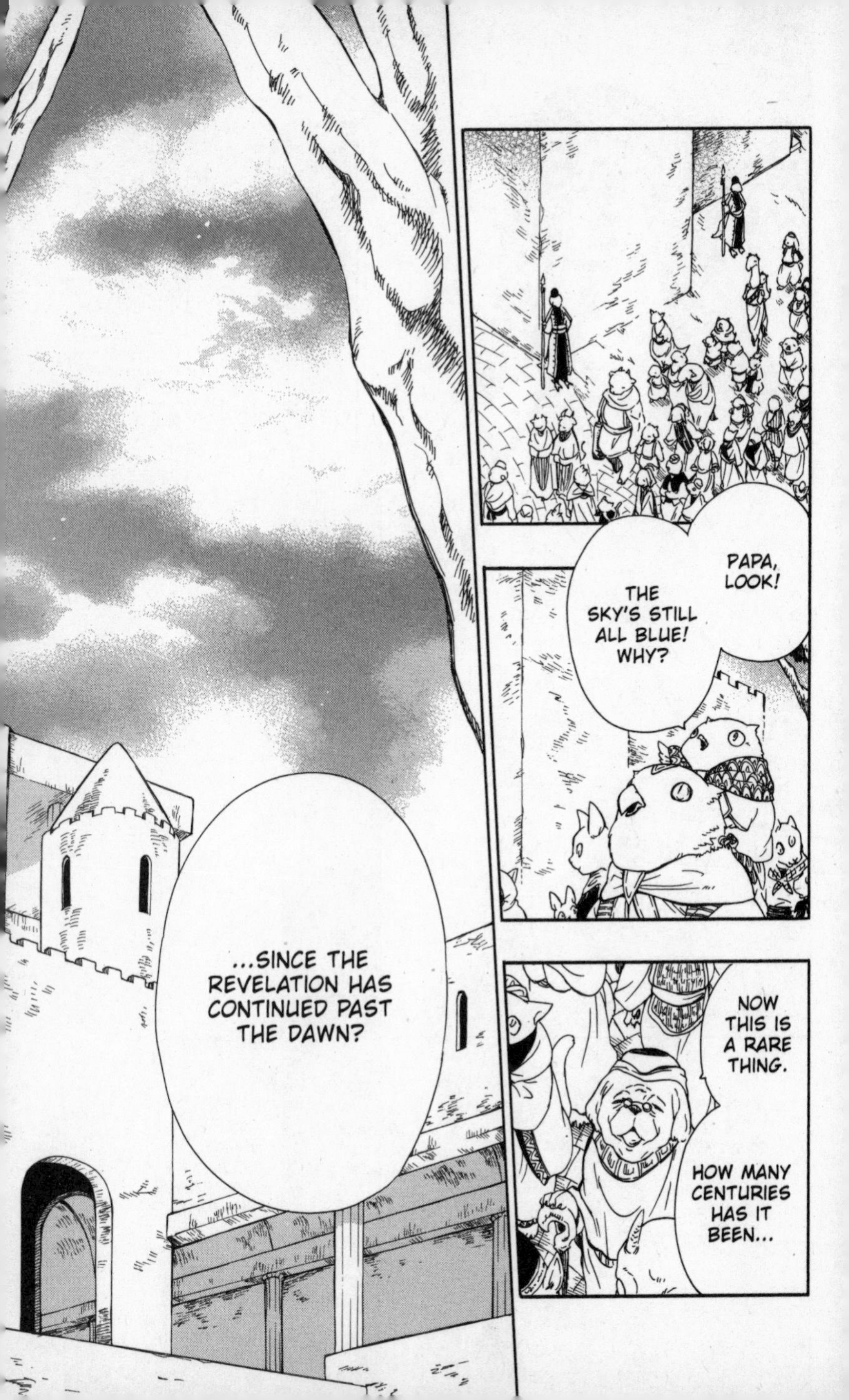
PAPA, LOOK!
THE SKY'S STILL ALL BLUE! WHY?
NOW THIS IS A RARE THING.
HOW MANY CENTURIES HAS IT BEEN...
...SINCE THE REVELATION HAS CONTINUED PAST THE DAWN?

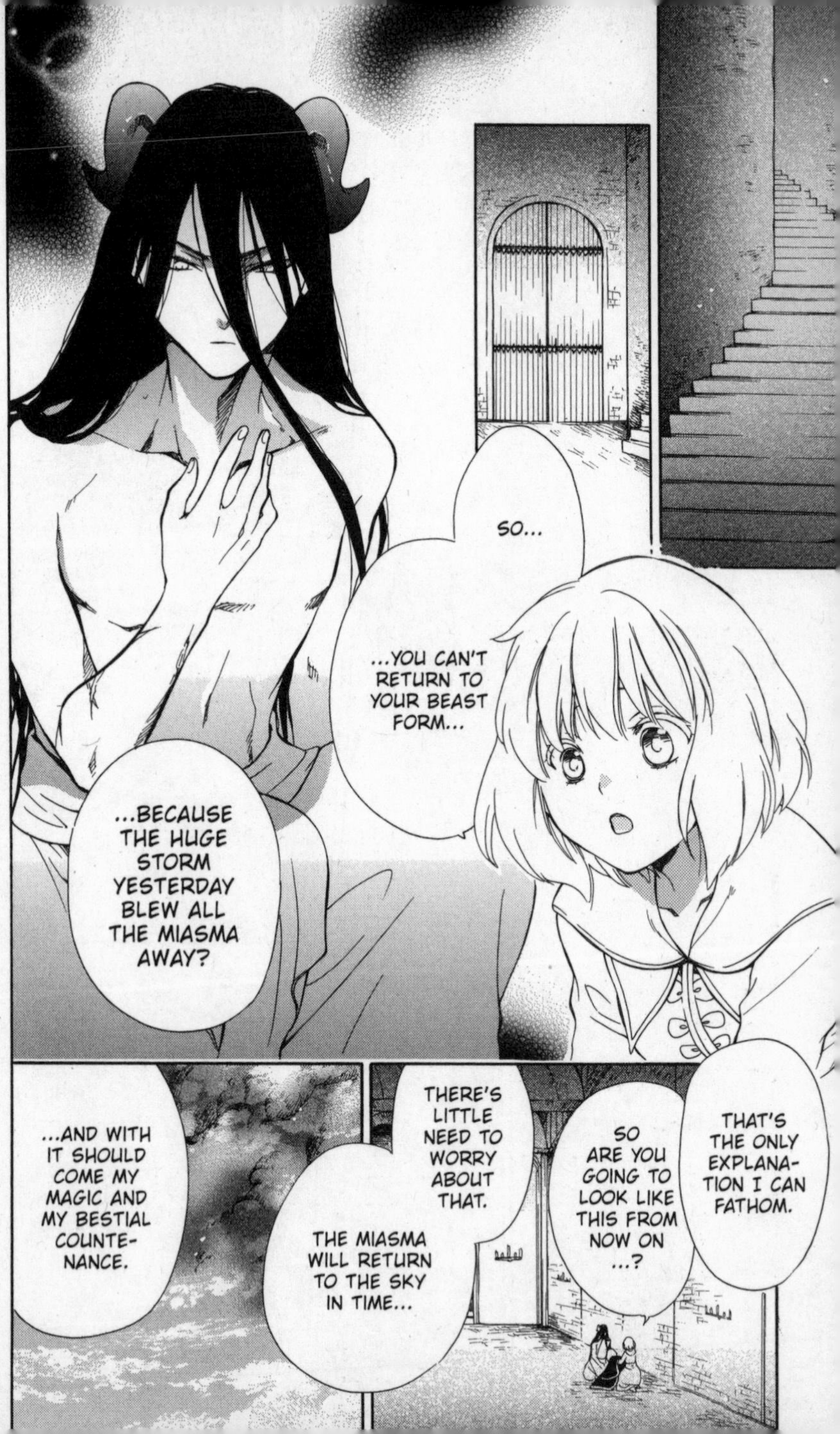
SO...
...YOU CAN'T RETURN TO YOUR BEAST FORM...
...BECAUSE THE HUGE STORM YESTERDAY BLEW ALL THE MIASMA AWAY?
THAT'S THE ONLY EXPLANA-TION I CAN FATHOM.
SO ARE YOU GOING TO LOOK LIKE THIS FROM NOW ON ...?
THERE'S LITTLE NEED TO WORRY ABOUT THAT.
THE MIASMA WILL RETURN TO THE SKY IN TIME...
...AND WITH IT SHOULD COME MY MAGIC AND MY BESTIAL COUNTE-NANCE.

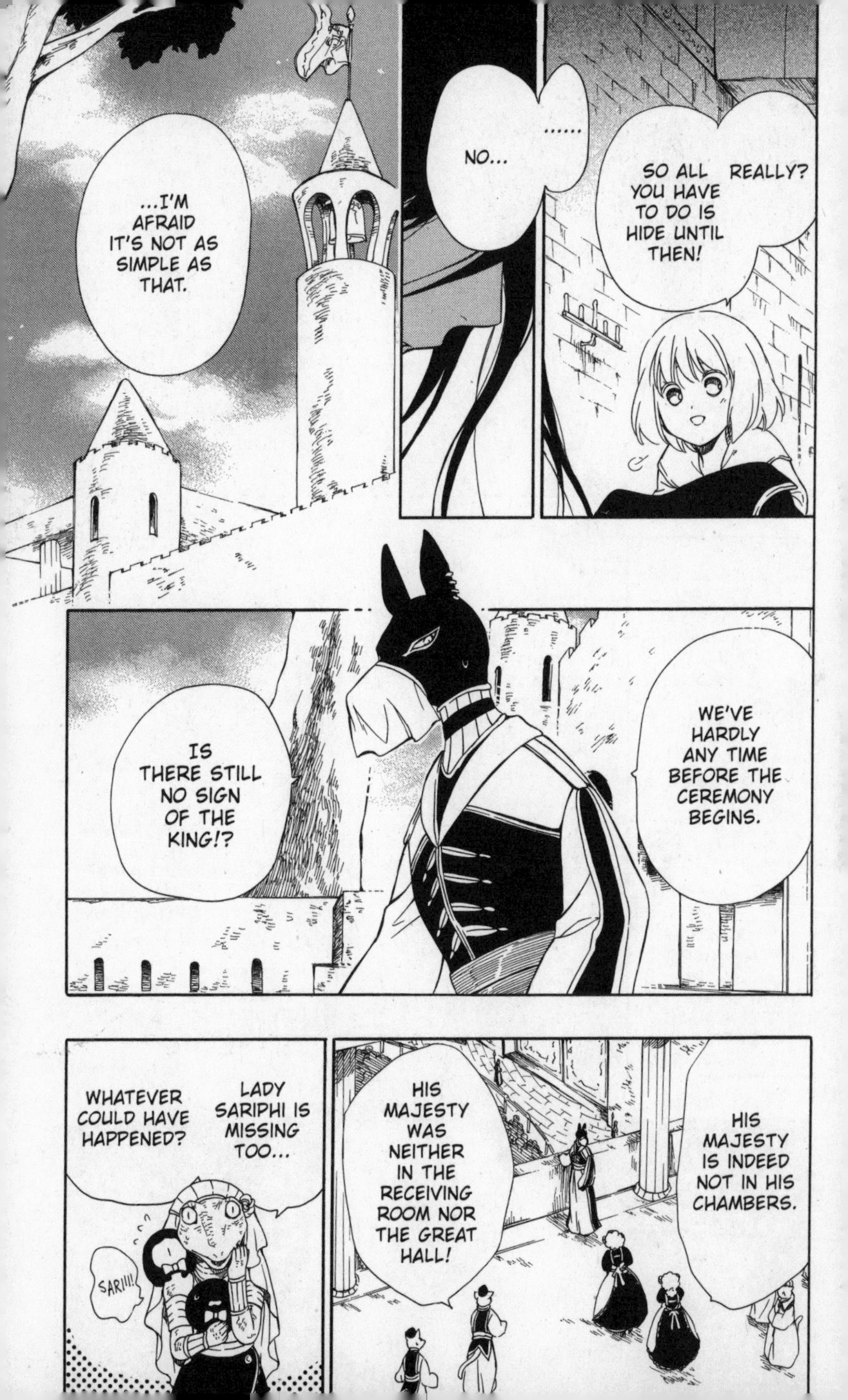
REALLY?
SO ALL YOU HAVE TO DO IS HIDE UNTIL THEN!
......
NO...
...I'M AFRAID IT'S NOT AS SIMPLE AS THAT.
WE'VE HARDLY ANY TIME BEFORE THE CEREMONY BEGINS.
IS THERE STILL NO SIGN OF THE KING!?
HIS MAJESTY IS INDEED NOT IN HIS CHAMBERS.
HIS MAJESTY WAS NEITHER IN THE RECEIVING ROOM NOR THE GREAT HALL!
LADY SARIPHI IS MISSING TOO...
WHATEVER COULD HAVE HAPPENED?
SARI!!!

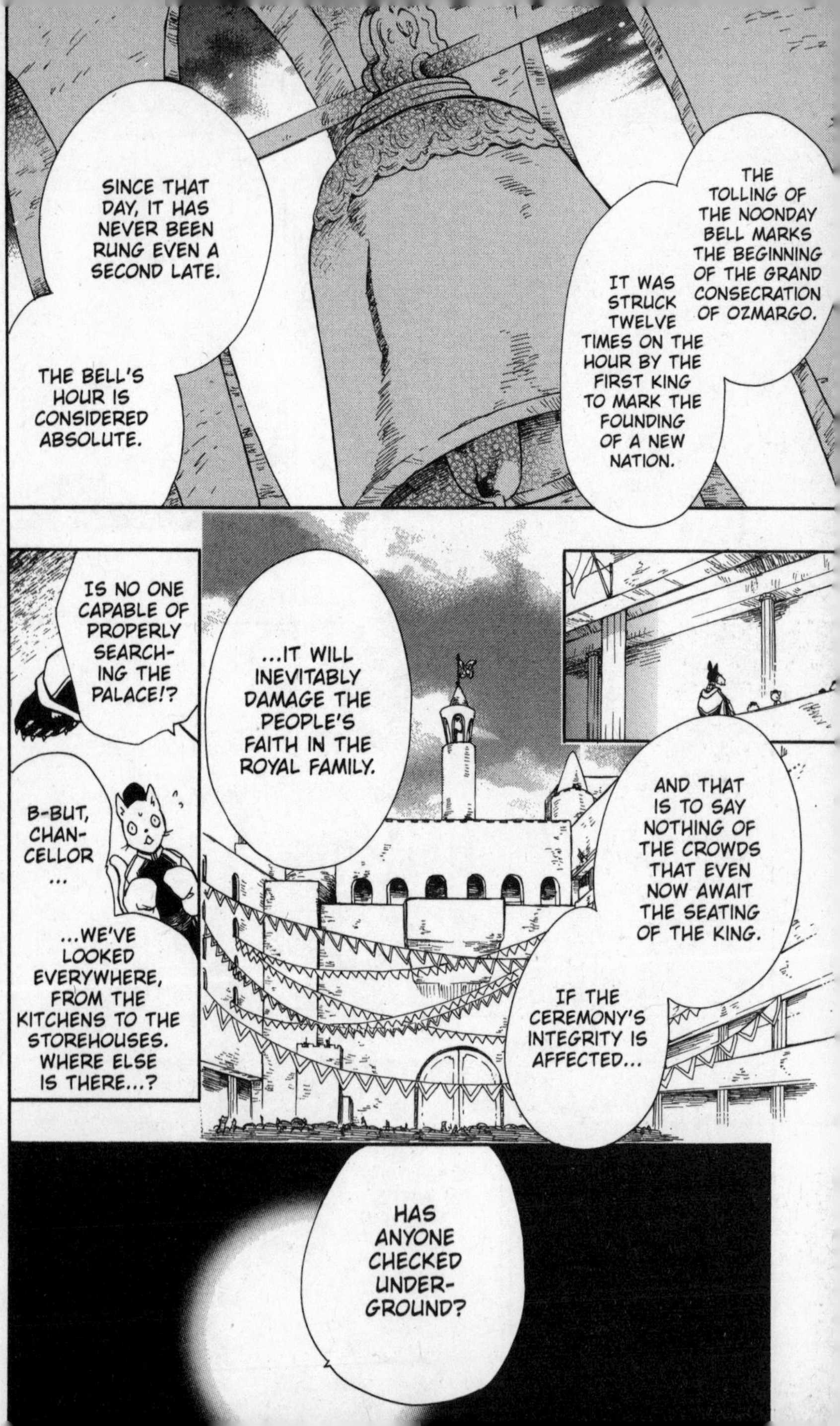
THE TOLLING OF THE NOONDAY BELL MARKS THE BEGINNING OF THE GRAND CONSECRATION OF OZMARGO.
IT WAS STRUCK TWELVE TIMES ON THE HOUR BY THE FIRST KING TO MARK THE FOUNDING OF A NEW NATION.
SINCE THAT DAY, IT HAS NEVER BEEN RUNG EVEN A SECOND LATE.
THE BELL'S HOUR IS CONSIDERED ABSOLUTE.
IF THE CEREMONY'S INTEGRITY IS AFFECTED...
...IT WILL INEVITABLY DAMAGE THE PEOPLE'S FAITH IN THE ROYAL FAMILY.
AND THAT IS TO SAY NOTHING OF THE CROWDS THAT EVEN NOW AWAIT THE SEATING OF THE KING.
IS NO ONE CAPABLE OF PROPERLY SEARCH-ING THE PALACE!?
B-BUT, CHAN-CELLOR...
...WE'VE LOOKED EVERYWHERE, FROM THE KITCHENS TO THE STOREHOUSES. WHERE ELSE IS THERE...?
HAS ANYONE CHECKED UNDER-GROUND?

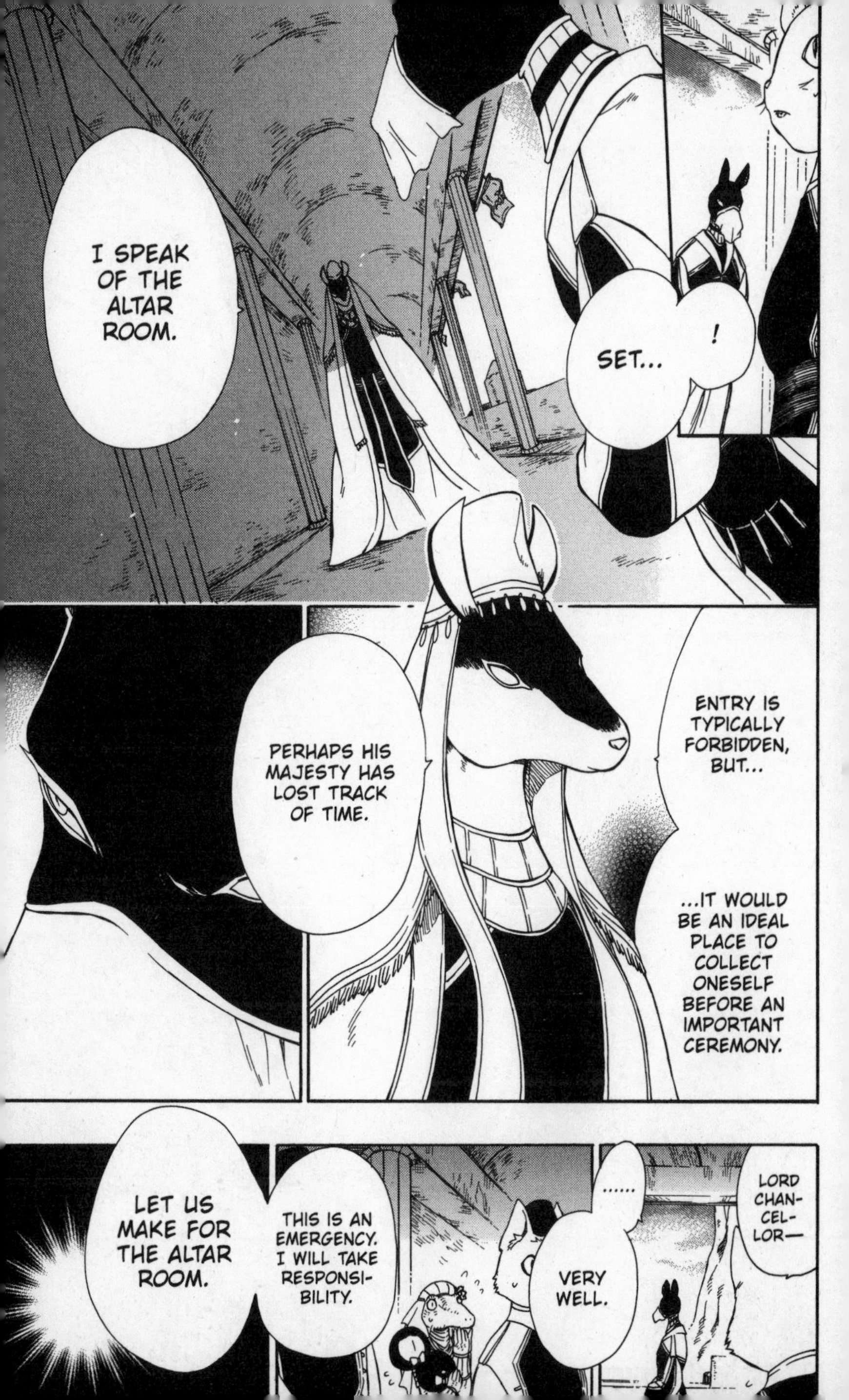
SET... !
I SPEAK OF THE ALTAR ROOM.
ENTRY IS TYPICALLY FORBIDDEN, BUT...
...IT WOULD BE AN IDEAL PLACE TO COLLECT ONESELF BEFORE AN IMPORTANT CEREMONY.
PERHAPS HIS MAJESTY HAS LOST TRACK OF TIME.
LORD CHAN-CEL-LOR—
......
VERY WELL.
THIS IS AN EMERGENCY. I WILL TAKE RESPONSI-BILITY.
LET US MAKE FOR THE ALTAR ROOM.

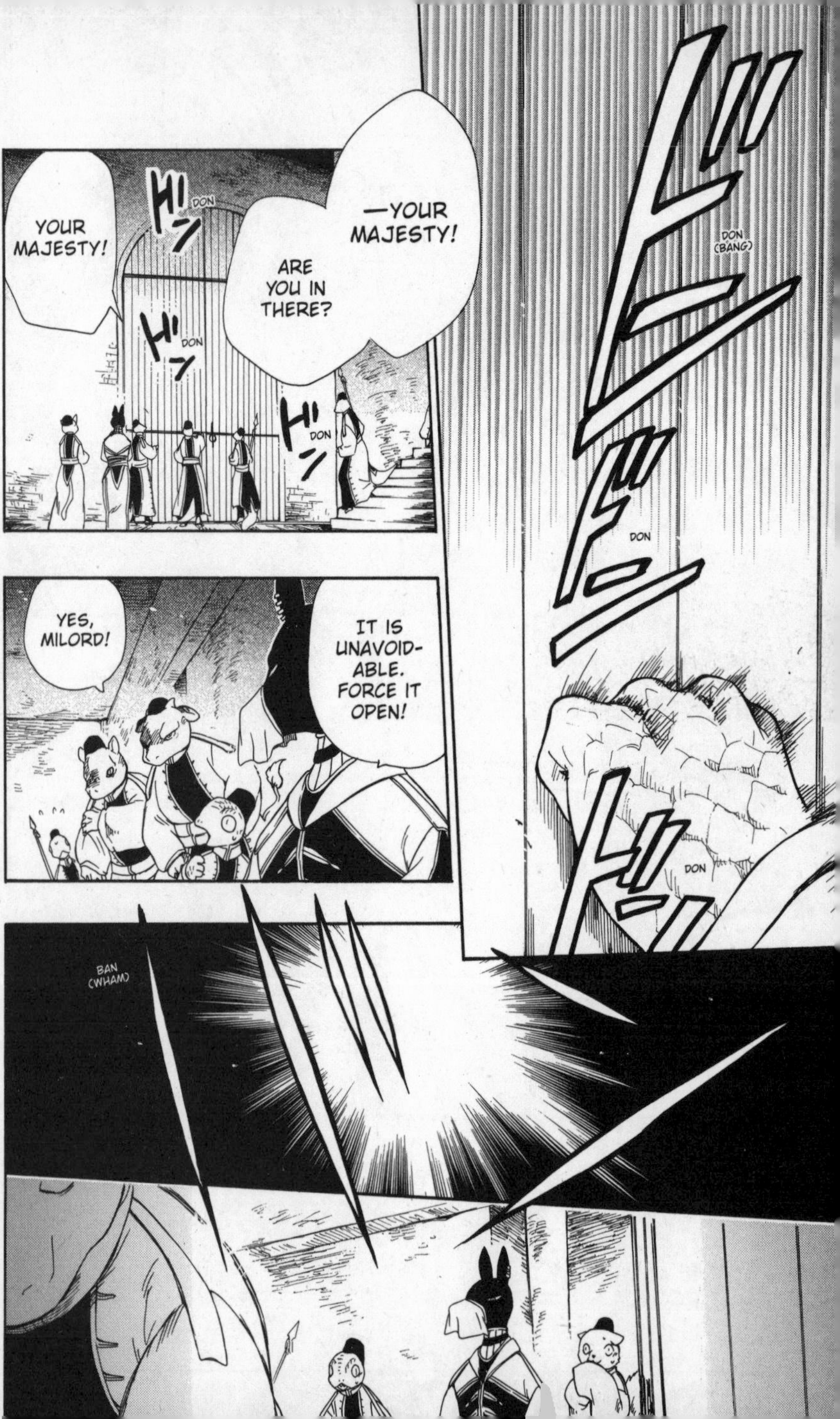
DON (BANG)
DON
DON
—YOUR MAJESTY!
ARE YOU IN THERE?
DON
YOUR MAJESTY!
DON
DON
IT IS UNAVOID-ABLE. FORCE IT OPEN!
YES, MILORD!
BAN (WHAM)

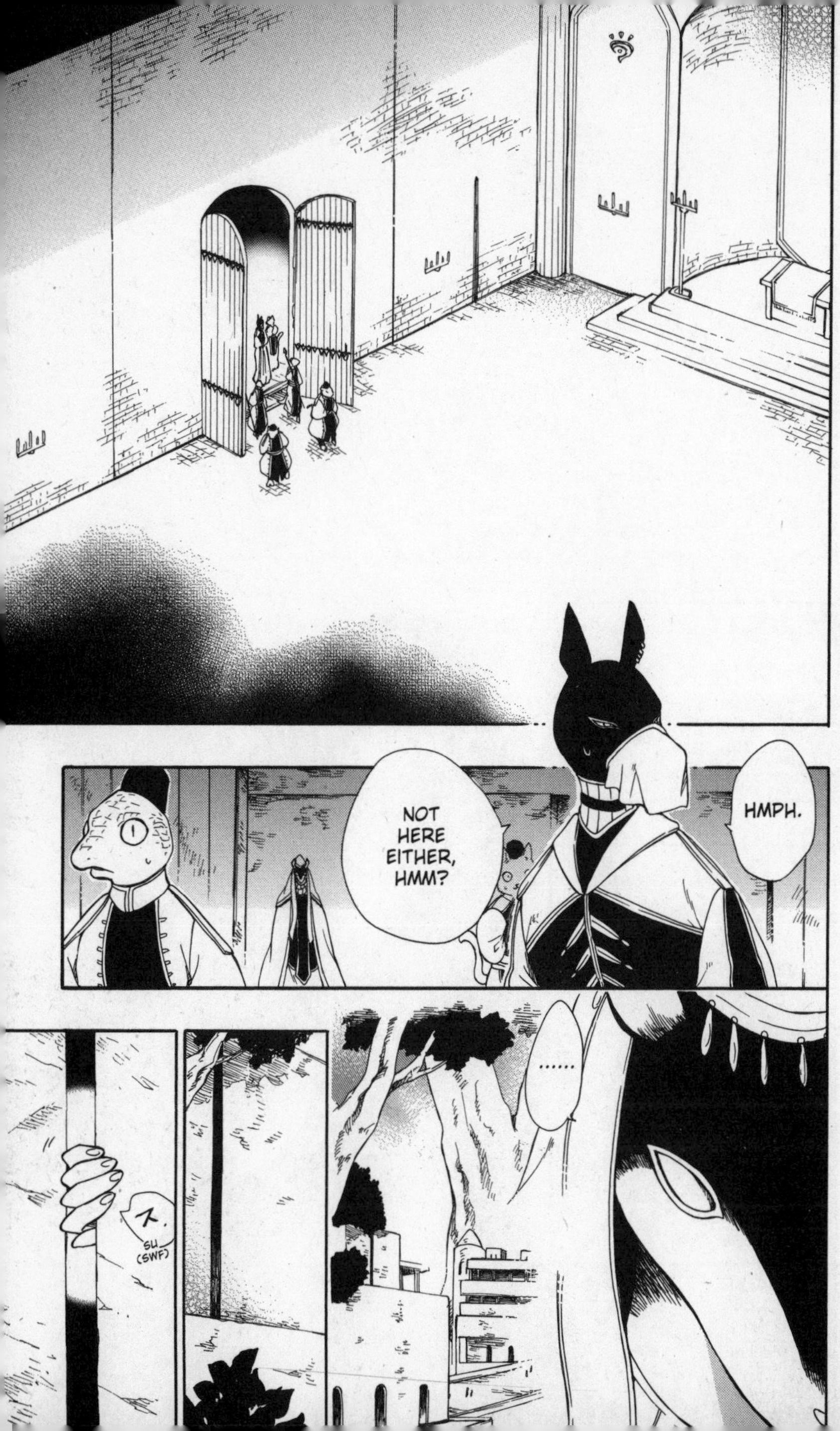
HMPH.
NOT HERE EITHER, HMM?
……
ス.
SU (SWF)

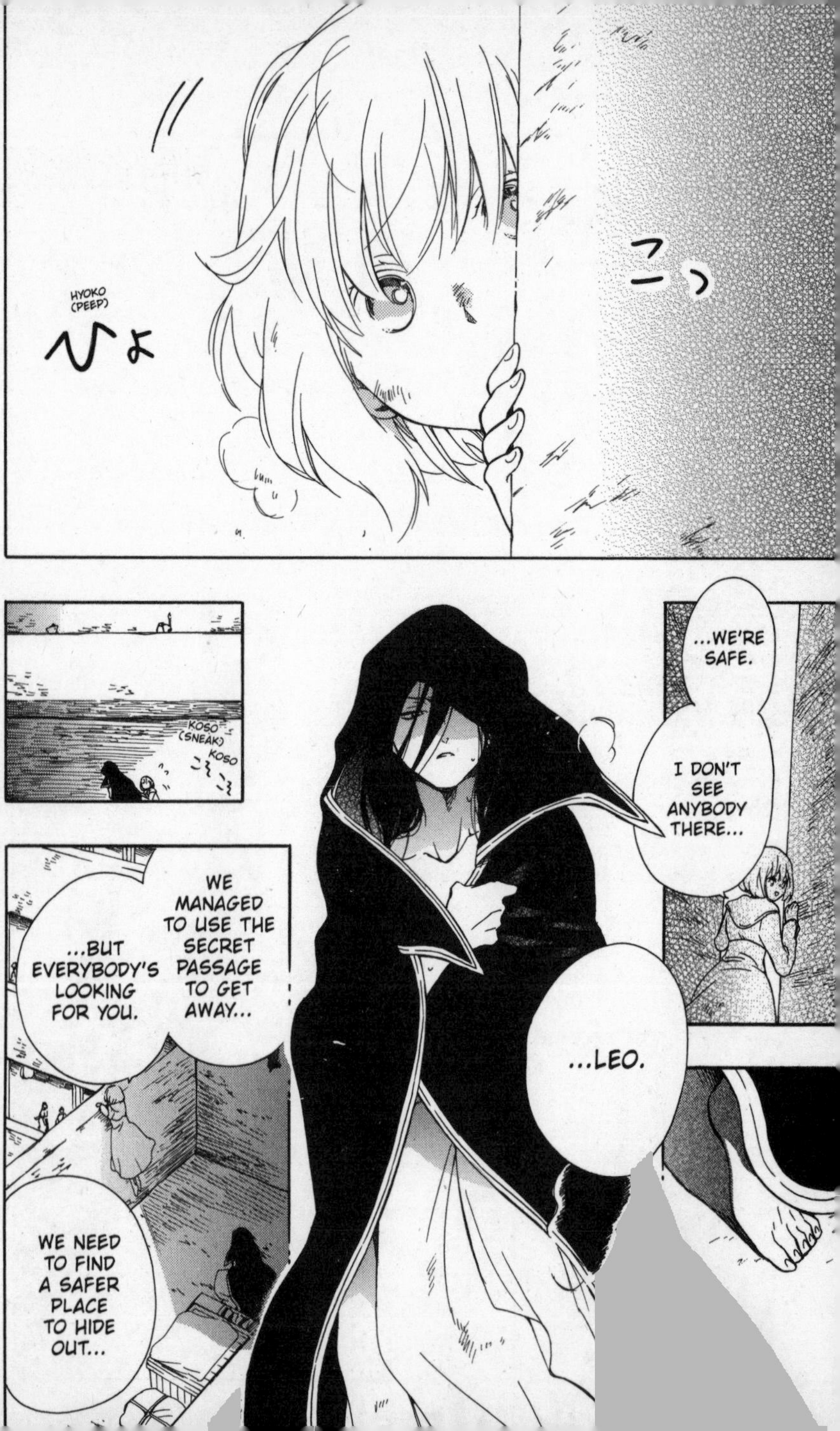
HYOKO (PEEP)
ひょ
...WE'RE SAFE.
I DON'T SEE ANYBODY THERE...
...LEO.
KOSO (SNEAK) KOSO
こそこそ
WE MANAGED TO USE THE SECRET PASSAGE TO GET AWAY...
...BUT EVERYBODY'S LOOKING FOR YOU.
WE NEED TO FIND A SAFER PLACE TO HIDE OUT...

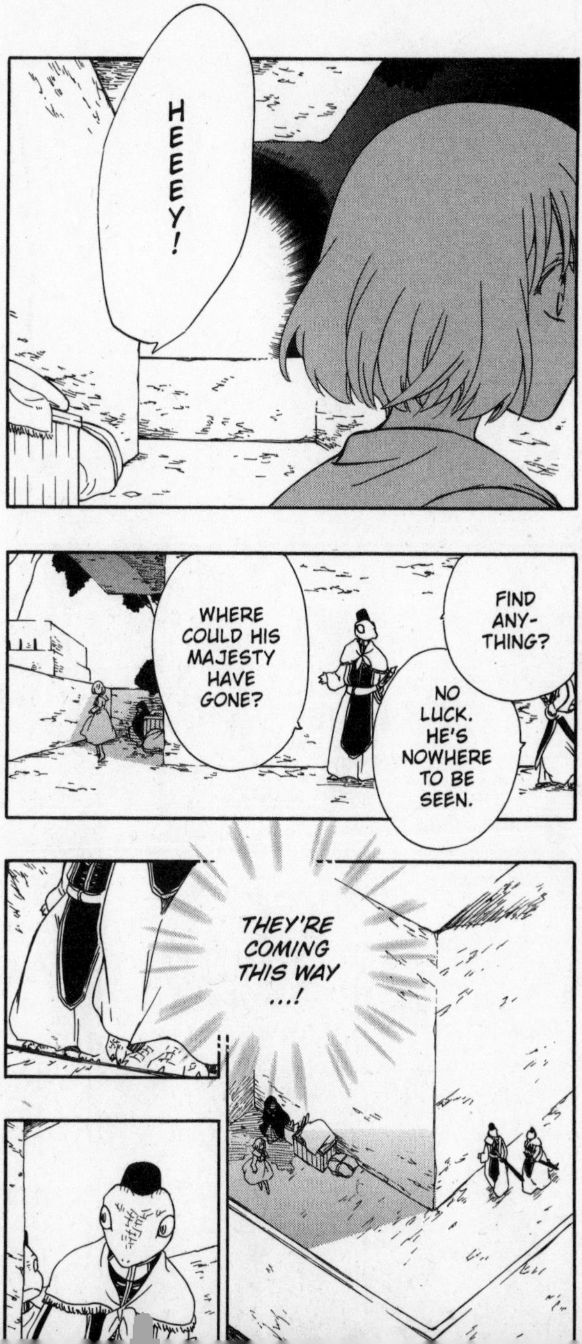
HEEEY!
FIND ANYTHING?
NO LUCK. HE'S NOWHERE TO BE SEEN.
WHERE COULD HIS MAJESTY HAVE GONE?
THEY'RE COMING THIS WAY ...!

AND SO, VOLUME FIVE COMES TO AN END. THE EDITOR WHO'S SUPPORTED ME SINCE BEFORE MY DEBUT IS MOVING ON, SO I'D LIKE TO TAKE THIS OPPORTUNITY TO THANK THEM FROM THE BOTTOM OF MY HEART. S-SAN, YOUR CHOOSING MY SUBMISSION IS WHAT BEGAN MY LIFE AS A MANGA ARTIST. THANK YOU SO MUCH FOR GUIDING THIS NOVICE FOR SO LONG.

AND TO MY NEW EDITOR, S-SAN (ANOTHER S-SAN!): I LOOK FORWARD TO WORKING WITH YOU!

NOW THEN, I PRAY I'LL SEE YOU ALL AGAIN IN VOLUME SIX. FAREWELL!

TOMOFUJI

(AND THANKS AS ALWAYS TO MY ASSISTANTS S-SAN AND O-SAN!)

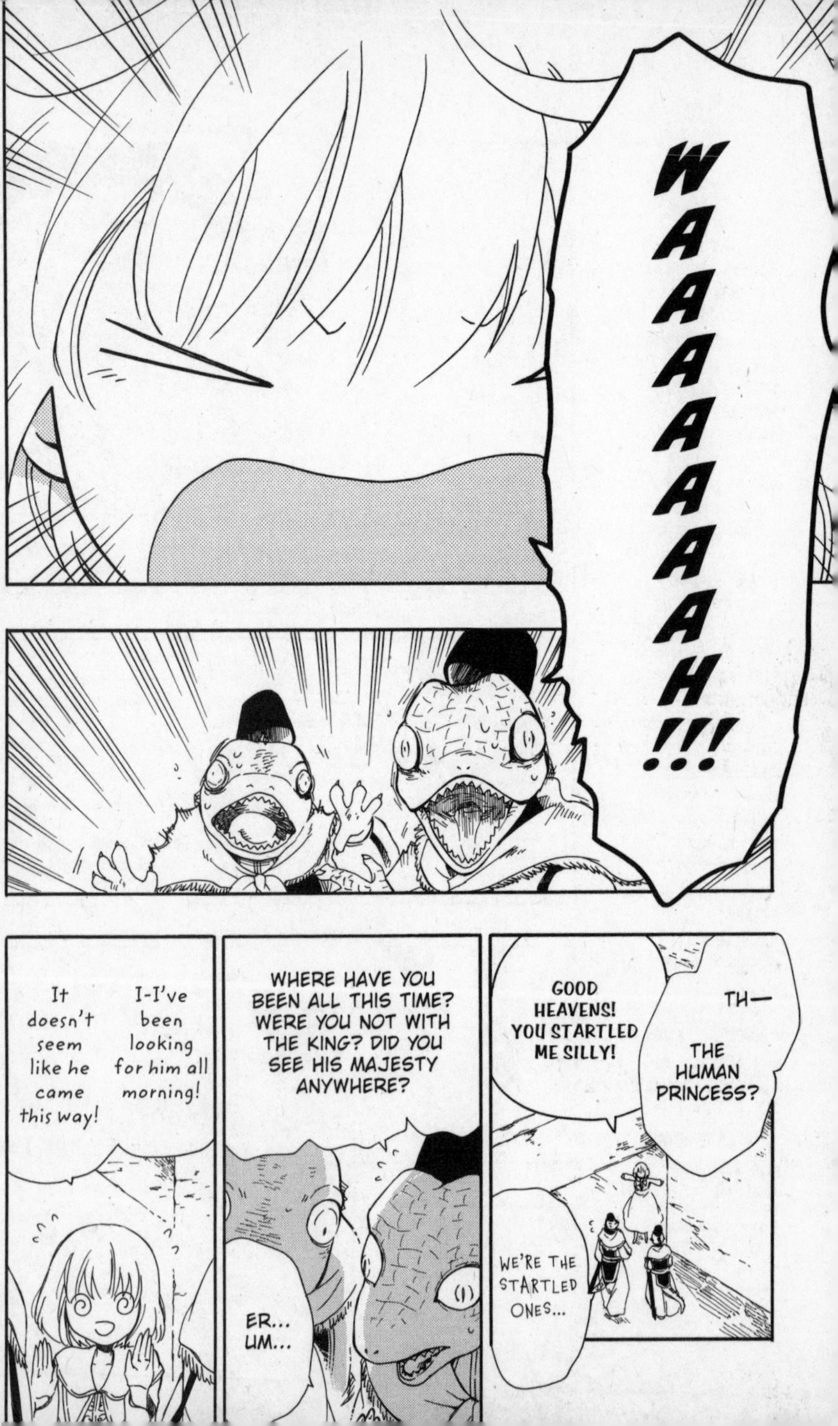
WAAAAAAAAH!!!
TH—
THE HUMAN PRINCESS?
GOOD HEAVENS! YOU STARTLED ME SILLY!
WE'RE THE STARTLED ONES...
WHERE HAVE YOU BEEN ALL THIS TIME? WERE YOU NOT WITH THE KING? DID YOU SEE HIS MAJESTY ANYWHERE?
ER... UM...
I-I've been looking for him all morning!
It doesn't seem like he came this way!

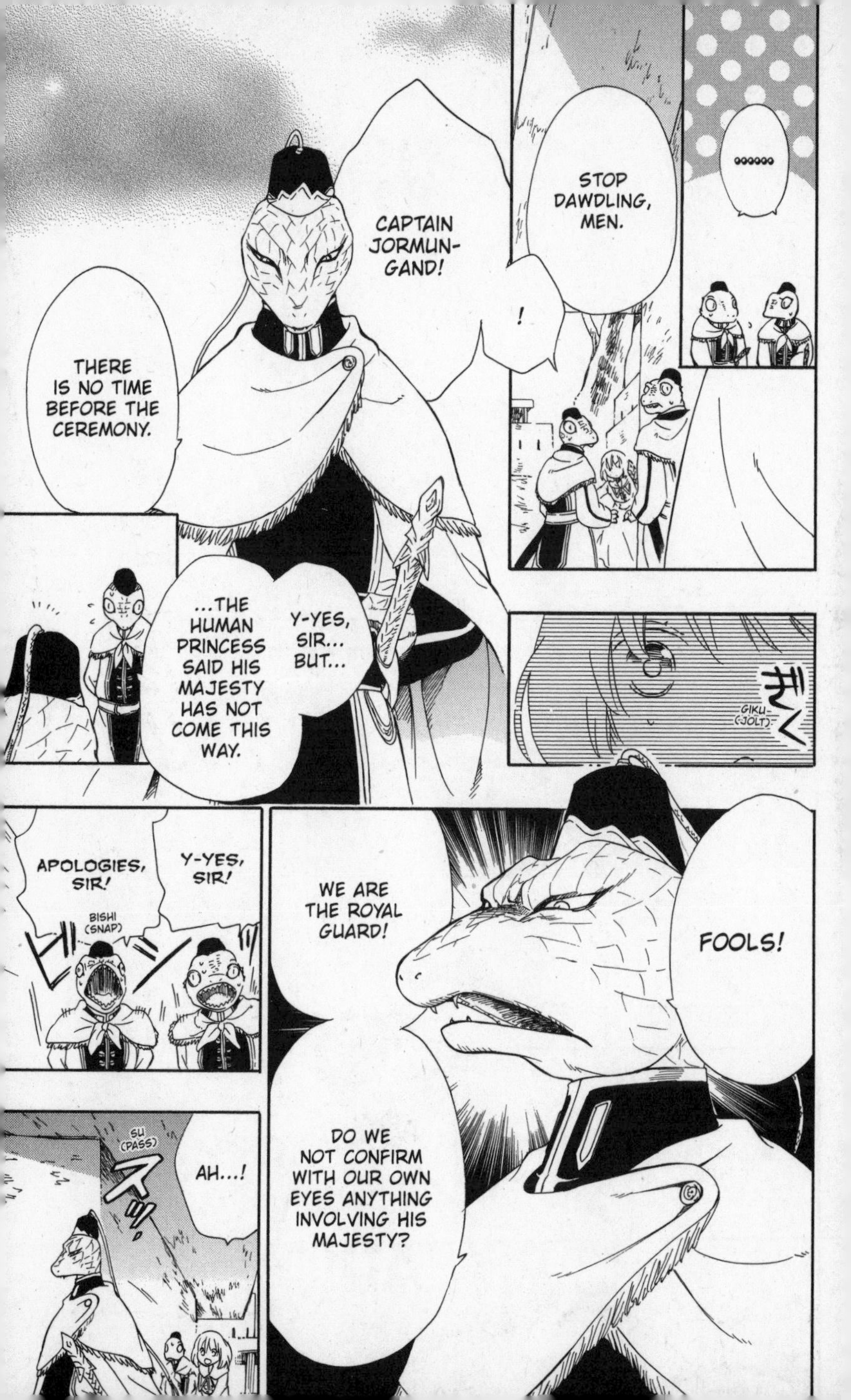
......
STOP DAWDLING, MEN.
!
CAPTAIN JORMUNGAND!
THERE IS NO TIME BEFORE THE CEREMONY.
GIKU (JOLT)
Y-YES, SIR... BUT...
...THE HUMAN PRINCESS SAID HIS MAJESTY HAS NOT COME THIS WAY.
FOOLS!
WE ARE THE ROYAL GUARD!
DO WE NOT CONFIRM WITH OUR OWN EYES ANYTHING INVOLVING HIS MAJESTY?
Y-YES, SIR!
APOLOGIES, SIR!
BISHI (SNAP)
AH...!
SU (PASS)

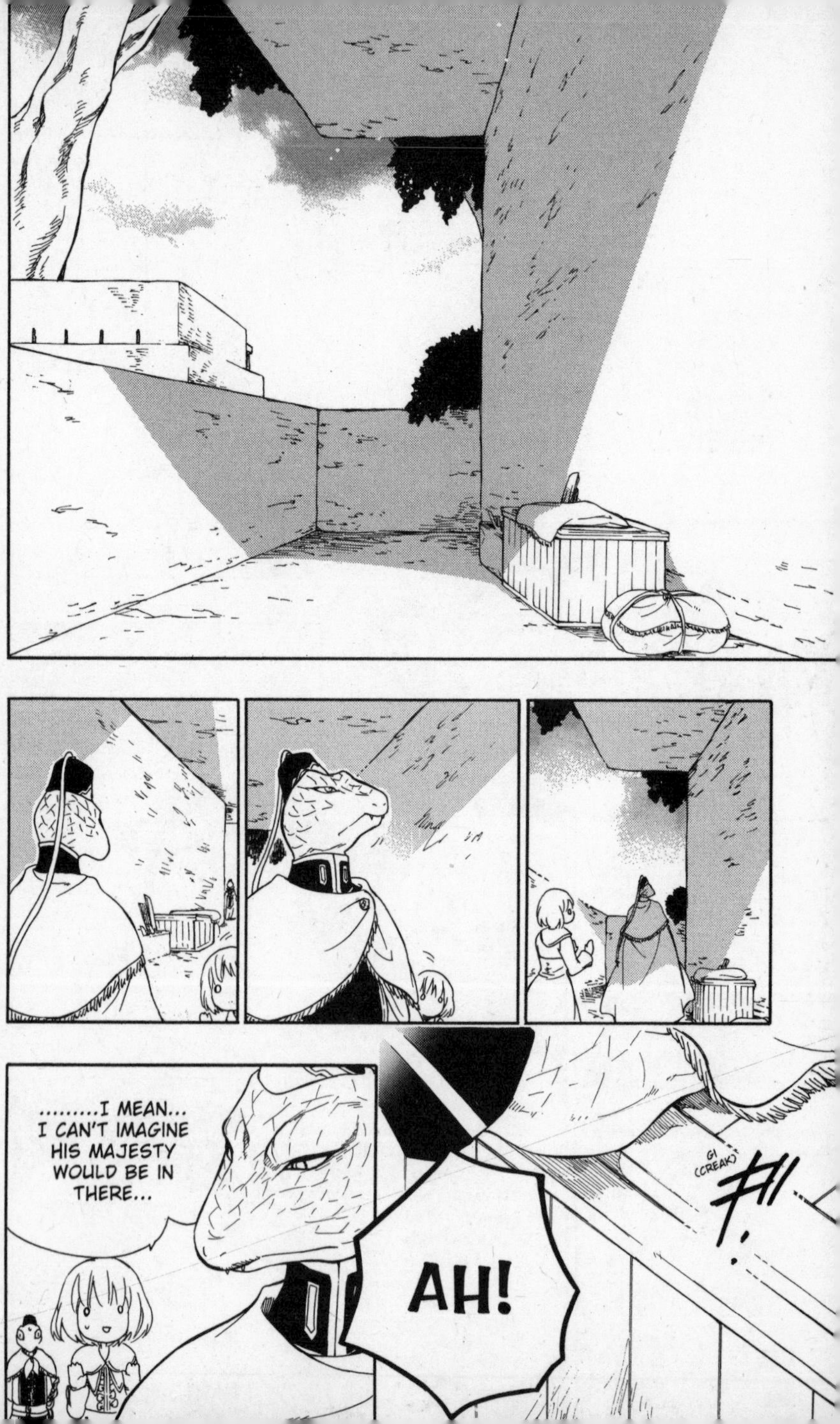
GI (CREAK)
.........I MEAN... I CAN'T IMAGINE HIS MAJESTY WOULD BE IN THERE...
AH!

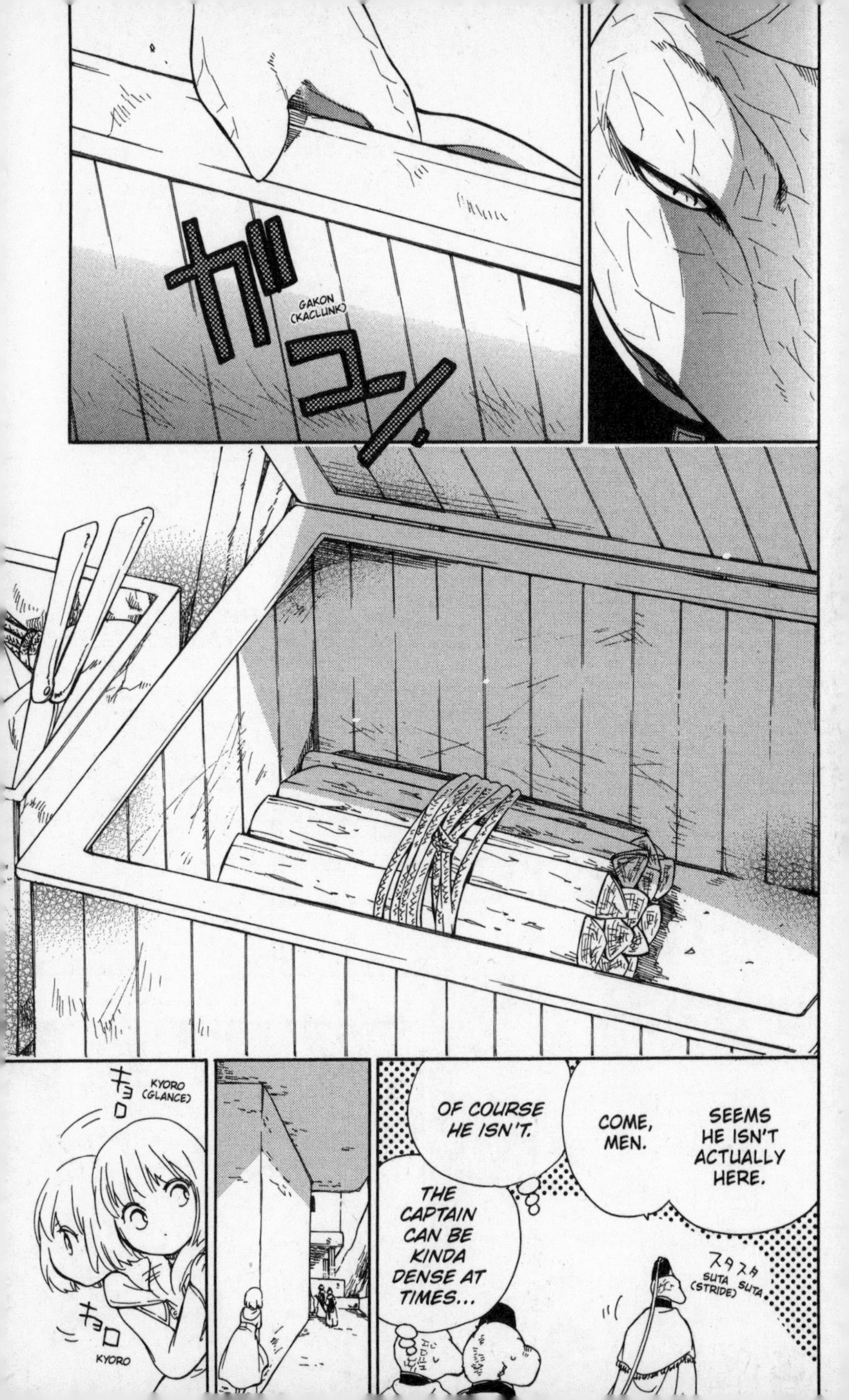
GAKON (KACLUNK)
SEEMS HE ISN'T ACTUALLY HERE.
COME, MEN.
OF COURSE HE ISN'T.
THE CAPTAIN CAN BE KINDA DENSE AT TIMES...
スタスタ SUTA SUTA (STRIDE)
キョロ KYORO (GLANCE)
キョロ KYORO

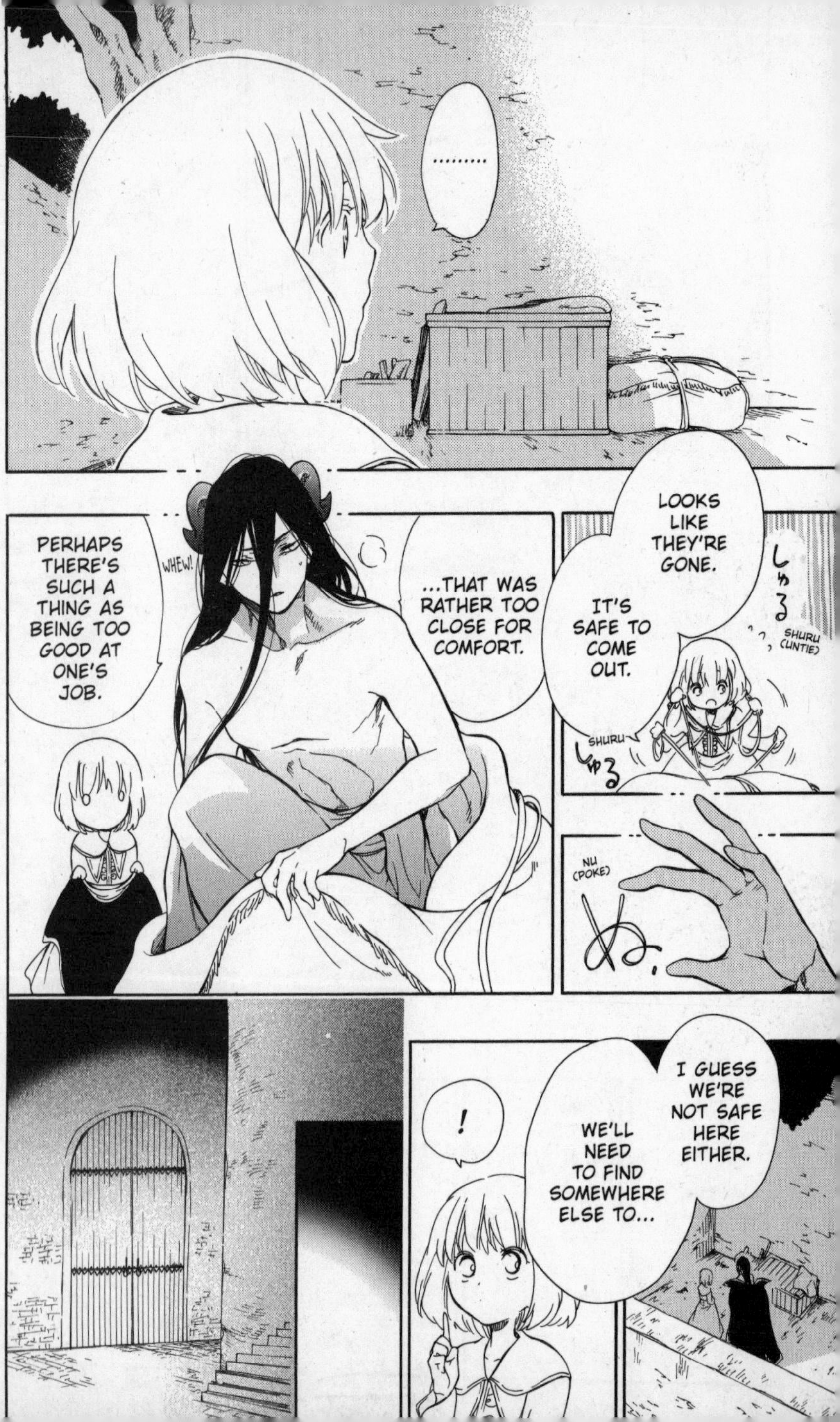
....
LOOKS LIKE THEY'RE GONE.
IT'S SAFE TO COME OUT.
しゅる
SHURU (UNTIE)
SHURU
しゅる
NU (POKE)
ぬ
...THAT WAS RATHER TOO CLOSE FOR COMFORT.
WHEW!
PERHAPS THERE'S SUCH A THING AS BEING TOO GOOD AT ONE'S JOB.
I GUESS WE'RE NOT SAFE HERE EITHER.
WE'LL NEED TO FIND SOMEWHERE ELSE TO...
!

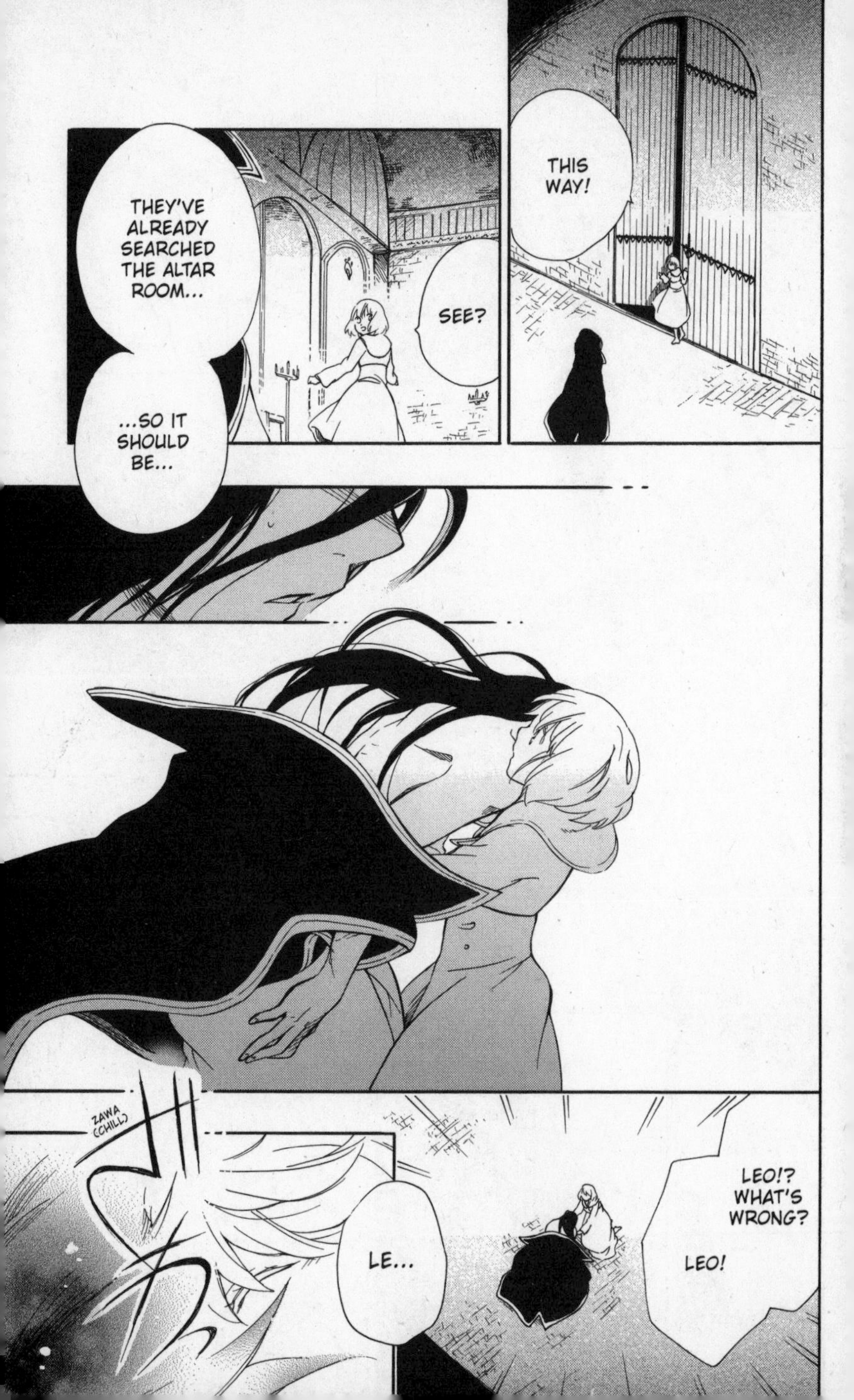
THIS WAY!
SEE?
THEY'VE ALREADY SEARCHED THE ALTAR ROOM...
...SO IT SHOULD BE...
LEO!? WHAT'S WRONG?
LEO!
LE...
ZAWA (CHILL)

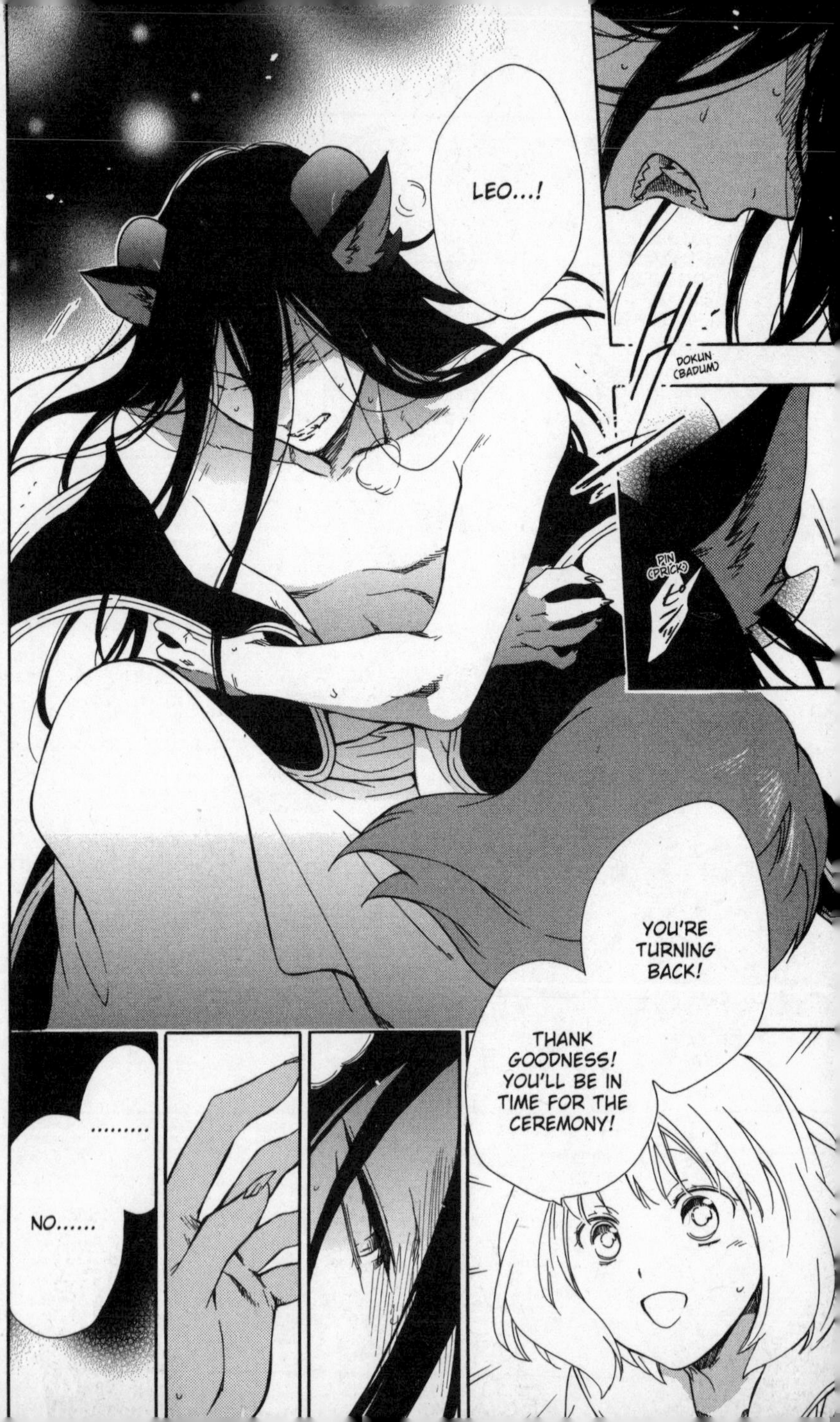
DOKUN (BADUM)
PIN (PRICK)
LEO...!
YOU'RE TURNING BACK!
THANK GOODNESS! YOU'LL BE IN TIME FOR THE CEREMONY!
....
NO......

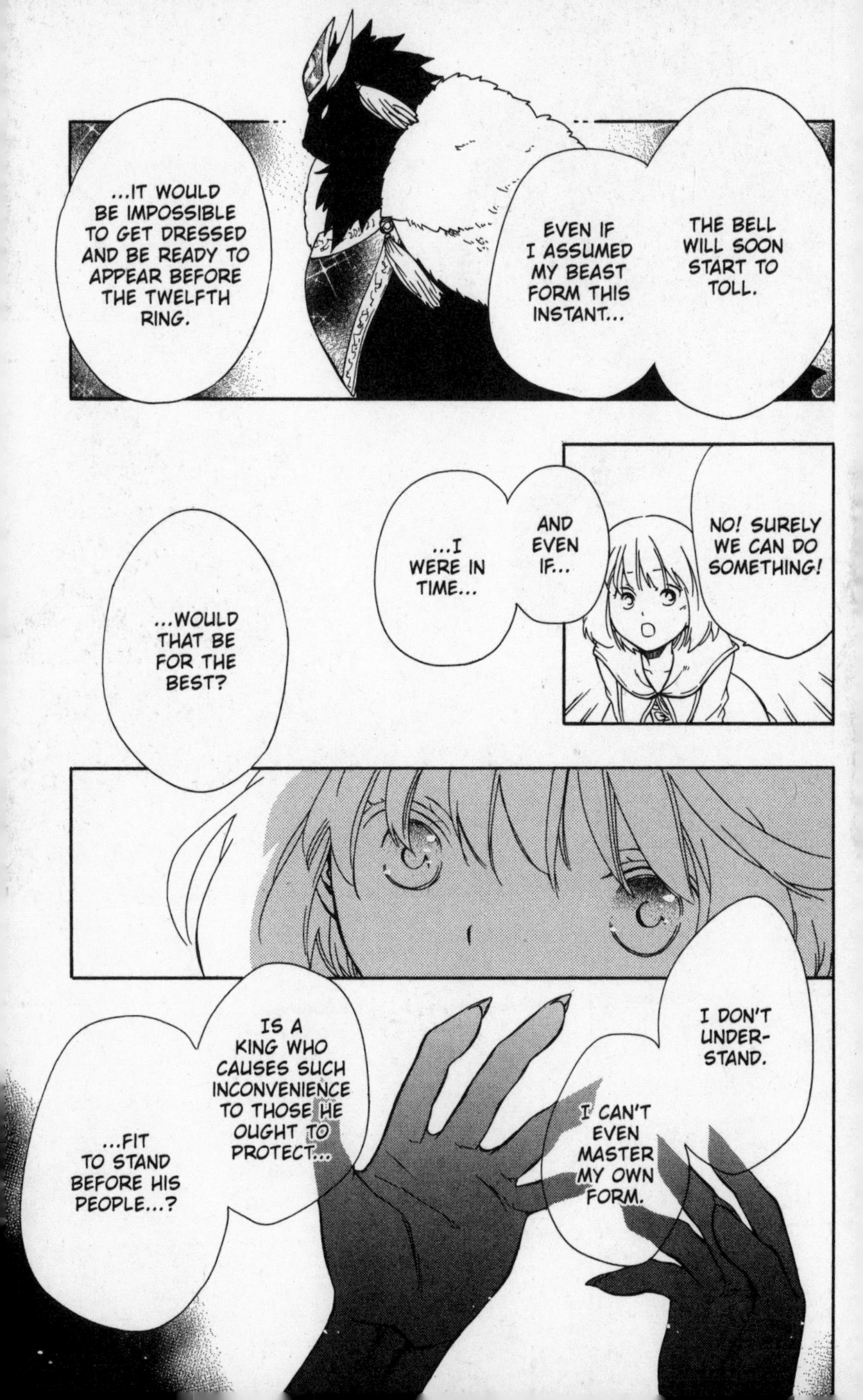
THE BELL WILL SOON START TO TOLL.
EVEN IF I ASSUMED MY BEAST FORM THIS INSTANT...
...IT WOULD BE IMPOSSIBLE TO GET DRESSED AND BE READY TO APPEAR BEFORE THE TWELFTH RING.
NO! SURELY WE CAN DO SOMETHING!
AND EVEN IF...
...I WERE IN TIME...
...WOULD THAT BE FOR THE BEST?
I DON'T UNDER-STAND.
I CAN'T EVEN MASTER MY OWN FORM.
IS A KING WHO CAUSES SUCH INCONVENIENCE TO THOSE HE OUGHT TO PROTECT...
...FIT TO STAND BEFORE HIS PEOPLE...?

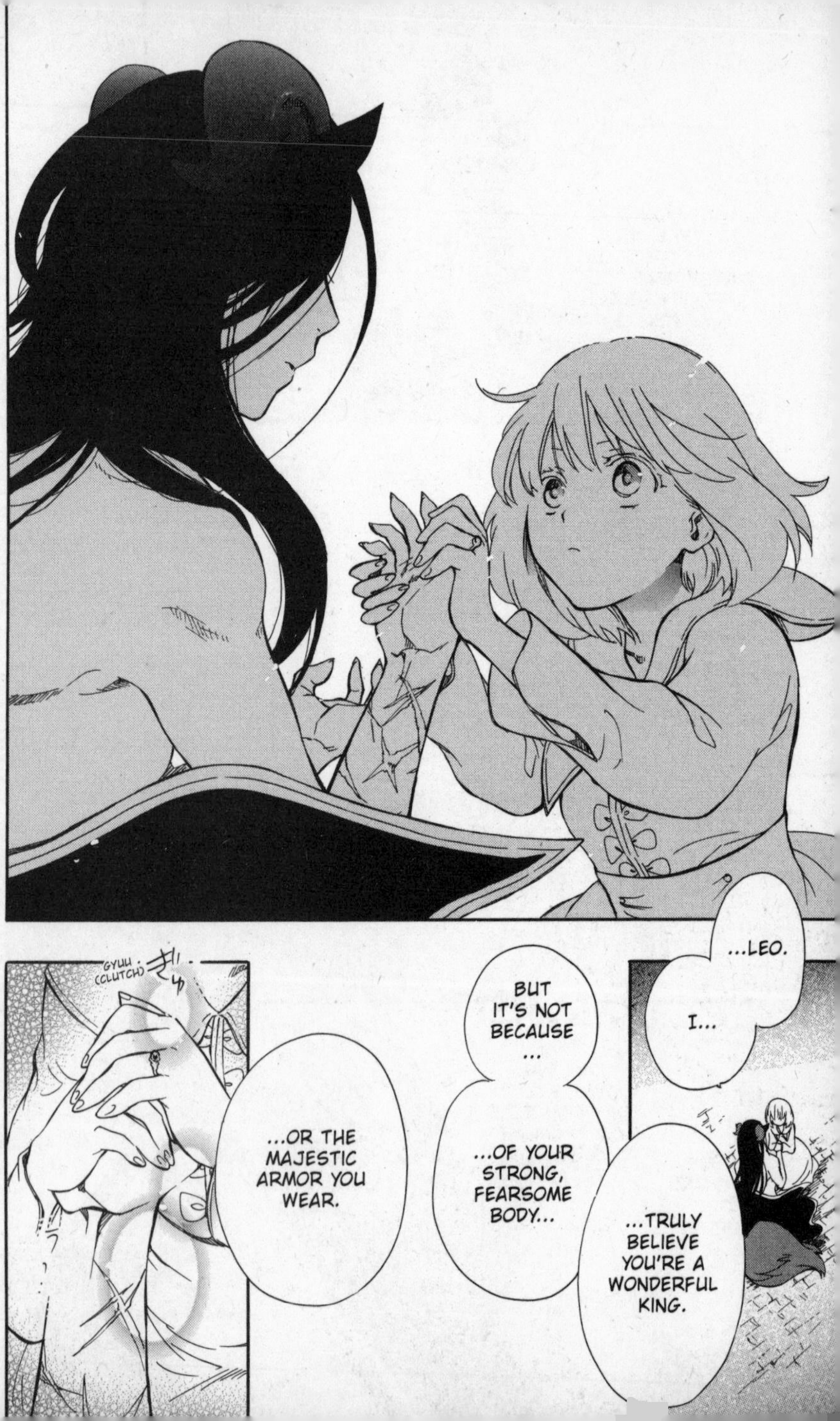
...LEO.
I...
...TRULY BELIEVE YOU'RE A WONDERFUL KING.
BUT IT'S NOT BECAUSE...
...OF YOUR STRONG, FEARSOME BODY...
...OR THE MAJESTIC ARMOR YOU WEAR.
GYUU (CLUTCH)

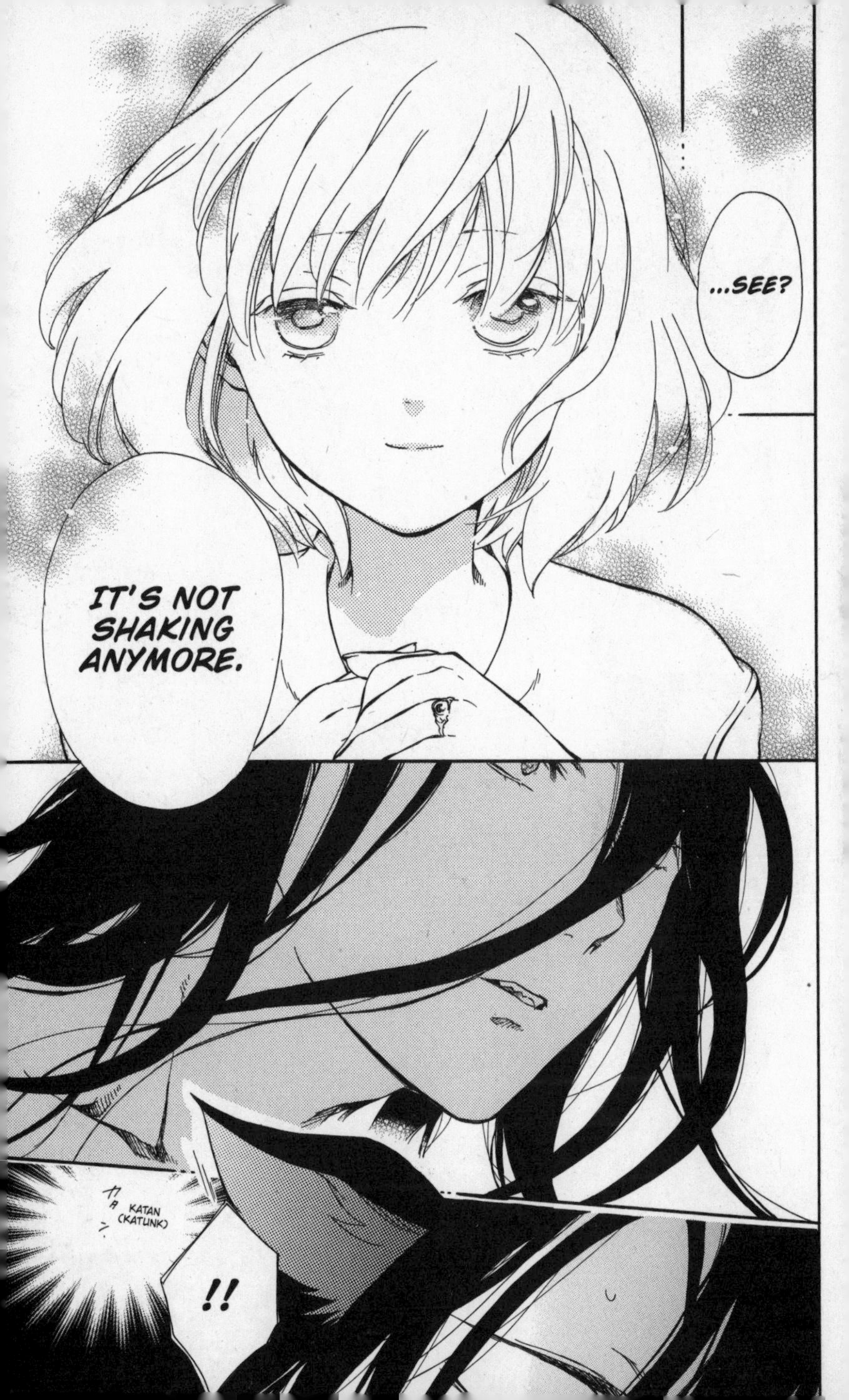
...SEE?
IT'S NOT SHAKING ANYMORE.
カタン
KATAN (KATUNK)
!!

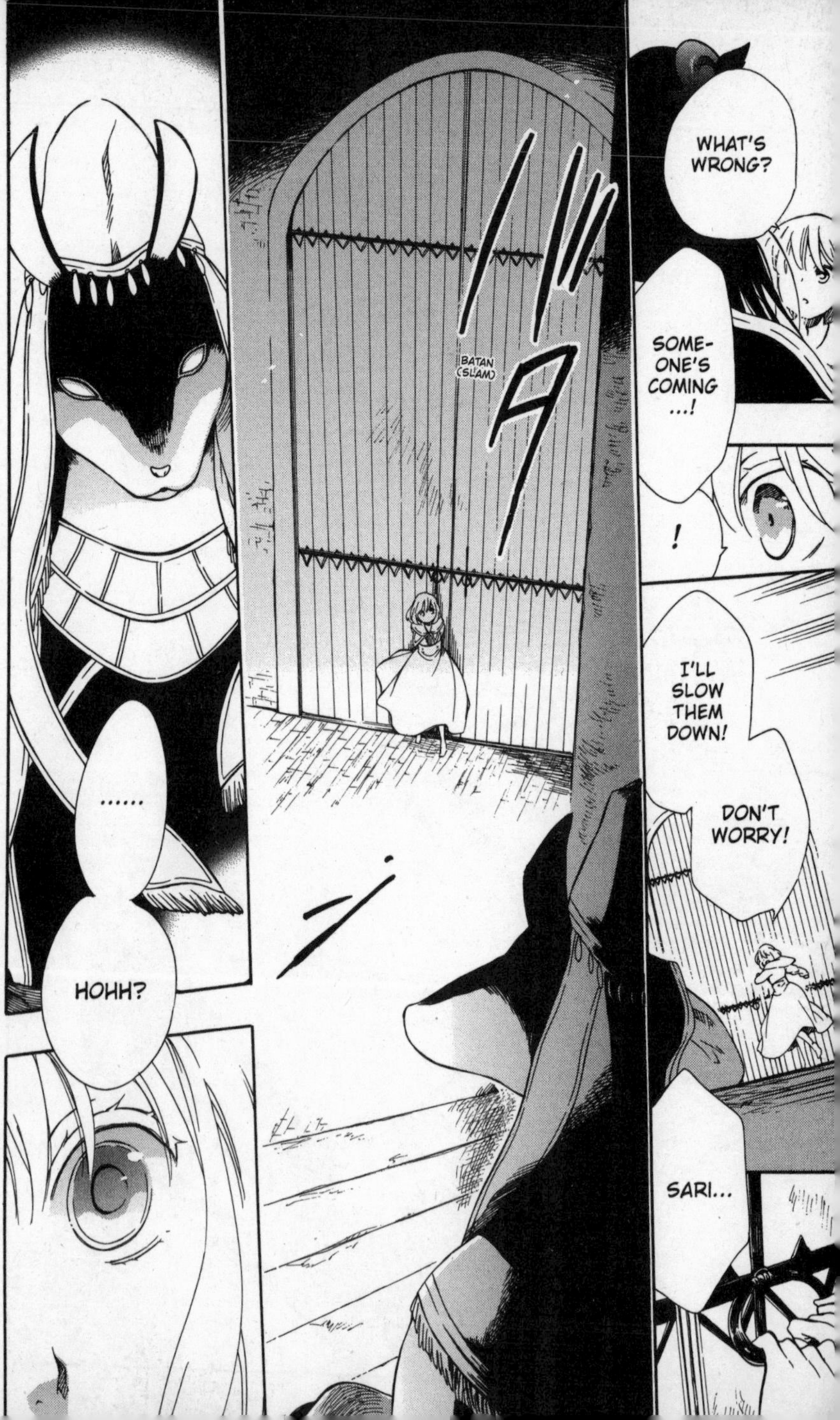
WHAT'S WRONG?
SOME-ONE'S COMING ...!
!
I'LL SLOW THEM DOWN!
DON'T WORRY!
SARI...
BATAN (SLAM)
......
HOHH?

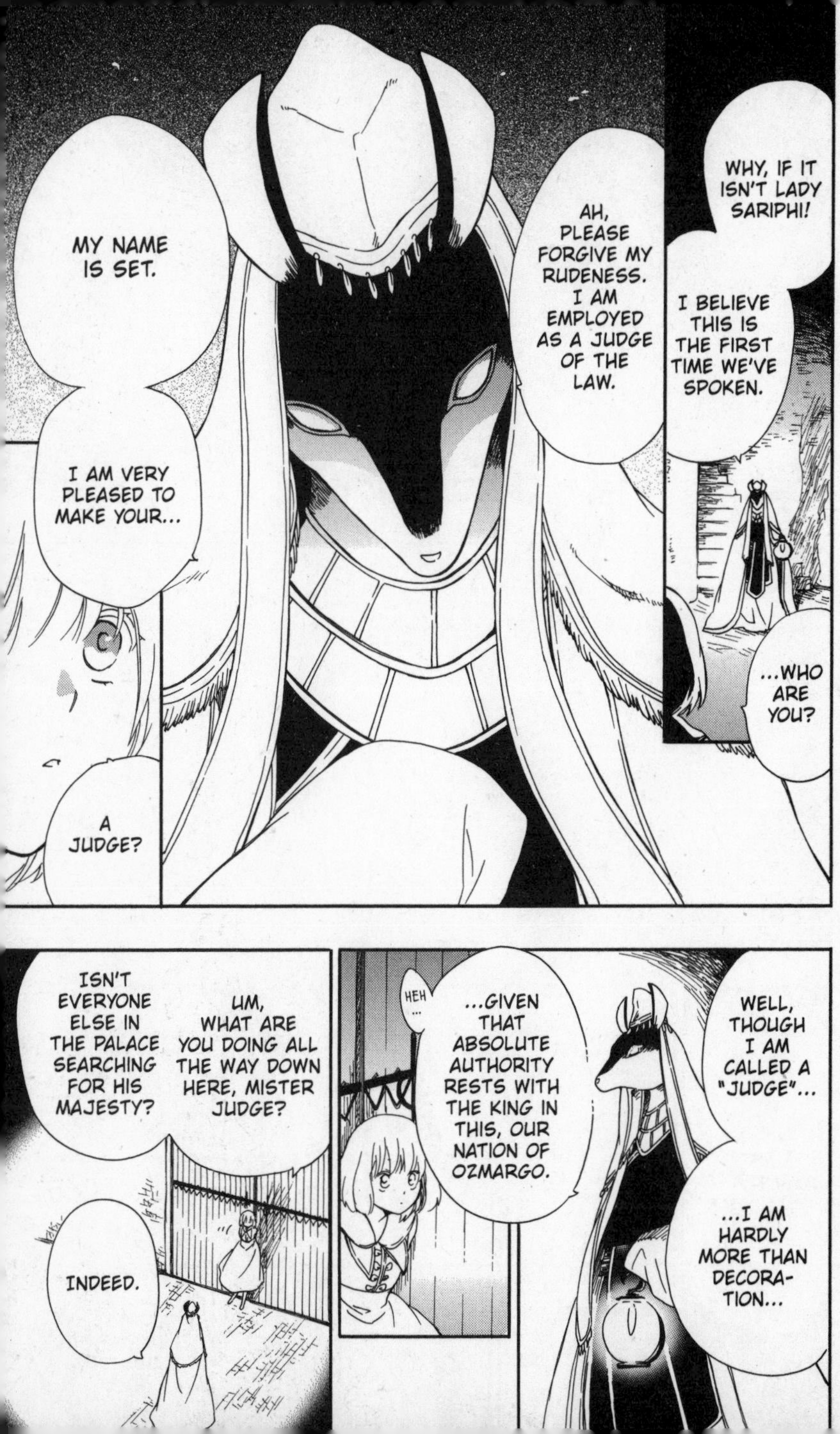
WHY, IF IT ISN'T LADY SARIPHI!
I BELIEVE THIS IS THE FIRST TIME WE'VE SPOKEN.
...WHO ARE YOU?
AH, PLEASE FORGIVE MY RUDENESS. I AM EMPLOYED AS A JUDGE OF THE LAW.
MY NAME IS SET.
I AM VERY PLEASED TO MAKE YOUR...
A JUDGE?
WELL, THOUGH I AM CALLED A "JUDGE"...
...I AM HARDLY MORE THAN DECORATION...
...GIVEN THAT ABSOLUTE AUTHORITY RESTS WITH THE KING IN THIS, OUR NATION OF OZMARGO.
HEH...
UM, WHAT ARE YOU DOING ALL THE WAY DOWN HERE, MISTER JUDGE?
ISN'T EVERYONE ELSE IN THE PALACE SEARCHING FOR HIS MAJESTY?
INDEED.

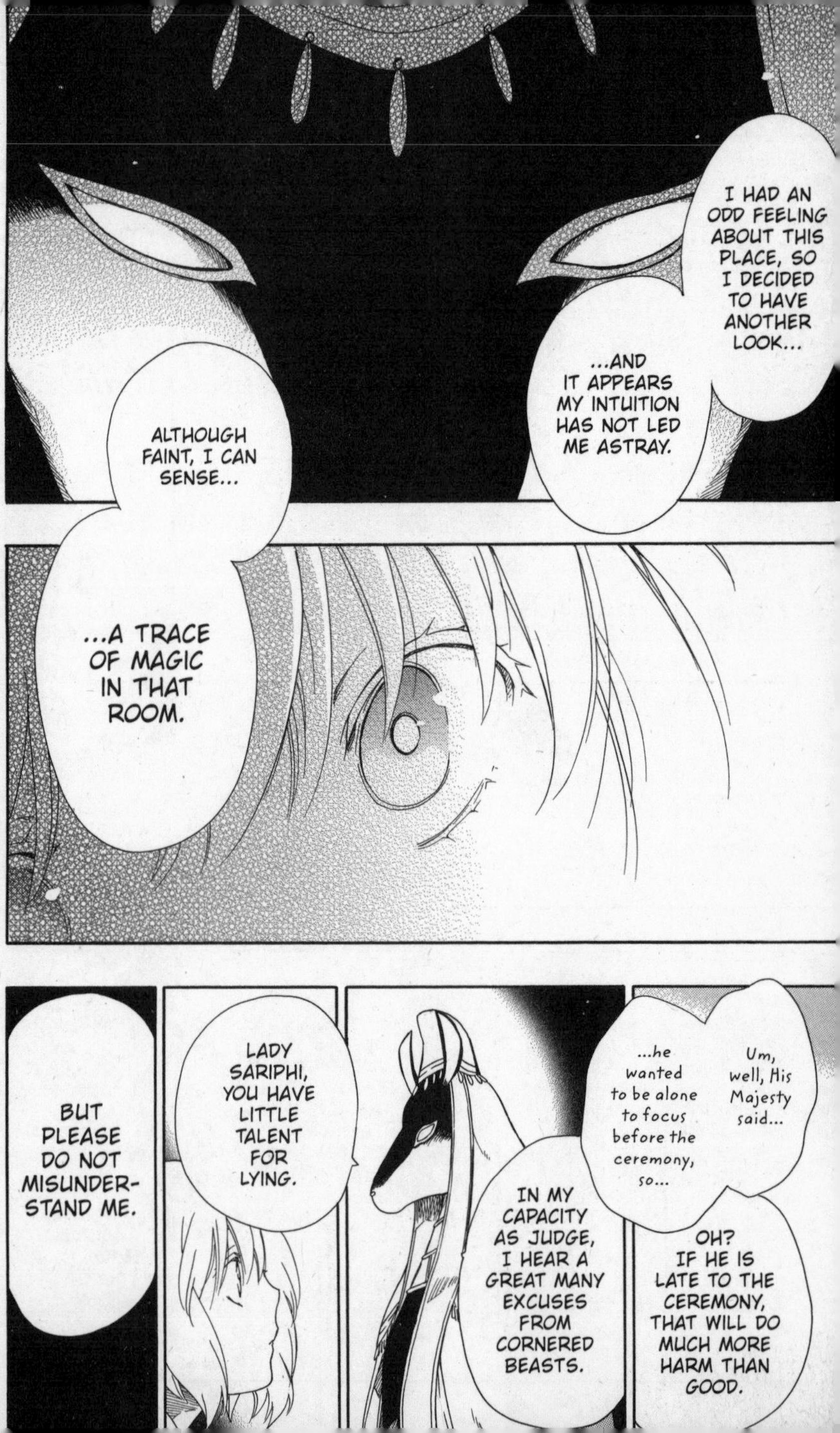
I HAD AN ODD FEELING ABOUT THIS PLACE, SO I DECIDED TO HAVE ANOTHER LOOK...
...AND IT APPEARS MY INTUITION HAS NOT LED ME ASTRAY.
ALTHOUGH FAINT, I CAN SENSE...
...A TRACE OF MAGIC IN THAT ROOM.
Um, well, His Majesty said...
...he wanted to be alone to focus before the ceremony, so...
OH? IF HE IS LATE TO THE CEREMONY, THAT WILL DO MUCH MORE HARM THAN GOOD.
IN MY CAPACITY AS JUDGE, I HEAR A GREAT MANY EXCUSES FROM CORNERED BEASTS.
LADY SARIPHI, YOU HAVE LITTLE TALENT FOR LYING.
BUT PLEASE DO NOT MISUNDERSTAND ME.

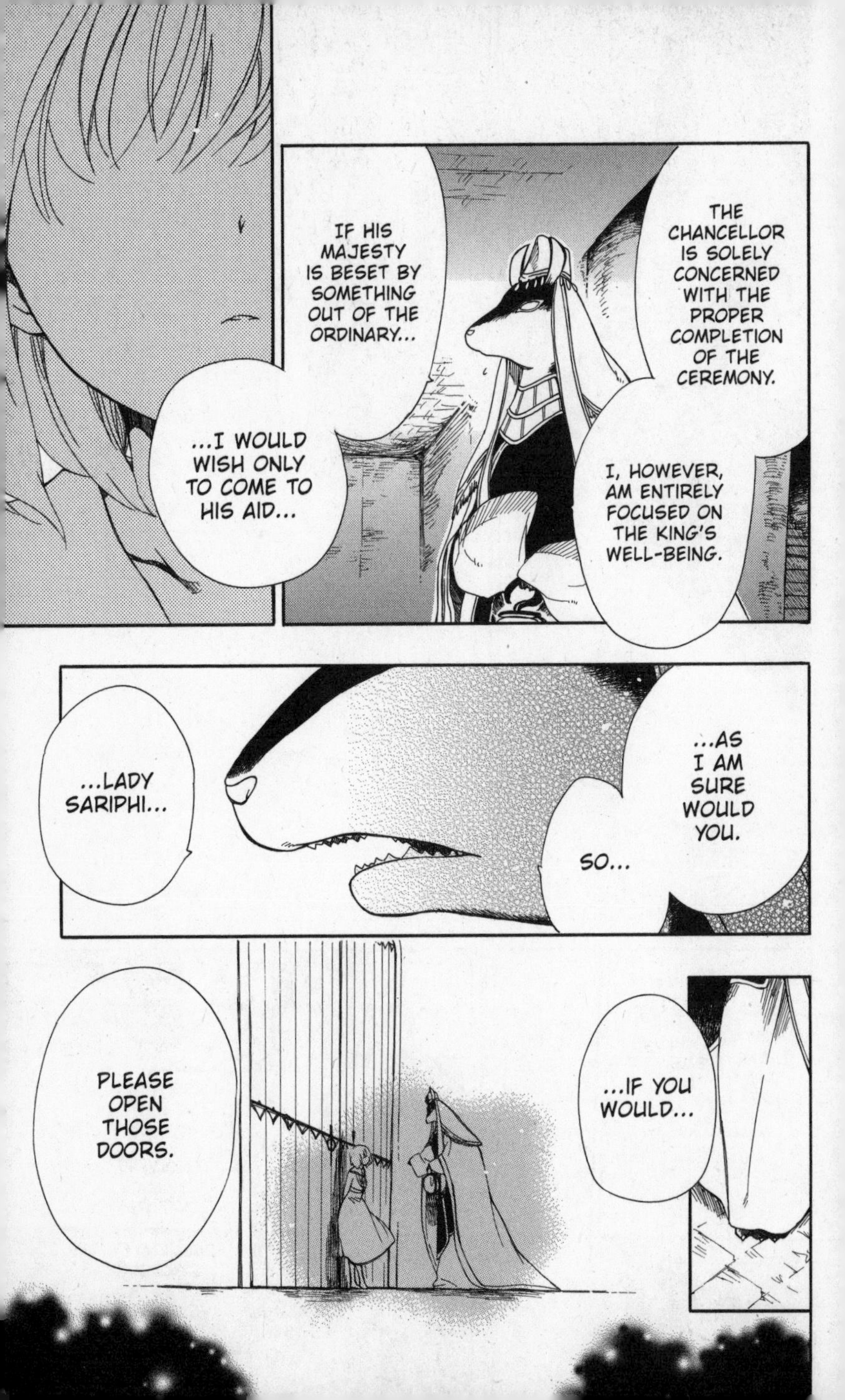
THE CHANCELLOR IS SOLELY CONCERNED WITH THE PROPER COMPLETION OF THE CEREMONY.
I, HOWEVER, AM ENTIRELY FOCUSED ON THE KING'S WELL-BEING.
IF HIS MAJESTY IS BESET BY SOMETHING OUT OF THE ORDINARY...
...I WOULD WISH ONLY TO COME TO HIS AID...
...AS I AM SURE WOULD YOU.
SO...
...LADY SARIPHI...
...IF YOU WOULD...
PLEASE OPEN THOSE DOORS.

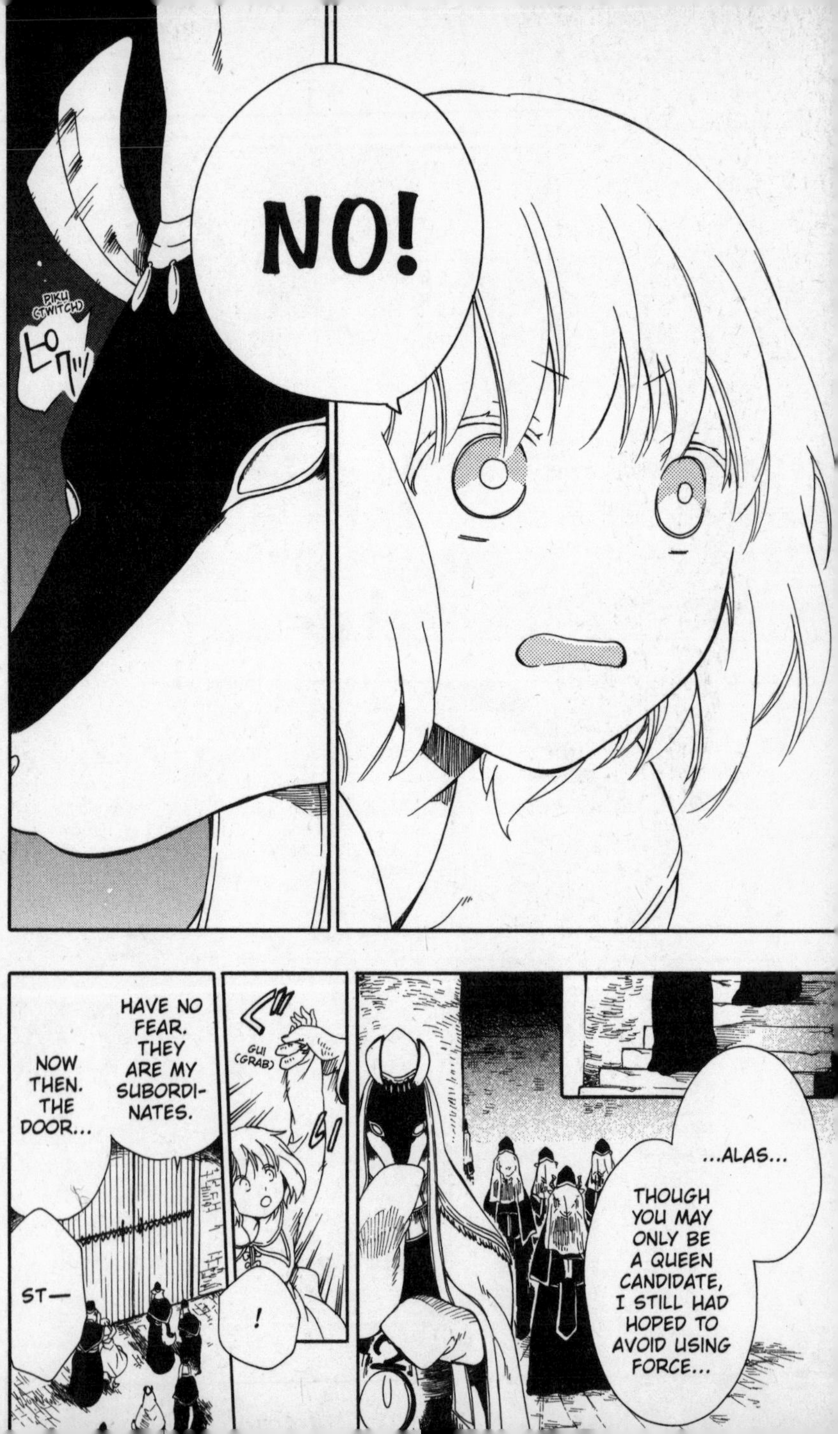
NO!
PIKU (TWITCH)
ピクッ
...ALAS...
THOUGH YOU MAY ONLY BE A QUEEN CANDIDATE, I STILL HAD HOPED TO AVOID USING FORCE...
GUI (GRAB)
!
HAVE NO FEAR. THEY ARE MY SUBORDINATES.
NOW THEN. THE DOOR...
ST—

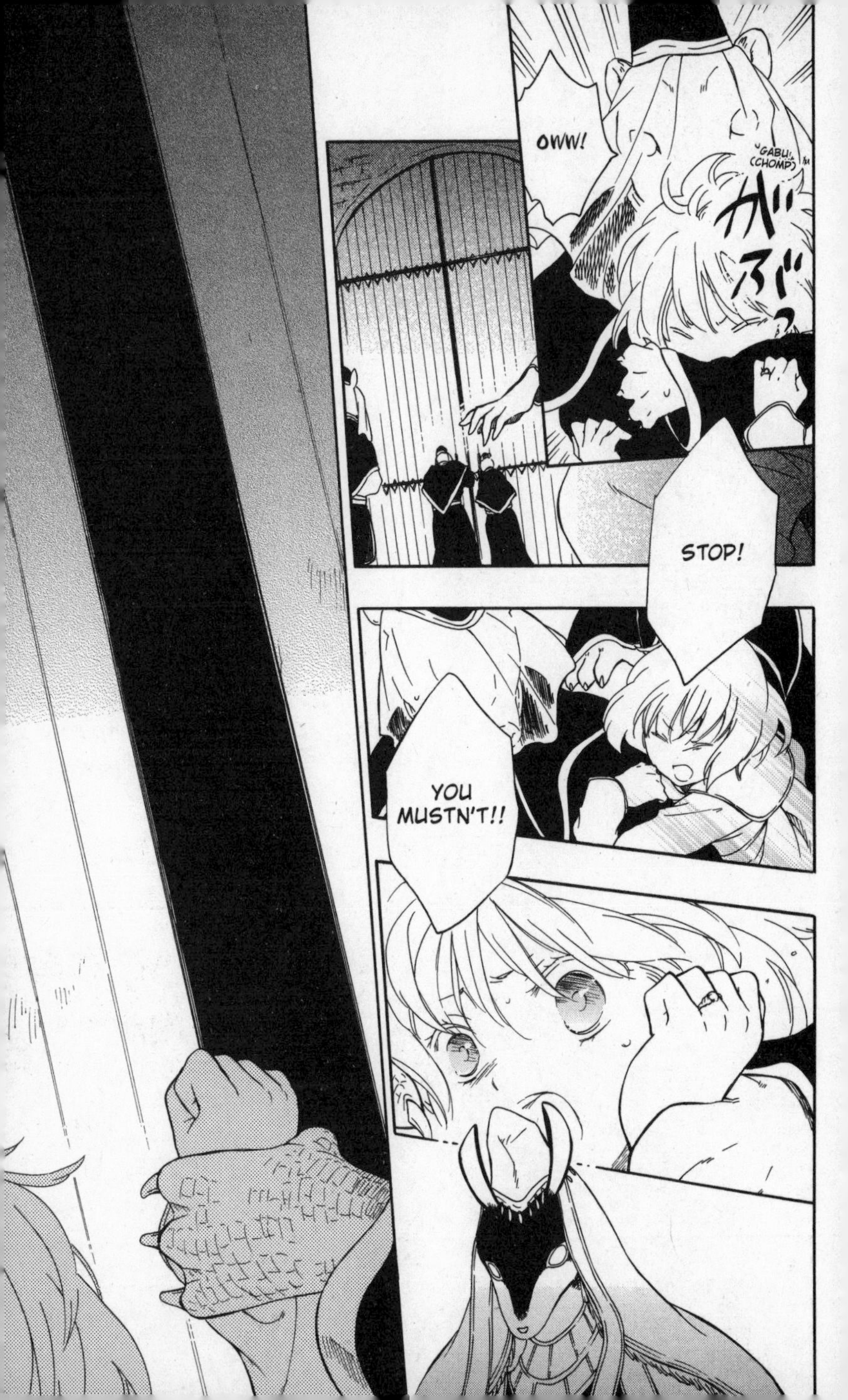
GABU! (CHOMP)
がぶっ
OWW!
STOP!
YOU MUSTN'T!!

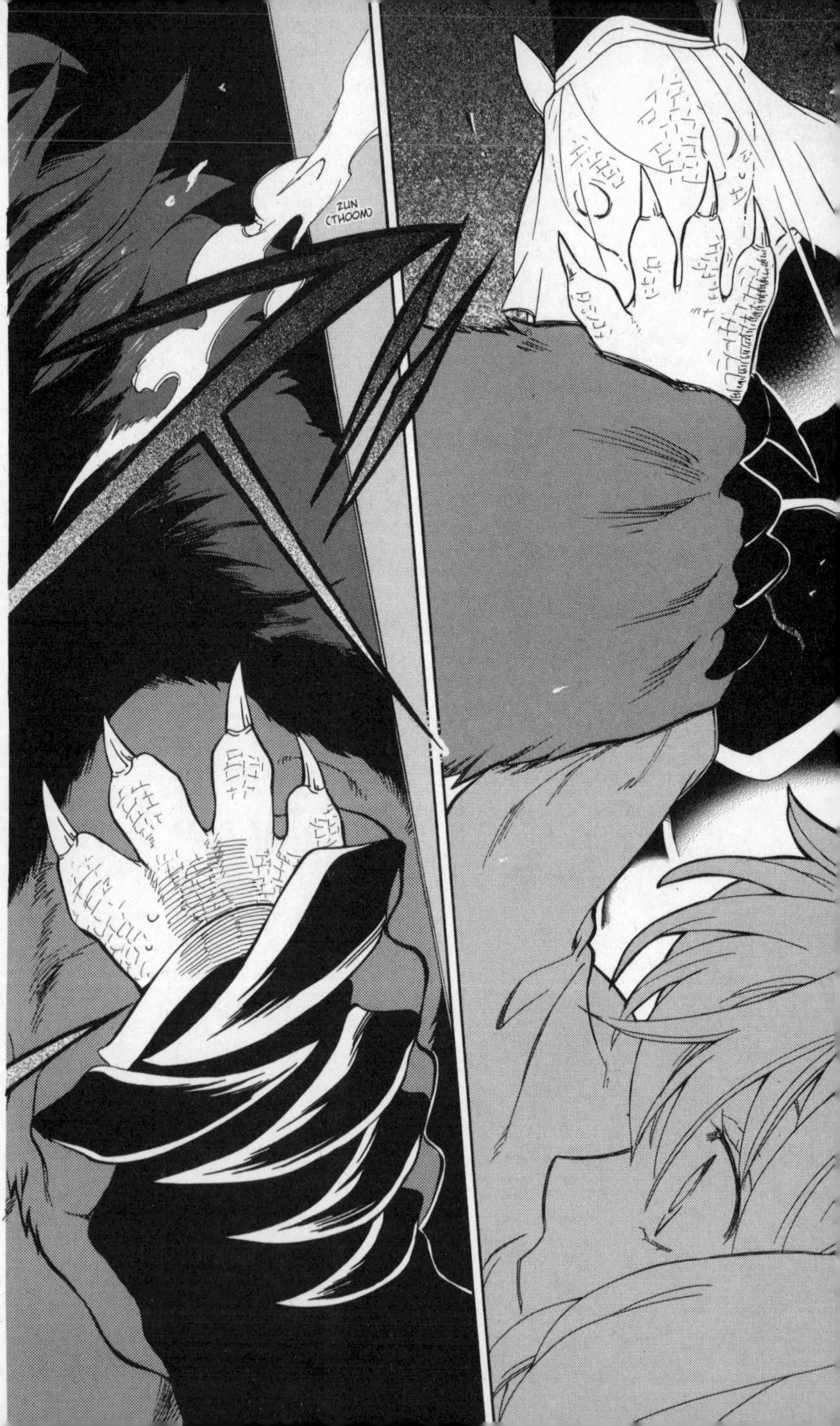
ZUN
(THOOM)

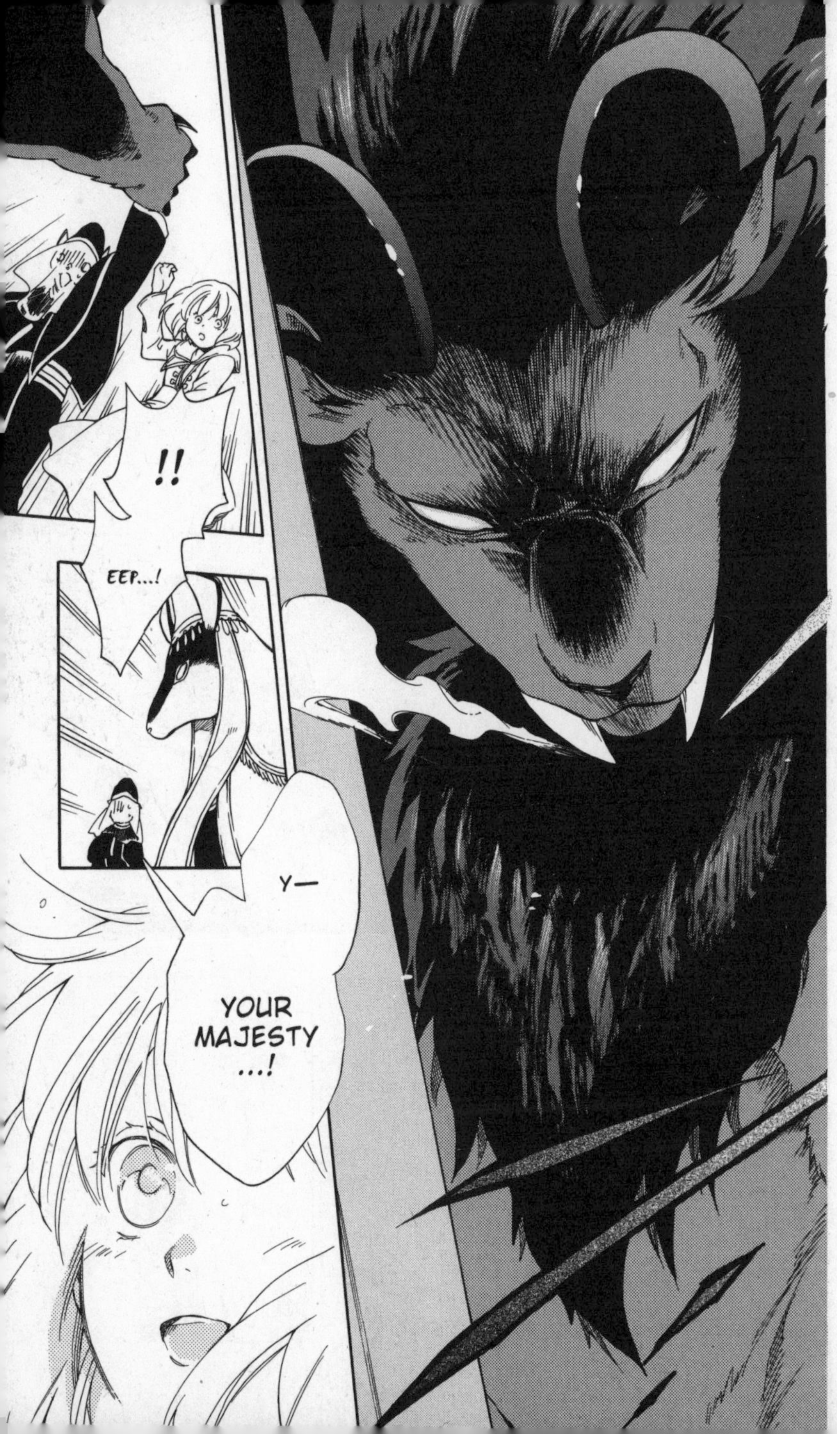
!!
EEP...!
Y—
YOUR MAJESTY ...!

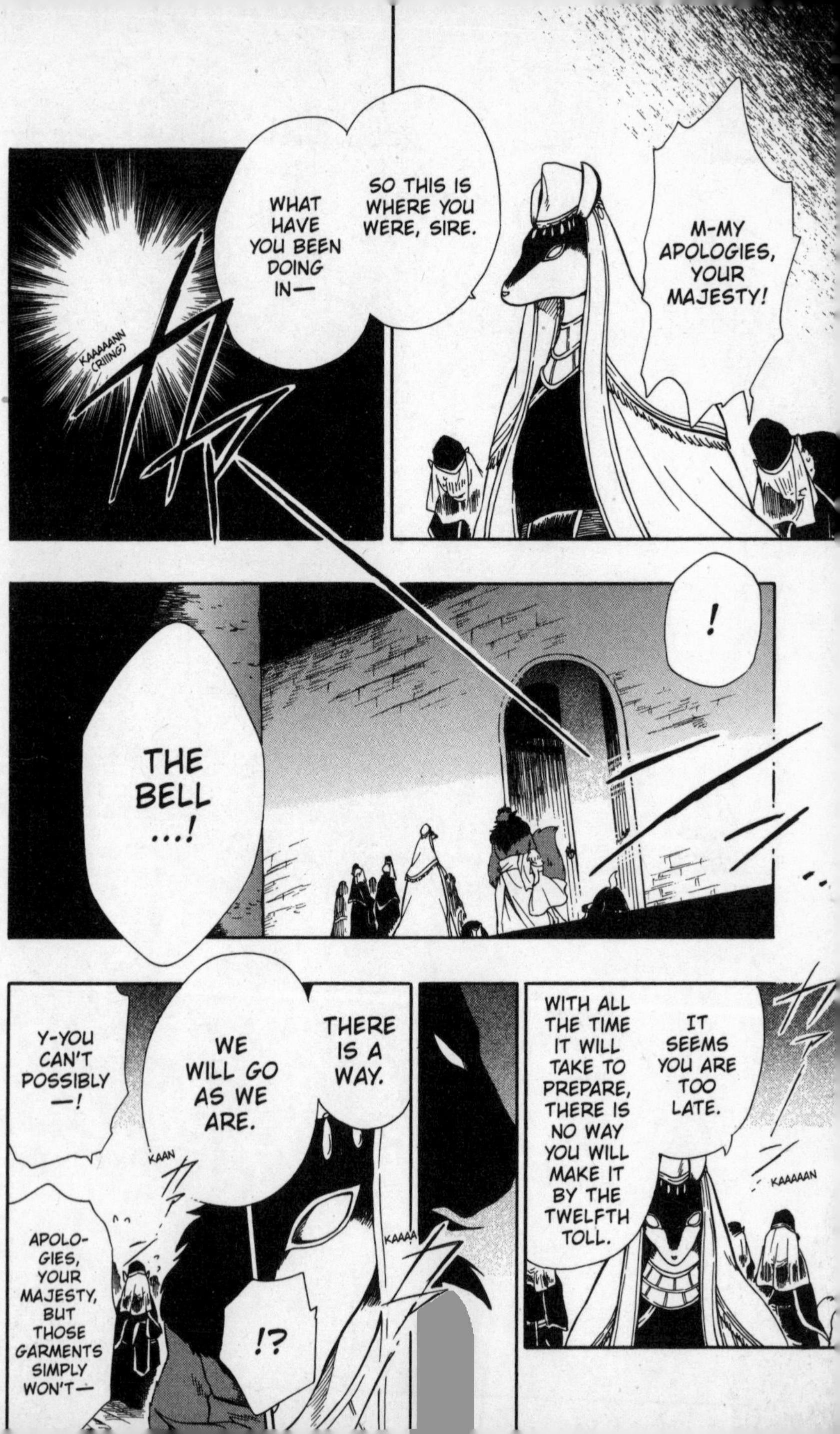
M-MY APOLOGIES, YOUR MAJESTY!
SO THIS IS WHERE YOU WERE, SIRE.
WHAT HAVE YOU BEEN DOING IN—
KAAAAANN (RIIING)
!
THE BELL ...!
IT SEEMS YOU ARE TOO LATE.
WITH ALL THE TIME IT WILL TAKE TO PREPARE, THERE IS NO WAY YOU WILL MAKE IT BY THE TWELFTH TOLL.
KAAAAAN
THERE IS A WAY.
WE WILL GO AS WE ARE.
KAAAA
!?
KAAN
Y-YOU CAN'T POSSIBLY —!
APOLOGIES, YOUR MAJESTY, BUT THOSE GARMENTS SIMPLY WON'T—

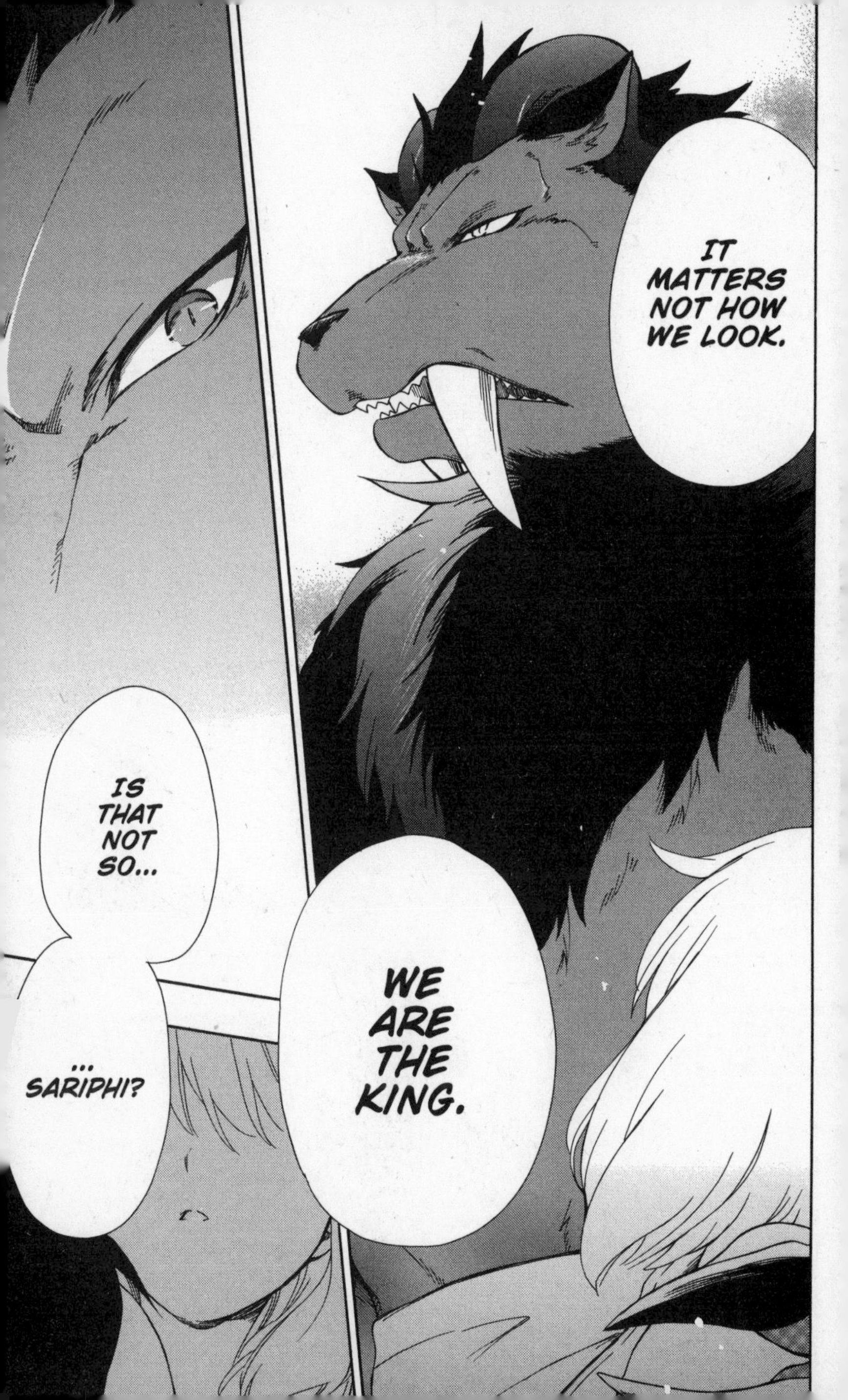
IT MATTERS NOT HOW WE LOOK.
WE ARE THE KING.
IS THAT NOT SO...
...SARIPHI?

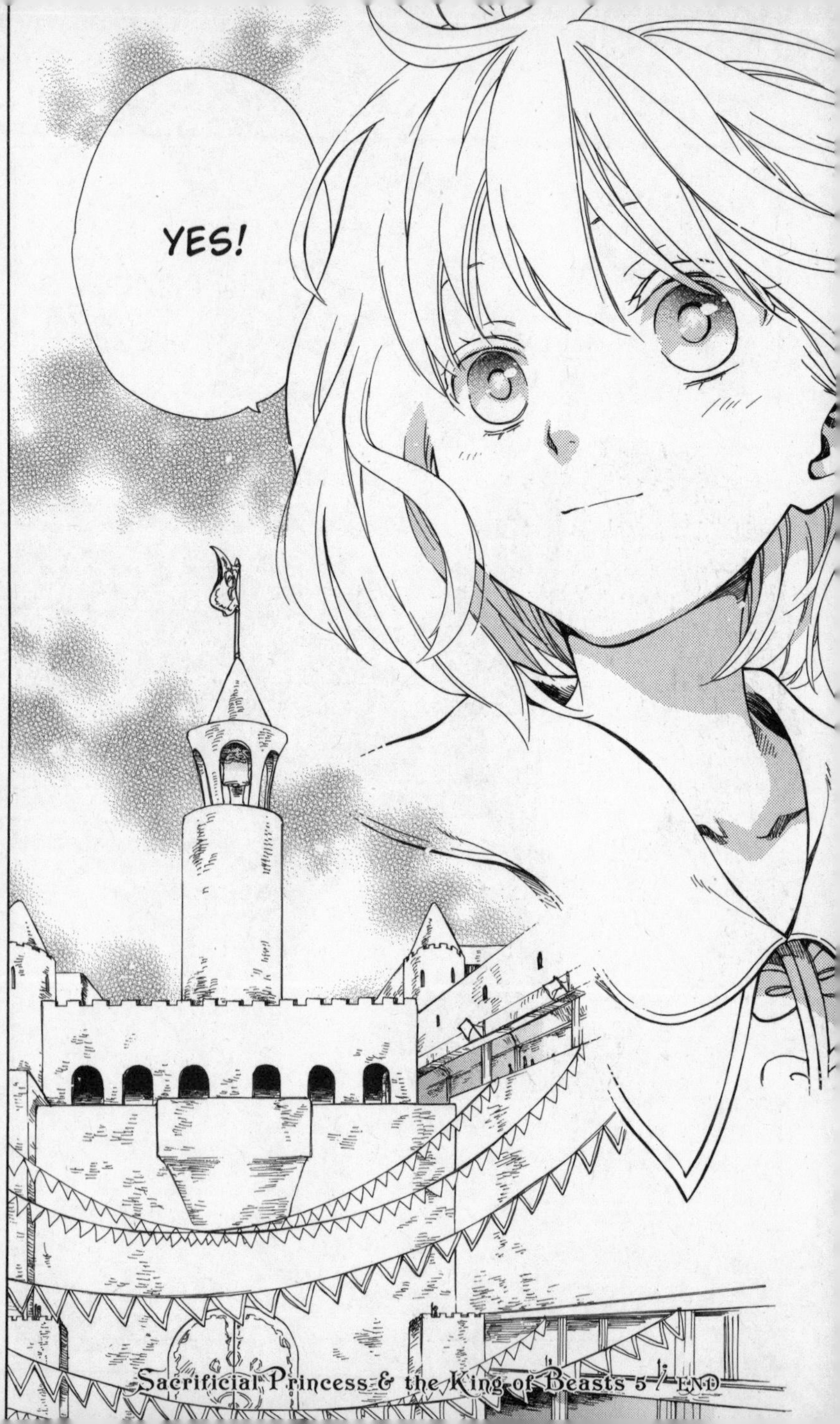
YES!
Sacrificial Princess & the King of Beasts 5 / END

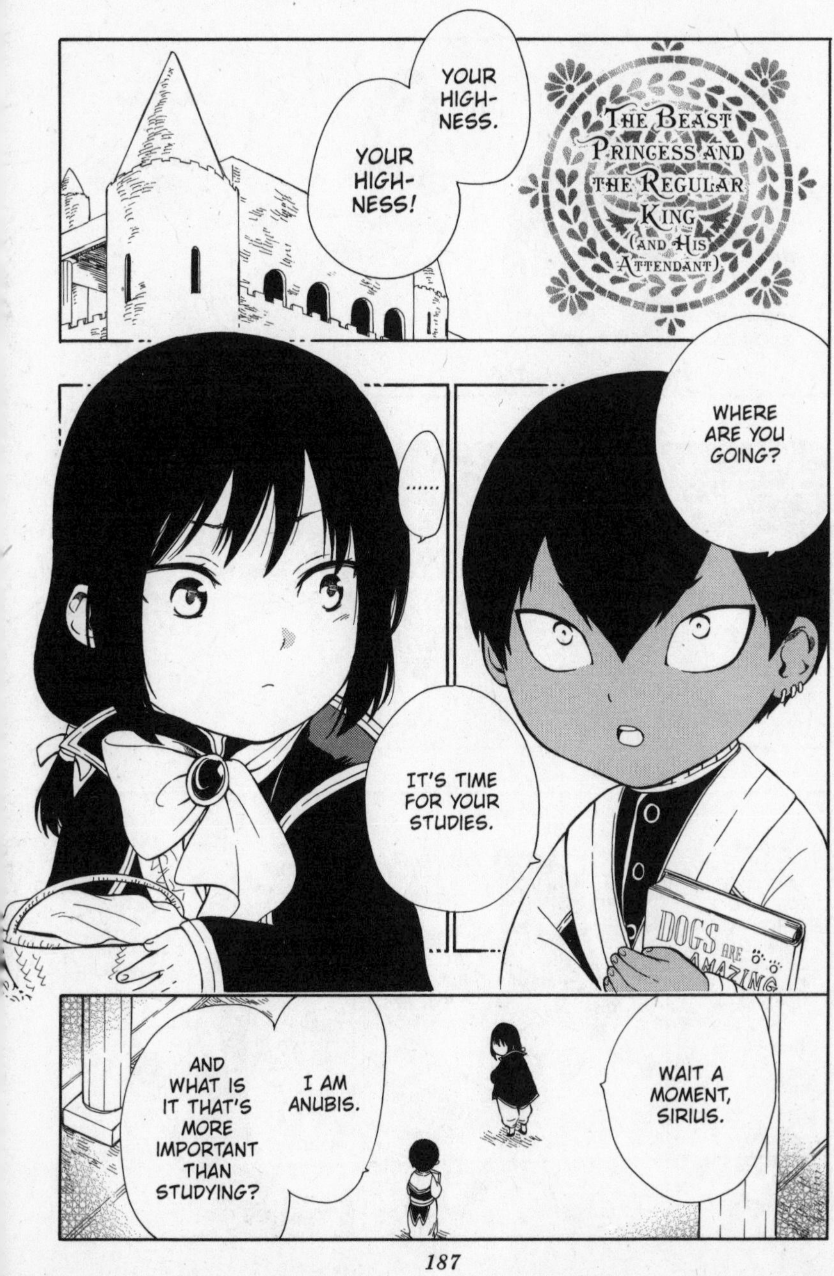
THE BEAST PRINCESS AND THE REGULAR KING (AND HIS ATTENDANT)
YOUR HIGH-NESS.
YOUR HIGH-NESS!
WHERE ARE YOU GOING?
IT'S TIME FOR YOUR STUDIES.
DOGS ARE AMAZING
......
WAIT A MOMENT, SIRIUS.
I AM ANUBIS.
AND WHAT IS IT THAT'S MORE IMPORTANT THAN STUDYING?

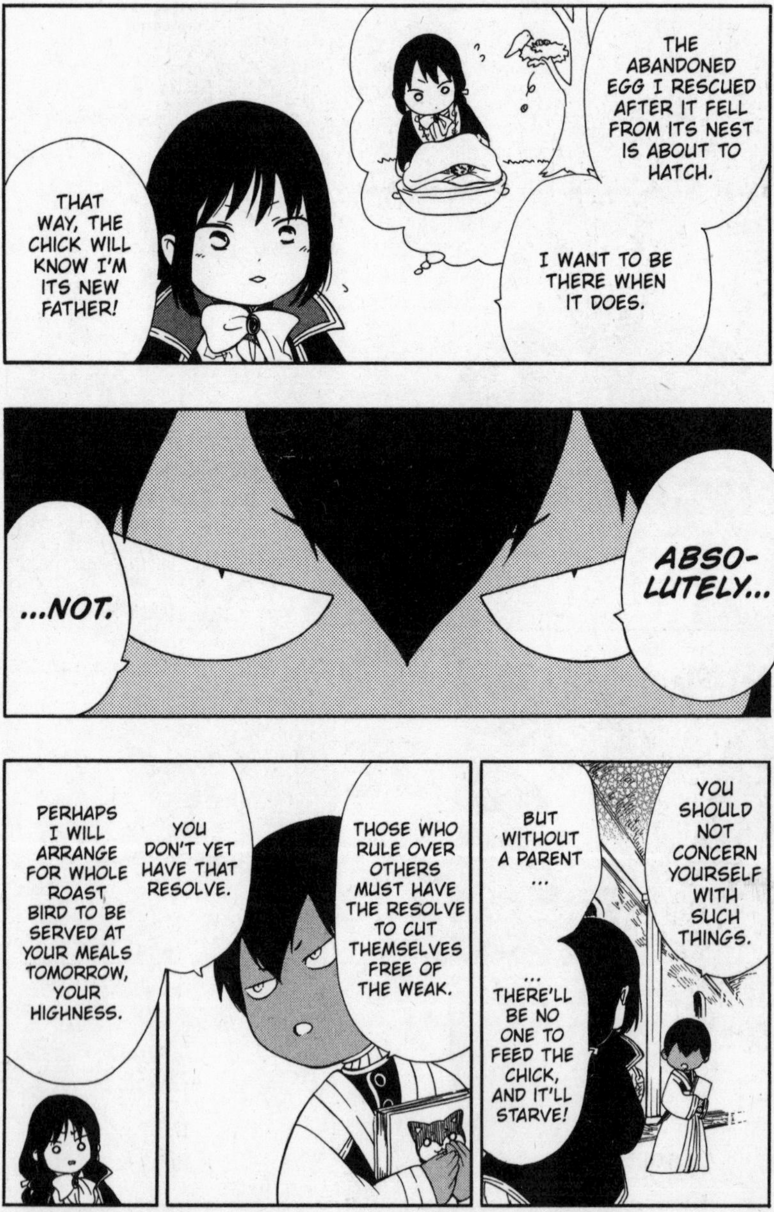
THE ABANDONED EGG I RESCUED AFTER IT FELL FROM ITS NEST IS ABOUT TO HATCH.
I WANT TO BE THERE WHEN IT DOES.
THAT WAY, THE CHICK WILL KNOW I'M ITS NEW FATHER!
ABSO-LUTELY...
...NOT.
YOU SHOULD NOT CONCERN YOURSELF WITH SUCH THINGS.
BUT WITHOUT A PARENT...
...THERE'LL BE NO ONE TO FEED THE CHICK, AND IT'LL STARVE!
THOSE WHO RULE OVER OTHERS MUST HAVE THE RESOLVE TO CUT THEMSELVES FREE OF THE WEAK.
YOU DON'T YET HAVE THAT RESOLVE.
PERHAPS I WILL ARRANGE FOR WHOLE ROAST BIRD TO BE SERVED AT YOUR MEALS TOMORROW, YOUR HIGHNESS.

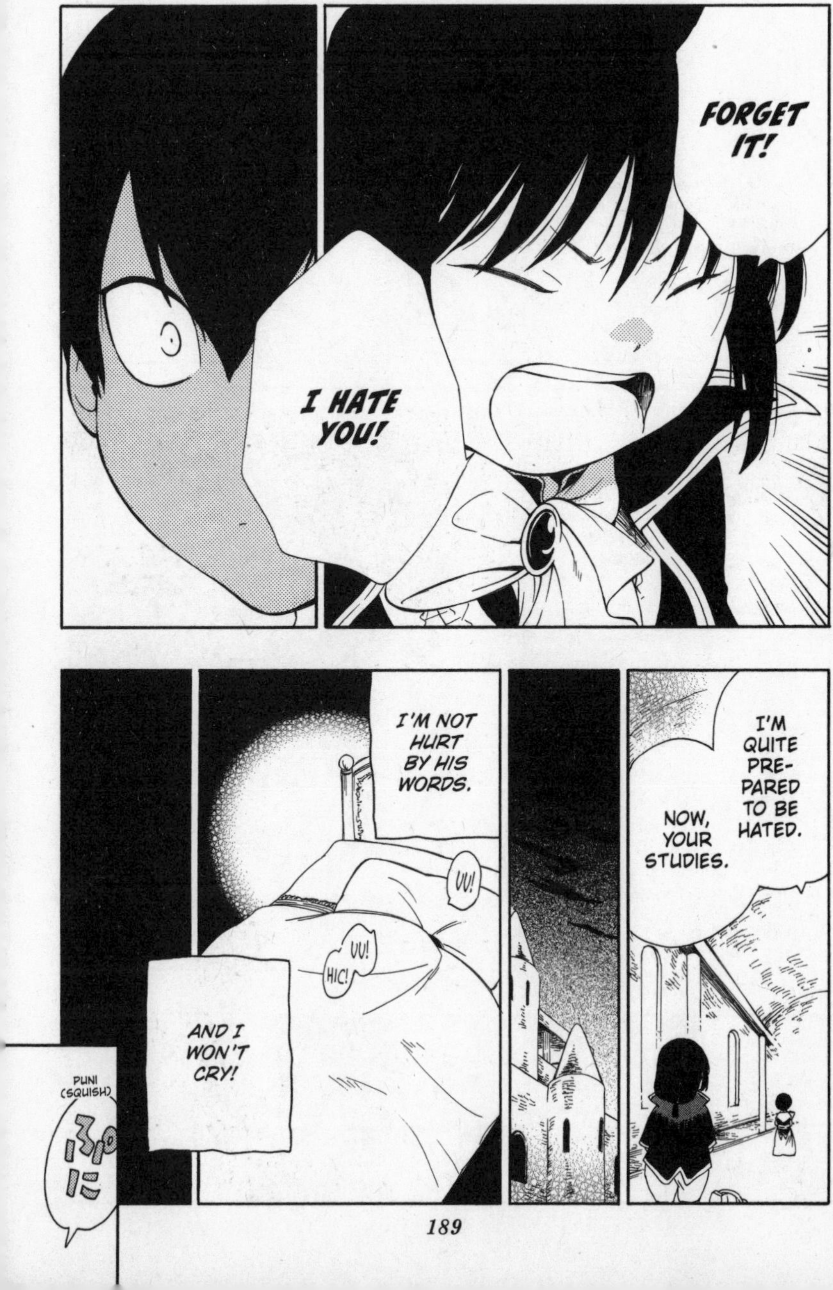

FORGET IT!
I HATE YOU!
I'M QUITE PRE-PARED TO BE HATED.
NOW, YOUR STUDIES.
I'M NOT HURT BY HIS WORDS.
UU!
UU!
HIC!
AND I WON'T CRY!
PUNI (SQUISH)
ぷに

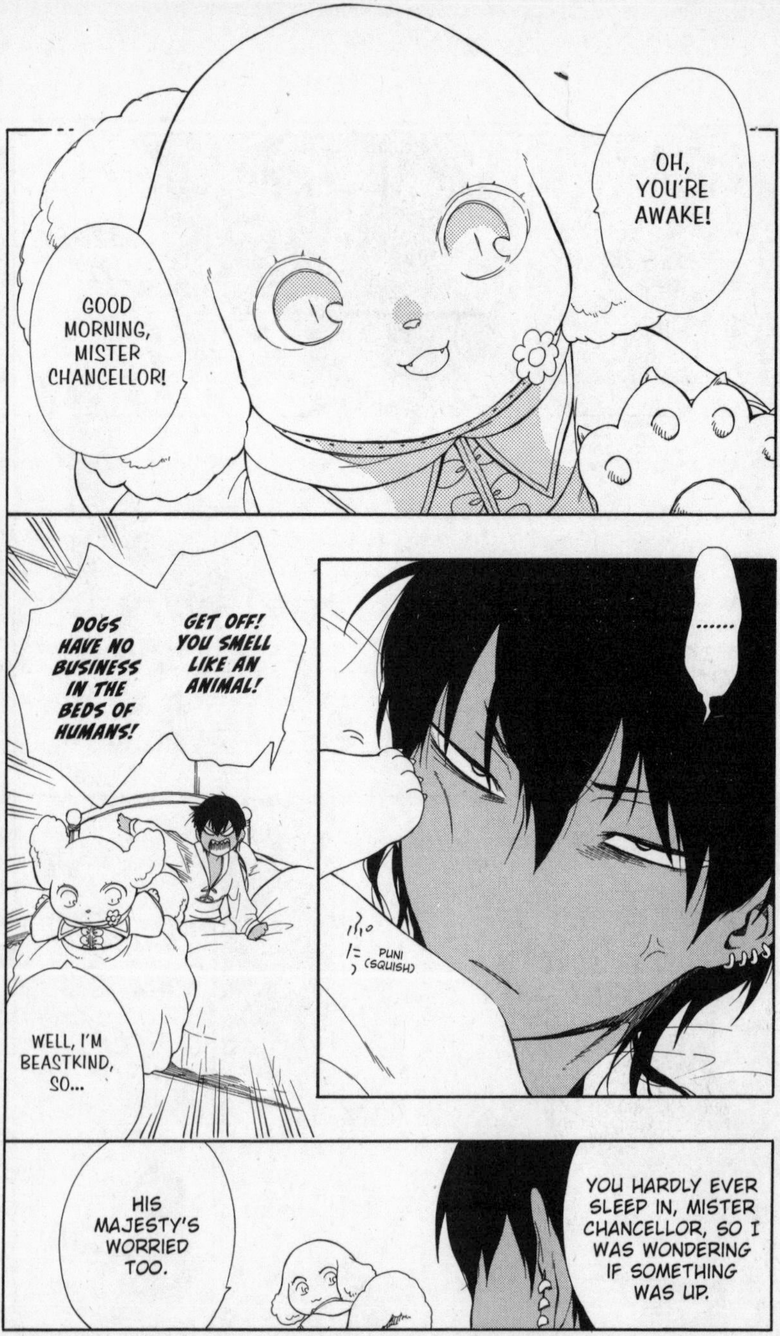
OH, YOU'RE AWAKE!
GOOD MORNING, MISTER CHANCELLOR!
......
ふにっ
PUNI (SQUISH)
GET OFF! YOU SMELL LIKE AN ANIMAL!
DOGS HAVE NO BUSINESS IN THE BEDS OF HUMANS!
WELL, I'M BEASTKIND, SO...
YOU HARDLY EVER SLEEP IN, MISTER CHANCELLOR, SO I WAS WONDERING IF SOMETHING WAS UP.
HIS MAJESTY'S WORRIED TOO.

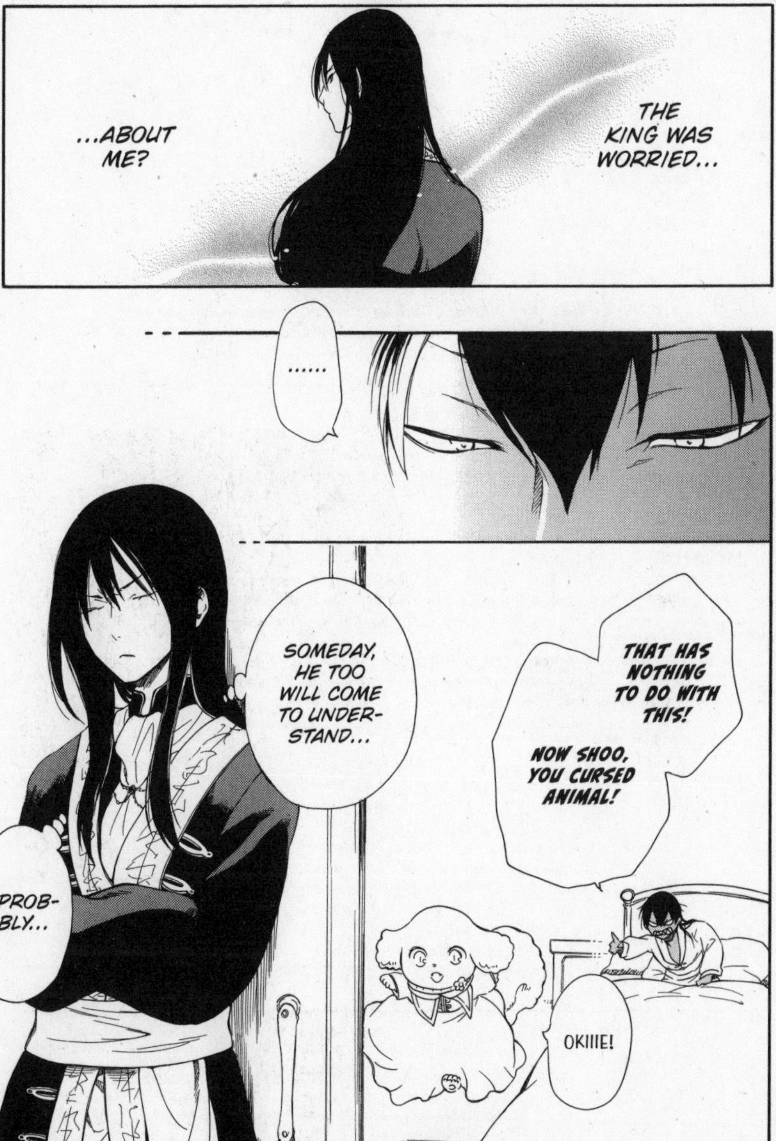
THE KING WAS WORRIED...
...ABOUT ME?
......
THAT HAS NOTHING TO DO WITH THIS!
NOW SHOO, YOU CURSED ANIMAL!
OKIIIE!
SOMEDAY, HE TOO WILL COME TO UNDER-STAND...
...PROB-ABLY...

SACRIFICIAL PRINCESS AND THE KING OF BEASTS

5

Yu Tomofuji

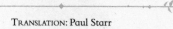
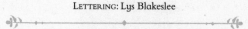

TRANSLATION: Paul Starr

LETTERING: Lys Blakeslee

NIEHIME TO KEMONO NO OH by Yu Tomofuji
© Yu Tomofuji 2017
All rights reserved.
First published in Japan in 2017 by HAKUSENSHA, Inc., Tokyo.
English language translation rights in U.S.A., Canada and U.K. arranged with
HAKUSENSHA, Inc., Tokyo through Tuttle-Mori Agency, Inc., Tokyo.

English translation © 2019 by Yen Press, LLC

Yen Press
1290 Avenue of the Americas
New York, NY 10104

Visit us at yenpress.com ❦ facebook.com/yenpress ❦ twitter.com/yenpress
yenpress.tumblr.com ❦ instagram.com/yenpress

First Yen Press Edition: April 2019

Yen Press is an imprint of Yen Press, LLC.
The Yen Press name and logo are trademarks of Yen Press, LLC.

Library of Congress Control Number: 2018930817

ISBNs: 978-1-9753-0369-3 (paperback)
978-1-9753-0435-5 (ebook)

10 9 8 7 6 5 4 3 2 1

WOR

Printed in the United States of America